WHERE SLEEPING GIRLS LIE

FARIDAH ÀBÍKÉ-ÍYÍMÍDÉ

WHERE SLEEPING GIRLS LIE

FEIWEL AND FRIENDS
NEW YORK

A Feiwel and Friends Book
An imprint of Macmillan Publishing Group, LLC
120 Broadway, New York, NY 10271 • fiercereads.com

Our books may be purchased in bulk for promotional, educational, or business use. Please contact your local bookseller or the Macmillan Corporate and Premium Sales Department at (800) 221-7945 ext. 5442 or by email at MacmillanSpecialMarkets@macmillan.com.

Library of Congress Cataloging-in-Publication Data is available

First edition, 2024
Book design by Trisha Previte
Feiwel and Friends logo designed by Filomena Tuosto
Printed in the United States of America

ISBN 978-1-250-80084-8 (hardcover)
1   3   5   7   9   10   8   6   4   2

ISBN 978-1-250-34555-4 (special edition)
1   3   5   7   9   10   8   6   4   2

FOR MY SISTERS:
MALIHA AND TAMERA

Dear Reader,

***WHERE SLEEPING GIRLS LIE* IS** about a lot of things. It's about the necessity of community and the importance and joy of platonic relationships. It's about the ghosts that haunt us and that we haunt back. It's about the many valid ways we respond to painful experiences.

More than anything, this book is about survival, and as you might notice from the sizable gap between the release of *Ace of Spades* and the release of this second book, it took me many years to write this in a way that felt like I would be honoring the story, the characters, and any readers who might see themselves in this story. (Also, second books are just bloody hard.)

When asked about whether I write myself into my stories, I always answer that I don't because I'm more of an observer than a memoirist. However, *Where Sleeping Girls Lie* is definitely one of my most personal stories to date. While I have not inserted myself exactly into any of these characters, some experiences and feelings depicted are things I unfortunately relate to deeply. I wanted this book to showcase a main character who lives a full life despite any past traumas, much like I try to, and so in the spirit of this, *WSGL* is not just one kind of story. It is part suspense-mystery, part contemporary romance coming of age, part antihero journey.

When I write stories, I'm always writing to specific feelings at the time, as well as people and places. With *Ace of Spades*, I was primarily writing to queer Black young adults attending PWIs and being pulled under by the weight of white supremacy, drowning while feeling unseen and unheard. With *Where Sleeping Girls Lie*, I write to young girls who feel so much anger, and need desperately for someone or something to tell them their rage is important, and that the capacity to heal from deep wounds is not at all impossible. While writing this book, I kept thinking of Oluwatoyin Salau and women like her who deserve so much more than this world gives them. *Where Sleeping Girls Lie* is my attempt at not only healing some of my own wounds but also helping others seek out the tools to do so as well.

I want this book to be so many things, but of course, what I want is not as important as what this book might mean to you, and so I ask you to take care as always while reading and I hope you enjoy the characters and the story as much as I enjoyed writing them.

With love,
Faridah

"'If he be Mr. Hyde,' he had thought, 'I shall be Mr. Seek.'"
—*Strange Case of Dr. Jekyll and Mr. Hyde*, Robert Louis Stevenson

"No hour is ever eternity, but it has its right to weep."
—*Their Eyes Were Watching God*, Zora Neale Hurston

THE WORLD WAS SILENT WHEN SHE DROWNED.

The weight of the stars, of the universe, and of her mind were like an anchor pulling her closer toward oblivion.

As her lungs caught on fire, and her vision went black . . .

. . . her heart began to slow.

Her final thoughts lingered, wading through the tangled mess of veins and empty, empty space.

And then she whispered the same words they'd later find on the note she'd left:

"I'm sorry."

I'm sorry. I'm sorry. I'm sorry. I'm sorry. I'm sorry. I'm sorry. I'm sorry. I'm sorry. I'm sorry.
I'm sorry. I'm sorry. I'm sorry. I'm sorry. I'm sorry. I'm sorry. I'm sorry. I'm sorry. I'm sorry.
I'm sorry. I'm sorry. I'm sorry. I'm sorry. I'm sorry. I'm sorry. I'm sorry. I'm sorry. I'm sorry.
I'm sorry. I'm sorry. I'm sorry. I'm sorry. I'm sorry. I'm sorry. I'm sorry. I'm sorry. I'm sorry.
I'm sorry. I'm sorry. I'm sorry. I'm sorry. I'm sorry. I'm sorry. I'm sorry. I'm sorry. I'm sorry.
I'm sorry. I'm sorry. I'm sorry. I'm sorry. I'm sorry. I'm sorry. I'm sorry. I'm sorry. I'm sorry.
I'm sorry. I'm sorry. I'm sorry. I'm sorry. I'm sorry. I'm sorry. I'm sorry. I'm sorry. I'm sorry.
I'm sorry. I'm sorry. I'm sorry. I'm sorry. I'm sorry. I'm sorry. I'm sorry. I'm sorry. I'm sorry.
I'm sorry. I'm sorry. I'm sorry. I'm sorry. I'm sorry. I'm sorry. I'm sorry. I'm sorry. I'm sorry.
I'm sorry. I'm sorry. I'm sorry. I'm sorry. I'm sorry. I'm sorry. I'm sorry. I'm sorry. I'm sorry.
I'm sorry. I'm sorry. I'm sorry. I'm sorry. I'm sorry. I'm sorry. I'm sorry. I'm sorry. I'm sorry.
I'm sorry. I'm sorry. I'm sorry. I'm sorry. I'm sorry. I'm sorry. I'm sorry. I'm sorry. I'm sorry.
I'm sorry. I'm sorry. I'm sorry. I'm sorry. I'm sorry. I'm sorry. I'm sorry. I'm sorry. I'm sorry.
I'm sorry. I'm sorry. I'm sorry. I'm sorry. I'm sorry. I'm sorry. I'm sorry. I'm sorry. I'm sorry.
I'm sorry. I'm sorry. I'm sorry. I'm sorry. I'm so sorry. *I'm sorry. I'm sorry. I'm sorry.*
I'm sorry. I'm sorry. I'm sorry. I'm sorry. I'm sorry. I'm sorry. I'm sorry. I'm sorry. I'm sorry.
I'm sorry. I'm sorry. I'm sorry. I'm sorry. I'm sorry. I'm sorry. I'm sorry. I'm sorry. I'm sorry.
I'm sorry. I'm sorry. I'm sorry. I'm sorry. I'm sorry. I'm sorry. I'm sorry. I'm sorry. I'm sorry.
I'm sorry. I'm sorry. I'm sorry. I'm sorry. I'm sorry. I'm sorry. I'm sorry. I'm sorry. I'm sorry.
I'm sorry. I'm sorry. I'm sorry. I'm sorry. I'm sorry. I'm sorry. I'm sorry. I'm sorry. I'm sorry.
I'm sorry. I'm sorry. I'm sorry. I'm sorry. I'm sorry. I'm sorry. I'm sorry. I'm sorry. I'm sorry.
I'm sorry. I'm sorry. I'm sorry. I'm sorry. I'm sorry. I'm sorry. I'm sorry. I'm sorry. I'm sorry.
I'm sorry. I'm sorry. I'm sorry. I'm sorry. I'm sorry. I'm sorry. I'm sorry. I'm sorry. I'm sorry.
I'm sorry. I'm sorry. I'm sorry. I'm sorry. I'm sorry. I'm sorry. I'm sorry. I'm sorry. I'm sorry.
I'm sorry. I'm sorry. I'm sorry. I'm sorry. I'm' sorry. I'm sorry. I'm sorry. I'm sorry. I'm sorry.
I'm sorry. I'm sorry. I'm sorry. I'm sorry. I'm sorry. I'm sorry. I'm sorry. I'm sorry. I'm sorry.
I'm sorry. I'm sorry. I'm sorry. I'm sorry. I'm sorry. I'm sorry. I'm sorry. I'm sorry. I'm sorry.
I'm sorry. I'm sorry. I'm sorry. I'm sorry. I'm sorry. I'm sorry. I'm sorry. I'm sorry. I'm sorry.
I'm sorry. I'm sorry. I'm sorry. I'm sorry. I'm sorry. I'm sorry. I'm sorry. I'm sorry. I'm sorry.
I'm sorry. I'm sorry. I'm sorry. I'm sorry. I'm sorry. I'm sorry. I'm sorry—

PART I

THE GRAVE
OF DREAMS

"It never looked as terrible as it was and it made her
wonder if hell was a pretty place too. Fire and brimstone
all right, but hidden in lacy gloves."

—*Beloved*, Toni Morrison

GO FISH

THE NIGHT IT HAPPENED, THERE was a party.

Though parties weren't unusual for the students of Alfred Nobel Academy, this one certainly was.

Every now and again, there'd be a secret off-campus soiree at a house one of the Senior Hawking boys rented out. Something gossipworthy would happen, like a third year who'd have one too many drinks and end up making out with his ex-boyfriend in public. Or a fourth year getting so high they'd forget where they were and would end up streaking around the pool, baring it all for everyone to see.

Then the following Monday, all the shenanigans from that weekend would become the hot topic throughout the boarding school, hushed whispers about the fortunate few floating through the hallways, the classrooms, and the dorms.

What made this night particularly strange, though, was what occurred when no watchful gazes or cameras—*to her knowledge*—were there to document it:

A girl climbing down from a balcony. Her trembling fingers gripping the handles of the spiral staircase. The night swallowing her cries whole as she stumbled toward the car that was waiting for her.

She didn't dare look back.

Looking back would be acknowledging what had happened.

What she had done.

The gray car was hidden in a corner on the quiet path that led up to the house, blending in with the shadows, visible only to those who knew to look for it.

The click of the car door echoed loudly as she climbed into the passenger seat, shutting the door quickly before anyone could see.

Another girl was settled in the driver's seat, concern carved into her dark features—her short blonde hair styled in gentle waves, rippling across her head, blurring and rippling more with the trembling girl's tears.

"Did you get the—" The blonde girl paused, noticing her friend's tearstained cheeks. "What happened?" she finished.

The girl silently wiped her face, avoiding her gaze.

"Sade?" the blonde girl said in a gentle whisper.

Sade finally looked up and stared into her eyes.

"H-he's dead."

NEW GIRL

SADE HUSSEIN WAS USED TO being lied to.

When she was seven, she was told that the woman she saw sneaking out of her father's room early in the morning was the tooth fairy and definitely *not* her nanny. When she was ten and she found her mother slumped back in the bathtub, unmoving, with a bottle of pills resting on the ledge—she was told that her mother was taking a very long nap and would wake soon. When she was fourteen, she begged her father to let her go to a normal school and make friends with real kids her age, instead of her only real friend being her maths tutor who let her sleep during class sometimes. She was told by her father that high school wasn't what it seemed. That it was the furthest from the magic that the movies had led her to believe.

But as the black town car pulled into the gates of Alfred Nobel Academy and the giant castle-like boarding school came into view, neither the rain nor the memory of her father's warning could dull her excitement.

The school looked like a palace.

The brownstone walls, fancy peaks, and crisp greenery near the front that seemed to stretch on for miles had captured her attention entirely. Even the driver's eyes widened at the sight of the enormous building, a far cry from the narrow town house she grew up in.

A knock on the window pulled them both out of their trance as a man wearing a security uniform leaned over the car.

Sade wound her window down.

"Name and purpose?" the security guy asked her.

"Sade Hussein, student," she said, and followed up quickly with, "It's my first day."

He nodded, then muttered something into his walkie-talkie. "All right. You can go on up. There should be someone waiting for you by the entrance," he told her.

"Thank you," she replied.

The car continued along the path, and Sade tried to take in more of the school surroundings.

Perfectly trimmed rosebushes, evenly cut grass, and wild cherry trees. In the distance, she could see rows of beautiful buildings. Old and new.

"I think this is as far as I can go," the driver said, the car coming to a stop in front of the main building.

"How much is that?" she asked.

The driver looked at her through the rearview mirror. "It's covered, compliments of your father," he said, the last part uttered quickly in a hushed tone, as though just the thought of him could raise the dead.

It was strange how even from beyond the grave, her father still had that effect on people.

It was as though people didn't truly believe he was gone.

The great Akin Hussein, bested by his very own heart. It didn't seem real.

She didn't blame them either—even she felt his presence still looming. Watching her every move like he had always done.

But she knew with absolute certainty that he had to be gone.

After all, she wouldn't be here if his heart was still beating.

Sade gave the driver a tight smile and dug into her purse for some cash. "Here," she said, handing the driver two crisp fifty-pound notes.

He was about to protest.

"I'd feel much better if you took this."

The driver hesitated before accepting the cash.

"Thank you," she said getting out of the car, careful not to crease the stubborn material of her black tweed custom Chanel dress.

As the driver unloaded her suitcases from the boot, the main entrance of the school swung open, revealing a tall, skeletal-looking woman with a high bun, pencil skirt, and a severe expression carved into her face.

"Sade Hussein?" the woman called out sharply as she approached the car, pronouncing both her first name and last name wrong: *SADIE HOO-SEN* instead of *SHAH-DAY HOO-SAYN*.

Sade noticed the woman eyeing her clothes with a disapproving look, grimacing at her shoes.

"It's *Sade Hussein*," Sade corrected, realizing only after saying it that that was probably a mistake. From her years of watching shows and reading books about high school, she knew that teachers rarely seemed to like being told they were wrong. Unlike her tutors, who always rewarded her tendency to be nimble-witted, this woman did not look pleased.

"You're late," she told her.

"Sorry. There was traffic on the way—"

"Four weeks late," the woman interrupted.

Sade said nothing to that, despite the reasons for her lateness boring a hole into her skull and weighing her shoulders down. She had a feeling the woman wouldn't care for her excuses, justified or not.

"There are rules, Miss Hussein, that every student is expected to adhere to. I'm not sure how things were at your last school, but here we do not accept tardiness, nor do we accept turning up on your first day dressed out of uniform. Please let this be the last time you find yourself . . . in traffic," the woman said, the veins in her neck purpling. She paused, as though waiting for Sade to speak up, but then carried on when only silence followed. "Your parents should have received all the documents and passed them along to you . . . and yet your house form is incomplete. We'll have to sort this all out today and you will most likely miss classes, falling even further behind. I expect you haven't done any of the reading to catch up either, seeing as you couldn't even complete the basic task of dressing properly for your first day of school. Seriously, did your parents not—"

"They're dead," Sade said coolly, interrupting her this time.

The woman looked uncomfortable. "Sorry?" she asked, as if it wasn't already clear.

"My parents—they're both dead. My mother died when I was ten and my father died a month ago, a few days before I was meant to start here. I was told it wouldn't be an issue and that it would be in my file. I assumed you would have read it—my apologies for making that assumption," she replied with a forced smile.

The driver awkwardly cleared his throat. "I have removed all your luggage from the boot, miss. Would you like me to transport your suitcases to your dormitory?" he asked her.

Sade's gaze moved from the woman's shocked expression to the driver's uneasy one.

Alongside her father's multimillion-pound estate, Sade had also inherited the burden of grief and the awkwardness that came with it.

"How much for you to move my bags?" she asked him.

He looked even more uncomfortable. "It's fine, miss, compliments—"

Sade's voice became unsteady. "How much?"

The driver kept quiet, and Sade sighed heavily before digging into her purse and handing him a cluster of twenty-pound notes this time, not bothering to count.

She turned back to the woman, her smile faltering. "Where do I get a uniform?"

● ● ●

5

THE INSIDE OF ALFRED NOBEL Academy was even more beautiful than the castle-like exterior. It was like stepping into a daydream.

Sade's eyes wandered as she stood in the entrance of the main building, taking in how flawless it all was. The hardwood floors; the tall, rounded glass windows; the ceiling that had paintings of what she thought were angels, but upon a second glance, wasn't so sure.

She felt as though she had just stepped into a museum instead of what was to become her home for the next two years.

It looked exactly like the pictures she had seen online.

"Right." The woman—who she had since learned was the school's matron and was named Miss Blackburn—interrupted her thoughts.

"You can go into that room there to fill in the house form. The form contains a simple selection of questions that will assess you on your needs and the best environment for your living at ANA. Try to answer as truthfully as possible. We take this very seriously and it is extremely rare that we allow transfers to other houses—not that we get many people wanting to transfer. The form is very comprehensive, and usually incredibly accurate."

Sade had read up on the school's houses. All eight of them: Curie, Einstein, Hawking, Mendel, Franklin, Turing, Jemison, and Seacole. Each house seemed to serve a specific purpose and, in turn, had students who fit that purpose. There was the house for academics, the house for sports prodigies, and so on. She wondered what house she'd be sorted into.

Miss Blackburn led Sade into the room with a single walnut-colored desk, a booklet, and a number two pencil. There was a door behind the desk, labeled SECURITY ROOM.

"When you're done, knock twice on the wall, then slide your form through the slot over there. It will be marked, and I'll bring you a uniform once the test results are back. It shouldn't take long. Any questions?" Miss Blackburn asked, passive-aggressively blinking at Sade.

Sade shook her head, despite feeling like she was in some kind of weird dystopian novel whereby the form was actually a test meant to determine her entire future or something. She placed her shoulder bag on the ground.

"Good," Miss Blackburn said, smiling tightly.

Sade took a seat at the desk.

Miss Blackburn turned to leave, then paused at the door and looked down at Sade's paper then back at her face. "Choose wisely," she said before leaving, the door slamming shut behind her.

• • •

MISS BLACKBURN WAS RIGHT; THE form took no time at all—though the questions were *very* strange.

There was a question that asked whether she preferred rainfall or sunshine, which didn't really make much sense to her. After all, it wasn't as if they could control the weather of the dormitory she was assigned. Another question had asked her if she preferred large windows or small ones, and another asked her to select her favorite woodland creature.

When she was done, she knocked twice, then slipped her test through the gold slot in the wall, swearing she felt a strange tug from the other side. When Miss Blackburn had told her it would be marked, she assumed she meant by a computer of some sort.

But the tug felt human, and Sade wondered whether there was a little old lady they kept behind the wall to do nothing but mark these forms. She wouldn't be surprised if there was. Because, while beautiful, something felt off about Alfred Nobel. Perhaps it was that everything was *too* flawless.

Sade was used to luxury, so she knew that wealth came with an abundance of secrets. She could bet that Alfred Nobel Academy had a lot of them. Buried six feet under, beneath the perfectly trimmed rosebushes by the entrance.

A knock sounded, and Miss Blackburn stepped back into the room with what Sade assumed was a folded uniform in her manicured hands.

"I have instructed your driver to take your things to your room," Miss Blackburn said. "I guessed your size," she continued, handing Sade the uniform, "but if you need something tailored to your tastes, you can go down to the school shop once you've settled in."

Sade eyed the clothes in front of her. The uniform seemed to be comprised of a lot of black. Black skirt, black sweater, and a black tie. It looked more like funeral attire than anything else.

"Thanks . . . Do I have to wear it now or can I change into it later?"

Miss Blackburn's gaze burned into her. "It's up to you."

Sade had a feeling that Miss Blackburn wanted her to change immediately, clearly still offended by her lack of proper dress. She wasn't sure what was so offensive about a tweed dress and laced Doc Marten boots.

"Any more questions?" Miss Blackburn asked.

Sade nodded. "I have two. Which house am I in?"

Miss Blackburn stood up straight. "Ah yes, you're in Turing House."

Like she did with the other houses, Sade had read up on Turing House briefly. It had been described as the house for the jack-of-all-traders, students with no particular special interest in any one subject; sister house to Seacole; and unlike most of the other houses, Turing had produced the least famous alumni.

7

How exciting, she thought.

"Turing, like the scientist?" Sade asked, wanting to sound interested. She remembered the tragic story of Alan Turing, the queer scientist, from one of her history lessons on World War II.

"Yes. As are all the other houses—named after scientists, that is. You'd know that if you had read the booklet. But what is your other question?" Miss Blackburn asked, obviously still holding a grudge over the fact that Sade hadn't come prepared. Which wasn't exactly true. She had looked up the things she thought would best serve her purpose here, but had clearly missed the mark on the things Miss Blackburn deemed pertinent knowledge.

"Could I get a tour of the school? I don't want to get lost," she said.

"Of course. Your house sister will be showing you around—she's outside waiting for us."

"House sister?" Sade questioned.

Miss Blackburn nodded. "You're assigned a house sister and house brother—in your first year, usually, but since you're a late arrival we've had to assign you some last-minute house siblings." Miss Blackburn must've noticed Sade's confused expression, because she added, "It's tradition. Normally a student in the year above you takes on the responsibility, but in your case, you've been assigned someone in your year—conveniently, she's also your roommate, so I'm sure the two of you will be well acquainted by the end of the term."

Sade blinked at that. She had never shared a room before. "Is this optional?" She'd already grown accustomed to her status as a tragic orphan at the ripe age of sixteen and wasn't looking for any new family.

"No," Miss Blackburn answered sharply. "As I said, it's tradition. I've assigned you someone from Hawking House to be your house brother. He's in classes for the rest of the day, but I'll make sure to introduce you both sometime this week."

Traditions. House siblings. Sade still wasn't feeling the idea of a forced family. This was starting to seem less like boarding school and more like a weird cult. Though, maybe this should have been expected given that the school motto was literally *Ex Unitate Vires*, which translated to "In Unity there is Strength."

A very cultish-sounding slogan if you asked her.

Miss Blackburn spoke again, probably sensing her continued confusion. "It can be difficult adjusting to boarding school. House families are one way we ensure our students have a support system during their four years with us. Seeing as you're in your third year, and this is your first time attending a boarding school, I think it would be rather beneficial. Elizabeth is outside waiting for us."

Sade picked up her shoulder bag and draped the uniform over her arm before following Miss Blackburn out into the hallway, now littered with students. Sade noticed their identical black uniforms and their different-colored ties as they rushed past her.

"Sade, this is your house sister—and roommate—Elizabeth Wang. She will be showing you around and answering all your burning questions," Miss Blackburn said, gesturing to the pretty, dark-haired girl in front of her.

Sade took in the girl's somewhat disheveled appearance. Her smudged eye makeup, her chipped black nail polish, and the solid rips along her tights. The girl watched her too, a strange expression slowly creeping onto her face as she stared at Sade.

It was as if she had seen a ghost.

"Hi," Sade said with a friendly smile.

"Hello?" Elizabeth replied after a moment's silence, still regarding her strangely. There was a subtle inflection at the end, as though her greeting was also a question.

"See, you're already off to a great start," Miss Blackburn said without an ounce of enthusiasm or care in her voice. "Sade, please drop by the reception after dinner to collect your welcome pack and house key. Ms. Thistle will be there to give it to you. I didn't have time today to put it together before your arrival."

Sade nodded, adding this to her mental list.

"All right then . . . quick tour?" Elizabeth finally said, her face relaxing now and her clear Irish accent vibrating between them. She seemed to have snapped out of whatever had overtaken her.

"That would be great," Sade replied, feeling Miss Blackburn's gaze still burning holes into her dress. "But if it's okay, I think I'd like to change into my uniform first."

MONDAY
CAGED BIRDS

AFTER CHANGING INTO THE VERY stiff uniform, Sade followed Elizabeth out of the main hall entrance and right past a building labeled STAFF QUARTERS.

"I thought we should probably start at the dorms. Turing's about a five-minute walk down this path—it's a pain if you wake up late in the mornings and need to rush out, but it could be much worse. We could be in Einstein House," Elizabeth said as they walked behind the main building and down a long, narrow stone path littered with wet leaves and fallen conkers from trees.

From where she stood, Sade could see that there were several buildings at the back of the school, most of which were buried deep behind the main building. Some were adjoining, and others stood alone.

"This is John Fisher, the founder of this fine establishment," Elizabeth continued, gesturing at a giant stone statue of an old white guy with a curled mustache and an old-fashioned coat and top hat, who stood in the middle of the path. "Hot, right?"

Sade raised an eyebrow at her. She thought he looked creepy, but then again, she always found statues to be a bit disturbing. Though maybe not as disturbing as Elizabeth's statement.

Elizabeth cracked a smile. "I'm kidding. I'd rather get all four of my wisdom teeth removed again than snog old man Fisher here. Besides, he'd probably hate my guts since he was not that fond of women or people of color. Two boxes I fortunately check."

John Fisher looked down at Sade and Elizabeth as though he was sneering at them.

"I can see that," Sade said.

They continued down the winding path, and Sade took in more of the architecture. One building stuck out to her: newer and distinctly un-castle-like. She noticed NEWTON SPORTS CENTER written in bold on the side of it.

Her mind drifted for a moment, sinking into the pits of a year-old memory. "Is there a swimming pool in there?" she asked.

"Miss Blackburn really wasn't kidding when she said you knew nothing," Elizabeth said as she turned to look at the building. "Alfred Nobel is famous for its swim team; Newton has the second-biggest pool on campus and is mostly used for practice. They're actually building a bigger practice pool inside right now."

Sade could hear the distant sound of construction work coming from inside the center.

"The Spitz Center, located behind the school chapel, has the largest pool and is used for tournaments and games . . . Are you a swimmer?" Elizabeth asked.

Sade felt the memory stir again, clawing at the edges of her mind.

The girl's body. Lifeless. Cold. Her lips blue, her braids sprawled in the water. A pool of thick red blood surrounding her head like a halo—

"I used to be," Sade replied.

"Well, in that case, you're in luck. There are only two houses on campus that are super close to Newton: Hawking and Jemison," Elizabeth said, pointing to a building on the left and then another on the opposite side that looked like a miniature version of the sports center. It was modern, with glass and solar panels, and a sign read JEMISON HOUSE in the front. Hawking House was white and gigantic, at least two times the size of Jemison.

"Most Hawking and Jemison residents are on the various sports teams. But . . . the third-closest house is ours, Turing. So you won't have to go too far to get to Newton if you ever wanted to go swimming after classes."

Sade nodded, half listening to her, half taking in Hawking House, seeing shadowy figures behind the drawn curtains in the house's windows disappearing and reappearing again and again.

When they finally arrived at Turing, Sade did a double take at how stunning it was. The house looked like a haunted castle. Unlike the main building, the stone here was nearly black.

"Here we are," Elizabeth said, taking out her key card and swiping it at a panel near the entrance.

Sade followed through the double doors, her boots creating an echo as she stepped onto the black-and-white checkered flooring that reminded her a lot of a chessboard.

At the center of the main entrance of Turing stood a large spiral staircase, and behind that, a French elevator. On the wall, there was an enormous painting, and unlike the ones she'd seen earlier, this one Sade could actually make out. It was a portrait of a tired-looking man, and underneath there was a sign that read ALAN TURING.

To the sides of the house's foyer, there were two doors. One with a gold plaque engraved with the words DINING HALL and the other COMMON ROOM.

Despite this being her first time in here, she had seen this entrance what felt like hundreds of times, from her obsessive late-night browsing of the school website.

Everything looked just like the photos.

A loud *ping* pulled Sade from her thoughts as Elizabeth took out her phone to check what Sade assumed was a message. Elizabeth stared at her phone for a few moments before slipping it back into her pocket.

Sade noticed the change in Elizabeth's expression, but before she had time to decipher it, Elizabeth had replaced her grimace with a smile.

"This is Turing, where you'll probably spend most of your time at ANA," Elizabeth continued, her voice weirdly shaky at first, before quickly regaining its balance. "We have breakfast and dinner in the house dining room, and then lunch in the main building with all the other students. Through there is the common room, where people usually hang out after classes or before dinner, then upstairs are the dorms. First floor is for first years, second for second years, and so on," Elizabeth said. "Because Alfred Nobel is an international school, we very much have an international system. Think of first years as freshman and fourth years as seniors. It's weird, and I'm sure very different from your last school, but you get used to it quickly."

Sade nodded. "It is very different. I was homeschooled before, so this is all new to me."

Elizabeth raised an eyebrow. "So you're telling me that this is your first time having to put up with the bullshit that is high school? I envy you."

I envy you.

It was funny that Elizabeth said that. Sade had been thinking the same thing: how lucky Elizabeth was to have been here, to have been free, for so many years already.

But she was here now.

She was finally free.

That's what mattered.

"I'll quickly show you to our room," Elizabeth said, leading Sade into the lift. Sade watched her pull the gates shut before pressing the button to the third floor.

French lifts always made her feel uneasy. Unlike normal lifts, these were like cages. You could see and feel the rise of the shaft as the lift ascended. Could feel the rumble and tug of the machinery.

Thankfully, the ride up didn't take too long. Before she knew it, they were walking down the hallway to the room that they would share for the next year.

Sade was still processing the idea of sharing a room, such an intimate space, with a stranger, that she didn't notice Elizabeth had stopped.

Nor did she register her sharp intake of breath or see the look on Elizabeth's face.

When she did finally notice the lack of movement, she first looked at the door with the engraving ROOM 313 and Elizabeth's name written under the number in white chalk, then at the thing Elizabeth's eyes were trained on.

The dead rat on the mat outside the door.

Sade stood frozen next to her.

The animal was still and pale, its tail curved around, its head squashed like it had been bashed in and planted there. Its eyes were small and lifeless as it stared up at her helplessly.

"Is that a—" Sade began, shock coursing through her, but she was cut off by Elizabeth.

"Hold on a second," Elizabeth said calmly, taking out her bronze room key and opening the door to room 313.

Sade watched as Elizabeth stepped over the dead rodent and disappeared into the room, leaving her outside alone. *Or well, relatively alone,* she thought, maintaining eye contact with *Jerry.*

Elizabeth reappeared a few moments later with a used shopping bag. She made a face as she gingerly wrapped the bag around the carcass and scooped the rat up into it before tying it and placing it in the bin in the corner of the hallway.

"All done!" she said with what seemed to be a forced smile. "Let me show you to our room. Sorry in advance for the mess; I didn't realize you'd be getting here until today," Elizabeth said as the door opened once again, leaving Sade to process what had just happened.

There was a dead rat. And Elizabeth was so casual about it. Was this something that happened often? *Did someone put it there?*

"Are there usually decaying rodents in the hallway?" Sade asked, eyeing the room and the floor suspiciously.

There was silence for a beat and then Elizabeth's voice came out through the door, slightly muffled. "Well, ANA is a very old school. Don't worry too much, though; it's a rare occurrence. I'm hoping there won't be any more dead rats after today."

If you say so . . . , Sade thought.

She crept slowly into room 313, avoiding the wet patch on the ground where the outline of the rat's corpse was still visible.

She watched as Elizabeth moved quickly to the pile of disregarded clothes on the floor, shoving them into a random corner. The room was dark still, the curtains drawn tightly, blocking all the sunlight. Elizabeth was too preoccupied with ridding the floor of her clothes to notice.

Sade flicked the light switch, and the details of the room came into view.

It had two beds, pushed to either side. Two wardrobes, her suitcases resting beside one of them and waiting to be unpacked, two desks, and a small table with a pile of used mugs stacked on top.

Elizabeth followed Sade's eyeline over to the mugs and she quickly swiped them, putting them outside on the floor in the hallway.

When she walked back into the room, her face was a deep red color and she looked flustered.

"Sorry, again. I really would have cleaned if—" Elizabeth started.

"It's fine," Sade interrupted, before adding, "I like your décor."

Elizabeth's side of the room was filled with personality. There were band posters, a cow-shaped kettle next to a ridiculous thousand-pack of Yorkshire tea bags, a sunflower rug on the ground, and random plants strewn about.

Elizabeth's eyebrows raised. "Oh, thank you—feel free to use anything on my side of the room. We aren't meant to keep electrical appliances in our dorms, but I have a bit of a tea addiction and so it is a necessary risk I'm willing to take."

Sade smiled at that. "I won't tell anyone about your secret tea stash."

Elizabeth held out her pinkie. "You promise?"

Sade looked at Elizabeth's fingers and remembered that they had been in close proximity with the dead rat moments ago. And so instead of hooking her own pinkie around Elizabeth's, she simply nodded and said, "Scouts honor."

Elizabeth beamed, satisfied with Sade's response.

"A little warning about me since we're sharing secrets. I have the slight tendency to sleepwalk when I'm stressed, and on occasion, I sleep with my eyes open," Sade added.

"Noted," Elizabeth replied, seemingly unbothered by this fact.

They had an understanding.

"Well, now that's sorted, I suppose I better show you the rest of the school, then. We have a lot to cover."

AFTER ANOTHER HOUR AND A half of wandering around the campus, Sade deduced Alfred Nobel Academy was too good to be true.

Some highlights of the tour included the school aquarium, the lucky fountain in the front that she had somehow missed when she had arrived, and the Starry Night Library—which apparently housed several special editions of her favorite books.

By the time they were finished, it was already lunchtime and Sade could hear the sound of students shuffling about, a low rumble of voices rising nearby.

They were now by the main entrance again. Elizabeth was getting Sade her lunch card from Miss Blackburn, leaving Sade to come down from the high of the tour. She found herself taking in the main entrance hall again, like she had done before, this time through a new set of eyes. The room was not as impressive as she had originally thought it was, now that she had seen the other rooms and buildings at the school. The wooden panels across the walls were dull and a little scratched. The rounded windows weren't as striking as the stained-glass ones in the Starry Night Library. And the chandelier above did not glitter as much as the ones in the dining hall.

As she looked up, though, she caught sight of the painting she had seen earlier and, squinting, could make out a few shapes and figures.

"Cool painting, right?" Elizabeth asked, looking up with her now.

Sade nodded. It was more than cool. It was somehow both glamorous and sad at the same time. Something about the colors. They were soft but also harsh, and the way the faces were drawn were as eerie as they were beautiful.

"It's called *The Crying Lady*. It was commissioned by the headmaster at the time, who was apparently having an affair with the painter. I always loved the story behind it," Elizabeth said.

"What's the story?" Sade asked, taking in more details she hadn't spotted before. Like the tears streaming down the faces of the women in the painting, the pained expressions behind their eyes, and the forced smiles on their lips. Their expressions unmasked their lies, hidden behind their beautifully drawn faces.

Sade noticed the birds for the first time too. Different colors, ranging from blue to red to copper yellow. Each bird caged and each cage gripped in the hand of one of the weeping women.

"The artist, Madame Alarie, wife to the abusive alcoholic Monsieur Alarie, decided one day that she'd had enough of his bullshit and poisoned his dinner," Elizabeth said.

Sade looked at the birds, focusing in on the blue one—the one that, unlike the others, seemed to have its mouth open. She noticed that its cage was slightly open too.

The story felt like it completed the painting somehow; Sade could see it clearly now.

"Madame Alarie sounds like a legend," Sade said.

"I agree," a smooth voice said from behind the both of them.

Sade startled and turned to find the source, a pink-haired boy with brown skin and a wide dimpled smile. His arms wrapped around Elizabeth, chin resting on her shoulder.

Sade noticed the immediate change in Elizabeth's expression; it was like his presence

15

was a light switch, her face brightening at the sight of him. She wondered if he was Elizabeth's boyfriend or something.

"Fucking hell, you scared the shit out of me," Elizabeth yelled, hitting the pink-haired stranger on the head.

"I'm sorry—won't happen again," he said with a grin that told Sade that it would most definitely happen again. "Is this your new roommate?" he asked, pulling away from Elizabeth.

She nodded. "Baz, Sade, Sade, Baz."

The boy—Baz—smiled at Sade and waved. "I like your name," he said.

Sade had never had someone compliment her name before. "Thanks, I like yours too—is it short for something?" she asked.

He nodded. "Basil, like the herb. My mother likes salad."

Sade nodded slowly, unsure of whether this cheerful boy was being serious or not.

"How did your German test go? I received your urgent *sandwich* texts," Elizabeth said to Basil, and then turned to Sade. "We send each other sandwich emojis when there's an emergency. It's like an extra dramatic SOS."

"It was dreadful. On the sandwich scale, I would say it was a three."

This made Elizabeth's expression shift suddenly into mild shock, like this made perfect sense. "Fucking hell, that bad?"

Sade, on the other hand, still wasn't quite following.

He nodded solemnly. "At least I won't have to see Mr. Müller until Wednesday. He can yell at me then, even though it's his fault for assigning a test that was at a level-three sandwich crisis."

"I'm sure it won't be that bad," Elizabeth said as she ruffled his hair, patting his head softly. "Speaking of sandwiches, we should head to lunch."

"Oh good, I'm starving," Baz said brightly, the German test suddenly forgotten.

Sade nodded along, despite not being all that hungry; her nerves from that morning as well as the memory of the dead rat had kept her appetite at bay.

She gave the painting on the ceiling a final glance before tearing her eyes away from it and following the pair down the corridor.

THE LUNCH HALL—WHICH LOOKED more like a ballroom—was filled with uniformed students, chatting and eating in small clusters.

Sade took a plate of the daily special: pan-roasted pastry rolls layered with herbed tomato puree and a creamy blend of artisanal cheeses, and pomme frites on the side—

otherwise known as *pizza rolls and fries*—and followed Baz and Elizabeth over to a table in the corner of the room.

Baz immediately grabbed the ketchup and squeezed a large quantity onto his plate of fries, giving it the unsavory appearance of congealed blood.

Sade stared at her plate, slightly put off by it now.

"So *who are you exactly*, Sade?" Baz asked suddenly.

She looked up, taken aback. It was a weirdly phrased question. "What?" she replied, not really knowing how else to respond.

He stared at her while continuing to drench his fries in ketchup. She could no longer see the fries anymore; his plate was merely a mountain of red.

"What were you doing before you came here?" he asked with a quizzical look.

It was a loaded question. She wasn't sure whether to give him the rehearsed answer or the truth.

She wasn't sure the truth was something he'd even believe.

She could feel Elizabeth and Baz watching her expectantly.

A half-truth it is.

"I was homeschooled before. My dad traveled a lot for work, so it was easier that way."

Baz's eyebrows raised like he was impressed. "What's that like?"

"Homeschool?" she asked.

He nodded.

Sade thought back to her memories of home and then replied: "Honestly, quite boring."

"Well, I can assure you there's nothing boring about this school," Elizabeth muttered with scorn, cutting into her pizza rolls now.

Baz smiled at that. "How are you finding ANA so far?" he asked, passing what remained of the ketchup along to Elizabeth.

"I like it—Elizabeth gave me a tour of the school grounds; it's really stunning."

Baz smiled and gave Elizabeth a look. "Has she given you the real tour of the school yet?"

Elizabeth sighed. "Ignore him—he's full of shit."

Sade quirked an eyebrow. "What's the real tour?"

"The only one that matters. The tour of the people, the cliques, the gossip, everything you'll need to know in order to survive this place. Knowledge is power."

"See, full of it," Elizabeth said with a small smile. Baz elbowed her softly before turning back to Sade.

17

"You want the tour?" he asked in an almost whisper, like he was daring her.

Sade took the ketchup now and squeezed some onto her own plate. "Go on," she replied.

Baz grinned, then scanned the room, before nodding at one of the tables in the corner. "Over there we have the Oxbridge and Ivy League lot—the ones who think they're better than everyone. When in fact, they're as messed up as the rest of us—just happen to be good at exams. That girl over there, the one with the blonde highlights, she got mono from her boyfriend and gave it to his ex-best friend and sworn enemy," Baz said quietly.

Sade watched the girl sitting beside a blond guy she assumed must have been her boyfriend, noticing the way the girl kept glancing at another guy across the table from them—who looked as guilty as she did.

"Then over there, you have the theater nerds; their specialty is randomly breaking out in song and pissing everyone off in the process. But I digress. That guy back there, I heard that at the last Hawking party, he almost killed the orange-haired fellow over there because of a 'missing' stash of *pills* . . ." Baz gestured to a redheaded guy at a different table.

"He's on the swim team, which is significant because swimmer boy is the stepson of the headmaster and would probably be exiled if found with said drugs . . ."

Baz was throwing so much information at her that it was getting increasingly hard to follow.

"What's a Hawking party?" she asked instead of trying to understand what he had just said.

"They're essentially high school frat parties thrown by the lowlifes who occupy Hawking House," Elizabeth muttered, eating her pot of jelly and scrolling through her phone.

"A lot of people would kill to get an invite, Lizzie—myself included. I heard that at the last party, one of the fourth years gifted a Rolex watch to each guest," Baz said, his eyes wide.

"Baz, you already have a Rolex," Elizabeth said.

"Yes, but it's not the same as being gifted one by an attractive senior named Chad."

"Sounds like a lot of fun," Sade said.

"Far from it," Elizabeth replied just as Baz exclaimed, "I bet it is."

The two began to bicker and Sade found herself zoning out, now watching other groups in the lunch hall and making her own observations. It was like witnessing a social experiment, this seemingly primitive instinct to split off and go into these little groups. It was so different from her home life and reminded her of movies she had grown up watching. She wondered whether people were aware of how many clichés they fulfilled on a daily basis.

Between the cliques, the unpleasant matron, and the drama, Sade wouldn't be surprised if she turned around and a camera crew along with a studio audience were there watching her first day of high school unfold like a scene out of *The Truman Show*.

A sudden shift in the air pulled her from her thoughts.

The loud rumble of voices in the hall began to soften, heads turning to the entrance of the room.

Sade turned too, wondering what had caused the abrupt change.

And that's when she saw them: the three girls who had captured everyone's interest.

Sade watched as they took their seats at one of the tables in the center, seemingly unaware of the way their presence transformed the room.

"Who are they?" Sade asked Baz, staring at the girls, eyes drifting to the blonde with the brown skin and those 1920s finger waves in her hair. She looked as though she had stepped out of a painting—they all did.

"The wildly attractive girls who just walked in?" Baz asked, looking in the same direction as her.

Sade nodded.

"People call them a lot of things: she-devils, the wicked bitches of the west, and my favorite, the *Unholy Trinity*. Dramatic names, but pretty accurate if you know even a little bit about them. I heard that they get together on the weekends and perform demonic rituals in order to keep their skin blemish-free."

"Baz, don't tell me you actually believe that," Elizabeth said, giving him a deadpan expression.

"Hey, I'm a social anthropologist. I'm just reporting what I hear!" he replied, holding up his hands.

"Are they popular?" Sade asked. In every movie about cliques, there was always the popular ones.

"I guess so, yeah. Not in the same way the Diamond Ring are—those are the girls whose families come from the oldest money you can imagine," he said, gesturing to a group of glamorous-looking girls at a different table. "The Unholy Trinity are more popular for being pretty, which is honestly a goal of mine," Baz said.

Sade chewed on one of her fries, watching the blonde again, feeling the hairs on her arms raise and her chest vibrate.

She looked at the other two: a South Asian girl with dark olive skin and long black wavy hair that seemed to flow down past her lower back, and in between them both, possibly the most objectively beautiful girl she had ever seen. And Sade clearly wasn't the only one who had noticed. The girl had everyone glancing her way, though she seemed unconcerned with the hold she had over the people of the lunch hall. She had long, bone-straight black hair; dark skin; and reminded Sade of a younger, curvier Naomi Campbell.

Baz spoke again in a lowered tone. "The one with *the hair* is Juliette de Silva. She's the goalie of the girls' lacrosse team and has an encyclopedic knowledge of everyone and everything . . . *Allegedly* her dad *owns* the guy who owns the big tech company that rhymes with *canoodle*."

Sade wasn't sure if Baz was being serious, but from the look on his face there didn't seem to be irony in his words.

"The blonde, scary one is Persephone Stuart. I heard that she once chopped off a guy's . . . *appendage* . . . in his sleep because he stared at her too long, and now she keeps it in a jar in her room," he continued, rather casually. "And the one in the middle is their leader, April Owens—she actually used to be Elizabeth's roommate."

Elizabeth didn't look too happy with Baz offering up that information.

"What happened?" Sade asked.

Elizabeth gave Baz a death glare before stabbing her lunch with a fork. "Nothing. People change roommates all the time; it's not that big of a deal—can we stop talking about them now? They're just girls."

Sade remembered Miss Blackburn's comment earlier about transfers being a rare occurrence but decided to drop it, not wanting to make Elizabeth upset and ruin what might potentially be her only friendship for the rest of her time at Alfred Nobel Academy.

Elizabeth's face dulled once again. Sade wondered what the history was there. It was clear it was nothing good.

Baz looked like he felt bad. In what seemed to be a peace offering, he silently pushed his jelly pot over to Elizabeth and she accepted it with a faint "thank you." It made him smile.

Something about the way the two interacted felt intimate. The sort of intimacy that you share with those you've known for an entire lifetime. Sade felt something twist inside and she swallowed the permanent lump in her throat.

Tearing her eyes away from them, she examined the hall once more, focusing on others instead of her own internal demons.

Without meaning to, her gaze landed on the unholy trio again, and she let herself get lost in them.

It was so easy to.

It made sense that their beauty was what they were well-known for. Even she was under their effortless spell.

Her eyes focused in on April, who was applying a thin layer of gloss to her lips. Then on Juliette, who was laughing at something someone must have said. Then, slowly, her gaze shifted toward the blonde she had spotted first, stopping short when a pair of curious eyes trained on her as well.

The blonde—Persephone, Baz had said her name was—was sipping from a glass, her head slightly tilted, her eyebrow arched as though she was considering something.

But most important, she was watching Sade too.

MONDAY
GLASSHOUSE

SADE HAD ONLY BEEN AT the boarding school for a few short hours, but she already had the feeling that something bad was about to happen.

She could feel the dread piling up in her stomach, the squeezing in her chest that usually followed one of her irrational thoughts about an impending doom encroaching on her otherwise dull life.

It was a panic attack. An irritating side effect of her disorderly thoughts and feelings.

This was a mistake, the voice in her head whispered. *You should never have come.*

That pesky voice fed her lies and exacerbated truths. It usually grew louder when she was confronted with something new or scary—like a completely new home, new school, new *everything*.

A memory floated aimlessly in her mind. Coming and going as it pleased, it made the dread in the pit of her stomach rise even more.

Whenever she'd have a particularly bad panic attack, her mum would always take her face in her hands and kiss her forehead, whispering, "*Hey, now, adie kekere . . . the sky has not yet fallen.*"

Somehow, hearing her mum say those words, hearing the nickname she'd given her, adie kekere—chicken little—would pull her out of her personal sinking ship.

Now that her mum was no longer here to calm the storm, her brain found other imperfect ways to deal with the dread. Sometimes she'd wake up screaming, her subconscious tortured by night terrors. Other times, she'd simply sleepwalk. Wandering around the house, searching aimlessly for an unknown thing. Mostly, though, it would just manifest in *this*. These misplaced anxiety attacks.

It was like constantly being haunted by herself, with no reprieve from the ghosts inside her.

The same dread-inducing memory persisted. First pausing, as though the disc in her mind was faulty, then rewinding, playing, stopping at the same twisted frame over and over again—

"You okay?" Elizabeth asked, looking concerned, while a puzzled Baz stared down at her too.

Sade sank her nails into her palms, relaxing at the feel of her nerve endings singing, grounding her in the entryway of Turing once again.

She nodded. "Sorry—got lost for a moment there—what were you saying?"

"I asked if you wanted to see the greenhouse. It's not fancy, but as the president of biology club, I'm the only student with access, so I like to chill there sometimes," Elizabeth said.

"You're the president of biology club?" Sade asked.

"Well . . . she *was* before they kicked her out for killing the class rabbit," Baz said.

Elizabeth whacked him. "One, it was the class hamster, and two, I did *not* kill Mr. Fluffy. That's a rumor. But anyway, I still have the keys. Want to come up with us?" Elizabeth said, dangling them in front of Sade.

It was already past seven p.m. Sade was hoping to do more exploring of the school grounds by herself before curfew, seeing as the tour could only cover so much. After lunch, Basil had gone back to his classes and Elizabeth had shown Sade around more rooms and buildings on the large expanse of the school grounds while they waited for Basil's last-period classes to end. Despite spending the entire day showing Sade around, Elizabeth had barely scratched the surface of the school's amenities and there were still places Sade wanted to see.

Her mind went back to the shadows in the Hawking House window from earlier.

"Sure," Sade replied, not wanting to turn Elizabeth down and jeopardize her first real chance at friendship.

Besides, she still had some time.

"Actually I'll have to take a rain check. I have rowing practice until nine," Baz said.

"Oh yes, how could I forget," Elizabeth replied with a sly smile. "Baz joined the rowing team this year because of that guy from Hawking . . . What was his name again? Kyle . . . Kieran—"

"His name is Kwame, and I didn't join because of him, I joined because I find the waters calming. But anyway, as much as I enjoy speaking with you both, I need to go," he said, wearing an expression that told Sade that it was definitely about this Kwame guy.

"Bring me back something with chocolate," Elizabeth said as he hugged her.

"I'll try," he said, kissing her forehead gently before pulling back.

Sade watched, feeling like the third wheel to a married couple. She'd noticed them exchange glances throughout the day, as though they were reading each other's minds, and noticed the way Elizabeth's guarded exterior peeled away when Baz was near. Seeing their friendship was . . . nice. Sade had once known what it felt like to have someone so close they could see every single one of your thoughts in a single glance. She knew what it was like to love someone so deeply they were the only person in the entire world who saw all the sharp, jagged edges of you and didn't run away.

Baz then turned to Sade. "Are you a hugger?"

Sade shook her head. "Not really."

Baz nodded, looking pensive for a brief moment. "We'll have to come up with a secret handshake," he said.

"A secret handshake?" Sade replied, her eyebrows furrowed.

"Yes, and it will be really awesome."

"I don't know if I'll remember all the steps, but sure," she said.

He seemed satisfied with that. "Send me a sandwich if you're in need of my services—otherwise, I'll see you guys later," he said, walking backward now. "It was nice hanging out with you today, Sade," Baz finished with a smile, before giving them a final wave and walking away, down the hall and out of the entrance of the Turing dormitory.

They both watched him go, Elizabeth's face returning to the one Sade had met earlier that day. The one with the cold expression and sad eyes. It was as though, when Baz left, the mask she had been wearing quickly eroded away.

"Let's head on up—the greenhouse is on the roof of the science building," Elizabeth said, moving her hair out of her face and tying it up with a gold hairband.

"Cool." Sade was unsure whether or not to ask if Elizabeth was okay. After all, they hardly knew each other.

Still, Sade couldn't shake the feeling that something was wrong. But as she followed Elizabeth, she reminded herself of the lesson life had taught her.

Not all her feelings reflected reality and not everyone needed saving.

As they walked out of Turing, Sade felt the panic from earlier rise and fall, floating gently on the surface, daring her to sink. The same haunting memory surfaced along with it, followed by the familiar hiss of the voice in her head.

You should never have come.

THE GREENHOUSE WAS FILLED WITH monsters.

Or as Elizabeth called them: *Monstera deliciosa*, otherwise known as the Swiss cheese plant.

". . . It's not so much about its edibility but rather its resemblance to cheese; very hard to kill too, known to be resilient and low maintenance, easy to keep as a plant pet," Elizabeth continued, gesturing to the large plants in the corners of the greenhouse with holes in their leaves. "Like I do with the others, I try to water this one every seven days; otherwise, no one else will—the caretaker is useless. Without me, most of these plants would shrivel up and die."

The greenhouse had many plants like this, with strange names and even stranger appearances. Sade had reached out to touch one and she swore it bit her.

Elizabeth had spent the last twenty minutes introducing Sade to all the weird and wonderful plants that were housed here. It was clear the plants meant a lot to her.

Sade's favorite so far was the hooded skullcap—despite its name, it was not, in fact, shaped like a skull.

"I'm probably boring you with this plant talk," Elizabeth said.

"Not at all, I found it informative," Sade replied, which was true. She had never heard someone sound so interested in plants and nature. "So you like biology?" she asked.

Elizabeth nodded. "I want to be a botanist when I'm older. Unlike people, plants are honest. If they're hungry, they tell you."

Sade had never thought of plants in that way. "That's really deep."

Elizabeth looked at Sade and gave her a small smile. She reached behind some of the potted plants and pulled out a small pot with blue flowers.

"Here," she said, handing the pot to Sade. "These are forget-me-not flowers."

Sade took it reluctantly.

"A 'welcome to ANA' present," Elizabeth added.

Sade examined the weird blue plant. "Thanks."

"You should name it. I find that plants respond better when you name them," Elizabeth said as she walked out of the small greenhouse and took a seat on the rooftop.

Sade looked down at the forget-me-nots. "I'll have to think about a name. Don't want to name it the wrong thing and it grows up to be a rebellious teenager because of that."

"That's always very important to consider when naming your plant child," Elizabeth said in agreement, stretching her legs out and letting them dangle off the roof.

Sade noticed the stickers randomly dotted around Elizabeth's boots. Four-leaf clovers.

"I like the stickers, on your shoes," Sade said.

Elizabeth looked down with her. "Oh, thank you. They're meant to bring good luck."

Sade definitely needed an abundance of that.

She looked away from her roommate's boots and over at the roof's edge. From the rooftop, she felt like one of the birds from the painting in the reception area. But instead of iron, her cage was made of glass and filled with wild plants.

From up here, she could see most of the campus, and what seemed so big early on now felt smaller from this new perspective.

"Are you going to sit?" Elizabeth asked.

Sade nodded, taking a seat next to her. "Sorry, got caught up in the view. It's really nice."

"It is. Sometimes I come here when I need to clear my thoughts and it does wonders. Everything feels less important when you're standing on a rooftop. One minute you're sad about getting a B on your English final, then the next you're up here and you think . . . fuck Shakespeare, I want to be a biologist anyway," Elizabeth said with a smile.

Sade laughed. "So profound."

"Right? I should be the poster child for scholarship kids everywhere. My motto: Do the bare minimum necessary to keep your scholarship as well as your sanity," Elizabeth said, holding up her water bottle like a fake microphone. "Feel free to come here, though, if you ever need to get away from all the madness that is ANA. I'll let you in."

"Are you sure? I wouldn't want to intrude on your special place . . ."

Elizabeth waved her off. "Don't worry; this isn't my only special place."

Sade nodded slowly. "Will take you up on that offer then, I think."

"Great," Elizabeth said, and then she folded her legs in and placed her chin on her kneecaps.

As they sat and watched the school beneath them, silence crept in slowly and Sade could feel her loud thoughts creeping in with it.

"Baz is really nice," she said, pushing the quiet away to keep the thoughts from going too far.

"He's the best," Elizabeth replied.

"Are you guys together?" Sade asked.

Elizabeth's eyes widened and she snorted loudly, "God, no—I'd rather have kidney stones than date Basil dos Santos. I love him, and he's a great friend but a rather lousy boyfriend. Besides, I'm not really his type."

"Oh, I'm sorry—"

"You're not the first to think it, so I don't blame you. For the longest time, even his own mother thought we were secretly dating. I see Baz more like my little pink-haired twin as opposed to someone I'd voluntarily kiss," Elizabeth said.

"How long have you guys known each other?" Sade asked.

"Since we were kids. My mum was his grandmother's nurse, and we were raised together. I never had any siblings, so Baz has always felt like my unofficial younger brother."

Sade smiled at that. "I had someone like that, before," she said.

"From back home?" Elizabeth asked.

Sade nodded, still staring down at the school beneath them. Her vision was criss-crossing and blurring.

"Do you think they'll keep in touch?"

Sade paused and glanced at Elizabeth briefly. "They died."

"Oh . . . I'm sorry."

"It's okay, it happened a while ago," Sade said simply, as though she were stating something mundane and reasonable.

There was nothing mundane or reasonable about death.

And yet people seemed to have a habit of doing that around her.

Dying.

Although Sade was so used to it now that grief sometimes felt almost like an intrinsic part of her. She once joked about changing her name to Rogue. Because like the character from *X-Men*, her touch was lethal.

She could sense Elizabeth's awkwardness. People usually became awkward around her whenever she mentioned her many dead relatives and friends. It was as though they could sense that she was a bad omen and were planning their escape.

"I guess I do know what it's like to lose someone like that . . . It sucks. I don't know what I'd do if I lost Baz; he's pretty much all I have left. He's also my only friend, so I think I'd be a lot lonelier than I am now," Elizabeth said haltingly.

"It is lonely. I'll take all the friends I can at this point. Accepting any applications?" Sade said semi-jokingly.

"I'm pretty sure Baz has already adopted you, so you officially have two new friends—if you want us that is, we are an odd pair . . . There's probably a good reason people don't approach us at school," Elizabeth said.

Sade thought about it. Despite wanting friends, she wasn't sure whether she deserved them. Especially given her pretty awful track record.

Her father always warned her about high school. That people would take one look at her and know she was a cursed thing. But she didn't answer to him anymore.

She was here. She was going to be normal. She was going to make friends.

"I'd like that," she replied after a moment or two, holding her hand out for Elizabeth to shake.

Elizabeth shook her hand. "You were warned."

Sade laughed. Before she could make a comment about her history of making bad decisions, Elizabeth's phone pinged loudly, like it had earlier. Once again, it wiped the smile from the girl's face in an instant.

"Is everything okay?" Sade asked. Elizabeth looked as though she had seen another dead rat, or maybe something much worse than that.

Elizabeth's head shot up and she nodded. "Y-yeah, I uh—have to go and do something, forgot to collect my lab homework this morning. Didn't you have to pick up something from reception?" she asked.

Sade's eyes widened, realization smacking her in the face. "I was meant to collect my welcome pack and house keys. Do you think Miss Blackburn will murder me for being late? I have this feeling she hates my guts already," Sade said, standing now with Elizabeth.

"You'll probably meet Ms. Thistle there; Miss Blackburn doesn't work in the evenings . . . And don't worry about her—she hates all of us," Elizabeth said, the mask Sade had noticed peeling away earlier now firmly cemented to her skin. Whoever that text was from brought a hardened expression to her new face.

"I can take you down to the reception if you'd like?" Elizabeth said.

Sade shook her head. "It's okay. I kind of want to wander around. I think it'll help me get used to my new surroundings."

"You go ahead, then—I need to lock up the greenhouse."

Sade nodded. "Thank you again . . . for showing me around today," she said.

"Anytime. I'll see you later in our room?" Elizabeth replied abruptly, all familiarity wiped from her voice.

"Yeah . . . see you," Sade said, then moved away from Elizabeth, toward the exit of the roof.

Before leaving, Sade glanced back at Elizabeth, who now seemed to be tapping at her phone.

Sade felt compelled to turn around, walk back up to her, and ask her what was *really* wrong. Because it was clear that something was.

But they had only just become friendly with each other. They didn't yet have that relationship.

She glanced at Elizabeth one last time before she left. A newer mask now clung to Elizabeth's skin.

This one made of glass.

SEA OF TROUBLES

MS. THISTLE WAS THE COMPLETE opposite of Miss Blackburn, much to Sade's surprise.

Where Blackburn was all storms and dark tailored suits, Thistle was bright knitted sweaters, polka-dotted cat-eye glasses, and a warm smile that matched her equally warm brown skin.

Sade was relieved to find that not all staff at the boarding school were predisposed to hating her after all.

The bright evening receptionist went into one of the large, labeled filing cabinets behind her desk and handed Sade a bulky folder filled with information about the school, the key to the Turing entrance, her dorm room key, and a map.

"Thank you, Ms. Thistle," Sade said with a smile.

"No problem, sweetheart. Just make sure you don't lose your dorm key; Miss Blackburn doesn't like me giving out replacements."

Sade made a mental note. *Lose your key. Face Miss Blackburn's wrath.*

"Got it," she said.

"Miss Blackburn told me that you already met your house sister, Elizabeth. I asked your house brother to come down after dinner too, but I guess he forgot. Wouldn't put it past that boy," she said, muttering the last part quietly. "Anyway, we'll have to try again sometime this week! Let me know if you have any questions or queries? I'm always here to help," Ms. Thistle finished, shuffling some papers and placing them next to her keyboard.

"Thank you—will let you know if anything comes up," Sade said, shoving the folder into her tote bag along with the key. She turned to leave but paused and turned back to Ms. Thistle. "Actually . . . I do have a question."

Ms. Thistle looked up at her. "Yes, of course, ask away."

"How does access to other houses work? If I made a friend in another house, could I just visit anytime?"

Ms. Thistle nodded. "You are allowed to visit other houses before curfew. Sometimes the doors might be closed—in which case someone will need to let you in, but if it's open and it's before curfew, then you certainly can!"

Sade gave her a smile. "That's very useful to know. Thank you, Ms. Thistle."

"No problem. I'm sure you'll make friends in no time and, if not, you're always welcome to hang out here. I hope you have a nice night, dear."

Sade waved goodbye finally, wishing her a nice night also, before walking out of the entrance she had used minutes ago.

She held up the map, scanning the key to find the building she required.

After a few wrong turns, she found it and folded the map up, tucking it inside her bag. She then followed the stone path around the main building to where she had stood earlier in the day with Elizabeth, near the statue of the academy's founder and the building that read NEWTON SPORTS CENTER.

The air was cold, and she had the eerie sense of being watched by someone . . . or something.

She turned around, expecting to see students lingering or devilish shadows dancing in the corners. But there was nothing there, just the looming presence of Hawking House.

She brushed the feeling off and headed inside the sports center.

Her footsteps echoed on the tiled floor and she was immediately struck by how quiet it was inside. She remembered the distant sound of building construction coming from within the center earlier. How dead it was now, in comparison.

Displayed on a board by the entrance was a map to the different floors and rooms in Newton. She scanned it for directions to the pool. This floor seemed to have indoor basketball and tennis courts, with the pool on the basement floor.

As she made her way down, the deafening quiet of the center seemed to only grow.

There was something unnerving about it. *Where was everyone?*

When she got to the basement floor, she followed the arrows on the walls and found herself in front of a giant glass panel.

Inside she could see what seemed to be a large natatorium with green-and-white tiling on the walls and a hole where the swimming pool should be, with scaffolding and material splayed about, surrounding the area.

She figured this had to be the pool that Elizabeth had mentioned earlier, the new one that was being built.

She glanced around, searching for the other, and noticed more arrows on the walls with a laminated sign that read POOL.

This time, when she followed the arrows, they led her to another glass-paneled wall, and through the glass she could see the familiar clear rippling surface of a swimming pool.

She pressed her palm to the door, hesitating, then stepping inside.

The familiar smell of chlorine hit her nostrils and she felt herself relax, before walking into the empty hall.

For the first time that day, she felt like she was at home.

In the distance, she thought she could hear the low rumble of a conversation, breaking up the quiet, but wasn't sure. She hadn't seen anyone around before. It was possible that it was something else: sound sometimes traveled weirdly in a swimming hall.

The swimming pool was twice the size of the one she had back at home. The one she used to practice in day and night.

Deeper too.

She stepped close to the ledge, staring down at the bottom of the pool, watching her distorted reflection ripple back and forth.

She bent down slowly to touch it, tracing the outline of her face.

If she squinted at the water, she could see it. The red pools of cloudy, fresh blood, spilling and mixing with the chlorine. Not that it was real. None of it was. Not the blood, the body, or the reflection staring back at her.

"You shouldn't be here," a voice said, echoing through the hall.

Sade startled, her hand fracturing her reflection.

She stood up and turned to find the source. A boy with dark skin and closely cropped hair, wearing nothing but Speedos and an impish grin.

He looked . . . familiar, but she couldn't pinpoint how or why.

"Wh-what?" she said.

"I said . . ." He stepped forward, and she followed the dance, stepping backward. "You shouldn't be here, dressed like that. You're wearing outside shoes," he said, gesturing to her Doc Marten–clad feet.

She had been so wrapped up in finding this pool, she'd forgotten.

"I'm so sorry—I can leave now—"

He shrugged.

"The damage has been done . . . might as well stay," he said before taking a leap into the pool.

She felt some water from the splash graze her fingers, so she moved back once again.

Even though he seemed okay with her staying, she wanted to leave, embarrassed by the fact that she walked in here dressed like this. If her old swim coach could see her now, she would be disappointed.

He resurfaced and swam toward the ledge, near where she stood. "You're new," the stranger stated.

"Is that a question?" Sade asked.

"Not really, just an observation. We don't get many newbies," he said.

"So I've heard," Sade said, remembering what Miss Blackburn said earlier about how selective the school was.

He stared at her for a few moments, as though he was trying to read her thoughts. "What's your name?"

"Sade."

"Like the singer?"

"No, like my grandmother."

"Your grandma's a singer?"

Sade narrowed her eyes at him.

"I'm joking." The stranger looked at her with a playful expression, like he wanted to tease her some more.

"I'm gonna go," she said, holding on to the strap of her bag.

He pushed himself back, floating on the water. "Okay, then."

"Okay, then," she replied, wanting the last word.

She turned to leave the room.

"Hey, new girl," she heard him say, prompting her to turn back and look at him.

"Yes?"

He smiled at her. "Welcome to ANA."

AFTER SPENDING ANOTHER TWENTY MINUTES wandering the mazelike halls of the sports center, she finally found her way out, emerging from the back rather than the front entrance she had used before.

In an attempt to not get lost again, she took out the map in her bag, trying to figure out which direction Turing House was.

The sound of doors opening and closing, as well as the gentle pitter-patter of footsteps from inside the sports center, rang out through the night.

She peered through the exit, hoping to catch a glimpse of someone, but saw nothing. It was as though a shadow had passed by, instead of a real human being.

It was probably past nine p.m. at this point, and yet it felt so much later.

Sade returned her focus to the map, following the path now all the way to her dorm.

Turing looked like a gothic tower in the moonlight. There was something unsettling yet warm about its darkness, and if it wasn't obvious before, this made it clear that Turing was perfect for her.

She stepped into the French lift and rode up to her floor, taking out the key to her room.

Room 313.

She paused to look at the door properly. It had Elizabeth's messy handwriting on the small chalkboard sign that hung beneath the door number. The sign read: *Elizabeth Wang's Room.* And underneath that there was a sticker that read BEWARE with a picture of a duck holding a knife.

She smiled at the detail. She hadn't noticed it when she was there earlier. Possibly too preoccupied by the dead rat.

"What are you doing out here?" a voice called, causing her heart to rattle.

Sade turned toward it.

A pale white girl with long brown hair and a stern expression stood staring down at her with her arms crossed.

"Going into my room . . . ," Sade replied.

"It's nearly past weekday curfew. You shouldn't be out at this time," the girl said.

Sade didn't bother responding, but instead stared at her, wondering why it was she cared so much about the curfew. After all, wasn't she also out of her room?

The girl squinted at Sade, and a look of realization crossed her face. "Are you the new third year?" she asked.

Sade nodded slowly, unsure of the relevance of that information.

"I'm Jessica, the house prefect—Miss Blackburn told me you'd arrived today," the girl said, eyeing her. "Since you're new and this is your first offense, I'll let you off this time. Just don't let me catch you out here again after curfew, okay?" she said.

The girl could only be a few months older than Sade, yet she acted as though she had years on her.

Sade gave her a thumbs-up and the girl—Jessica—replied with a tight smile and retreated back down the hall.

She shrugged off the interaction and stepped into the dorm, the door closing behind her.

She crept through the dark room, not wanting to wake Elizabeth, and quietly got changed into her nightclothes before climbing into the rigid single bed.

She turned to the side, looking at the clock in the corner, which now read 9:26 p.m.

Sade's gaze landed on Elizabeth's bed, noticing the outline of a lumpy figure under the covers.

It seemed Elizabeth was already asleep.

She should probably do the same, seeing as she had her first day of classes tomorrow.

A gentle breeze floated into the room from the open window, bringing with it the October chill.

Too lazy to do anything about the window, Sade settled down, resting her head on her pillow and filling her mind with the words of a familiar du'a, as she often did at night, until she finally felt herself getting drowsy.

In the corner of the room, the shadows flickered, morphing into one solid, familiar figure.

A girl. Always the same. With long swooping braids, identical to her own, a white nightgown, and a solemn, translucent expression.

The girl who would tiptoe into Sade's nightmares and beg Sade to save her.

It was part of her nightly routine now. Sade would close her eyes and the girl would appear.

She would *always* appear.

Sometimes, Sade's body would forget she was dreaming, and she'd get up, walking in her sleep, searching for the girl. Not wanting to let her slip away again.

Most times, though, the girl would just linger, watching over Sade. Holding her.

And while to others, a nightmare like this would scare them enough to keep them from sleeping, it brought her comfort. Made her feel less alone.

Before the world went dark, Sade felt her, the shadow girl from her nightmares, crawl into bed with her and hold her close.

TUESDAY

NEW BEGINNINGS

ELIZABETH WASN'T IN THE ROOM when Sade woke up.

She wasn't at breakfast either.

She had probably gotten up earlier or gone to hang out with Baz, so Sade got ready for her first day of boarding school alone.

It was very unlike her routine back at home. There, she would wake up at the crack of dawn for swim practice with her coach, go for a run, get dressed in normal clothes, and spend the day being tutored in one of the study rooms, where they'd also eat breakfast and lunch, before rounding the day off with another grueling practice with her swim coach. Her muscles were used to a constant cycle of breaking and tearing, so her body probably thanked her for this change in routine.

In the Turing House dining hall, most people were still dressed in their nightgowns, and a few others like Sade in their uniforms. After a *small* breakfast—seeing as most of the options were not halal—she went back to her room, wanting to do her hair before heading to class.

She stood in front of the mirror, slicking down her edges to give her braids the appearance of being newer than they were. She hadn't gotten her hair rebraided in over a month. Between her father's funeral and starting at Alfred Nobel Academy, there hadn't been enough time for it.

She opened one of her suitcases and rummaged around for some shoes, jumping a little when she heard a sharp knock.

"Coming!" she yelled, grabbing a pair of her black Mary Janes and slipping them on, before rushing over to the door.

When she opened it, a white, blonde, brown-eyed student appeared with a pink slip in hand.

"Miss Blackburn wants to see you before class," the student said, handing Sade the slip.

Sade had been hoping to avoid another interaction with Miss Blackburn so soon after the last, but as usual the odds were never in her favor.

"Okay, thanks."

The student nodded and then promptly walked away.

Sade looked at herself one last time in the mirror, swallowing her first-day jitters.

She kept her mum's saying in mind, *the sky has not yet fallen,* as she picked up her bag and headed out.

"YOU'RE LATE," MISS BLACKBURN SAID to Sade, who was still breathless from rushing down, before handing her a class schedule.

"I came down as soon as I received the note—"

"As I said yesterday, your excuses won't get you far here. Please don't let this happen again," Miss Blackburn cut in, her eyes already elsewhere as she scrawled in a leather-bound diary. Sade considered asking Miss Blackburn whether she'd like her to teleport down next time but decided against it, figuring that she valued her life enough not to.

A knock sounded on the door and Miss Blackburn finally looked up.

"That must be your house brother. I wanted to introduce the two of you as soon as possible," she said, pushing herself out of the chair.

Sade turned to the door as Miss Blackburn pulled it open, revealing a tall, familiar stranger.

Sade locked eyes with him, noticing the shocked expression on his face, which quickly dissolved into a small, questioning smile.

"It is such a pleasure to have finally been graced with your presence, Augustus; we had some trouble tracking you down yesterday," Miss Blackburn said dryly, folding her arms.

"Anything for you, Miss B," the boy, Augustus, said.

Miss Blackburn moved aside and gestured at Sade.

"This is Sade Hussein. She's a transfer student and your new house sister. Sade, Augustus Owens, our deputy head boy," Miss Blackburn said, introducing Sade formally to the boy she had met at the pool the previous evening.

Now that he was fully clothed, she could look at him without it being weird.

Well, at least less weird than before.

He was dressed in the same black uniform; however, his sleeves were rolled up and his tie was black and blue. He had dark brown skin; tight curls; and a sharp, angular face.

He reminded Sade of a sculpture, rather than a person.

"Nice to meet you, Sade," Augustus said, holding out his hand for her to shake. She noticed a few cuts on his knuckles.

She stared down at the pattern of bruises, then back up at his face before placing her hand in his.

"Likewise," she said.

"Great," Miss Blackburn said, looking down at her watch. "Your classes start in a few minutes. If I were you, I would start making a move. Especially you, Sade, given your *history*."

Augustus held open the office door for her. "After you," he said, and so Sade stepped out and he followed.

She finally looked down at her schedule. She had assumed she would have gotten it last night with the welcome pack, but Ms. Thistle had told her that they were still working out the logistics of her subjects with the teachers given her late arrival.

She had only been allowed to pick four subjects to take this year, so she had picked English, Mandarin, History, and Psychology.

It seemed that English was up first.

"You have Mr. Michaelides first period, tough luck," Augustus said, startling Sade a little. He was leaning over, reading her schedule with her.

"Is he strict or something?" she asked.

"No . . . just extremely boring. The guy can talk for *hours* if you let him. I usually bring a sudoku puzzle to his class just in case," he said.

"Sudoku? Are you seventy-five?" she asked.

Augustus laughed. "Yup. You got me. I guess it is true what they say, Black don't crack."

Sade found herself wanting to roll her eyes at the corniness of his response. "Right," she replied, pulling her bag over her shoulder.

"That looks heavy; have you been shown to your locker yet?" he asked.

Sade nodded. "Yeah, my house sister did yesterday. But it's honestly fine. I won't have time to put my things away before class and I think I'm already going to be late."

She looked down at the schedule and then up at the hallway for any indicators of where her class would be.

"The Austen Building is straight through there if you were wondering. It's not hard to miss," Augustus said, pointing at a large oak door.

"Oh, thanks."

"No problem, just doing my house brotherly duties," he said, tipping an invisible hat.

"Well, I better be going—don't want Miss Blackburn to kill me. Thank you again, Augustus," she said.

"It's actually just August, like the month. Like you, Miss Blackburn believes I'm a seventy-five-year-old man trapped in a seventeen-year-old's body," he said.

"Why don't you correct her?" Sade asked.

"Because I don't have a death wish," he replied.

"That makes sense."

August stared at Sade silently for a moment. It was clear that he was analyzing her. As she was doing to him.

"I should go," Sade said, moving closer to the door.

"Yeah, of course—good luck," August said.

"Thank you," she replied, turning now.

"Wait . . . ," he said, and she turned back.

"Yeah?"

He rummaged through his satchel and took out a small book. She watched him rip out a page and write on it before handing it to her.

The page was filled with numbers and blank boxes and, on top of that, his phone number.

She looked up at him as he backed away now with his hands in his pockets and a glint in his eye.

"In case you get bored," he said, then turned and walked in the opposite direction, leaving Sade in the hallway alone.

SADE GOT TO CLASS APPROXIMATELY seven minutes late, as the teacher, Mr. Michaelides, was in the middle of discussing some character's untimely demise.

She tried to seem apologetic as she crept toward a vacant chair at the back of the small classroom. She quietly placed her bag on the floor and took out her notebook and pen.

"Ultimately, his hamartia, his fatal flaw, was his ambition, and hers—her greed," Mr. Michaelides said, his Canadian accent reverberating throughout the room. He paused now to look at Sade through his glasses. "Thank you for joining us—Sade? I assume."

She nodded, and he smiled.

"Welcome! I'm always pleased to have another literature lover join my class. Everyone, this is Sade. Sade, this is everyone. Do you have a copy of the text?"

She shook her head and he grabbed a battered text from his desk.

"You can use my copy for now, I have it all up here anyway," he said, tapping his temple as he handed her a copy of *Macbeth*. "Have you read it before?"

"Yes," she replied. Her tutors had made her read all Shakespeare's plays. Her favorite was *The Tempest*, though *Macbeth* was a close second.

He smiled again. "Good. Well, we are just looking over the themes and preparing for the presentations at the end of the week. Since you're behind . . ." Mr. Michaelides scanned the classroom and then gestured to someone in the corner. "Persephone will help you get up to speed. She will work with you for the rest of the term on all our assignments."

Sade turned to look at Persephone, and the blonde girl from that group Baz had called *the unholy somethings* stared back at her.

Persephone didn't look too pleased. "Mr. Michaelides, how do you expect me to focus on my own presentation and assignments if I'm also helping someone else?" she asked.

Sade hadn't expected her voice to sound that way. Slightly raspy with this blend of different accents, melding together, rising and falling. Some words spoken with British English intonations, others not.

"Persephone, I think we both know that won't be a problem. Didn't you tell me that you were already done with your presentation?" Mr. Michaelides asked with a glint in his eye, his arms folded over his chest.

"Yes, but I have other work—"

"So it's decided then. You will help Sade catch up with everything she missed so far, yes?"

Persephone stayed quiet for a few moments before nodding.

Mr. Michaelides smiled wider. "And that's why she's our deputy head girl, always so helpful and understanding. Now, moving on to the theme of relationships in the text. I will divide you into pairs to discuss your thoughts on the representation of relationships in the play . . ."

Sade looked around the room. Including herself, there were eight students taking this class.

Mr. Michaelides paired them off, putting her with a pale, freckled redheaded guy named Francis.

"What did you think about the relationship between Macbeth and his wife?" Sade asked him after neither of them had said anything for a long, painful minute. Francis seemed preoccupied with staring out the window.

He shrugged, fingers tapping on the desk, leg bouncing as his gaze stayed fixed on whatever had caught his eye outside. She glanced at the window, trying to see what it was he was so focused on. But there was nothing there.

"I guess I'd say it was toxic, that they both used each other," Sade said, replying to her own question.

Francis sat forward, resting his chin on his hand now, still focusing on the window and not on her.

She placed her hand on his shoulder, patting him gently. "Francis?"

He jumped, staring at her shocked, as though until that moment he hadn't realized that she was next to him.

"What?" he said gruffly, eyebrows bunched together.

She looked pointedly down at the play on the desk. "We're meant to be discussing the class question," she answered.

He looked down at the text and then back up at her, his gaze unfocused. "Oh, right," he said, scratching his head and sitting back. "What was the question again?"

"Macbeth and Lady Macbeth, their relationship," she repeated. He stared at her blankly, his eyes bloodshot.

"I don't know . . . whatever you think, I guess," he said, his voice trailing off as his head turned back toward the mysterious window. She had lost him once again—not that she ever had him. Francis was clearly someplace else.

She watched him carefully. His battered fingerless gloves. The way he bit his nails, the slight tremor in his fingertips, yellowing nails indicating he was a smoker—confirmed both by the smell that clung to his clothes and the cigarette placed on top of his ear—as well as his untidy uniform.

Francis was a mess.

Spaced out. Off in another world, or perhaps on something that was clearly more important than this lesson ever could be. She wondered if there was even a point in trying to engage with him or if she should simply continue to make her own notes instead.

The latter seemed to be more productive.

As she started to make notes, Sade noticed Francis sit up sharply as though he had been electrocuted. Then, out of nowhere he stood up, the chair clattering behind him.

"Francis? Is everything okay?" Mr. Michaelides asked, everyone's eyes now on the both of them and Francis's still on the window.

Francis looked at Mr. Michaelides's worried face, coming back to himself.

"Y-yeah . . . I need to uhm . . . use the bathroom," he said, before grabbing his bag and walking out of the classroom.

Well, that was weird . . . , Sade thought.

Mr. Michaelides cleared his throat. "Sade, you can join Ezra and Liv's group until Francis returns," he said, gesturing to their table.

Sade nodded, grabbing her notebook and a chair to move over to the table, where a lanky, pale, freckled boy was seated opposite a short, dark-skinned girl.

She sat down next to Liv, but instead of joining in on their discussion, she found herself looking out the window, trying to see where Francis had been looking. In the distance she could make out the faint outline of two figures.

They seemed to be arguing about something.

Sade squinted, her eyes zoning in on one of them, who seemed to have a crumpled uniform and bright red hair.

CLASS ENDED, AND FRANCIS DID not return.

Sade walked out of the classroom, pushing the worksheets from her chatty teacher into her bag.

"Hello," a soft, familiar voice called out.

Sade looked up to see the blonde unholy girl. She was wearing a brown jacket over her white dress shirt, her purple tie slightly loose around her neck. She stepped closer to Sade, with her arms folded. Sade noticed the silver septum ring in her nose.

"I'm free tomorrow after last period. I'll meet you in the main library to help you with the presentation and let you know tomorrow when I'll be free to meet on other days," the girl—Persephone—said.

"Oh . . . okay," Sade replied, realizing that Persephone hadn't asked her for her own availability. They locked eyes and Sade felt tiny pins prick across her face and arms. It felt like Persephone's gaze could permeate her skin. Like Persephone could take one look at her and see everything. All her thoughts, her dreams, her nightmares. All with a single glance.

It was very intimidating.

Persephone finally pulled her eyes from her face and unfolded her arms. "Don't be late," she said before turning away from Sade without another word. Not even a *see you later*.

Sade watched her for longer than was probably socially acceptable, having to eventually force herself to look away.

She took out her schedule once again.

She still had to somehow survive the rest of her first day of lessons.

• • •

AS SHE CAME TO FIND over the next few hours, school was a lot more intense than Sade had previously thought.

She spent the time between the final bell and dinner locked away in the library. While homework was in some ways important, it wasn't nearly as important as the other things she needed to accomplish, and she needed to plan how she was going to tackle it all.

When she arrived back in Turing, she could hear the sound of other students getting ready for dinner, some in the common room and others already in the dining hall.

She locked eyes with the painting of the house's namesake, finding his exhausted expression relatable.

She made her way up to her dorm room, stopping short when she spotted a pink-haired person seated at the foot of the door, staring down intensely at what appeared to be a Nintendo Switch.

Baz was jabbing the buttons hard, his tongue poking out as he concentrated on whatever game he was playing.

"Baz?" Sade said, causing him to look up, wide-eyed, almost as if he was surprised to see her, despite this being her dorm room.

"Oh, hey—you good?" he asked.

"Yeah . . . you?" she replied, still unsure what he was doing here.

He stood up now, pocketing his Switch. "Have you seen Elizabeth today? She hasn't been answering my texts."

"Was she not with you this morning?"

Baz shook his head. "I haven't seen her since yesterday when I left you guys."

That's strange, Sade thought, having a bad feeling about this.

"Maybe she's in the room—have you tried knocking?" she asked.

He nodded. "No answer. I even went to our normal hangout spot after class too, and she wasn't there either. I was hoping you had seen her."

"I haven't. Maybe she's hanging out with another friend?"

Baz smiled at that. "Elizabeth doesn't really *do* people."

This didn't really surprise Sade. The Elizabeth she had spent the day with yesterday didn't seem like much of a people person.

Baz ran a hand through his pink curls and sighed. "She does this sometimes. Goes away for a bit, usually when she wants to be alone. I'm sure she'll text me when she's feeling better," he said, like he was trying to convince both Sade and himself but failing.

"Maybe you can tell a teacher if you're really worried," she suggested, and Baz gave her a look as though she was weird for suggesting it.

"Maybe," he said, in a way that told her he probably wouldn't be doing that. "Anyway, I'll let you go to dinner," he said, holding out his hand now.

Sade raised an eyebrow. *Did he want her to shake his hand?*

He reached out and took her hand, slapping it against his.

"That shall be stage one in our very complicated handshake," he declared.

"Right," Sade said, somewhat glad he'd remembered she didn't like hugs. She hadn't realized he was serious about the handshake, but then again, from the little she knew of Baz, she probably should have anticipated that.

"Could you let me know if you do see her, though?" Baz asked.

Sade nodded. "Yeah, of course. I can text you?" she said.

His eyes lit up and he took out a battered flip phone and passed it to her.

"I accidentally dropped my regular phone in tea during dinner. Repairs are probably going to take *forever*, and so I'm sadly stuck with my grandmother's old Nokia for now," he said.

"How did it drop into tea?" Sade asked as she tapped out her number into the ancient device before handing it back to him.

He shrugged. "It's just one of those things that happen, I guess." And then without any warning, he lifted the phone up to take a picture of her for the Contacts page. The flash nearly blinded her. "I'll call you so you have my number too."

"Okay," Sade said, still recovering from the phone's flash.

"See you later," he said with a wave, before walking in the opposite direction toward the spiral stairs that led to the ground floor she had just come from.

Sade opened the door and found the room exactly as she had left it that morning. Empty.

She brushed off the weird feeling creeping up on her, the feeling that something bad was going to happen. The feeling that maybe something bad had *already* happened. Instead, she went down to dinner, where she sat by herself in the busy hall, eating lasagna and trying to block out that same weird feeling.

Surely, if Baz thought something bad had happened, he'd report it, right? He was Elizabeth's best friend after all; he'd know if something was wrong.

Maybe she just needed to be alone, like he said.

Her mind went back to the weird expression on Elizabeth's face whenever her phone would ping with a notification. The dead rat, her sudden shift in mood on the rooftop.

Dark thoughts about what it all might mean niggled away at her.

• • •

43

THAT NIGHT AS SADE LAY still in the dark, watching the door, waiting for Elizabeth to walk through, she felt a heaviness resting on her chest. It was harder and harder for her to breathe.

She kept watching the door. Kept waiting.

But Elizabeth never came. Somehow, it felt as though Elizabeth had simply fallen off the face of the earth. One moment she was there, showing her around Alfred Nobel, introducing her to Baz, taking her up to the greenhouse on the roof. Then the next, gone.

Sade wondered what the normal thing to do was when someone seemingly vanished from school. Her instincts told her to tell someone, but she remembered Baz's hesitation and considered that maybe that wasn't a normal response. Wouldn't the school notice if one of their students hadn't shown up to her classes? Surely the house prefect would note a change like that; she seemed like the type to keep track of that kind of thing.

If Elizabeth didn't show up by the end of tomorrow, she'd tell Ms. Thistle.

Just in case.

She looked over at the plant Elizabeth had gifted her the day before. Now resting on their bedroom ledge.

You should name it, Elizabeth had said.

Sade decided that she'd name it once Elizabeth returned. They would name it together.

As her eyes grew heavy, the girl she saw each night resurrected from the shadows. But this time she didn't come to Sade.

This time she stayed in the corner. Her face contorted into a smile as tears bled from her eyes.

"*I'm sorry*," Sade whispered.

But it was too late.

WEDNESDAY
GONE GIRL

THE NEXT DAY, SADE WOKE up alone once again.

Elizabeth's bed was empty, and Sade's mind was full of worry.

Elizabeth was probably fine and would indeed show up by the end of the day. Sade had always been one to overthink things. If Baz wasn't that worried, then maybe she shouldn't be either.

Shoving her concern into the corner of her mind, Sade went down for breakfast, got dressed in her uniform, and headed out of Turing.

She was so busy reading her schedule that she didn't notice it at first.

The sound of tires on gravel.

The crowd of people.

The hushed whispers.

It wasn't until she reached the main building and finally saw the men in black police uniforms being led by Miss Blackburn into her office that she realized what was going on.

She, along with some of the other students gathered around, watched Miss Blackburn as the matron held the door open for the officers. Sade's heartbeat stopped when Miss Blackburn's head whipped around, her gaze landing on her.

Miss Blackburn squinted her eyes at Sade, silently questioning her.

Then she looked away, staring at the other students gawking at the police.

"Shouldn't you all be making your way to your first lessons? Come on, hurry along, there's nothing to see here," she said.

But it was clear that that was not the case.

It seemed that police officers weren't a common presence at Alfred Nobel Academy.

Sade knew her next thought was an irrational one, but she couldn't help thinking it.

That somehow, they were there for her.

• • •

THE HOURS WENT BY AND Sade tried to forget about the disturbance that morning.

It was the class before her lunch period, and she was in Mr. Michaelides's English lesson.

Today they were discussing who the villain of *Macbeth* was and whether the main characters were truly in the wrong.

Sade was paired up with Francis again, who, thankfully, was present for today's class—both physically and mentally. He seemed a lot more relaxed than he had been the day before.

"Lady Macbeth is the villain," Francis stated, leaning back in his chair with a pencil balanced on his nose. "She forced Macbeth to do all this shit he didn't want to do because he was whipped. Not his fault that he loved her and she abused his love."

Sade raised an eyebrow. "More like *he* abused her. She was treated like his property; she didn't even have her own name. Her name is literally *Macbeth's woman*. Of course she'd want some agency and power."

Francis rolled his eyes. "Don't come at me with that feminist BS."

Sade suddenly missed Francis ignoring her and not opening his mouth to speak. Before she could retaliate and tell him exactly why her feminist BS mattered, there was a knock on the classroom door.

"Come in!" Mr. Michaelides said.

A tall, gangly student walked in with a white slip and presented it to him.

Mr. Michaelides accepted it, lowering his glasses to read. "Sade Hussein, you have been summoned to the headmaster's office," he said.

The whole class turned to look at her.

And while it was only nine pairs of eyes, if you included Mr. Michaelides and the student who had come to deliver the slip, it felt like the whole world was watching and judging her, making assumptions about what crime she may or may not have committed to warrant a summons to the headmaster's office.

Her mind filled with worries and her stomach, with dread.

She grabbed her things and started making her way to the front of the class. Mr. Michaelides told her that he'd catch her up on anything she'd miss. She thanked him, then headed off to the headmaster's office with the student.

On the way there, her thoughts filled with thousands of theories as to why she was being called to the headmaster's office.

It occurred to her that she didn't even know what he looked like. Right now, Webber was a faceless, scary entity who wanted to reprimand her for reasons unbeknownst to her.

What if she had broken some sacred unspoken rule and was being expelled after barely two days of being here?

Being expelled was not an option.

Going back to the house of horrors she grew up in, with its haunted hallways filled with the ghosts of all the dead and the memories of things she long wished to forget.

That was not an option.

She tried to gauge the look on the student's pale, freckled face, trying to see if it was neutral or judgmental, but she got nothing. Maybe they didn't know why she had been called either.

They arrived at the office of Headmaster Webber. His name was engraved in gold in the door.

The student knocked twice and a stern, familiar voice reverberated through. "Just a moment."

There were heavy footsteps from behind the door, and it felt like an eternity had passed by the time the door opened.

She was welcomed by the stone-faced expression of Miss Blackburn, who ushered her inside impatiently. She led her over to the corner of the large room, where a middle-aged white man with dark brown hair and a square jaw sat behind an oak desk, waiting. In front of him was a nameplate that read HEADMASTER WEBBER.

He sure did like to show his name off, it seemed.

Beside him on either side of the desk stood two police officers.

Sade swallowed; her heart was racing as sweat gathered at her temple.

"Take a seat; we won't keep you long," the headmaster said.

Sade forced herself forward, sitting carefully in the seat in front of him.

"You're probably wondering why you have been called to my office. Don't worry, you're not in trouble, we just wanted to ask you a few questions. I'll let PC Park and PC Laurence take over now. Just answer their questions honestly, and you'll be fine," Webber said, giving her a big smile that she assumed he meant to be reassuring but instead felt creepy and Cheshire-like.

A tall officer with *Park* written on his uniform stepped forward. "We were informed that you are the roommate of Elizabeth Wang, correct?"

Sade nodded slowly, her heart hammering away more, making her feel light-headed.

"How long have you known Miss Wang?"

"We met yesterday and she showed me around the school."

"So you guys weren't close?" the officer asked.

"No, I'm new to the school. I just started," Sade replied, wondering if Elizabeth was okay.

"When did you last see or speak to Miss Wang?"

"Did something happen to her?"

"Please just answer the question, Miss Hussein," the officer said.

"Uh, I guess I last saw her just before bed on Monday—she was sleeping, so we didn't speak or anything. The last time I spoke to her was after dinner. We hung out for a bit at the greenhouse on the roof of the science building," she said, worried that mentioning this would get Elizabeth in trouble. Was she even allowed to go up there anymore?

"What time would you say that was?" Officer Laurence asked.

"Around eight p.m., I think?" Sade replied.

"And what time did you get into bed?"

"Just after nine," she said.

Officer Laurence tilted his head. "Just after nine? And you were in bed the whole night?"

Sade wondered where this was going. "I think so."

"You *think* so?" the officer repeated.

Sade thought about her night terrors and her sleepwalking and felt something sink inside.

She wasn't sure if she was in bed all night.

Sometimes she'd sleepwalk for hours, roaming the grounds like an aimless ghost, before climbing into her bed and waking up like nothing happened.

It had been a habit of hers for years now.

It wouldn't be the first time she couldn't confirm her whereabouts at night and certainly not the last.

"Yes, I was in my bed all night," she said, trying to sound certain, even though she wasn't.

She couldn't be. She never remembered her sleepwalking misadventures. Most of the time she wouldn't get up to much; she'd simply stumble around the expanse of her bedroom only to be found passed out on the floor the next morning, feet away from her bed.

Other times, there'd be evidence of her late-night misadventures—like the time she'd got up in the middle of the night and eaten a whole tray of brownies. She'd woken up the next morning with the taste of chocolate in her mouth and received the scolding of a lifetime from the family cook.

The officers exchanged a curious glance. One made a note in a yellow legal pad.

"Thank you for your help. We greatly appreciate it."

"Is everything okay?" Sade asked, heart still beating wildly.

"Well, there's no easy way to say this," PC Park started, pausing to think over his words carefully.

"We believe something has happened to your roommate."

Sade felt her heart stop. "What?" she asked, to both no one and everyone.

"Nothing is confirmed as of yet, but we have launched a formal investigation into the case and hope for some answers in the next few days." It felt as though they were speaking in code.

"An investigation into what?" Sade asked.

This time Headmaster Webber spoke, a regretful expression on his face.

"I'm afraid Elizabeth is missing."

I SLEEP, I DROWN & DISAPPEAR[1]

Dear Diary,

Last night I think I died. But I'm not so sure.
I don't remember a lot of it.
It's like I keep stumbling into a dark room, searching for the switch to make things bright again. To make me remember. But the switch isn't there. Was it there before?

---

[1] An anagram

THE SINKING SHIP

THE REST OF THE DAY was filled with judgmental stares and whispered insinuations.

Soon after the meeting that morning, rumors began floating around the school about Elizabeth's disappearance. It seemed like everyone suddenly suspected the *new girl*.

Even teachers regarded her strangely, cautiously eyeing her in the hallways and during classes as though she might jump and kidnap them too.

Now all Sade wanted to do was get away from everyone, at least until the rumors subsided.

But unfortunately, thanks to her English teacher, she already had plans.

"Sorry I'm late," Persephone said, out of breath like she had run to the library to meet Sade on time. Yet despite this, she still looked perfect. Her hair was cornrowed into several plaited lines and not a single strand out of place.

It was as if she was incapable of imperfection.

"It's okay, I haven't been waiting long," Sade said.

Persephone nodded. "Should we find a table, then?"

"Sure," Sade said.

After a few minutes of searching, they found a small table tucked away in a corner between two bookcases.

Sade took a seat and Persephone followed, before taking out her folder and her laptop.

"Here are my notes from the last month of class, and all the things you need to know for the assignments coming up this year and key dates and deadlines. The presentation on Friday is pretty straightforward; we're just presenting all the discussion points listed . . . here," she said, pointing a manicured finger at one of the sections in her notes.

"Thanks," Sade said, overwhelmed by everything she still had to catch up on, as well as the anxiety that hadn't quite settled from the meeting with Webber earlier.

"No problem. I can give you a copy of my presentation if you'd like?" Persephone asked, staring at Sade expectantly.

Sade felt her neck warm at the sudden eye contact. She forced her head to bob up and down, having lost the ability to speak.

"Let me just head to the photocopier. There's usually a line at the one on this floor, so I might be a while," Persephone said before pushing herself out of her seat and taking her folder with her. "Do you want anything from the vending machine while I'm there? I'm going to grab a water."

"I'm fine, thanks," Sade said, and Persephone nodded before turning away from her and heading toward the stairs.

Unlike the Persephone she had met in class and seen briefly in the lunch hall, this iteration of her seemed a lot nicer. Less guarded.

Sade watched her go, focusing on her silhouette as she disappeared and not on the stares of the passing students or the silence that followed once they realized it was her. The new girl who was supposedly behind the disappearance of her roommate.

In particular, the table opposite seemed to have a problem with whispering their thoughts and had instead opted to speak them at a normal volume.

"*My friend at Turing said that she saw them have a fight about something,*" one said.

"*I heard at her last school they had to expel her because she stabbed some girl in the shoulder,*" another chimed.

Sade felt like someone had written the word *guilty* on her forehead in permanent marker. She wasn't sure how being Elizabeth's roommate made her guilty or made it seem like the lies about her were so believable.

Maybe it was simply the fact that she was new. A blank slate.

Much easier to paint her in anyone's image. To write an elaborate history for her. To give her a motive.

She decided, after overhearing one of them suggest that she was a drug dealer, that she would wait for Persephone elsewhere.

She stood up, which of course got the attention of the group of loud gossipers, and walked over to the doors that led to the emergency stairwell, where she hoped she could hide away for some time without the scrutiny of strangers.

As she neared the doors, though, she heard the sound of someone on the phone.

A familiar voice.

She pushed the doors open slightly, spotting Baz's familiar pink mop of hair. "Yes, Auntie. I'll keep you updated, get well soon, love you, bye," he said, sounding quiet and glum.

Sade slipped through the doors slowly as he hung up, wiping his eyes with the sleeve of his black sweater.

He looked up from his seated position on the stairs, startling a little when he saw her. "Jesus," he said, looking genuinely scared.

She wondered if he could see the mark on her forehead too. The invisible words spelling out her alleged crime.

"Sorry, I didn't know you were in here," she said.

He shook his head. "It's okay." Baz's eyes were red, like he hadn't slept at all last night.

Seeing him now, it was clear that he knew Elizabeth was missing and that he was worried, much more so than he had been yesterday.

She moved toward him, taking a seat. "Are you okay?" She hated asking that question when she knew the answer was so obvious. It was something she hated being asked herself, especially after the many tragedies in her life.

Are you okay is what people ask when they don't know what else to say. It's an easy question for the asker, but an unbearable one for the asked.

"I don't know." He sniffed. "I was on the phone to her mum, and I had to act like everything was okay. Her mum doesn't know the half of it."

"Didn't the school tell her everything?"

"They did. I just mean, I knew—you know? I knew something was off, and now she's gone somewhere and I knew."

"Don't do that," Sade said. "It's not your fault—"

"Then whose bloody fault is it?" he asked, looking at her now.

She could see how wet his entire face was. His bloodshot eyes. How much he blamed himself for this.

She knew that look too well.

"I don't know, but blaming yourself for something that's out of any of our control doesn't help."

"I should have stayed with her. I shouldn't have gone off to rowing practice; I knew something was off," he muttered, she assumed to himself.

Sade had known something was off with Elizabeth too. And she also did nothing.

"I should have stayed . . . ," he whispered again.

Sade could feel her brain itch, a memory beginning to claw at her:

"You should have stayed with her." She heard someone yell distantly. But she knew it was coming from inside. She knew it wasn't real. It was just an echo of the past.

"You let her die, you did this."

"No—I didn't mean to—"

The crack from *his* hand echoed in her mind, pulling her back into the present, where Baz was next to her, his head somehow having made its way onto her shoulder. She noticed how much he was shivering, so she wrapped her arm around him gently.

Then Sade said something that she'd regret: "She'll be okay. They'll find her."

There was really only one rule in situations like this. Don't make promises that you know won't be kept. Only a god could make such a promise, and she was as mortal as they came.

They were words meant to comfort him. But there was nothing comforting about the stronghold of delusion or false hope.

WHEN SHE GOT BACK TO her room later, there were five officers in uniform spread about the space, examining the potential crime scene.

"A lot of tea in this one's room, eh?" one officer said offhandedly to one of the other officers, whose laugh reverberated around the room, escaping into the halls. He saw Sade staring at him and smiled at her, then went back to making comments and cracking jokes, as though it was all perfectly routine. As if they weren't searching the room of a missing student but instead playing some kind of scavenger hunt game.

Her eyes flickered over to her own side of the room as the officers shuffled around, slipping past her suitcases, her chest of drawers, and her bed. She could hear the sound of her heart ringing in her ears and felt her stomach flip as she kept her eyes glued to the drawers.

After an hour or so spent watching the officers rummage around Elizabeth's things, Sade was allowed to enter the room again.

They'd apparently finished their search and collected any samples of Elizabeth's DNA they could find, and they were now on their merry way.

Miss Blackburn had come up at some point to watch over the officers, and when they were done, she was there to show them out.

Before she left, she turned to Sade, the usual grimace on her face. "The officers have given the room the all clear, but due to the circumstances, I'd understand if you'd like to swap rooms. Let me know and I'll happily arrange that for you," Miss Blackburn said.

Sade stared blankly ahead at the room, feeling the guilt from not reporting Elizabeth's disappearance sooner burning into her. "I'm okay here, I think," she said, finding that she'd much rather wait for Elizabeth to return than have to settle into another space with another stranger.

"Very well," Miss Blackburn replied before exiting the room swiftly, taking the police with her. The nosy, watchful gazes of the girls in room 314 and 315 followed the group down the corridor.

Once back inside and finally alone, Sade headed straight for the dresser and the drawers she'd been anxiously glaring at. She tugged the top drawer open, surveyed its contents, and then shoved them to the back, away from the prying eyes of outsiders.

With a sigh, she fell back heavily on her bed, sat still, and eyed Elizabeth's side of the room like it was a puzzle.

The police no longer saw the room as a potential crime scene, so why did it still feel like one?

The quiet was all-consuming, reminding Sade of how empty this room truly was without anyone but herself in it.

It was weird, since she'd barely shared this room with Elizabeth. But the room felt her absence and loudly reminded Sade of it.

She slowly got up, drawn toward Elizabeth's side of the room. She ran her eyes over Elizabeth's things, reaching out to touch the headboard of her bed, noticing scuff marks from its age. Before she knew it, she was opening Elizabeth's drawers and taking a peek inside, searching under the bed and even the mattress for clues.

Nothing seemed out of the ordinary. She took a step back, feeling bad for doing it. Invading Elizabeth's space. Crossing that boundary.

She needed a break from this room it seemed.

Sade moved toward her own suitcases, rummaging through her things and pulling out her swimsuit, cap, and goggles. Feeling a little jittery, she left the room and headed to the only place in the world that always brought her peace.

The swimming pool.

Back at home, in her father's house, and even outside it, being near water, being in a pool, was her sanctuary, always. Until it was not.

She decided to skip dinner and instead head straight to Newton; her dinner would be some snack from a vending machine. She'd rather have a processed cinnamon roll than be stared at and talked about for however long it took to finish today's special.

As she walked through the halls of Newton over to the old swimming pool, she could hear the not-so-subtle hammering from the construction and the sound of the builders talking. Luckily, being in the other pool seemed to dull their noise.

Sade felt jittery as she pulled her swimming suit on for the first time in a long while, fingers shaky as she gripped the nylon material. She wasn't sure if it was the result of her nerves from being so close to a pool again or if it was her excitement.

Either way, the feeling made her nauseated.

She walked out of the changing room and into the chlorine-filled pool, where someone seemed to be doing laps across the deep end.

She took a seat on the bench and watched them, envying the ease with which they swam. Their arms sliced the water, their form as straight as an arrow.

When they finally came up for air, she recognized the face of the swimmer. It was her supposed brother, or at least the one Miss Blackburn had forcibly thrust upon her.

"Hey, new girl," he said, noticing her now.

"I have a name," she replied.

He smiled. "My bad. You coming in today?" he asked.

She assumed by *in* he meant the pool.

She wasn't sure. She hadn't done this in such a long time. She was almost certain she had forgotten how.

If that was even possible.

"I'm not sure . . . ," she said.

"Why not?" he asked.

"I think I've forgotten how to swim."

He started floating on his back. "So what you're saying is . . . you're scared?"

She didn't like the way he said that. It was like he was calling her weak. "*No*—"

"Then what is it, new girl?" he asked.

She narrowed her eyes at him, realizing that he was daring her. "I'm not scared," she said, pulling her goggles down, securing them as she walked to the steps. The water beneath her wavered, and it made her feel queasy. But she didn't back down, didn't want Mr. Douche-face to win.

Her legs vibrated against the slippery ladder, nervous energy coursing through her as she slowly lowered herself into the pool, while ignoring her beating heart.

As her feet touched the bottom step and she felt her swimsuit mold into her in the water, the fibers clinging desperately to her skin, she felt herself begin to relax. The water was warm and welcoming.

It felt like coming home.

"See, new girl? Not scary at all," August said before splashing at her gently.

She tried to move away quickly but wasn't fast enough to dodge the water, and it spilled all over her face and swim cap. She splashed him back, but he ducked, surfacing again a little way from her.

"I win," he said.

"You cheated. I didn't know we were playing a game, so it doesn't count!" She caught herself smiling. Somehow the water had momentarily washed all her worries away. The taunting voice inside, the whispers in the library and the halls, even Elizabeth were all forgotten in an instant now that she was here in the water with this strange boy again.

"Okay, fine. Let's play a game," he said, pulling his goggles up, which she noticed were old and worn-looking. "Two lengths. Fastest wins."

"That works for me," she said. Lengths were always her strong point. She was fast, and she knew it. This would be easy.

The pair swam to the deeper end of the pool, clambering out to find their starting positions. The boy began counting down.

"Three . . . two . . . one . . . ," he said, and then she dove into the pool headfirst. Felt the water embrace her, pulling her in like an old friend it had longed to touch.

She swam like her life depended on it, cutting through the water, holding and releasing her breath over and over again. She felt invincible. Her body felt stronger in the pool than it had before.

Once she got to one end, her legs began to burn, but she propelled herself forward again, pushing through and letting her muscle memory do the work. They reached the end of the lap, her hand smacking the tile first.

August came up for air, shock on his face as he breathed heavily. "Where did you learn to swim like that?"

She shrugged. "My coach won silver at the Olympics and trained us to her standard." Sade allowed herself a coy smile at August.

"You should join the girls' swim team," he said.

"What?"

"You're really good. The official tryouts for this year's team already happened, but I'm sure if they saw you swim, they'd have to consider you," he said.

She hadn't thought of competing since the last time she trained or even swam. Almost a year ago now. It used to be her whole life. Something about considering his suggestion—even for a brief moment—felt natural.

"Oh . . . I don't really do that anymore. I don't want to make it into something serious."

He looked even more taken aback, ready to challenge her on that. "Really?"

She nodded, hoping he'd drop it. No good came from unearthing the past.

"Well, if you change your mind, I'm sure I can persuade the coach to let you try out," he said.

"Are you on the team?" she asked.

"Yeah, I'm a reserve at the moment, but I'm training hard to be the captain in my fourth year," he said.

"Gonna need a lot of practice, then," she said, resulting in her being splashed again. This time she was able to dodge it in time.

"I can't prove it, but you definitely cheated. I want a rematch."

"Lengths again?" she asked.

"No . . . Something harder," he said. She could see the cogs in his mind spinning. "Who can hold their breath the longest underwater."

"Okay," she said.

She felt the itch in her brain return. It felt like the sky was falling.

"Right—three . . . two . . . ," he started, taking longer pauses between each number.

"One," she finished for him, and they both sank beneath the surface of the water.

Sade kept her eyes closed at first, wanting to get used to the feeling of being under again.

The itch persisted.

She opened her eyes and smiled at August, letting him know how easy this was for her.

He raised his eyebrows and folded his arms in response. He swam deeper, touching the bottom with his hands and doing a handstand.

She surveyed the pool, trying to think of something impressive to do, but she quickly got distracted by the flicker of something nearby.

She squinted into the depths, now noticing a red cloud blending with the blue of the water.

The same red spilling across the floor of the pool.

The same red staining her palms.

And then, she looked up and saw it.

The dead body floating in the pool alongside them.

7

WEDNESDAY
UNHOLY

SADE SCREAMED, BUT THE WATER muted any sound that came out of her mouth.

Her chest was ablaze as she choked, chlorine pouring into her lungs.

She couldn't breathe.

She could hear someone calling her name as the world began to slip away.

"SADE." The voice rang out again.

She no longer felt the warm water hug her close, just skin. Cold, cold skin.

"Hey, it's all right," he said, and Sade realized she was being lifted up by August.

She coughed and water sputtered out and she felt her lungs expand once again.

"Are you okay?" he asked.

She looked back down at the water, now clear. Devoid of blood and lifeless bodies, so she nodded. "I'm fine."

She realized she was still trapped in his arms and moved away from him now.

"What happened?" he asked, concern written into his features.

What happened? It was a loaded question.

Hard to really explain to anyone who didn't live inside her head why it was she imagined things she shouldn't.

What had happened? The sky had merely fallen, crushing her under its vast weight.

"You won," she answered, then moved toward the steps. She climbed out of the water, pulling off her goggles, her thighs heavy.

On the edge of the pool, she could see splatters of crimson-red blood skirting around the tiles. She knew it was her mind playing tricks again, convincing her of false realities.

"You don't want a rematch?" August asked, looking slightly hopeful.

She shook her head. "I think I'm done playing for today; maybe some other time," she said before smiling at him and walking away without a goodbye.

When she was alone in her cubby, her legs finally gave, and she dropped to the floor, thankful for how well the water was able to mask her tears.

THURSDAY

THE NEXT MORNING, THE STUDENTS of Alfred Nobel Academy awoke to news of an emergency assembly.

It was obvious even to those who rarely paid any attention to the goings-on at the school what the "emergency" was about.

Rushing breakfast, Sade followed the crowd of excited, curious voices to The Great Hall—which Sade had learned on her tour with Elizabeth was named after Alexander the Great himself.

I wonder what it is about this school and its obsession with naming rooms after dead white men. It's a bit concerning, Elizabeth had said after telling Sade this fact, looking very unimpressed with it all.

It felt weird now, returning to the hall without her. It had only been three days, yet it felt like Elizabeth had been missing for much longer than that.

The hall was large enough to fill a small stadium, with marble floors and warm cherrywood walls. The room was structured like a lecture theater, with seats dotted all around focused on the center stage for the speaker.

Sade could feel eyes on her again.

It seemed people were still keen on believing the rumors about her kidnapping or doing *worse* to her roommate. She could even see the scorn in their gazes, as though it was her fault they had to be here instead of being trapped in a boring lesson about organic chemistry.

She scanned the large room for any faces she recognized, not that she had any friends to sit with, but more so hoping that a familiar face might judge her less.

She spotted Basil in the corner and felt relief. Baz didn't suspect she was a kidnapper—or at least she hoped he didn't—and so he wouldn't mind her sitting near him. His hair, as usual, stuck out like a sore thumb.

"Hi," she said.

"Hey," he replied, still looking as tired as he had the day before. But despite this, he seemed weirdly happy to see her, greeting her with a small smile and wave.

She took the seat next to him.

"Quiet down please, find a seat quickly, let's make this assembly as painless as possible," Mr. Webber said into the microphone on the stage.

The volume in the hall persisted and Miss Blackburn tapped the mic before yelling: "BE QUIET!"

The hall immediately fell silent. Students quickly clambered into seats, and conversations between friends ceased.

"Erm, thank you, Miss Blackburn," Headmaster Webber said as he took the stage.

"As some of you might be aware, there has been an incident. A third-year student, Elizabeth Wang, has been missing since Monday. The local police, in cooperation with the school, are working hard to find Miss Wang and ensure she's safe. If you think you might know something about Elizabeth's whereabouts or if you think you might've seen her that evening, you can fill in a comments card anonymously and pass it on to Miss Blackburn, who will relay that information to me and the police."

Sade thought back to her own interaction with the police and wondered what they thought of her. Whether they thought she was a suspect.

Should she have said more?

They hadn't interviewed her again, so she assumed she was in the clear.

But then why did this deep guilt keep gnawing at her?

She looked around the large hall once again, noting the cameras in all four corners. How does a school lose a person anyway? Isn't there CCTV all over?

Why did it feel like there was more to the story?

"Your parents have been informed of the goings-on and I have assured them that our priority is the safety of every single one of you . . ."

"More like his priority is our parents' money and sponsorships," Baz muttered.

"You are now all free to go. Miss Blackburn will dismiss you in row order to prevent any accidents, thank you," Headmaster Webber said before rushing away from the chaos and out through a door at the back by the stage.

When it came to their row, Sade and Baz walked out together into the crowded hallway and out of the building.

"What do you have first period?" he asked her, grabbing a small pack of miniature Jammie Dodgers from his pocket, before opening the wrapper and shoveling the shortbread cookies into his mouth.

"Uhm . . . Mandarin in Chomsky Building, you?" she said.

"I have German in the C block too; I'll lead the way," he said, his voice muffled by the biscuit.

She was grateful that Baz was here. She had familiarized herself with some of the school grounds but still had trouble finding her way around. At least now she might finally be on time to a class.

"Mandarin sounds hard; have you studied it before?" he asked as they walked through a door to another building and then to a quieter hallway.

"I lived in Beijing for a few months when I was twelve, so I know a little," she said. "Are you good with languages?"

"Portuguese is my first language since my family is from Brazil, then English, and I guess I learned a little bit of Irish in primary school, but other than that, I'm pretty useless," he said.

"You know two and a half languages! That's not useless," she said as they turned a corner.

"My German teacher would beg to differ," Baz replied. "He's all like, *Your German is as confusing as your name, Basil* and *Stop sleeping in my class, Basil* and *You owe me homework, Basil!* Stuff like that."

Sade laughed. "He really sounds like a nightmare," she said.

"I know, right. He won't let me be," Baz said.

They turned another corner, this hallway completely devoid of people and classrooms and filled with discarded boxes and old-school desks.

"Uh, Baz . . ."

"Yeah?"

"Is the C block nearby?" she asked, aware, suddenly, of the passing time.

He stopped abruptly. A weird look crossed his features as he turned to face her. "No," he said. "Kind of . . . it's all relative—"

"Where are we?" she asked him, feeling more than a little bit creeped out.

Baz quietly stared at her, searching her face with his eyes for something. "Can I trust you?"

She nodded slowly.

"I think something bad has happened to Elizabeth," he said, eyes bloodshot.

"What do you mean?" she said, feeling her stomach sink.

He ran a hand through his curls. "I can't prove it, but I just have this strange feeling. And I know they won't believe me. Webber thinks Elizabeth ran away in the middle of the night. Somehow snuck off the school premises—"

"Is that something she's done before? Snuck off in the middle of the night?" Sade asked.

Baz looked so helpless and small. He sighed. "Maybe. But she'd tell me if she was going to do that. And even on the rare occasion that she sneaks off during the day, her phone is never off. I've called her so many times, but it keeps going to voicemail. I keep wondering if . . . I don't know . . ."

He stopped speaking, like he was scared of admitting something out loud.

"If what?" Sade asked, her nervous system beginning to stir.

He sighed before speaking again. "If someone took her. I know it sounds dramatic."

Sade shook her head. "It doesn't, not to me."

Baz looked relieved.

Sade could tell from watching him that he desperately needed someone to believe him. And she did believe him.

Because she had that strange feeling too.

"Where does she usually go . . . when she leaves the school?" Sade asked, wondering why this was something students were just able to do.

The school was surrounded by a lot of forest. It would be so easy, she suspected, to escape without anyone ever knowing.

"She usually just goes alone to the local town, mostly to the cat café they have there. She always returns within a few hours. She's never been gone this long," he said, rubbing his eyes.

"Do you have any idea why she would leave so often?" Sade asked.

"She always says that being at ANA sometimes feels like being in a cage. I guess leaving is her way of breaking free. I remember once she went for longer than usual, lost track of time I guess, and got a suspension warning for leaving in the first place. Webber brought this up when I spoke to him yesterday. Made it seem like she was some unpredictable delinquent and that her disappearance didn't matter at all."

Sade raised an eyebrow. She hadn't realized that he'd spoken to Headmaster Webber yet. "You spoke to Webber?"

Baz sniffed and nodded. "Yeah, and it was pointless. I asked him what they knew and he basically said some bullshit about how he couldn't give me any personal details, they were exploring a number of avenues, but couldn't dedicate very many resources to it, and that given her *history* it was likely the case would take a while. It's not like she's the only student who sneaks off campus, and I know he knows that. He just doesn't care."

Sade picked apart his words, trying to think of anything that could help at all. She didn't doubt that Webber was useless. She wasn't naive to the idea that authority figures weren't always deserving of their positions.

And yet something felt weird about this—about Baz's story.

She didn't quite buy the idea that Elizabeth left the school for hours on end to go into town simply to get away from the Alfred Nobel bubble. She had the greenhouse, for one. That seemed to be her refuge. "You're sure Elizabeth wasn't meeting up with anyone?"

Baz shrugged. "I don't think so. I think I'd know if she was meeting someone, we tell each other everything," he said.

"Everything?" Sade repeated.

He nodded. "More or less." He seemed so sure about it. Like he knew with almost absolute certainty that he and Elizabeth had no secrets between them. But the thing was, everyone had secrets. Things too dark, too ugly to share with the people they loved most.

She knew this more than anyone.

It was possible that Elizabeth had secrets like that too. Things she didn't want Baz to know.

Sade thought back to the look on Elizabeth's face. The fear behind her eyes, and a weird sort of . . . determination. Like she had decided on something finally.

If Baz knew everything about her, surely he wouldn't be here speculating now.

"What do you think we should do?" she asked him.

"I was thinking we could do a search," he said. "I know the police are doing their own, but they can't know everything, right? I might be able to figure things out that they can't. I can show people around town her picture and see if anything comes up. I feel like there's something going on, and I can't sit around and do nothing. It feels like I'm betraying her." His eyes were glazed over like he was moments from crying. He also had the same fear, the same determination that Elizabeth had had.

Baz was right. They had to do something.

"A search sounds good," she said. There was a chance that Elizabeth was okay and that they were overthinking things. But there was also a chance that they weren't. She'd been missing for three days now.

And doing nothing would be worse than doing too much.

"I was thinking of doing the first search after school if you're free?" he said, his voice mangled by nerves.

She nodded. "Yeah, of course. I'll be there."

"Thank you, Sade. It means a lot," he said with another sniff, and then he glanced down at the time on his phone. "We better get going; class starts soon. Sorry for kidnapping you."

She waved him off. "Always happy to be kidnapped for a good cause," she said, trying to lighten the mood and stop the dread from creeping in again.

This made him smile and she felt like she had accomplished something.

As they walked out of the abandoned corridor, guilt still weighed heavily on her as she considered something else about Elizabeth and her disappearance.

Something darker.

What if Elizabeth had left in the middle of the night, had gotten hurt somehow, and Sade was the only one who could have helped her?

What if Sade had failed again?

AFTER ARRIVING ALMOST TEN MINUTES late to her Mandarin class, Sade didn't think her day could get any worse.

Between a failed pop quiz and the constant ogling she received whenever she went anywhere—which she couldn't tell if it was triggered by her newbie status or her blossoming reputation as resident roommate killer—she was exhausted by the time lunch rolled around.

Sade decided to go to the lunch hall for the first time since Monday, figuring that people were going to think things about her regardless of whether it was the truth or not, and she should at least eat properly before being sentenced by the public.

As she'd already come to expect, most of the lunch hall food was not halal, and so again she found herself having pasta.

She got her tray, swiped her card, placed her bag and cardigan down on a chair, and took a seat at the same table the three of them had shared on Monday. She, Elizabeth, and Baz.

This time she was by herself.

People seemed too into their conversations to notice her presence.

She felt herself relax, stabbing now at the pasta in her bowl and scrolling through her phone aimlessly, looking for a distraction while the lunch hour went by.

She had sent a text to Baz, asking if he was coming to lunch, to which he had replied that he was going to take a nap in the nurse's office. He had looked almost on the brink of collapse earlier, so she was glad to hear this, even though it meant she would be by herself. She'd become used to eating lunch by herself at home, but for some reason, eating by yourself in a room full of people proved to be a somewhat lonely experience.

Sade was so preoccupied with her search for something noteworthy on her phone that she didn't notice the hall begin to quiet. Nor did she feel the prying eyes of the students from the tables surrounding her.

She didn't feel *their* presence either.

The three girls loomed over her as she scrolled.

It wasn't until one of them cleared their throat that Sade snapped out of it.

"Are these seats taken?" the one in the middle asked, a sweet smile on her face.

It was the unholy girls.

Sade shook her head, still stunned. Her eyes drifted toward Persephone, who didn't seem happy to be there.

"Thanks," April said, taking a seat in front of Sade.

The girl on her left, Juliette, followed suit, and Persephone stayed standing for a few moments. Her hand gripped an Octavia E. Butler novel, and her face was pinched as she finally sat down.

"Sade, right? I'm April. This is Jules and Sephy. We heard you were new here; we don't get many transfers," she said.

"Yeah, I've, uhm . . . heard," she replied. She put her fork down, feeling self-conscious all of a sudden.

"Where did you used to go?" April asked. Up close, April was even more perfect. Her skin was free of blemishes, and her hair was perfectly curled. She looked like a doll.

"I was homeschooled," Sade replied, realizing she had been staring at April too long.

"That's so fascinating. I've never met someone who was homeschooled before. Has it been hard adjusting to boarding school life?"

"Kind of; it's been a pretty intense week," Sade said, which caused something to flicker behind April's eyes.

"I can imagine," she said.

"She was your roommate, right?" Juliette said abruptly, while twirling her hair.

Sade guessed she meant Elizabeth. "Yeah," she replied.

"Were you guys friends?" Juliette asked.

She considered the question, recalling their deal on the rooftop of the science building:

You officially have two new friends—if you want us . . . , Elizabeth had said.

It seemed so simple at the time, but now the whole ordeal hardly felt like it was something written in stone. Were they friends?

She didn't know.

"Kind of . . . I guess. I didn't really know her for very long—"

Juliette interrupted Sade midsentence. "I watched a documentary once about a girl who was stabbed to death by her college roommate. It was really sad. Some roommates are really weird, though, so you almost can't blame people . . . Not that I'm saying that you did anything, but if you did, I wouldn't tell anyone," she finished with a smile that seemed harmless but made Sade feel on edge.

April laughed. "Jules, you can't just accuse people of murdering their roommate.

65

It's not polite." She arched a perfectly plucked eyebrow at Sade, as though daring her to whisper her deepest, darkest secrets to them.

"But anyway, we thought since you were new and everything, we'd invite you to sit with us at lunch tomorrow if you'd like? We would invite you today, but we were just leaving," April said.

Sade was taken aback, unsure of whether she was being serious or not.

April's fingers tapped on the table as she awaited Sade's response, and Sade noticed an unusual pattern of what seemed like fresh burns along her forearm. Her hand moved from view, under the table and away from Sade's prying eyes.

"Is that a yes?" April questioned.

And Sade realized then that she had been quiet for longer than was socially acceptable. "Sorry, yeah, sure," she said, watching as April's shark smile broadened.

Sade glanced at Persephone, who she had been avoiding looking at this entire time. Persephone was staring at her, a bored expression on her equally perfect face.

"Wonderful!" April said, standing. "I hope the intensity of this week doesn't scare you away. Things are usually a lot less . . ."

"Murdery?" Sade replied jokingly. But none of them laughed.

". . . a lot less serious," April finished.

Sade realized joking about murder probably wasn't helping her look any less guilty.

"We'll see you tomorrow?" April asked.

Sade nodded. "Yes, tomorrow."

April grinned, and then said in a lower register that almost seemed menacing, "Perfect, I look forward to getting to know you, Sade."

"You too," Sade said, her voice hiking up an octave as she anxiously swallowed.

She watched the three of them stand once again and walk away.

What do those girls want from me? She wasn't sure.

But maybe the question shouldn't be what they wanted from her, but instead, what insight might Sade gain from them?

FINDERS KEEPERS

THE FINAL BELL RANG, SIGNALING that the school day was officially over.

Sade had agreed to meet Baz at the reception area for the search party; only when she arrived, it was empty.

No teacher manning the desk, or pink-haired boy waiting for her.

She leaned against the help desk and took out her phone, about to send Baz a message when—on cue—her phone vibrated in her palm with a text from the devil in question.

New message from Basil: I'll be there in 3

She sent back a thumbs-up, then swiped off the messaging app and scrolled to the other apps on her phone—looking again for something to pass time. She could hear students circling the halls, leaving the main building to go to their various after-school activities or to their houses.

She found herself on one of the many social media apps she had on her phone but didn't really use for anything other than prying into the lives of others.

She saw a notification, alerting her that Baz had followed her, along with two of the unholy girls, Juliette de Silva and April Owens.

She was certain that Persephone probably had a profile and chose not to follow her for the same reason she had given her the cold shoulder at lunch today.

She wasn't sure what she did to piss the blonde off and wasn't entirely sure she cared. She had way too many things on her mind to be obsessing over why a beautiful stranger disliked her.

Things like Elizabeth.

She accepted Baz's follow request back and then went to his following list and searched for Elizabeth, eventually finding her after scrolling through the long list of people Baz followed.

She clicked onto her page and, as Sade had suspected, Elizabeth's page was mostly outdated.

She only had three photos up.

The most recent photo was from a year ago: her reading a Stephen King novel while seated in a shopping trolley. The next, from around the same period. This one of Elizabeth alone, in a room with a green-and-white-tiled background, wearing these giant sunglasses and staring directly into the camera. She seemed to be wearing a tank top, but Sade couldn't tell.

The last photo was from a year and a half ago. A selfie of her and Baz. Her hair was pink, Baz's hair a blue afro, a huge smile on her face as he pressed his lips to her cheek.

None of the photos told Sade much. Just that Elizabeth didn't seem all that interested in social media.

She closed the page and typed in *Alfred Nobel Academy* on maps, looking at the satellite view of the academy and the surrounding town. It looked like a maze.

So easy to get completely lost in.

"Hello," Baz said, his voice pulling her out of her thoughts and her eyes away from her phone. He looked cheerier than he had earlier. The bags under his eyes were less prominent now and his face was filled with color.

Sade almost jumped at the sight of Miss Blackburn behind him. It looked like she was watching Sade with a small scowl. Though that might just be her regular face.

"Hey," she said, trying to ignore the looming presence of Miss Blackburn.

"Ready to go?" he asked her.

She nodded stiffly. "Yes."

Baz must've noticed her uncomfortable expression, because he turned back to stare at the cold matron too.

"Miss Blackburn said she'd chaperone us," Baz explained.

Sade nodded, unsure whether the explanation made a difference.

It was uncharacteristically nice of the matron to let them leave the school grounds to look for Elizabeth. Then again, maybe her saying yes was to avoid looking like a knob.

"You have until just before seven. I have an episode of *EastEnders* to catch at seven," Miss Blackburn said, looking down pointedly at her watch.

Baz nodded. "We better get going, then," he said with a wide smile. Both his expression and the green hoodie with what seemed to be froggy ears attached contrasted starkly with Miss Blackburn's black trench coat and frown. The hope he had radiating off him in large waves was alluring. So much so, Sade felt it infect her slightly, eating away at her nervous, morbid thoughts. He linked his arm with Sade's and they followed Miss Blackburn out of the school entrance.

"I wonder if there'll be enough time to get dinner in town. I'm craving fish and chips," Baz said.

"Seven," Miss Blackburn repeated sternly.

"Yes, miss," he replied with a mischievous glint in his eyes.

They got to the school's parking lot, hidden away on a different path near the entrance, filled with identical black cars, all with the license plate A N A and a number after it.

They looked a lot like something Batman might drive.

Miss Blackburn pointed her car keys at A N A 5, and the car beeped twice, then the doors automatically slid open.

"Get in," she said, striding over to the driver's seat.

They obediently climbed inside the *Batmobile*, and Miss Blackburn made them put on their seat belts before pressing her foot to the gas pedal, pulling out of the parking lot, and driving down the path Sade's driver had taken when they'd pulled into the school gates only days before.

She looked over at Baz, who was staring intently at his phone's screen, at a picture of Elizabeth. It was one she hadn't seen on her profile. He looked focused. His foot tapped on the carpeted floor of the car, thighs shaking, anxious energy swirling around and out of him.

She could almost hear his thoughts. *This has to work. I have to find her.*

She tried not to think about what might happen if they didn't. Tried not to think about how with every passing moment, the likelihood of finding Elizabeth alive decreased exponentially. She could have run away and gotten hurt—or worse, kidnapped—and then like other lost girls, she could fade into the ether, never to be seen or heard from again.

Baz inhaled sharply, as though Sade's negative thoughts were seeping out from her and weakening his convictions. She decided to look away from him and instead out the window, wanting to settle her own nerves.

The blur of the surrounding forest whizzed by as they drove off the school grounds and into the local town. Sade sank back into her seat and let her mind slip away—attempting (and failing) to ignore the flashes of light she kept seeing out the window, appearing and disappearing, and then getting closer as the car was propelled forward.

It was a girl in a white nightgown watching her leave the school. A disappointed grimace was etched into her bright mahogany skin.

Sade considered shutting her eyes, but she knew the girl would only follow her there too, stalking her mind and forcing her to remember the bigger picture.

You should never have come.

The girl in the white dress was now pressed up against the glass, blocking all the light from outside.

I'm sorry, Sade wanted to say to her, as she had done time and time again. And as she would continue to do until the words carved a hole in her throat and tore out what was left of her.

But saying sorry was never enough.

The only worthy wager was to be paid in blood.

Even if it was her own.

THE LOCAL TOWN WAS CLOSE enough to the school that it didn't take them long to get there.

Having not paid much attention before, Sade was surprised by how normal it looked. There were rows and rows of quintessentially English old-timey medieval buildings, made modern by the shops that occupied them. She half expected to see a horse and carriage ride past her at some point. But as was expected for a town with one of the country's most expensive boarding schools nearby, all she saw were Teslas.

Miss Blackburn parked in front of a local florist, and they exited the car, with strict instructions not to wander off too far into town.

Then they were at their first stop.

The cat café was at the junction of the main road, and it looked more like a computer room than a café—with rows and rows of elderly people on old desktops typing away.

Baz showed the owner, who looked very much like a cat himself, a picture of Elizabeth.

"I work here all week and can't say I recognize her, no," the owner said.

"She comes here a lot," Baz said, pressing on. "Are you sure?"

The owner heaved a sigh and squinted at the photograph again, then continued with a look on his face that made Sade uncomfortable. "I'm sorry, kid. I think I'd recognize a lady as beautiful as that."

Baz's face screwed up. "She's seventeen."

"So? Is it a crime to comment on that now?" the guy asked, like there was nothing wrong with talking about a girl like that. Especially one who was missing. "Anyway, I told you I don't recognize her. As I said before, I work here all week and would definitely remember her even if she wasn't a regular. I've got a photographic memory," he said, tapping his temple and giving them a creepy smile.

Sade didn't believe him and it was clear that Baz didn't either. "Can we see your CCTV tapes, then?" Baz asked, folding his arms now.

The owner looked irritated. "Listen, kid. I did you a favor answering your questions. Unless you've got a police badge or a search warrant, you have no right demanding all these things. If you're not going to buy anything, I want you out of my shop, now."

Baz didn't seem like he was ready to give up on the shop just yet.

"Let's just go. There's still a lot of places we can check out," Sade said, tugging on Baz's sleeve.

"Better listen to the girl. Sometimes they know what they're talking about," the owner said with a wink. Baz's eyes narrowed, but surprisingly, instead of saying a quip back at him, he turned and walked toward the door.

For a moment, it seemed as though he was going to storm out, but then he pulled a chair from the front of the shop and climbed on top of it.

Sade's eyes widened as Baz began to shout.

"The owner is a sexist pervert and if I were you, I'd take your business elsewhere," Baz said for all the shop to hear, including the kittens.

This triggered multiple heads to turn around.

The owner looked at a loss for words, but before he could do something like call the police or chase them, Baz took Sade's hand and pulled her from the shop, sprinting away.

When they finally came to a stop at a corner of the high street, away from the owner's line of vision and slightly out of breath, Sade finally spoke.

"Baz, he could sue you for slander!" Sade said, exasperated. She found his actions both shocking and humorous.

Baz shrugged, still catching his breath. "That perv can piss right off; I don't care. Wouldn't be the first time I've been sued anyway," he said, before taking out a crumpled piece of paper from his pocket. "Right, next on the list is the juice bar around the corner."

"Wait," Sade said as Baz started to walk forward, pausing now to look at her.

"Yeah?"

"Did you not find the cat café weird?"

Baz's eyebrows furrowed. "Weird how? Was it the smell? I noticed that too—"

Sade shook her head. "No, I mean the computers. When you said cat café, I imagined a normal coffee shop with cats roaming about. Why would Elizabeth go there? Aren't there computers at school?"

Baz nodded, looking pensive for a few moments. "We're monitored on the school computers. Even our personal laptops and phones have a program installed into them to monitor activity. People often get around this by sneaking in devices the school doesn't know about. Elizabeth didn't have a personal laptop, so I guess it makes sense that she'd come there."

"I don't think my phone has that program on it."

"They usually search our devices in the first week of term. Since you came later, the school probably forgot to search yours, what with everything that's happened this week. I'd say that's a lucky escape. At least you won't have Headmaster Webber calling you in for writing inappropriate fan fiction on your laptop," he said.

Sade raised an eyebrow at that but didn't press further, as some things were better left unsaid.

She didn't like the idea of being so closely monitored. She had already spent so many years of her life under the scrutinous gaze of her father.

It did make her question, though, what was it that Elizabeth might've wanted to hide?

She typed in *the cat café* on her phone, and the search results pulled up the café they had just been to, however, it was now listed as the *Cyber* Cat Café, with the description: *A place to enjoy our coffee, stroke a cat, and access the internet for a minimal time-based fee.*

"If Elizabeth did come here to use the computers, maybe there are things on her search history. Things that could help us figure out where she might be now."

"Wouldn't it be regularly cleared, though, since it's a public server? Maybe I should go back and ask more questions about the computers—"

"No, you should definitely *not* do that. For one, I think it's safe to say that we are now banned for life from that place. I think we should report it to Miss Blackburn, ask her to tell the police or something. They can look through his CCTV footage, or ask to search the computers, check if anything is dodgy about it."

Baz shrugged and then said, "Okay."

Sade glanced down at Baz's list of locations to search. "Did Elizabeth say she went to the juice bar often?"

Baz shook his head. "This one's just a guess. She's into organic stuff, so I figured it might be worth a shot."

"That's smart, very Sherlockian," Sade said, which made Baz smile a little.

Baz looked back at the cat café in the distance with a weary expression and then at the juice bar, pocketing his list now.

"Ready to go then, Watson?" Baz asked Sade. She could see the fear returning in his eyes, coupled with the drive to figure this all out.

She wasn't sure what would happen if they spent the day searching and got the worst kind of answers. The kind that only prompted more questions or the kind that led them to a dark possibility that she didn't even want to entertain.

Sade nodded, determined to help him find the right kind of answers. The ones that wouldn't cause more pain and heartache.

"Whenever you are, Holmes."

AFTER A LOT OF WALKING around from store to store in the freezing cold, with no more information on Elizabeth's whereabouts than when they started, the already dampened mood was further sullied by the rainfall.

"Great," Baz muttered as his list began to run and fall apart.

"Were there any more places on the list?" Sade asked, shivering as she held her bag above her head to protect herself. They hurried into the doorway of a closed charity shop for shelter.

He shook his head, his hair stuck to his skin. Some of the recently used pink dye was bleeding down and leaving subtle streaks on the sides of his face. "We better tell Miss Blackburn that we're done with the search," he said, his voice wobbly like it might break. It felt like they had gone on some kind of pointless wild-goose chase with nothing to show for it.

Apparently, there *was* something worse than a bad answer.

No answer at all.

She could tell from the look on Baz's face that he thought he'd failed Elizabeth.

"You did your best," she said.

He wiped his face and looked away from her. "I don't know if I believe that. I think if I did my best, I would have found something helpful. I can't even guess where she might be. She's meant to be the person I know the most in the world, and these past three days have shown me that maybe I don't. Maybe I'm just a shit friend."

Sade had seen them together. There was no way Elizabeth didn't mean the world to him.

"You're definitely not. There's no doubt that she was your best friend—"

"Is," Baz interrupted. "*Is* my best friend."

"Is," Sade repeated, unsure why she said it in the past tense. Why it slipped out so easily.

"I'm sorry; it's been a long day," Baz said, looking out into the rain as it punched the ground and intensified. It didn't seem like the storm would dwindle anytime soon, so he stepped out. "Let's just go."

She followed him over to Miss Blackburn's car, parked on the side of the street, where Miss Blackburn was reading a newspaper in the driver's seat.

He knocked on the window, and the woman turned back briefly, then pressed a button in front of her that made the doors slide right open.

"Ready to go?" Miss Blackburn asked.

Baz nodded solemnly and Miss Blackburn pursed her lips, watching them with a foreign expression.

She looked . . . sorry.

"Okay, well. It's getting dark. Let's try to get back as quickly as possible," she said.

Baz and Sade slid into their seats once again, and Miss Blackburn shoved her newspaper into the glove compartment, then started the engine.

Sade sat back, waiting to feel the vibration beneath her and the swift motion of the car's movements, but instead, all she heard was the staggering sound of the engine roaring, dying, then roaring again.

Miss Blackburn let out a sigh before trying the ignition again and failing miserably.

"Something's wrong with the engine. I'll have to call the emergency line," she announced, then muttered, "These electrical cars are useless."

As if the day couldn't get any worse, it somehow had.

Sade looked at Baz, who was staring at the ground silently, his brows bunched together like he was thinking too hard. The rain pelted on the roof above him like his own personal dark cloud.

"I'll be right back," Miss Blackburn said, holding the phone to her ear and pushing open the door, before slamming it again.

Sade rested her head against the window, the rain raising her usual levels of dread. As she attempted to zone out, the girl appeared once again—like she often did when Sade let her mind be vulnerable.

This time, only her hands were visible.

She knocked on all the windows of the car, tapping and waiting for Sade to notice her. When the girl was sure she had, she began to draw something on the windshield.

Two dots and a downturned line.

A frown.

The car door suddenly opened again, and Sade jumped, stifling a scream. Miss Blackburn climbed back in, her usually tidy hair now soggy and sticking to her forehead and neck.

"Right, the emergency line is sending someone over to help, said they'd be thirty minutes max," she said.

"Can't they send another car up from the school?" Baz asked.

Miss Blackburn shook her head. "It's better we wait."

Help didn't come for another hour and a half. By the time the emergency car service had arrived, the rain had settled slightly but Miss Blackburn's face had only become scarier. Even the emergency engineer looked scared for his life as she spoke to him. Miss Blackburn had stepped out of the car, and Sade could hear him stammering as he told her what the problem was.

Baz was quiet for most of it, his expression vacant.

It wasn't until Sade heard his stomach rumbling that he finally spoke up again.

"Sorry," he said. "Didn't eat today."

Her eyes widened in alarm. "At all?"

He nodded, resting his head back. "Basically. I ran out of Jammie Dodgers before first period."

"I'm sorry," she said after a moment.

He smiled lazily, looking her in the eye now. "If there's one thing the Irish and English like to do, it's apologize for nothing."

She almost apologized for apologizing but stopped herself. "Very true; it's a bad habit, I guess."

Baz nodded. "If only the English would make it a habit of theirs to apologize for actual things they've done, but alas," he said just as Miss Blackburn reentered the car again, completely drenched in rain and carrying a white plastic bag she hadn't left with.

As she maneuvered her way into the driver's seat and got comfortable, the material of her clothes produced a funny sound on the seats.

"Finally, we can go," she said, roughly shoving the seat belt in.

"Oh, before I forget, since we've definitely missed dinner now, I got you both something to eat on the way back," Miss Blackburn said, reaching into the white bag and handing back two parcels of what smelled strongly of codfish.

"Thanks, miss," Baz said to her, while Sade eyed the food suspiciously, before finally thanking her too.

Miss Blackburn nodded and started the car, heading down the main road once again.

As they ate their food in silence at the back, Sade considered the facts.

The world didn't begin and end in the bounds of this town. If she'd gone of her own accord, it was entirely possible that Elizabeth had snuck away and gotten a bus out of there. Possibly even a train. Elizabeth could be anywhere in the country, perhaps even the world.

Sade wasn't sure if saying this would help Baz or just hurt him.

It was hard to think that you might never see someone again. Though, with her luck, you might see them again, in your daydreams and nightmares. Wearing white dresses and tampering with the remains of your sanity.

The school grounds were quiet when they got back. The students were in their dormitories, winding down before the day's end.

Miss Blackburn walked them back over to the reception, where she signed a release form stating their whereabouts this evening.

Ms. Thistle seemed to be away, so it was just the three of them in the quiet entrance.

"Right, I better be off now. Sorry again that the search didn't produce the results you hoped for. But I'm kept up to date with all the details on the case and will be sure to let you know if they find anything new," Miss Blackburn said with a tight smile.

Sade could see from the clock on the wall that it was already past eight—almost nine—and imagined that Miss Blackburn resented being made late. Though, Sade would admit, it was surprising that the matron entertained helping them at all today.

Maybe she wasn't as bad as she'd seemed.

"Thanks, Miss Blackburn. I actually had a question about the searches that the police were doing . . . Do you think they'll check the town and the shops there too? Specifically, the cat café," Baz asked.

Miss Blackburn raised an eyebrow. "Why? Did you see something?"

Baz shook his head quickly. "No, nothing. I was just wondering," he said, eyes widened like a deer caught in headlights.

Miss Blackburn nodded questioningly. "Well, from what I understand, they already searched all the shops in town, and interviewed anyone working there. Including the cat one."

Baz frowned. "Why did you let us go into town if the police had already done it?"

Miss Blackburn stared at him silently before answering. "So that you could put your own mind at ease, Basil. I know Miss Wang was your friend, and your roommate and house sister, Sade. So I allowed it. I hope now you can let the adults do their jobs. It is what they're trained for, after all," Miss Blackburn finished, her stare icy and her voice patronizing. "I'll be leaving now, but do let me know if you have any legitimate concerns or remember anything useful that can help the police find Miss Wang."

And then without another word, Miss Blackburn walked past the pair, leaving them in the corridor alone.

Sade took back what she had thought earlier. Miss Blackburn was still as cold as ever.

"What a grinch," Sade said after a few moments.

Baz cocked his head to the side. "A grinch?"

"Yeah, you know. Someone who is heartless."

Baz paused for a moment, staring at her. "Sade, do you not swear?"

Swear words were something her father had always discouraged.

"Sometimes . . . ," she said, her face growing hot. She hadn't considered that this wasn't normal.

Sade felt Baz nudge her lightly with a smile. "I think that's sweet, Watson. Though, I must warn you that after hanging out with me for a few weeks—you will be a certified sailor. But I agree, she *is* a grinch."

The two walked over to the dorms in a heavy, cold silence. The rain was now a light drizzle and the evening's sky was dark and dense and black.

Baz's dorm, Seacole, was opposite hers, so once they got to Turing, Baz didn't have to go far.

Before he left, he held his hand out to her. She looked him in the face, confused, and then remembered the handshake she'd agreed to learn. After a brief pause, she reluctantly slapped her hand against his. He raised both his hands up and curled them into fists. She bumped her own fists against his, prompting him to nod, satisfied at her response.

"Stage two in the secret handshake, complete," he said.

"Ah," she replied.

"Thank you, by the way," he said, then added, "For today."

"Anytime," she said, wanting to apologize, but resisting the urge to. She wasn't quite sure what she was sorry for.

Sorry that I didn't help you find any leads?

Or, *Sorry, I might have seen Elizabeth leave the room that night, and stopped whatever happened to her, but might've been too sleepy to notice?*

Or perhaps:

Sorry for being here instead of her . . .

"I'll see you tomorrow. At lunch?" he said.

She nodded.

"Yeah, I'll see you."

He waved and turned, walking down the path to Seacole House.

Sade watched him open the doors and disappear into the house, before going inside her own house.

Turing wasn't as quiet as the main building. She could hear people moving about on the floors above, as well as the gentle clashing of pots and pans and dishes being picked up by the staff in the dining room.

As she stepped into the French lift and rode up to her floor, she had the odd feeling that something was off.

That feeling was made real when she stepped out of the lift and rummaged around her bag for her room key but couldn't seem to locate it.

She shook her bag to see if she could hear the familiar clinking of metal, but no such sound was produced. Dread piled up inside. It was likely that she dropped her key while they were out in town all evening.

She remembered Ms. Thistle's warning about losing her dorm key; she would have to face Miss Blackburn's wrath. It was bad enough that she already thought Sade was incompetent—this would simply put the nail in the coffin.

She stared at the door, weighing her options.

She could go ask for a replacement key, or she could stay outside all night. Neither sounded pleasant. Now would be a great time to know how to pick a lock.

She stepped toward the door once again, hoping that by some miracle, she accidentally left it unlocked this morning. But as indicated by her fruitless rattling of the knob, the door was indeed locked.

As she moved to back away, she felt something solid beneath her feet. She looked down at the mat she stood on, then stepped off it and nudged it to the side with her shoe, remembering the dead rodent from Monday.

Relief spread through her when the underside of the mat revealed a key. Likely a spare. Elizabeth must have kept it there in case of emergencies. And this was definitely an emergency. She'd rather sleep in the hallway than let Miss Blackburn know of her carelessness.

She reached over and picked up the key from the ground, eyebrows furrowing together when she inspected it.

It had what seemed to be a small S written in black marker on the base.

Just like her own key, which had an S for *Sade* written in either Miss Blackburn's or Ms. Thistle's writing.

This one was S for *spare* she figured.

What are the odds?

She shrugged off the weirdness and rolled the mat back over before inserting the key into the lock and turning it.

Inside, the room felt colder than it had in the morning. The window she had shut after breakfast was now open, gusts of wind flowing into the room, causing the curtains to dance and the hairs on her arms to raise.

In the dark, she could make out the shape of her dresser, with its drawers sprung open as though someone had been riffling through her things. Panic began to rise inside.

Sade quickly switched the lights on, noticing now how spotless Elizabeth's side of the room was. The once disheveled bedsheets were tucked neatly into the mattress, her disregarded clothes folded away into her opened dresser.

Someone had been in here.

She scanned Elizabeth's side of the room again, expecting her to emerge from her hiding place.

She imagined her appearing suddenly with a smile, saying: "Like what I've done with the place?" unaware of the chaos her disappearance had caused.

But the room was still empty. Sade was still alone.

She looked at her side now, searching for more signs of forced entry.

And that's when she spotted it: the wooden box on her bed.

9

THURSDAY
THE MUSIC BOX

THE BOX SAT OMINOUSLY ON top of Sade's bed.

Still and silent, like it was watching her.

She half expected it to grow legs and chase her out of the room. Or worse, for it to start beeping and explode in her face.

But instead, it sat there, unmoving. Waiting to be touched.

Sade had watched enough spy movies and horror flicks to know that touching a strange box that had seemingly been left for you was always a bad thing. But still, she found herself moving slowly toward it until she was right in front of it.

She let out a breath, inching forward to touch it. Her manicured fingers grazed the wood and its intricate carvings of flowers and spirals, which crisscrossed the outside of the box.

Someone has been in here, she thought again.

Someone left this box on my bed.

A voice, her voice, urged her to take the box, open it, see what was inside.

She grabbed the box, flicking the latch before easing open the lid. Immediately, a slow, charming song started to play as a girl made from glass twirled in the center.

A message was engraved into the open lid in gold. *For my dear Elizabeth.*

Sade felt her heart stop altogether.

This box was Elizabeth's . . . So why was it on Sade's bed?

The bad feeling sank its teeth into her again, crawling up her arms. She didn't believe in coincidences. Her life thus far had been a series of carefully laid mousetraps, set by the universe. And the joke was constantly on her.

Sade had a feeling this box was the universe's next act in the series of tricks it had in store for her this lifetime.

But who gave the box to Elizabeth? A relative maybe, or a friend . . . Sade thought about Baz for a moment.

Except why was the box here now?

As she stared at it closely, she noticed another latch inside, underneath the twirling girl. This one was much smaller than the external one.

She flicked it up, and the twirling girl folded in on herself as the second lid opened.

This hidden compartment revealed what seemed to be scraps of paper and handwritten notes.

She recognized the handwriting as Elizabeth's, from the way she had written her name on the chalkboard that hung on the room door. The same handwritten script was scrawled all over.

Sade picked up one of the notes. The writing looked more like rushed squiggles than actual words. From the random sentences, she could make out the word *Fisherm*... something, most likely *Fishermen?* But other than that, it might as well have been gibberish.

Sade spotted a black envelope tucked beneath the scraps of paper and notes. She reached in, pulling it out.

The envelope was thick and felt expensive to the touch. On the front of the envelope was the outline of a fish, engraved in silver, and on the back, one of those old-fashioned wax seals with a similar fish symbol. She tugged the letter open, spotting something written on the paper in silver.

For Elizabeth

.-. .- - ... / - .... .- - / .... --.- .. .- .. .-.. / -.... . -.-. --- -- . / .- /
-- . .- .-.. / -....- / .- / --.- .. --- - . / -... -.-- / - ..... . /
.-... . --. .-. -.-. .-. -.-- / .--- --- .... -. / ..-. .. ..-. --..-- /
--- ..- .-. / ..-. --- ..- -. -... .-. -..--- / - ..... . / --- .-. .. --. .. -. .- .-.. /
..-. .. ..-.. -- .- -. . / .... -- .... . .-.. ..-. .-.-.- / .-. .- -- . --- -.... .-. /
.... / .-- --- .-. -... .... / .-- .. ..-.. -.-- --..-- /
.. -. - .-. -.- .- .-.. .. --.. / - ..... . -- --..-- / .- .... / -.-. --- ..- / .- .-.. /
-. --- .-- / .-. .- .-. .- / --- ..-. / - ..... . / .... --. ....-. / .-. .-. -. -.- .... /
--- ..-. / - ..... . / .-- --- .-. -.. .-.- -..-.- / -... .. .- .-. / .... - .. -- . -.. /
--. ..- . .... - --..-- / .. / .- -- / .-- -- / .--. .-.. .- -. .... -.. / - --- /
.. -. ..-. --- .-. -- / -.-- --- ..- / - ..... .- - / .-.- --- ..- / ..... .- ..-. . /
-.... . . -. / .... . .-. . -.-. . -... / .- .... / --- -. . / --- ..-. / - ..... . /
.-... ..- -.-. .-. -.-. -.-- / ..-. .-.. -.-- / ---- / .- - - . -. -... / .- /
.... .- .-- -.-. .. -. .-. --. / .... --- .. .-... . . .-.-. / .--. .-. .- .-. . .... /
..-. .. -. .-.. / - ..... / .-... . / -.... . .... .-.. .. .... / -.... . . .. -. -.. / - .... /
.. -. .... .. - . . -... / .-- . / .-.. --- --- -.- / ..-. .... --- .-. .-. .-. -.-. -... / - --- /
..... .- ..-- .. -. . --. / -.-- --- ..- -..--- / .-.- -. .-.. / .-. .-. .- . --- -.... . .-. --..-- /
-.. --- -. .----. / .... --.- ..- .. .- .-... .-.-.- / -..... - ..-. --

Sade frowned at the page, looking at the combination of hyphens, periods, and forward slashes. The first combination went dot, hyphen, dot, dot, hyphen, hyphen, ellipses . . . It seemed to be some sort of encoded message . . .

A sharp knock on her door made her jump, and Sade quickly shoved the box and the envelope under her duvet.

She went to open the door and found the house prefect, Jessica, outside.

"I noticed your lights were still on," she said.

"I was studying," Sade lied.

Jessica raised an eyebrow. "Lights are meant to go out at nine thirty."

It was that time already? "Sorry, I didn't know—"

Jessica interrupted with a tight smile. "Just don't let it happen again, okay?"

Sade felt the urge to close the door in her face. "Okay," she said instead.

Jessica gave her one last dismissive glance before turning away.

"Wait—uhm, Jessica," Sade said.

The prefect turned back. "Yes?"

"I think someone came into my room today," Sade said. "My things weren't in their usual place. Is there any way you could look at CCTV or—"

"It was the cleaning lady," Jessica said, interrupting Sade once again.

"The cleaning lady?" Sade questioned.

"Yes, she cleans our rooms on Thursdays. Is that all?" Jessica asked, looking bored of this conversation.

Sade nodded uncertainly. The cleaning lady probably found the box in Elizabeth's things and forgot to put it back in its right location. Nothing deep or mysterious about it.

Yet she couldn't quite believe that.

"Good night, then," Jessica said, turning sharply once again and disappearing down the hall.

Sade went back inside her room and changed into her nightclothes before turning the lights off. She climbed into her bed, pulled the box out from under her duvet, and opened it back up again—swiping on her phone's flashlight.

The gentle sound of the music filled her ears as the girl twirled around in endless circles, and Sade quickly pulled the duvet over her head to muffle the sound and not alert Jessica that she had no plans of sleeping just yet.

She opened the envelope and searched for meaning again in the symbols.

It was clearly an invite of some kind.

For Elizabeth the invite began. What kind of message needed to be concealed in this way?

Her gaze went back to the music box. To the dancing girl. To her face, her hair, her expression. Something felt familiar about her. Something Sade hadn't noticed before.

The girl looked just like Elizabeth.

She read the engraving on the box again, noticing the faint sign of two extra letters.

For my dear Elizabeth—TG

TG.

Who was TG?

Did they send her this letter?

Suddenly, the gentle sound of feet pacing outside her door came, and she quickly pushed the letter back inside the box and snapped it shut, silencing the song.

She waited a few moments for the footsteps to fade before pushing the box under the bed and lying back heavily.

She would have to look through it more tomorrow when the threat of the house prefect wasn't so close.

As she closed her eyes and attempted to drift off, the conversation with Baz from Tuesday replayed in her mind:

Maybe she's hanging out with another friend? she'd asked.

Elizabeth doesn't really do *people,* Baz had replied.

If Elizabeth didn't *do people*, then why was it that she had a box that seemed to be from a mysterious person named TG?

Was TG this person's initials? Or was it something else entirely?

FRIDAY

A FAMILY AFFAIR

SADE WAS LATE.

Again.

This time, her lack of punctuality was caused by a night of tossing and turning, which resulted in her waking up a whole hour later than she usually did.

She rushed her morning routine, had a cereal bar for breakfast, and ran to the A block like her life depended on it—which if Miss Blackburn could somehow see her, it did.

She scurried into the middle of Mr. Michaelides's lesson, breathing heavily as she apologized for her lateness. The class all stared at her, unimpressed expressions on a few faces. Especially Persephone, who looked at her like she could scorch her with her gaze alone.

It seemed that Sade had interrupted Persephone's *Macbeth* presentation.

The presentation she only now realized that, in the chaos of the last few days, she'd forgotten to finish.

Great, she thought. Just what she needed to round the week off, her first detention.

She quickly took an empty seat, pulling out her USB, which contained her very poorly put together presentation that consisted of an introduction slide and not much else.

"... Lady Macbeth is often seen as villainous, but I don't think she is . . ." Persephone's voice echoed in the room as an image of a girl dripping in blood projected behind her. "I think she is a woman disrupting dominant ideas of womanhood, destroying the patriarchy, and defying the male gaze."

The image on the presentation was replaced by a king on a throne made of human bones.

"If she's a villain, then Macbeth is one too. And if Macbeth gets to be a flawed but ambitious hero, she does as well. Thank you," Persephone finished, triggering light applause around the classroom.

"Brilliant as usual, Miss Stuart," Mr. Michaelides said.

She didn't smile or react to his praise. Persephone's silence was loud and as sharp as a knife.

Mr. Michaelides awkwardly cleared his throat. "I have always loved feminist readings of *Macbeth*! Up next, Francis Webber, and then Sade Hussein."

Sade raised an eyebrow at the mention of Francis's surname. *Webber.* Like Headmaster Webber? She hadn't made the connection before.

Francis got up and stood in front of the class, the smell of cigarette smoke and something earthy clinging to him and lingering in the air. His auburn-colored freckles and his bright orange hair were luminous in the projector's light.

She remembered Baz's mention of the headmaster's stepson on Monday during the crash course in the school's cliques, but hadn't realized that the stepson in question was Francis.

The pair seemed nothing alike.

Persephone sat down in the seat next to Sade, and Sade snuck a glance at her like she often found herself doing.

Persephone had this constant poker face.

It was hard to tell what she was thinking. Sometimes Sade thought Persephone was staring back at her, like she had on that first day. Then other times, like yesterday, it seemed like Persephone wanted to be anywhere but near Sade.

It could be that Persephone hadn't even been looking at her on Monday. Maybe she didn't think of Sade at all.

Sade looked away from the unholy girl now, zoning out as Francis droned on about his take on Lady Macbeth and Macbeth's relationship, unsurprisingly misogynistic dribble spilling from his lips as he spoke.

When he was done, people clapped and Mr. Michaelides gave him a tight smile. "That was certainly very different from Persephone's presentation," he said.

"I try to refrain from describing women as being *totally psycho* and *fugly*, so yes, very different," Persephone said.

Francis rolled his eyes. "Persephone's just mad because she scares all her potential boyfriends away with her charming personality."

"One, not that it's any of your business, but I'm a lesbian, so I have very little interest in your species, especially if they look and act anything like you do, and two . . ." She held up her middle finger as a response. Some students in the class snickered as Francis's face grew red.

"That's enough. I'm sure we can all have this lively debate without resorting to bringing up anything personal," Mr. Michaelides said, looking even more uncomfortable. It was clear he wasn't one to discipline or confront students often. "Sade, it's your turn now," he continued in an attempt to move things along.

Still reeling from Persephone handing Francis's ass to him, Sade almost forgot about her impending punishment. She snapped out of her shock and grabbed her USB before walking up to the front of the class.

Her presentation popped up behind her as she plugged it into the computer.

Here goes nothing.

She had studied this play so many times, at this point she didn't need the presentation to be able to talk about it.

"Whenever you're ready, Sade," Mr. Michaelides said.

She nodded, feeling herself growing warm as the gazes of her classmates bore into her. "Yes, uhm . . . Lady Macbeth," she began.

"Can't hear you," a boy said from the back, which garnered snickers from the class.

"I think Persephone made a lot of good points," she continued, speaking a little louder now. "But, uhm . . . I'd argue that Lady Macbeth is and should be considered a villain, maybe more so than Macbeth. However, even worse than the two characters, is the playwright himself: Shakespeare. This presentation is meant to be on the relationships and characters in Macbeth, and I'd like to talk about why Shakespeare is the villain and about his relationship between himself—the author—and his characters."

The whole class had fallen quiet. No fidgeting, no sly smiles or unimpressed faces. Just silence and blank expressions.

"Could you elaborate?" Mr. Michaelides asked, also looking a little blank.

Sade was mostly bullshitting her way through this presentation. But she remembered an exercise her English tutor, Ms. Samuels, always made her do.

The interview with the author.

It involved an interrogation-style interview with the author of whatever book she was studying that week, and because Shakespeare wrote a whole load of plays, she constantly found herself head to head with William himself—metaphorically, of course.

"Shakespeare was an unhappily married middle-aged man with a tendency to write very one-dimensional women, but fully fleshed men. I'd argue that the only way Shakespeare knew how to write a strong woman was to strip her of her femininity and make her cruel. He had to dehumanize her and reduce her to nothing in order for it to make sense why she was different. She's the antithesis of the perfect wife. She hates children, she wants dominance, and she speaks her mind . . . ," Sade rambled on. She wasn't sure where it was all coming from. Maybe years of having Shakespeare force-fed to her had finally broken the dam and released this flood of thoughts she apparently had.

She finally came to the end of her presentation: "Lady Macbeth isn't empowering, despite what modern feminist critics might say. She's Shakespeare's cautionary tale. You disrupt the patriarchy, you suffer."

No one clapped. The look of bewilderment on the faces of most of the students was still evident.

"Wow, that was a brilliant analysis, Sade. Very impressive," Mr. Michaelides said finally. It was a contrast to Francis's expressionless expression as he looked out the window, clearly uninterested. At least Mr. Michaelides seemed to like it and she had somehow avoided a detention.

She really needed to catch up on her towering workload to avoid this situation repeating itself. As the cards were rarely in her favor, it was unlikely she would be able to pull off something like that again.

As Mr. Michaelides went on about what they would be studying next week in class, Sade zoned out. Her mind was once again consumed by the box and the strange letter with its code and weird fish symbol.

What if there really was more to its contents?

She'd have to show Baz and see what he thought, if it could be a lead.

". . . *The Book Thief* is a great introduction to the Second World War and literature set around that time. We'll also be watching *The Imitation Game* next week. Which, if you didn't know, is a movie on how the great Alan Turing cracked the Enigma code during World War II." The bell interrupted. "Ah, I see I'm out of time. Come and collect your copies of *The Book Thief* from the front of the class; you have the week to read the first fifty pages before we discuss the text. Make sure you read up to chapter four for Monday's class."

People started to get up, grabbing a copy before shuffling out of the tiny classroom. But Sade sat still, her mind going over Mr. Michaelides's words.

Enigma code.

That code from Elizabeth's box . . . the repeating dots, the pattern they made.

How could she have missed this before?

Morse code.

The letter was written in Morse code.

When she was homeschooled, she'd had a brief lesson on the many codes used in the Second World War, and while she didn't know the code itself by heart, she knew it used dots and dashes.

She would have to find some kind of translation guide on the internet, but maybe the code would lead them closer to figuring out who sent the invite and, in turn, who else might know where Elizabeth could be. Hopefully it would confirm her suspicions that Elizabeth was hurt or, better yet, disprove them.

She wouldn't be able to crack it until after her classes, but she felt that she was finally getting somewhere.

Surely, such a cryptic letter would tell her *something*.

As she rushed out of the classroom, her thoughts were interrupted.

"Hey," a voice said.

Sade looked up and was met with the deep brown of Persephone's eyes. The girl was leaning against a nearby wall, staring Sade down. It was very intimidating.

"Hi," Sade replied.

"I liked what you said in class."

"Oh? Thanks."

They stared at each other for a few moments, which to Sade felt like hours. It was as if Persephone was sifting through her thoughts, trying to read her mind. With all she had locked away inside, Sade hoped she couldn't.

"I'll see you at lunch, then?" she asked.

Sade had almost forgotten about the invitation to lunch from yesterday. She nodded. "Y-yeah, I'll see you."

Persephone's lips tugged at the corners, not quite a smile, but something like it—though Sade could have imagined it. Persephone walked away and Sade stared after her.

Persephone seemed to be another code that Sade wasn't sure she could crack. But she felt like Persephone was daring her to try anyway.

THE UNHOLY TRINITY WEREN'T THERE when Sade arrived at lunch, so she grabbed her food and went to what was becoming her usual table. She was surprised to find Baz there building some sort of tower out of his Doritos.

"What are you doing?" she asked as she sat next to him.

"I'm building a tower," he replied.

"I meant here. I don't usually see you in the lunch hall."

"It's *bangers and mash* day," he stated matter-of-factly, like that explained it.

Sade made a face. "I hate mashed potatoes," she said.

Baz looked down at her plate of veggie lasagna and made a similarly disgusted face. "Says the person eating green lasagna."

"Hey—It's the only halal option on the menu," she said, and then took a massive bite of it with an exaggerated look of satisfaction. "Much better than lumpy potatoes."

"It should be illegal to hate mashed potatoes," he replied.

She smiled. "The joy of free speech!"

"Let's change the subject before I'm forced to disown you," he said. She'd been worried that the search might've made things worse. But he still had that determined look, like he hadn't yet abandoned all hope.

"Do you know anything about a music box Elizabeth owned? The cleaning lady accidentally left it on my bed yesterday when she cleaned the dorm."

Baz looked confused. "A music box?"

Sade nodded, his expression dampening some of the hope she had that it might be a relevant lead.

"She never mentioned any music box—I don't think I saw one in her room either. Are you sure it was hers?"

"Yeah, it had her name engraved into it. It was written weirdly, though."

"What do you mean?"

Sade cast her mind back to the box, remembering the carvings, the twirling girl, the notes inside. "It said, 'For my dear Elizabeth—TG.'"

Baz's face didn't seem to stir at the mention of TG. Maybe he didn't know what the mysterious letters meant either.

"It seems like someone gave it to her, maybe her mum or something?" Sade continued.

Baz shook his head. "No, it wouldn't be from her mum or a relative," he said with absolute certainty.

How was he so sure? "Why not?" she asked, sitting up straight.

He hesitated, his eyes surveying the area before he spoke, quietly this time.

"Elizabeth doesn't have the best relationship with her family. Her mum used to be my avó's, my grandma's, nurse before my grandma passed on, and Elizabeth saw my grandma more than she saw any of her own extended family. I'm not sure of all the details, but Elizabeth was pretty much raised by her mum and her great-aunt, Julie, but more so Julie. I speak to her mum more than she does these days, and she doesn't keep any reminders of her mum at school either. It's kind of a sore subject and also not really my story to tell, which is why I didn't mention it before."

"Oh," she replied simply, not expecting all that.

Baz scratched his head and returned to his tower. "Yeah, anyway, a lot of shit happened, and then her mum got really sick, and they had this big blowup in second year. Elizabeth doesn't even really go back home during the holidays. She usually stays here, goes home with me, or, before, she would go to her aunt Julie's. But as a rule, Elizabeth likes to keep school and home separate. She's always been like that, so it's highly unlikely that the box is from family," he finished with a small shrug.

Sade nodded.

She was similar to Elizabeth in that regard. Wanting to keep school and home separate. She understood the allure of starting anew and leaving all the baggage behind.

Almost all of it anyway.

"So the box could be from someone here, at school?" she asked.

Baz looked at her for a few uncomfortable moments. "I guess it could." He then looked away awkwardly. "Was there anything else about the box? Or other things you found?"

Sade nodded. "There were notes, but I couldn't really make out what they said. And a letter written to Elizabeth in Morse code—"

"Morse code?"

"I'm pretty sure. I can show you everything after school? See if there could be any clues?"

He nodded slowly, taking in all this new information. It was probably hard for him to process it. The fact that Elizabeth was obviously keeping things from him.

Is keeping things. Present tense.

She had to stop doing that.

Baz seemed to have given up on his tower, and now proceeded to eat it while blankly staring into the distance. Sade noticed a police officer speaking to one of the lunch ladies. The officers had been around a lot more since yesterday, walking past classes during lessons, roaming the halls after school. It felt like they were all being surveilled.

Sade continued with her lasagna, eating it slowly, knowing that with her appetite, she'd probably get sick of it soon.

"Sade . . . ," Baz said quietly, bringing her back into the room.

"Yeah?"

"Why is April Owens waving at you?"

Sade looked up, bits of the lasagna dangling from her lips.

April Owens was, indeed, waving her over, seated at the table in the center. A perfect smile plastered on her perfect face.

"She kind of invited me to sit with them—"

"Fuck off," Baz said, eyes wide.

Sade said nothing to that, unsure of whether Baz was telling her to leave or not.

"Are you serious?" he asked.

She nodded.

"What are you still doing sitting with me?" he said, staring at Sade like she had grown two heads.

"I quite enjoy your company actually—" she started, only to be cut off again by Baz.

"This is like turning down an invitation to meet with a royal or something. You need to go, quickly, before they change their minds."

"Fine, I'll go," she said, rolling her eyes as she got up.

Baz tugged at her sleeve as she turned to move.

"What?" she asked.

"Fill me in later," he said, and then let her go, sending her off to the wolves.

As Sade walked over to the table, the gazes of some of the other students in the hall followed her slowly.

The table was slightly larger than the one she was seated at with Baz, but today, unlike Monday when she had initially seen the unholy girls among others, they were the only people there.

"Hey! Take a seat," April said with a wide smile.

"Thanks," Sade replied, sitting on one of the vacant chairs. She felt sweat gather on her brow, like there was a giant spotlight aimed at her. It hadn't seemed that hot in here before, but being in front of them and the unclear expectation of what exactly they wanted from her made her insides burn with anxiety.

"How has your first week been so far? Minus the roommate situation, of course," Juliette asked her. It was a simple question, and yet somehow it felt like a test.

"It's been good mostly, stressful, but good," Sade replied.

"Yeah, the workload is rough at first, but you eventually get the hang of it," April said.

Sade nodded, relieved that she wasn't the only one who found the work hard. "How's this week been for you guys?" she asked, directing the question to the three of them, while trying not to notice Persephone staring at her silently from the corner.

"Uneventful," April replied.

"Same, but it feels like this time of year always is," Juliette said.

"What about my birthday?" April asked with a raised eyebrow.

"The only good thing about October," Juliette amended.

"It's your birthday this month?" Sade asked.

April looked at her, her eyes these blank dark pits. "Yes, the thirty-first," she replied with an empty smile.

It seemed quite fitting that April's birthday was on Halloween, seeing as the girl kind of scared her.

"Greetings, all!" a familiar voice called out.

She looked up to find August, who wrapped his arms around April, pulling her into a hug. He glanced up as though he could feel Sade's eyes on him, and smiled. "Hi, swimmer girl," he said to Sade.

He was joined by a stranger with sharp, pale features and near-white hair. The white-haired guy sat next to Juliette, but along with Persephone, April, and Juliette, his eyes were trained on Sade, interest clearly piqued.

"You two know each other?" April asked as August sat next to Persephone.

"She's my new sister," he said. Now more eyes were on the two of them.

"House sibling," Sade corrected, drawing her gaze briefly away from the boy with the snow-colored hair. "Seeing as my name isn't swimmer girl, I guess we don't know each other after all."

"A family affair," April said with a smile. "You'll have to excuse my twin; he is a bit annoying."

Sade hadn't made the correlation before. August and April Owens. *Twins*.

"And you'll have to excuse my sister; she forgets the world doesn't revolve around her," he replied. April threw a chip at him, and he dodged, laughing.

"Are you going to introduce new girl?" the white-haired guy interrupted.

Juliette perked up, taking out her phone before clearing her throat. "Sade Hussein, originally from Wandsworth but has lived in other cities and countries, was home-schooled before she came here, and . . . is a double Gemini."

Sade looked at Juliette in shock. How did she know all that?

"Don't be alarmed. Juliette knows everything and the sooner you accept it, the less surprising it gets," the white-haired boy said, following it up with, "I'm Jude, by the way. Jude Ripley. Head boy. Swim team captain—"

"We get it, hotshot—this isn't a job interview," Juliette interrupted.

Jude merely smiled at her. "Hey, I just wanted to make sure I properly introduced myself to the new girl."

Juliette rolled her eyes at him. "I think you've made your point now—Sade, don't confuse his conventional looks and smile with a nice personality. He stole my Build-A-Bear donkey in second year and still hasn't given it back."

Now it was Jude who was rolling his eyes. "I have no idea what you're talking about, Jules."

As Juliette accused him of being a thief once again, Sade stared at the boy for a few moments, taking him in.

He had these piercing blue eyes, the kind that were on the verge of being creepy but instead were just slightly unsettling. There was a ring of faded purple around his eyebrows, a bruise, covered up by what seemed to be concealer.

He looked exactly as she imagined a person with the name *Jude Ripley* would look.

". . . Listen, this boy here is not only a thief and a liar, but he thinks he's a celebrity too. Introduce yourself like a normal person for once, Jude. Not like we should be so thankful to be graced by your presence."

Jude smirked at her, then looked back at Sade, who felt more sweat pool on her forehead. "The opposite really—I feel like I have been graced with Sade's presence."

Her skin only burned hotter in the invisible spotlight. She forced herself to smile. "It's nice to finally be graced with your presence too," she said. Then added, "Jude Ripley."

His smirk folded into a broad, charming grin.

Sade noticed Persephone and her loud silence, focused now on the book she was reading instead of the conversation.

"Did you guys hear about the vigil for that missing girl?" Juliette asked.

Sade turned to her, feeling her heart skip at the mention of Elizabeth.

"I don't get the point of it; she isn't dead," April said, applying a thin layer of gloss to her lips now.

"You don't know that. She's been gone for nearly a week, and you know what they say about the likelihood of finding a missing person alive after seventy-two hours," Juliette added.

Sade had thought of the probability of it all. How with each passing hour, the chance of Elizabeth being okay became less and less likely. She needed to figure out that box and fast. It was her only lead at the moment. Her only lead for a girl she really didn't know at all.

"Why do you know so much about crime, Jules? Got a secret murder fetish?" Jude asked.

She shrugged. "I like true-crime podcasts; they help me sleep at night. I guess you *could* call that a murder fetish . . ."

As Juliette went on about her penchant for blood and corpses, Sade thought about the statistics of finding a missing person.

According to the internet, the first seventy-two hours were vital. The strongest chance of finding someone alive happened in that window. After that, the numbers just got depressing.

Every minute counted.

Sade saw wisps of red in the distance as a familiar redhead zigzagged through the small crowd by the tables nearby, seemingly hurtling toward the group.

It was Francis and he looked weirdly agitated. His eyes were red and his limbs shaky.

"Hey, French! Feels like I haven't seen you in forever," August yelled over the cafeteria noise as Francis neared the table.

Francis yelled back in an exaggerated way, "Maybe I've been avoiding you, Auggie."

April turned around and Francis's agitation seemed to melt away as he stared at her. She wrapped her arms around his neck and he proceeded to bend over to eat her face.

Sade tried to stay neutral and not let her disgust be so visible. She scanned the table to gauge the reactions of the others. Surely, she couldn't be the only one who saw that Francis was leagues below April. Then again, she never really saw the appeal of sexist assholes.

"Some of us are trying to eat here," Persephone said, finally speaking.

Francis retaliated by giving her the finger, still focused on kissing April. He was holding April's face with those ratty, discolored gloved hands of his. Sade was surprised April even let those gloves near her.

Love was a strange thing.

"Yeah, get a room," Jude replied with a smile, yet continued watching them.

The two finally came up for air and April turned back around. "Are you staying for lunch?" she asked him.

He shook his head. "Just wanted to grab the captain," he said, nodding at Jude.

Jude had his chin resting on his hand, and an eyebrow raised. "What about, French?"

Francis smiled. "Swimming, as usual. Coach said he won't let me swim next week, which is bullshit. I need you to convince him I can."

Jude sighed and looked back at the group, eyes meeting Sade's briefly. "Gotta go, lads. Duty calls," he said, standing up now. "Hope to see you around, Sade," he added, his blue eyes piercing into her.

She nodded. "I hope to see you around too."

HER LAST-PERIOD PSYCHOLOGY CLASS FINISHED a few minutes early, and Sade rushed back to her dorm room before the post-school crowd could form.

She'd texted Baz to meet her there once his classes had finished so they could open Pandora's box and look at all the mysteries tucked inside it, together.

Once she got to her floor, she pulled out her key, fingers shaking in anticipation.

She pushed the door open, hurried inside, and dumped her bag down on the floor before she reached under the bed for the box.

She turned on her phone's flashlight and got down lower, shining the light across the expanse of carpet beneath her bed, going back and forth over and over again. But there was no use.

The box was gone.

FRIDAY
FORGET-ME-NOT

SADE SEARCHED ALL OVER THE room for signs of the music box, despite her certainty that she had placed it under her bed.

It was simply gone.

Unless the box had grown legs and scuttered out of the room while she was in classes all day, it was obvious that someone had been inside the room and taken it.

But who?

"Do you know where I can find Jessica?" she asked a passing student as she stepped out of her room.

"She might be in her room? Room 412."

Sade thanked them and made her way up.

The fourth floor was identical to hers. The only difference she could make out was the carpet, which was mauve with floral patterns instead of the plain beige that lined the third floor.

She knocked on 412 and waited a moment as the sound of shuffling came from behind the door. Finally, it swung wide open, revealing Jessica in a bathrobe and some sort of face mask plastered to her skin.

"What is it?" she asked.

"I think someone came into my room—"

"Didn't we already have this conversation?"

"Yes, but that was yesterday. This is today. Something of mine is missing and I just wanted to see if there was any CCTV or—"

"No," Jessica said bluntly.

"No to there being CCTV or no to you checking?" Sade asked.

"Both. The only CCTV in the dorms is by the entrance and dining hall. For the sake of privacy, CCTV isn't used in the residential parts of the building."

"Could you check the CCTV by the entrance, then—"

"No," Jessica repeated.

Sade figured there was no point in arguing back or bothering her any longer.

"Is that all?" the prefect asked.

"Yes. That's all."

"Good," Jessica said, closing the door in her face. It appeared the fourth year did not find it at all disturbing that in the same week Sade's roommate went missing, she was here reporting that someone might have broken into her room. Twice.

Some house prefect she was.

The thought that someone might've been in her room freaked Sade out more than anything. Especially considering what they had taken, and the fact that they'd gone through her stuff. If she wanted answers, she would need to go digging for them herself.

Sade remembered seeing the security room by the reception area on the day she filled in her house-placement form. She just needed a way in.

She left Turing House, walking straight over to the main building, where she was relieved to see Ms. Thistle settling in for her shift and Miss Blackburn gone.

Ms. Thistle smiled at Sade and Sade returned the smile.

"Can I help you, dear?"

She questioned whether Ms. Thistle would listen to her if she asked to see the CCTV footage of the outside of Turing. She seemed a lot more understanding than Blackburn, yet still Sade wasn't sure she could risk the possibility of Thistle saying no. It was much easier to do this herself.

"No, I'm fine, just waiting for a friend."

This wasn't technically a lie. Though she had asked Baz to meet her in Turing's common room.

Ms. Thistle nodded brightly. "Glad to see you're making friends. Let me know if you do need anything, always happy to help."

"Thanks, miss," Sade replied, continuing to smile plastically until Ms. Thistle finally got up and went over to the photocopier in the back room behind the desk, and her face was able to return to its neutral anxious state.

She looked around, searching for any teachers watching the area, pausing when she looked up at the ceiling and noticed the little, weary eyes of the women staring down at her like they were judging her. She tore her eyes away from the painting and moved toward the room where she had filled in the house form on Monday.

Luckily, she found the room unlocked and quickly slipped inside before anyone could notice, closing the door behind her.

The room was empty, the desk she'd used still in the same place.

Behind it was the door to the security room, which was slightly ajar. She could see the glow of a blue monitor and the outline of a figure seated in front of the monitor in her direct line of vision.

She froze.

She hadn't thought this far.

She felt her heartbeat pulse as anxiety flooded her system.

The guy in the security room began to hum a tune, and Sade quickly scanned the area, searching for a hiding place.

She spotted a closet in the wall by the cabinets and crept toward it, before twisting the handle and squeezing herself inside the tiny space.

It was filled with boxes stacked on top of one another. She made sure not to move too much, as to not topple them over and potentially die under the weight of all the cardboard—all because of a hunch.

The humming stopped and was replaced by static from what sounded like a walkie-talkie.

"Hey, Harry—just a heads-up, I'm popping out for the bog," she heard the gruff voice of the security guard say.

She listened for the shuffle of feet on the carpet and the sound of a door opening and closing, and then when it felt safe to do so, she stepped out of the closet and quickly marched into the small security room.

The guy had said he was going to *the bog*. She assumed this meant he was taking a break or something, so she probably had about ten to fifteen minutes before he came back.

She had to work quickly.

Sade surveyed the desk in front of her. There were a number of screens and a keyboard—each button controlling a screen, it seemed, and each screen a camera on campus.

Sade found the button that said TURING and pressed it, which pulled current footage of the main entrance of the house up to the big screen in the center.

Using the mouse, she moved the cursor over to the rewind button on the screen and watched nervously as the footage began to reverse. She tried to see if she could spot anything or anyone suspicious.

At first it was nothing, with students in classes for most of the day. Then just after lunchtime, a hooded figure exited the building. Sade paused the footage, trying to get a better glance at them. But they were facing away from the camera. She instead focused on other things like their stature, the width of their shoulders, any hair sticking out. They seemed to be on the shorter side, though it was hard to tell from this angle. She let the footage play a little more, the image at the back of the hoodie coming into view.

A white, blurry logo of some kind. It almost looked like the outline of a rocket or . . . a fish.

Like the fish on the box's invite.

Very weird . . .

She took a photo of it with her phone.

The figure seemed to be hugging their chest, so she rewound the footage again and slowed it down. This time the figure's arms were slightly visible. It hadn't been clear the first time she had looked at it, but this time it was unmistakable.

The figure was holding a box.

One that had the same color and shape as the box she'd found in her room. She could even see the same carvings on the wood through the slightly blurred footage.

"I knew it," she whispered. Someone *had* been in her room.

She wished she could tell Jessica *I told you so*. But then she'd have to explain how she had gotten this information, which would lead to Jessica telling on her and then she assumed to her expulsion from Alfred Nobel Academy.

She needed Jessica or even a teacher to look at this footage and see.

Sade could hear the distant sounds of people walking in the hallway, the laughter of students, the sound of shoes hitting carpet, low whistling.

She needed to leave.

The whistling neared, and Sade heard the deep voice of someone approaching the room.

Her heart quickened as the door handle to the security room rattled, and she dived under the desk, narrowly avoiding being caught.

The door opened and the security guard stepped in, taking a seat on the chair and dragging it forward, his feet nearly trampling Sade's hands. She heard a click and the sound of a local news station rang out from what she assumed was a radio, filling the silence a little.

She hoped he didn't notice that the screen was on a different page from where he'd left it.

The man swiveled in his chair, almost stepping on her several times, and Sade realized how screwed she was. She had no idea how long he'd stay in there for. It could be hours and she hated small spaces.

She could feel the dread rise inside, and panic filter through.

This is what happens when you don't listen to me, the voice hissed at her.

Sade closed her eyes, trying to breathe as evenly as she could.

It was going to be okay.

She would get out of this.

She just needed to be quie—

Her phone buzzed silently and she felt her heart jump out of her chest briefly.

She hoped he hadn't heard that. Luckily, the gentle hum of the radio in the corner seemed loud enough to cover it.

She slowly lifted her phone up, turning down the brightness. It was a message from Baz. She turned her vibrate setting off before responding.

B: Where are you?

What a question, she thought. If only he knew.

S: In the main building, where are you?

B: I'm at Turing, waiting for you. I wanted to see the box and hear about your lunchtime date with the she-devils

The box. How would she tell him that this strange, mystical box was no longer in her possession because a strange, mystical figure seemed to have broken into her room and taken it? It would be better to explain in person.

S: I don't know why you call them that, they were actually kind of nice, she texted, only really replying to the latter half of his message.

B: Okay, so come and tell me how nice they were

Sade looked down at her phone and then up at the legs of the security guard.

S: I need you to do me a favor first.

B: What?

S: I need you to call reception and tell them there's been a fight or that something has happened in some other building. Something that'll make them call security.

B: Why?

S: Just do it, please?

At first the three dots indicating that Baz was typing appeared, and she feared that he'd ask more questions or say no, but instead he disappeared.

She hoped she hadn't been abandoned. Not that it was a new feeling; at this point in her life, it was getting quite repetitive.

Minutes passed and Sade was almost certain that Baz had ignored her pleas. She could be trapped here for god knows how long.

Just then, the sharp ring of the telephone sounded in the room and the security guard picked it up.

"Hello?" he said. "You what? How did that happen? Jesus Christ, I'll be right there."

She heard him hang up the phone before pushing himself up again and walking out the door.

Sade let out a sigh of relief. It seemed that Baz had come through for her after all.

She quickly crawled from under the desk and walked out of the security office, then out of the room she had done her test in, not anticipating running straight into Miss Blackburn.

"What on earth were you doing in that room, Sade?" she said.

The universe couldn't seem to give her a break. Just this once. "I uhm . . . I w-was just uhm—"

"Are you going to speak up?" Miss Blackburn said.

Sade could feel her hands shaking and a lump forming in her throat. "S-sorry, I was uhm, l-looking for you."

Miss Blackburn raised an eyebrow at her. "Whatever for, Miss Hussein?"

She had to think of something quick, before Miss Blackburn figured out that she was lying and gave her detention, or worse.

She looked around, searching for something to help her case.

She spotted the wall nearby with the engraved names of all the head girls and boys from the history of the school.

"I—I wanted to ask about how becoming a head girl would work? I wasn't sure if it was too soon to ask since I know head girl positions are only open to fourth years, but I figured I'd get an early start."

Miss Blackburn looked her up and down, eyes narrowed. "You want to be head girl?"

Sade shrugged. "I don't know, I'm just thinking about it. I know it helps university applications and so I thought, why not."

Miss Blackburn nodded slowly, seeming to buy her story. "Well, the teachers nominate a few students—those with the best grades, the right attitude. Then the students vote from that selection. I wouldn't worry about that for now, though, I'd focus on catching up with the work you've missed. You can start thinking about the coveted head girl positions once we start seeing straight As from you. But anyway . . . I must be going, there's an emergency in the science block. See you later, Miss Hussein," Miss Blackburn said, nodding at Sade before walking out of the building with a walkie-talkie held close to her mouth.

Sade felt she could finally breathe normally again.

She looked down at her phone now, a message from Basil waiting for her.

B: Done :)

S: What did you tell them? They seemed so panicked.

B: I told them that some idiot let all the hamsters and guinea pigs from the science lab out of their cages.

She could hear distant screaming, voices melding together, and a loud voice yelling.

"A RAT! I saw a bloody rat!"

The commotion continued. "No way," she whispered, eyes widening now.

S: Baz . . . did you release the animals from the science labs?

B: A magician never reveals his secrets

Sade stared down at her phone in shock.

Baz had to be the oddest person she had ever met.

B: Meet me in the Turing common room in 15. I need to wash hamster piss off my hands first.

APPROXIMATELY SEVENTEEN MINUTES LATER, SADE found herself in Turing House.

She would've been there sooner if she hadn't been stopped by a girl from her English class named Liv, who'd handed her a colorful flyer about a vigil happening tomorrow afternoon for Elizabeth.

"We wanted to show Elizabeth that people here care. They say runaways respond best to vigils," Liv said as she hugged the flyers close and smiled with all the forced sincerity in the world.

Was that the current theory about Elizabeth? Sade still didn't know what she believed herself. Runaway was the more optimistic option, but somehow everything else pointed to something more sinister.

"Did you put this together?" Sade asked her, staring down at the flyer now.

Liv shook her head. "No . . . I think one of Elizabeth's friends must've? I just volunteered to hand them out, seeing as it's a good cause and all."

One of Elizabeth's friends. That didn't make any sense. She almost wanted to roll her eyes in response.

People were so opportunistic.

"Elizabeth didn't have any friends," Sade found herself saying before she could stop and think about what that sounded like.

Liv's smile was immediately wiped away.

Sade tried to think of things to say that would make her sound less like a complete asshole. "I mean, I know she kept to herself."

Liv nodded. "I guess she was the quiet type; I didn't know her, though. But I think it's nice what they're doing, putting this vigil on." Was it nice?

She didn't think so, because empty gestures were exactly that. Empty.

No one seemed to care. Not really.

"You're right," Sade said to Liv. "It is nice."

Liv smiled once again. "Hope to see you there?"

Sade nodded. "Yeah, I'll see if I can make it."

On the flyer, there was a picture of what she assumed was Elizabeth's yearbook photo, where she had a miserable expression on her face. There were flowers and patterns on the sides, and, underneath, the time and place the vigil would be held. The flyer looked less like a flyer for a vigil and more like a wanted poster.

She folded it up and shoved it into her pocket before making her way to the Turing common room.

Baz had told her that he was with the house mascot, Marx, somewhere in the common room. She walked through the area with the couches and the foosball table and the students lounging around, into the room where the Turing mascot resided.

Baz was seated cross-legged on the ground, with the fluffy white cat nestled next to his thigh and what seemed to be a little guinea pig cradled in his arms. He wasn't wearing his uniform, and instead had on a brown sweater and jeans.

Sade closed the door behind herself slowly, and upon hearing the click of the lock, Baz looked up at her.

"Hey!" he said.

"Hi . . . ," she replied, locking eyes with the animal in his arms. "Is that a . . . guinea pig?" she asked, watching him scratch the top of its head.

"Yes," he replied, like it wasn't at all strange that he had one in his possession.

"Where'd it come from?" she asked, taking a seat opposite from him, on the rug.

"Found the poor thing wandering around campus, decided to bring it here with me. I think I'm gonna name her Muffin," Baz said with a smile.

By *found it wandering around campus* she assumed he meant: *She got lost after I unleashed the animals in the science labs, and I decided to grab this one.*

But who was she to judge? She hadn't been doing the most morally upstanding thing at the time. Besides, it was arguably her fault that this happened, seeing as she had asked Baz to create a distraction. Maybe she should have been more specific.

"Why Muffin?" she asked.

"I got a muffin from the vending machine, and homegirl here ate it all."

"Can guinea pigs even digest muffins?"

He shrugged. "We'll see."

The guinea pig shuffled out of Baz's arms and made its way over to Sade, sniffing her first before settling into her lap. Sade was never much of an animal person and she froze, keeping still as the guinea pig got comfortable.

"I never understood why they're called guinea pigs. They aren't really pigs, are they? Just big hamsters," she said.

"I guess it's just one of those confusing things," he replied, stroking Marx the cat now, who purred rather contemptuously at Muffin. "How was lunch?"

She knew by *how was lunch* he was really asking if something noteworthy happened. Which it hadn't, but she felt like saying that would be disappointing both for him and for her. She'd be lying if she said that something about being chosen by them didn't make her feel special.

"It was okay. They invited me back on Monday," she said.

Baz's eyes widened in excitement. "You're already climbing up the ranks and it hasn't even been a week yet. You must teach me your ways."

"To be honest, I think they're just being nice to me because I'm new here."

"I've never seen the Unholy Trinity pay other newbies any mind," Baz replied.

"Interesting," Sade said, now wondering why they invited her. She remembered the details of her first conversation with them. The fascination with Elizabeth and her disappearance.

Of course, it wasn't about her being new, it was because she was the roommate of a missing student. Nothing special about her as a person, just the fact that she might be a murderer.

"How about the box? Did you bring it down with you?" Baz asked, staring at her empty hands.

She shook her head. "It's gone."

He looked confused. "The box?"

"Yes, and I think someone deliberately took it from my room. I went into the security office to find out who. Turns out my hunch was right. I saw someone on the CCTV exiting Turing with a box in their hand, but unfortunately, I couldn't make out their face. But I'm thinking there must be a reason they took it—they must know something we don't about Elizabeth. Otherwise, why would someone steal a random box? Or go through the effort of breaking into my room, for that matter? How did they get in anyway? I'm rambling, sorry, I guess I hadn't processed it until now . . . It's been a long afternoon," Sade said, finally releasing a breath.

Baz looked like he was giving her words some serious thought. "That *is* really odd . . . and suspicious." He paused. "Though, I know Turing is notorious for theft. People are always losing things to the *Turing Thieves*. It's possible that one of them might've figured that you were new and would be an easy mark. Elizabeth used to hide her secret snack stash in places the Thieves wouldn't really consider."

The Turing Thieves? she thought, confused as ever. Was it possible that the box's theft had nothing to do with Elizabeth's disappearance but instead a notorious ring of house burglars? But then it felt as if someone had left it for her to find first . . .

"Was anything else of yours taken?" Baz asked.

She shrugged. "I didn't get the chance to check. I hope not."

"If anything, you can report it. Chances are, though, you'll never see it again . . . ," Baz said, voice trailing off, and his eyes wandering a little. "It *is* strange, though . . ."

"What is?" Sade asks.

"I haven't known the Turing Thieves to strike midterm. They usually wait until later, when students begin receiving expensive care packages from family and friends. Lots to take then. I also haven't known them to steal something like that. Usually, it's shoes, snacks, and jewelry. Useful things I suppose . . . Do you remember anything specific about the box, like that code or something? Maybe it could still lead us somewhere."

Sade thought back to the box, and the black envelope, and the strange coded letter. She took out her phone and searched for a Morse code translator before tapping out what she could remember.

"I think I remember only the first combination of symbols—a dot, hyphen, two dots, two hyphens, and an ellipses."

.-. .- - . . .

She pressed Enter, and the translator quickly changed the symbols into letters she recognized. The combination spelled out . . .

Rats.

She thought back to the dead rat on the first day, awkwardly slumped on the mat outside the dorm room. A strange coincidence, or perhaps a deliberate link. She couldn't tell, and either way, it wasn't a particularly useful coincidence.

"Not so helpful, I guess," she said.

"Maybe the Turing Thieves now have a thing for cryptic boxes. Or it's possible they didn't even know what they were stealing," he said with a dejected shrug, before looking down at her lap. "What's that?" Baz asked, pointing at her pocket and the pink paper that was now in Muffin's mouth.

She tugged it gently away from the guinea pig and hesitated before speaking, not knowing if the mention of Elizabeth would trigger him. "Nothing, just a flyer for that vigil happening tomorrow."

"Oh," Baz said with a nod.

Silence.

"Are you going?" she asked.

He shook his head. "I don't think so. To be honest, Elizabeth hates this sort of thing, not to mention most of the people who would be attending anyway. They're all posers who don't give a shit about Elizabeth or the fact that she's missing. What about you, are you going?"

Sade shrugged.

She supposed that there was a benefit to going that Baz didn't see. It might help them understand what happened that night. It might give her clues as to who gave Elizabeth the box in the first place.

All she had at the moment was the box. And she didn't know what it meant or who the mysterious *TG* was.

Saying all this to Baz seemed a bit insensitive, though, so she refrained. Not going was his rightful choice.

"You know April's brother, August, is my house brother?" she said, changing the subject.

Baz's eyebrows went up, almost all the gloom dissolving from his face in an instant. "No way? You've really become acquainted with all of ANA's royalty. The Owens family practically owns the school. I mean, they literally even own part of the land or something wild like that. Did you know Headmaster Webber is their godfather? It's all very incestuous."

I didn't know that, Sade thought, cringing at the memory of Francis and April kissing. "I also met the swim captain—Jude? Do you know much about him?" she asked. His pale blue eyes and his smile seemed to be seared into her brain.

Baz was looking down at Marx now, playing with his ears. "ANA's resident fuck boy," he mumbled.

"A fuck boy?" she asked.

"You know . . . a guy that fucks with the hearts of his conquests."

"I know what a fuck boy is, Baz," she said, laughing. "I guess it makes sense that he would be one. I've learned not to trust nice exteriors."

"*Nice exteriors* sounds like fancy talk for 'I think he's hot.'" Baz smiled, wagging his eyebrows. "Got a crush?"

"No," Sade said. "I'm just observant."

"Well, I wouldn't blame you if you did. Jude Ripley is the sort of guy that almost everyone has a crush on at some point. And I heard that when he's interested, he goes all out. He flew this girl, Dina Leslie, to Paris for the night once, only to break up with her the next day."

Sade could feel Muffin trying to eat her skirt, so she lifted the guinea pig off her lap before stroking its fur. "Sounds like an asshole," she said.

"At this point, which Hawking House boy isn't?" Baz replied with a bitter undertone. Sade suspected he had his own bad experiences with boys from Hawking House.

She looked down at the flyer for the vigil again.

Elizabeth was still the ticking clock in her mind.

Sade knew more than anyone that the difference between saving someone and losing them was simply a matter of time. How long does it take you to decipher the clues? To figure out the glaringly obvious? To stop the worst from happening?

Oftentimes, too long.

Next thing you know, you're spending every waking moment wondering what you missed. Wondering if there was any stopping it. Wondering if you could have saved her.

"Still thinking about Jude and his *nice exterior*?" Basil asked, nudging her out of her thoughts.

Sade forced herself to smile. In some ways, she was thinking about him.

She'd admit, she always did like Paris.

SATURDAY
NIRVANA

THE VIGIL WAS HELD IN the school's chapel on Saturday afternoon.

Candles adorned every wall of the dark room, their flames throwing strange shadows that mingled with the colored light trickling in through the stained glass windows. The students stood around the altar at the center, spilling out along the surrounding pews.

Sade wasn't sure what to do at an event like this, or even what to wear. Black felt too formal, an admission of something sinister. Bright colors, too insensitive.

She opted for a combination of the two: a plain forest-green turtleneck shirt, gray skirt, and chunky oxford boots.

Before she had left to come to the chapel, she spent what felt like hours pacing her room, going back and forth between attending the vigil or skipping it altogether. She was still turning over Baz's comments in her mind, and she felt guilty turning up for such a superficial event. Did she really know Elizabeth at all, herself? Was she just the same as everyone else, wanting to show her face for appearances?

But Elizabeth had been kind to her. And Sade knew how important it was that she and Baz kept searching for her. She needed to be here.

Sade scanned the chapel as she walked down the aisle. She was surprised when she spotted a familiar face standing by the altar. She walked up to him, tapping him on the shoulder.

"Hey, new girl," August said, turning to face her. He held a plastic cup. Apple juice, Sade assumed; there was a refreshments table at the side of the chapel.

Apparently, people struggled to grieve on an empty stomach.

"Hello, Augustus," Sade replied. He was standing on his own, next to a school picture of Elizabeth blown up into a poster and placed on a stand.

"Big turnout," Sade said.

He nodded, taking a sip of his drink. "Yeah, I guess a lot of people feel bad, you know? It's not nice hearing that something bad might've happened to a person you knew."

"Did you know her?" Sade asked.

August looked a little taken aback but shook his head.

"No, just paying my respects," he said.

Sade paused. Didn't people only pay respects to the dead? Didn't people believe that Elizabeth was still alive? She looked around again. At the students dressed in black. Vultures, coming to peck for gossip and grief.

Sade nodded. "Me too."

Nearby, a group of students were chattering about Elizabeth.

"I heard she was dating an older guy, skipped school to go and see him."

"Really? Well, whatever it is, I bet the boyfriend did it. It's always the boyfriend."

It's always the boyfriend . . . , Sade repeated in her mind. The words reverberated as though her brain were an empty, echoing cave.

She remembered how often Elizabeth would check her phone, and the look on her face whenever she got a text. She also remembered how convinced Baz was that Elizabeth didn't hang out with anyone else.

It's always the boyfriend.

What if Elizabeth *was* seeing someone? Someone no one knew about.

What if the music box and those letters written in code were from him to her?

What if it was TG?

What if TG knew about the music box somehow and was the one in the black hoodie who took it?

She brought out her phone and opened her messages with Baz, hesitating before typing out her message and sending.

S: Is it possible that Elizabeth was dating anyone?

"Texting someone special?" August asked.

She looked at him, locking her phone now and pocketing it. "Just a friend . . . ," she said, the cogs in her mind still spinning over the pressing questions.

"Hey, August," she said quietly.

"Yeah?"

"As deputy head boy, what would you do if someone told you they thought an item was stolen from their room?"

He raised an eyebrow. "First, I'd ask them if they were in Turing House. And then if they said yes, I'd tell them good luck," he said. "Did someone take something from you?" he asked.

A part of her almost regretted being sorted into Turing House, considering its reputation.

She hesitated before nodding. If anyone knew how to help her here, chances were it was the deputy head boy.

"In that case, I'd ask a teacher to check whatever CCTV is available, see if there's anything they can spot that looks suspicious," he said.

This had been her plan after yesterday, but she figured getting a second opinion could help with perspective.

She already knew the footage existed; she just needed a teacher to see it too so she could officially report it without incriminating herself. Then identify whoever stole the music box, and work out their connection with Elizabeth.

"I think I'll do that. Thank you, Augustus," she said.

"No problem, new girl," he replied with a nudge.

A random person that Sade was almost certain knew nothing about Elizabeth announced at the front that there would be a speaker who would be saying a few words shortly.

Baz was right about the vultures who would use this opportunity to look good.

"What was it that you think got stolen?" he asked.

Sade looked up at him. "A music box."

He nodded, looking thoughtful. "I take it it's important to you."

"It's not so much the box, but the things inside it. Those were important."

It was a half-truth, something she was used to telling.

"I'm sure it'll show up somewhere," he said.

She hoped so.

The sound of a microphone being tapped reverberated around the room. Headmaster Webber stood by the altar with a solemn look on his face.

"Sorry to interrupt your gathering, but I bring an update on Elizabeth's whereabouts. I received news this morning through correspondence with Elizabeth's great-aunt Julie that Elizabeth is with her in Birmingham and has decided to take a leave from her studies for now. Her mother has been made aware, and we as a school will be keeping her in our thoughts, hoping for her return when she's ready. As we now know Elizabeth is safe, the police will be vacating the campus today. We are grateful for their help in locating her. Thank you, all."

Whispers filled the room as Headmaster Webber stepped away.

Sade continued to stare at the place the headmaster had stood long after he'd gone, her vision crisscrossing as she processed the abrupt turn of events. She had to tell Baz.

"Well, that's good news," August said. She had almost forgotten that he was still next to her.

It was good news, and yet, why did it not feel like it?

She nodded absentmindedly. "Yeah. Really good news . . ."

She watched as people moved on, grabbing more refreshments from the sides, laughing and smiling with one another as though a moment ago they weren't all supposedly grieving over their missing classmate.

The vigil ended soon after, and Sade and August walked out of the chapel together, squeezed between the bodies of the rest of the students and the staff who had attended the gathering.

Once they got outside, she felt that she could finally breathe again.

"Well, I have to get going. I've got swim practice and Coach gets really irritated when I'm not early," August said.

"On a Saturday?" she asked.

"We take swimming very seriously at ANA. Coach trains us like sharks."

"I've heard," she said.

He smiled. "You know, I hear the girls' team is still looking for reserves. You should try out . . . if you want to, that is."

"Thank you, but I don't swim anymore," she said, feeling the irritating itch in her brain, the claws of a memory.

He tilted his head. "What about the other night? You were amazing—"

"That was just a one-off thing. I don't plan on doing that again."

"Doing what again?" he asked slowly. She could see confusion swirling in his eyes.

"I don't plan on swimming again."

To someone like August, swimming was like water was to a fish. He'd suffocate without it.

Sade knew people like him. She *was* people like him, until she couldn't be anymore. That night was her last; it had to be.

He blinked. "That's fair, I guess."

The two locked eyes and it seemed as though August wanted to say something but didn't know how. So he just stared at her.

Eventually, he pulled his eyes away and placed a hand in his pocket. "I'll see you around?"

"Sure," she replied.

Then she watched him walk away, disappearing into a door in the garden now.

Checking her phone again, Sade headed back to Turing House. Still no message from Baz. She typed out and sent another text.

S: Did you hear the good news about Elizabeth?

"Sade," she heard as she almost ran into a figure.

She looked up and was met with familiar thick eyeglasses and a friendly smile."

"Hi, Mr. Michaelides," she said, noting the cup of coffee clasped in his hand. Thankfully, she narrowly missed giving him second-degree burns.

"We're not in uniform, no need to be so formal. You can call me Adrian," he said.

She nodded politely but decided against correcting herself. She didn't feel all that comfortable calling a teacher by their first name.

"Off somewhere?" he asked, taking a sip of the hot liquid.

She was planning on stopping by Baz's dormitory on the way to Turing, but since he wasn't answering her text she wasn't sure anymore. "Actually . . . I had a question," she said.

His eyes perked up. "Go ahead."

"I think someone broke in and stole something from my room yesterday, a music box . . . Is it possible to look at CCTV of Turing House?" she asked.

"Oh, I'm sorry to hear that!" Mr. Michaelides said, brows raised in alarm. "I'll try to see if I can get access to the CCTV and let you know, is that okay?"

"Yes, thank you," she said, feeling relieved. Despite knowing Elizabeth was okay— or, if not okay, at least found, *somewhere*—Sade still had that funny feeling that something was wrong. It was probably her perpetual sense of dread again, but she'd rather be sure and let her mind finally rest.

"No problem, Sade—anyway, I must be off! I have to mark assignments. I'll see you on Monday," he said.

"Bye, Mr. Michaelides," Sade said.

He raised an eyebrow.

"Sorry—Adrian," she corrected.

"Goodbye, Sade," he replied with a smile before walking off in the opposite direction.

SHE KNEW IT WAS A bad idea, maybe even an illegal one, but as she sat in the quiet of her dorm room, Sade's thoughts began to taunt her with questions about Elizabeth. Why would she just up and leave in the middle of the night if she was going to stay with family?

Maybe it was something people just did. Maybe she just needed to get away.

Maybe Elizabeth was fine. After all, she was with her great-aunt Julie in Birmingham. She wasn't missing. She was with family.

So why is it that it still feels like the sky is falling?

As she stared at Elizabeth's side of the room, Sade let her thoughts win as something inside her snapped and she suddenly found herself walking over.

Glimpses of Elizabeth could be seen in the trinkets she kept. The posters of her favorite bands on the walls, the sunflower rug she had on the floor. It was all Elizabeth. All of it.

Something has to make it all make sense, she thought as she once again broke the boundary and went through Elizabeth's personal things, riffling for new answers.

Sade rummaged through Elizabeth's dresser, finding nothing but random pricey items of luxury jewelry that contrasted with the all-plaid and the ripped articles of clothing. Like the music box, they seemed misplaced with who she thought Elizabeth to be.

She continued to search, looking through her desk, under her bed and mattress, and . . . found nothing. No hidden notes written in Morse code or other gifts with engraved initials that said TG.

Shouldn't she be overjoyed? That Elizabeth was okay?

It made sense to exhale now. To stop this fruitless hunt.

But it was like her mind couldn't switch off.

As she stepped back, taking in the mess she had made and considering how to put it all back in place, she noticed that a corner of Elizabeth's Nirvana poster sagged down, the rest of the poster shifting with it. In her flurry she must have accidentally knocked it out of place.

She placed a towel on the bed before climbing on top of it and moving to shift the poster back in place.

She began easing the corners off carefully along with the Blu Tack, but when she got to the bottom right corner, she was surprised to find something stuck behind it. She pulled the poster off completely, and on the back, she found an envelope taped to it.

Weird.

She gently removed the tape, opening the envelope now and drawing out a small stack of photos.

The first was of Elizabeth in what seemed to be the greenhouse, wearing sunglasses and giving the camera the finger. She turned it over and, on the back, there seemed to be scribbles in Elizabeth's writing.

The next was of her former roommate in a dorm room, sitting on the windowsill and smiling at the camera.

The next was of Elizabeth in a black bikini, sitting in front of a wall with green and white tiles, still staring at the camera.

Why would she keep these photos hidden?

Sade continued going through the photos, noting how in every one, Elizabeth had her eyes fixed on the camera . . . Or maybe not the camera, but the person behind it.

A picture of Elizabeth in an oversized shirt, seated in a different dorm room, still looking at the photographer, still smiling.

When Sade pulled out the final photograph, she almost dropped it in shock.

She brought the photo closer, then turned it around to see if there was any writing on the back. This she could just barely make out.

Three months

"What is this?" she whispered to herself.

Her phone pinged, disrupting the silence in the room and making her heart skip a beat.

She pulled it out.

B: Sorry, took a nap—was up all night making a nest for Muffin

Sade was pretty sure guinea pigs needed a cage not a nest, but before she could respond to that, her phone pinged again.

B: What good news about Elizabeth??

Baz asked, bypassing her first message.

Sade felt a chill settle over her shoulders.

S: At the vigil Webber announced that she's with her great-aunt Julie in Birmingham, taking a sabbatical. It's weird because wouldn't she tell you that she was? You know her better than I do, though, so I don't know. I guess I'm glad she's safe.

She sent the text to Baz, wanting to add more, but needing to order her thoughts first.

She looked back down at the photo in her hand, and then she exited her chat with Baz and opened the picture-sharing app she barely used, going back to Elizabeth's page and the picture of her in the room with the tiles, comparing the two.

She hadn't seen it before, the reflection in the glasses, the cameraman.

Did you know her? she'd asked.

No, just paying my respects, he'd replied.

She looked down at the physical photograph in her hands of the two of them. A selfie.

Elizabeth was kissing his cheek and the boy was smiling up at the camera. The boy Elizabeth was likely dating, the one reflected in her glasses, the one holding the camera in all the pictures, the boy Sade had seen today who'd told her he didn't know Elizabeth.

August Owens.

Her phone buzzed once again, and somehow, the message that appeared on the screen managed to knock even more air out of her, pulling the world completely out from under her feet.

B: Elizabeth's great-aunt Julie died two years ago

13

GHOSTS CAN'T TYPE

BAZ BURST INTO HER ROOM, a look of alarm on his face and his new guinea pig nestled in his arm.

"Tell me what Webber said exactly," he said immediately upon entering. It had only been three minutes since he sent the message, so he must have either tele-ported after sending it or been somehow multitasking by holding a live animal, texting, and running.

Sade could feel herself trembling slightly. "He said he'd received news that Elizabeth was with her great-aunt Julie in Birmingham. That she was taking a break from her studies—What did you mean by she died? How is that possible?" Sade asked.

"I meant what I said. Her great-aunt died from brain cancer at the end of first year," he said, breathing quickly, his eyes slowly drifting to Elizabeth's side of the room.

Sade sat down heavily on her bed before her limbs could give out.

"It had to be in writing," Sade said quietly.

"What?"

"Well for one, he said they'd corresponded with each other, which would mean written, and two, her great-aunt is dead, right? The way Webber described the news, it definitely sounded like her great-aunt had been the one to let them know, not Elizabeth. And so whatever way they received the news, it had to be in writing. But why, especially if Elizabeth had been missing for five days, did they not dig further or ask any questions? You'd think the police would at least interview Elizabeth, or her great-aunt, or both, to close their case?"

"Ghosts can't type, so how is any of this possible?" Baz asked.

Sade remembered her own application to Alfred Nobel. How she'd filled it in her-self, signing off as her father with ease. It seemed Alfred Nobel didn't ask questions. Anyone could fake an email. She had done so herself.

"Exactly, ghosts can't type. Clearly, the school doesn't know great-aunt Julie is dead," Sade replied.

Baz's eyes widened. "Of course, they don't . . . Elizabeth's mum never told them."

Sade raised an eyebrow. "But wait, Webber said Elizabeth's mum was told that Elizabeth was with her great-aunt. If she knew Julie was dead, why wouldn't she say something?"

Baz ran a hand through his vibrant curls and took a seat next to Sade on her bed. He looked down at the ground for a few moments and then up at her once again. "Elizabeth's mum is sick. She knows Julie is dead—she's been told before—she just doesn't really remember it."

"What do you mean she doesn't remember?"

Baz sighed, pausing for a moment. "Elizabeth's mum was diagnosed with early-onset Alzheimer's a few years ago. It's why she and Elizabeth had that fight. Elizabeth tried to persuade her to get help, but her mum refused; she didn't want to be out of work or put into a care home. Things have only really gotten worse since then." There was a small squeak from Baz's arms as Muffin tried to wriggle out of Baz's grip. Baz reached into his pocket and produced a small container of what seemed to be muffin crumbs, placing it now in front of the guinea pig.

"I'm sorry to hear that," Sade said.

"Elizabeth doesn't like people knowing. I feel bad telling you without her permission, but I guess at this point, I have no choice," he said. "It's clear someone else sent that email. Either Elizabeth wrote it and is fucking with the school for whatever reason, or . . ." His voice trailed off.

Sade finished the sentence in her head.

Or someone who knows about Elizabeth's great-aunt Julie sent the email, and knows where Elizabeth is.

A loud ping went off in the room, and Baz took out his phone. He swore under his breath and quickly bolted up, holding Muffin tighter.

"Is everything okay?" Sade asked.

"Yeah, I'm just late for rowing practice," he said. "Clearly, nothing more important in life than making a boat move really fast. I have to get going before our coach sends someone to Seacole with a pitchfork, but thank you for letting me know about Webber. Time for a new plan A."

Sade nodded, standing and walking with him to the hallway. "Any ideas?"

"Find that email and then who sent it."

"How?" she asked. It wasn't like they could break into Webber's office and steal his personal computer or something. *Or could they?* "You want to hack the headmaster's emails?" she questioned, hoping he wasn't serious.

"I know a guy," he replied with a shrug.

"You can't be serious," she said, but from the expression he wore, he was. Even Muffin squirmed about, looking uncomfortable at the riskiness of his plan. "I'll message you with an update on what he says," Basil replied simply. Then he waved goodbye like he hadn't just casually planned a cyber heist.

It wasn't until she got back inside that she noticed the photos discarded on her bed.

In the flurry of the whole dead-aunt situation, she'd forgotten to show them to Baz or tell him her new theory.

That somehow, August was involved in all this.

These photos weren't necessarily incriminating, but his lies certainly were. August was hiding something, and Sade was going to find out what.

SUNDAY

THE TROUBLE WITH MUFFINS

SADE WOKE UP ON THE floor of her dorm room, as was customary after a night of sleepwalking, with a pounding headache and a text from Baz.

B: So apparently muffins are bad for guinea pigs.

Baz's message was the least strange thing that had happened in the last twenty-four hours, which was saying something.

Between the revelation that Elizabeth's dead great-aunt was somehow writing emails and the possibility of Elizabeth having a secret boyfriend and said secret boyfriend being August Owens, she wasn't sure how many more surprises from the universe she could take.

This all explained the headache and the sleepwalking. That much anxious energy could power an entire city.

Sade considered going to the pool to ask August to his face about Elizabeth, but she couldn't bring herself to leave her room. Her brain kept coming up with *what-ifs*. What if August was the one who had broken into her room? What if August knew more about Elizabeth's disappearance than he was letting on?

Suddenly, the outside world seemed a lot scarier than the four walls of her haunted dorm room.

S: What're you gonna do?

B: I need to take her to the vet

This message was followed by a knock on her door, and for the second time in less than twenty-four hours a semipanicked-looking Baz stood on the other side of it. He was wearing a shirt that said RIBBIT, a brown aviator jacket, and what seemed to be a green *frog* hat.

Third strange thing to happen in the past twenty-four hours: Baz's attire.

"I like your hat," she said, not knowing what else to say.

"Thanks," he replied.

His abrupt visit found her sitting on a bus next to him on the way to the local town.

Since they were third years, they were allowed to leave the campus on weekends. Baz had managed to sneak the guinea pig out by placing her inside his sweater, but now that they were on the bus, he had her out on his lap. Sade hoped the bus driver didn't notice and kick them off midjourney. She hated long walks.

When they finally got to the vet, Baz handed Muffin over with a solemn look in his eyes and they took a seat in the waiting room.

He rested his head back against the wall. "I'm such a shit person. I've only had her for a few days and now we're already in the emergency room."

Sade smiled at his dramatics. "Baz, first, this is a charming veterinary office, not the A&E, and second, she'll be fine. The vet said it's unlikely anything serious will happen."

He looked at her, still sad. "When people say things are fine, it usually means they're not fine," he replied.

Sade didn't have a response to that at first. After all, she knew it to be true. She took his hand and squeezed. "Listen, this time, I mean it," she said.

"If you say so," he muttered.

Low and behold, ten minutes later the vet delivered a very much alive and healthy Muffin back to a relieved-looking Baz, who genuinely seemed like he was going to cry.

He hugged Muffin close. "I'm sorry for nearly killing you, won't happen again, promise."

"You should probably get some actual guinea pig food for Muffin so she doesn't get hungry and go about eating things she shouldn't," the vet said.

Which Baz took to mean scouring the town center for pet accessories. It was clear to Sade, when Baz suggested placing Muffin in a Waitrose shopping bag instead of buying a cage, that she needed to step in.

After a few hours spent looking for items for Muffin to comfortably (and illegally) stay in Baz's dorm, the three of them were on the bus again.

Sade rested her head on the window, Baz seated next to her, his head on her shoulder and Muffin safely stowed away in the new portable cage Baz had bought.

An alert chimed on his phone and he sat up quickly, eyes scanning over the screen anxiously before disappointment settled on his face.

"Is everything okay?" Sade asked.

"Was just expecting a message from the guy looking into the source of the message about Aunt Julie, but instead all I got was an email alert from the Seacole house prefect telling me I got a package."

That was fast, she thought. They'd only spoken about hacking the school yesterday evening, and he already somehow had someone on the job.

"I didn't know that ancient devices could receive emails," she said with a smile, as he pocketed the Nokia.

He nudged her lightly, returning her smile. "You're laughing now, but when my once-tea-infused modern device returns, you'll see that it doesn't quite live up to Nokia's standard."

"If you say so," she replied.

It was raining heavily by the time they arrived back at school. It made her panic. Sade could feel that scraping of her brain, the beating of her heart. Rain sometimes reminded her of being submerged in water.

You're okay, the reassuring voice in her head whispered, causing her heart to slow, the tingling in her hands to fade, and the dread to be plucked away by the simple phrase.

As Sade draped her jacket over her head, Baz attempted to keep Muffin's cage dry, and together, they ran for shelter, eventually ending up in Baz's dorm, Seacole House.

The outside of Seacole was all moss-covered redbrick and Victorian roofs.

Inside, the red, earthy tones followed. There was a dark oak stairwell with exposed brick on the walls, dark wooden lockers, and a portrait of the house's own namesake, Mary Seacole.

The common room was filled with burgundy wallpaper and brown leather chairs with a brick fireplace in the corner.

It felt like the sort of room a serious person would reside in.

Unlike in Turing, where the common room was always populated with people, Seacole's was nearly empty.

"Welcome to Seacole House! Where no one likes to hang out because the other houses are apparently a lot more fun," Baz announced when they walked in.

Sade could see why. Despite its cozy yet serious vibe, it did feel really boring. There wasn't even a television. It was like the Seacole residents were being punished for something.

"Why were you sorted into Seacole House?" Sade asked. Baz was the opposite of bland.

He shrugged. "It's the house they put the people they don't know what to do with, I suppose. I'm not obsessed with sports like the Hawking and Jemison lot or academics like the Mendel and Curie bunch or art like Einstein and Franklin, and so Seacole it is."

That makes some sense, she thought. She sat on one of the leather couches, and Baz placed Muffin's cage beside her, shaking off the last droplets of rain.

"Gonna go and make us some tea; how d'you take yours?" he asked, pulling off his sweater now.

"No sugar, no milk," Sade said.

Baz looked horrified. "As black as your soul, I see," he said.

"Of course," Sade replied with a smile.

Baz shook his head and then disappeared into the little kitchen in the corner of the common room. As soon as he left, the clawing returned, and with it a terrible memory. *What really happened to Elizabeth* . . . the voice inside whispered.

So much and so little had changed in the six days that had passed.

Elizabeth was still missing and everything still felt kind of hopeless, especially now that the school was convinced that a ghost had Elizabeth in her care.

The venture into town had served as a nice diversion from her spiraling thoughts about yesterday's discovery, even though she'd felt the weirdness of being back in the town center so soon after the search party.

She tried to cast her mind back to the crowded chapel.

His warm brown skin, calming eyes, and smile gave no indication that he was a liar. *Just paying my respects*, he'd said so casually.

Was there a clue before? Something she had missed that indicated August was lying?

The best liars, Sade had found, were the ones who were also lying to themselves in some way. They'd lied so much to others, it was too easy to also eventually convince their own minds of the lie.

Baz stood in front of her with a small jug of milk nestled under his arm, two empty mugs, and a steaming pot of English tea gripped in his hand. "Earth to Sade?" How long had he been standing there for?

She blinked, Baz pulling her back into the room, and the first thought that came to mind slipped out from her lips.

"Elizabeth was dating August," she said.

Baz's eyebrows furrowed together. "What?"

"August Owens," Sade repeated.

His eyes went wide. "What makes you say that?"

She took out her phone and showed Baz the picture she had taken of the photograph that showed the two of them together.

Baz stared at the photo, his mouth slightly open. She could see him thinking. His brain whirring. Going over every single thing, every interaction, trying to piece it all together.

"Fuck," he said.

"What?" Sade asked, hoping he had remembered something that would make this all make sense.

"Tea burned me," he said, placing the items in his hands now on the coffee table one by one.

"Did Elizabeth ever mention August?" she asked.

Baz sat next to her, blank faced. "Sorry, this is a lot to process . . . I don't think so. I guess now and then she'd comment on how stupid his face looked, which come to think of it is what she says when she actually likes something . . . The signs were all there," Baz said, whispering the last part.

Sade knew he was still processing the possibility of his best friend secretly dating the school's golden boy, but she wondered if his mind had gone to the dark place hers had instantly gone to.

"Do you think . . . August has anything to do with her disappearance?" Sade asked.

Baz looked up at her. "I don't know," he said. "Seeing as I didn't even know that they hung out, maybe he did, maybe he didn't," Baz continued soberly. "I'd always heard through ANA whisper networks that August was with Mackenzie Peters—vice captain of the girls' swim team—up until recently. Elizabeth would have been in second year when this was taken; I can tell from the highlights in her hair. This might've been when she was still roomies with April. Maybe they were friendly and hung out then?"

Sade hadn't considered that thread. That they were just friends. Boys and girls could be just friends after all.

But that wasn't why she had immediately jumped to that assumption.

August's lies were why.

"At the vigil, I asked August if he knew Elizabeth and he said he didn't. He was clearly lying, which leads me to think that he knew her more than he wanted to let on. He's definitely hiding something."

"That does sound like he's hiding something," Baz said with a frown. "Maybe *he's* the email ghost."

Sade nodded. They had so little to go on, everything had to be considered.

"We'll find out soon enough. Hopefully I'll hear back from my source about the email soon. If not, we follow the August strand and see where that takes us," he said, his face a little flushed.

"How do you know that the hacker won't report you to Blackburn or Webber?"

"He promised he wouldn't tell anyone," Baz said simply, as though this person's word was somehow enough. She imagined that Baz was someone who probably saw pinkie promises as blood oaths too. "And even if he does, the worst that can happen is they suspend me. I don't care at this point; all I care about is finding Elizabeth. The email is how I do that. It's all I have right now."

Sade paused before speaking. "Actually, you also have Elizabeth's room." Her voice faltered. It wasn't her stuff to offer, or even go through. "I found the pictures there; maybe if you came over you could see anything that I or the police might've missed? Things she kept hidden—it could help with figuring out who else might know what happened to her."

Baz nodded. "That's a good idea," he said, a faraway look in his eyes as he stared off into the distance.

It felt like the common room kept shrinking in size as the weight of so many unknowns descended on them.

"Want some tea?" he asked, suddenly snapping out of it.

"Sure," she replied. She watched him pour the tea from the pot into a burgundy mug, before doing the same to an identical mug but adding milk and three sugar cubes to his. He handed her the dark brown liquid and picked up his own.

Silence returned as she watched him struggle to open a pack of biscuits.

"Are you okay?" she asked, not knowing what else to really say.

He shrugged. "I don't know. I just hate this school sometimes. If one of their elites went missing, there'd be helicopters searching for them day in and day out. They wouldn't just settle for an email. Headmaster Webber only cares about the issues that affect his pocket. Aka, our donors don't care and so neither do we. It's all so fucking predictable," he said as the packet finally burst open.

He shoved a jam-filled biscuit into his mouth and then held the packet out to her. "Want one?" he asked, mouth full of biscuit.

Sade reached in and took one. "Thanks."

A high-pitched squealing sounded from behind him.

"I think Muffin is hungry," Sade said.

"Think she'd like Jammie Dodgers?" he asked.

"Yes, but unless you want to take another trip down to the vet tomorrow, I'd suggest only feeding her guinea pig food."

"Good point," he said, brushing some crumbs off his jeans. He stood up, lifting the shopping bag they'd brought in from town.

"Just gonna get a bowl from the kitchen," he said before disappearing once again.

She looked at the photo of August and Elizabeth, her eyes focusing in on the details of it beyond their facial expressions and body language.

Like the tiles in the background. Why did they seem so familiar?

Baz returned with a plate filled with guinea pig food. He opened Muffin's cage and placed the plate in front of her. Muffin scrambled forward and started nibbling on bits of what looked like colorful cornflakes as Baz stroked her back.

"Sade," he said as they both watched the guinea pig eat.

"Yeah?" she replied.

"Do you think guinea pigs like tea?"

She hit him lightly with a cushion.

"Okay, okay, water it is."

"God, at this rate I feel like I'm Muffin's responsible parent," she said.

Baz laughed. "That's cool with me, I always wanted to be the fun parent instead of the grumpy one. I feel like maybe my pet-owning skills reflect my friendship skills too. I seem to be bad at both. Poisoned my guinea pig and lost my best friend, all in one week," he said with a sad smile, still stroking Muffin's back.

"That's not true," Sade said, feeling bad for indirectly calling him irresponsible.

He shook his head. "It might be true, who knows. Maybe I'm overreacting and the police are right. Maybe I never knew Elizabeth the way I thought I did. Maybe she's okay and sent that email herself and is with someone she trusts more than me. She always joked about dropping out, running away from this place . . . Maybe it wasn't a joke, maybe I just wasn't listening close enough," he said. The words had begun to come out hoarsely, sentences tangled as he spoke.

Sade didn't know what to say to that, or where it was all coming from, but at the same time she understood why he was saying it. It was guilt talking.

He felt responsible for Elizabeth, and every day that passed and she wasn't there, he blamed himself more for it.

"It's not your fau—" Sade started, but was interrupted by Baz.

"It's okay," he said with a sniff. "It is. She's like a sister to me. If something happened to her, it would be on me. Her mum told me to take care of her and I didn't." His face was wet now.

Sade felt the urge to reach out and wipe his tears away, stop him from falling into this pit of aimless self-blame. Muffin continued eating, unbothered by the sound of Baz's rambles or even the sight of his tears.

Pets were heartless sometimes.

"I'm so sorry, Baz," Sade said.

She didn't specify what for, but she was sorry that he felt this way and that the school didn't care.

"I'm sorry too," he said, his apology as vague as her own. But she was certain that he was apologizing to Elizabeth, and maybe even Elizabeth's mum—not her.

She was going to look for answers. The police and the school had given up, but she hadn't yet. And neither should he.

All of this was linked somehow. It had to be. She would simply find those connections, and everything would be fine. He would be fine.

"Can I give you a hug?" she asked him.

He looked up at her, eyes glassy and round. "I thought you don't like hugs," he said.

"I don't usually, not with strangers anyway," she said.

He nodded. "I'd like that."

So Sade shifted over and wrapped her arms around Baz, feeling his previously tensed muscles slowly relax.

"Thank you," he mumbled.

It reminded Sade of the times when she'd needed someone, and that person was always there to wrap their arms around her and tell her it was all okay. Until they weren't anywhere anymore, and she was left to deal with the world alone.

She knew how lethal loneliness could be.

And she didn't want Baz to feel that too.

15

MONDAY

ISCARIOT

THIS TIME LAST WEEK, SADE had been at her family's estate in London, nervously waiting for the driver to take her to her new life.

A life where she'd no longer be the black sheep of the family, or the pitiful orphan, spreading her bad luck to everyone. That wasn't her assuming things either; she'd heard these very sentiments at family gatherings. Her aunt Mariam used to spread rumors when she was younger of her being an evil spirit, born to bring misery to her family.

Despite her aunt's flair for the dramatic, Sade knew there was some truth to her words.

All the bad things that happened and continued to happen around her were clearly her doing. She was bad luck and she needed to leave to make things right.

She would start over at this new school.

She'd be no one's burden, no one's shame. She'd become a nothing. And in being nothing, she would be free somehow. Escape the past and the demons tethered to her shadow, tiptoeing behind her around her quiet, empty home.

You should never have come . . . The voice she'd grown accustomed to hissed bitterly.

There was no instruction manual for ridding yourself of your own self. She seemed to have simply brought the bad luck to Alfred Nobel Academy with her.

Now, a week since her departure from home, she was seated in her English class, wondering if this was all a mistake.

You should never have come. The hiss sounded like a constant alarm in her mind, going off at random and souring her thoughts with a simple sentence.

This feeling was further cemented by Mr. Michaelides dropping a sheet of paper on her desk with feedback from the presentation and her grade—a B minus.

Sade had never received a B minus in her entire life.

She felt the knife that was permanently jammed in her chest sink in some more and twist painfully, nudging now at her vitals.

"Hey, look! We got the same grade," Francis said with a wide grin. "I guess I'm clever after all."

How the hell did she get the same grade as *Francis*?

"We're going to spend the first ten minutes discussing the pages I asked you all to read over the weekend. Get into pairs quickly or I'll have to choose," Mr. Michaelides said.

The sound of chairs scraping against the floor sounded as people scrambled to grab their partners.

Francis dragged his chair in front of Sade's desk and sat down. "Hey, partner," he said.

Sade sighed, still glaring at the red mark on the sheet Mr. Michaelides had given her.

Once the shock had settled in a bit, she finally looked up at the freckled, punchable face of Francis. She hoped somehow that the universe would answer her prayers and not make her have to work with him again, but the universe was never all that receptive to her wishes.

Before she could offer him a reply, a dark cloud moved overhead, blocking the light above them both.

They looked up, eyes greeted by the looming presence of Persephone.

"I'm working with her," Persephone said, arms crossed.

Francis looked amused. "I called dibs."

"I don't care; leave now or face the consequences. Your choice."

Francis stayed still, like he was calling her bluff. But when she stepped forward, he shot up out of his seat and moved away. The smell of what Sade was almost certain was weed lingered.

How did the teachers not notice? Maybe being the headmaster's stepson meant no questions were asked when it came to these matters.

Persephone placed her bag on the floor, taking the seat across from Sade now. "Hey," she said.

Sade stared at her, heat itching at her neck and her heart quickening ever so slightly. It seemed that the universe was listening after all, or perhaps she was daydreaming. Which would make sense if it weren't for the fact that she rarely dreamed about something as pleasant as this.

Sade realized that she had just been staring at Persephone and hadn't yet responded to her greeting, so she quickly mumbled out a "hi."

Persephone's eyebrow quirked up in response and she stared back at Sade, then offered her a subtle smile.

With every interaction with Persephone, however small, Sade could feel the stakes of their silent game rising. Now, she could almost hear her thoughts.

Thinking about me?

To which Sade mentally responded.

Always.

"Did you do the reading?" Persephone asked, interrupting their nonverbal conversation.

Sade cleared her throat and nodded. "Y-yeah, I already read the book so I just skimmed through the first few chapters again last night."

"Same," Persephone said before taking out the text and flipping through the pages with her perfectly manicured fingers.

"What was that about, by the way?" Sade asked haltingly. "Asking Francis to leave."

Persephone tilted her head and gave Sade a peculiar look. "You looked like you needed saving," she said after a moment's pause. "And also, I like working with smart people. Makes life easier."

Sade tried not to look too surprised that Persephone thought she was smart. If only Persephone knew she got the same grade as Francis, maybe then she would have second-guessed coming over here and saving her.

"We should take notes on what we discuss in case Mr. M quizzes us. Do you have a spare pen?" Persephone asked, pulling Sade from her thoughts.

She nodded, reaching into her bag for her pencil case. Upon realizing that she hadn't packed it that morning, she gave Persephone the only pen she brought with her to class. Sade would have to use her blood as ink instead.

"Thank you," Persephone said as she took the pen, their fingers lightly brushing.

The rest of class went by in a mostly painless blur, as Mr. Michaelides lectured about themes, prose, and more homework.

Sade wondered what the purpose of so much extra work was anyway. When she was homeschooled, there was no need for home assignments for the obvious reason, but also because it seemed like a misuse of time.

The bell rang, cutting him off midsentence. It was rare that Mr. Michaelides was not still speaking when the bell rang. Sometimes it seemed that he didn't even hear it, too caught up in whatever he was saying. "I'll see you all tomorrow! Sade, can you stay behind please," he said, wrinkles gaining prominence as he smiled at her.

"Sure," she said before packing up her things and going over to his desk.

Part of her hoped he had gained access to the CCTV, then she could prove that someone *had* stolen something from her room, and then try to identify who had taken the box, and why. But that was unlikely; she'd only asked him two days ago, and Mr. Michaelides had no idea what the stakes were here.

"Just wanted to talk to you about your feedback. I hope you weren't too disheartened. I wish I could have given you a higher mark, but the assignment brief was to present to the class using visual aids, i.e., a presentation—which if you had done, I would have given you an A."

"Oh," Sade said, not expecting him to say that.

"I'm a harsh but fair grader, and I know you're very capable, so don't let a mistake like that rob you of a deserving grade next time, okay?" he said, placing his cold hand on top of hers.

She nodded, her eyes flickering down to his tanned fingers and the silver wedding band wrapped around his ring digit.

"Okay," she said.

"Wonderful," he replied, removing his hand now. "I'll see you tomorrow."

Sade's eyes lingered on where his hand had been, her stomach turning and the knife inside twisting some more, and then as his fingers crossed together, elbows on the table, her gaze shifted back to the silver of the wedding band.

After a moment, she looked up, bringing her attention back to his face. "See you tomorrow, Mr. Michaelides."

As she exited the classroom, still trying to shake away the strangeness she now felt, she was surprised to find Persephone there once again, standing by the row of dusky lockers.

"Hi," Sade said.

"I wanted to give you your pen back."

"Thanks."

"See you at lunch?" she said. Exactly as she had done on Friday.

Sade nodded.

THE SAME PATTERN FOLLOWED ON Tuesday.

Persephone stood by the lockers, taking a textbook out, greeting Sade without looking at her.

This time, their conversation lasted longer than a few seconds.

As Persephone riffled through her locker, they talked a bit more.

Sade made a comment about Francis, then apologized, not knowing whether Persephone actually disliked Francis.

To which Persephone laughed and said, "He's dating my best friend. Doesn't make him any less of a pothead or an asshole, so feel free to insult him all you like."

"Will do . . . ," Sade said awkwardly, and then followed up with: "Why'd you call him a pothead?"

Persephone shrugged. "Because he is one. Can't you smell it on him? Not sure why April likes to surround herself with people like that, but to each their own, I guess. Can't pick who your friends befriend."

This was surprising. She'd assumed that they were all friends. Juliette seemed to get along with the boys well enough.

"Is it the same with the others—April's brother, and the blond guy, I forget his name . . . ," she said, which was obviously a lie. *Jude Ripley.* How does anyone forget a name like that?

But they'd only had one conversation on Friday, so remembering his name, both the first and the last, felt too weird. Like she was indirectly confessing to something.

Persephone looked at her, unblinking, like she was trying to decipher the mess in Sade's mind, only giving up on it and turning away after a few moments. "They're all the same. August, Jude, Francis, the swim team boys. Addicted to chlorine, cocaine, and toxic displays of masculinity," she finished with a sarcastic lilt to her tone.

That explained Francis's bloodshot eyes and the constant tapping of his feet. Sade couldn't say she was all that surprised.

"Have they been dating long? April and Francis," Sade asked, still trying to figure out how on earth the pair worked. April seemed so much better than him. Smarter too.

Persephone went quiet and then finally answered with a brusque "No."

Her locker slammed loudly, and she turned to face Sade. As usual, curt: "See you at lunch?"

Letting Sade know that the conversation was finished for now.

WEDNESDAY WAS THE SAME. PERSEPHONE at her locker. A friendly conversation.

On their walk after class, Persephone asked Sade questions about herself. Like, what homeschool was like, how she was finding things at ANA, if it was true that there was a brand-new hot tub installed in Turing House.

Sade laughed at the last question, then asked, "How do you know I'm in Turing House? Are you stalking me?"

"Yes, I am actually," Persephone replied with a glint in her eye as they stopped in front of Chomsky block, where Sade's next class was.

When Sade's smile faltered, Persephone looked pleased.

Then she walked in front of her and whispered, "Your tie is black."

Sade's eyebrows furrowed. Why was she pointing out the color of her tie?

"What?" she asked, feeling warm at the proximity of Persephone's face to her own.

"That's how I know you're in Turing," she said, stepping back now. "I've got to head to class. I'll see you at lunch?"

Sade nodded slowly, feeling stupid for asking if she was stalking her. She glanced down at the purple and black of Persephone's tie, denoting that she was in Curie House.

Then Persephone gave her a final smile and walked away in the direction they had just come from.

Sade realized that Persephone had walked right past the block where her own lesson took place. It seemed the pair had a budding friendship or at the very least an acquaintanceship. However, after their friendly exchanges between classes, lunch would come around and things would get weird.

Like now.

Persephone barely acknowledged her or anyone else for that matter. Just sitting there silently reading a book, almost as if she was on a completely different planet from the rest of them.

Despite Baz's warning about the *Unholy Trinity*, as well as Persephone's random moments of coldness, she found herself warming to the group.

They made her feel included, even if their initial interest in her was because of Elizabeth.

On Monday, April, whom she found the hardest to impress, never knowing what the other girl was thinking with her unreadable expressions, had complimented her hair. She still wasn't sure it was a genuine compliment, seeing as it was approaching her sixth week with her braids in and there was only so much Blue Magic and hair gel could fix.

April barely seemed to offer compliments, though, so she took it as her being kind.

On Tuesday, April had invited her to Juliette's lacrosse match happening later that week. Sade had learned it was an intimate invite, only extended to her close friends—aka Persephone.

By Wednesday, Sade strangely felt like she belonged.

Her family was wrong. She wasn't misfortune personified. She was someone people seemed to want around, despite what her aunt Mariam said or the whispers inside that told her she shouldn't be here.

As she ate her pasta and listened to Juliette rant about a grade she received in French class, Sade could feel eyes on her.

This wasn't the first time.

She had caught Jude staring not-so-subtly at her on Tuesday too. She had pretended not to notice his glances, but today she chose differently, turning to stare back at him too. She saw the light shade of pink that crept up his neck, followed by the movement of his eyebrows as he nodded at her. Then he suddenly got up, breaking eye contact with her and taking his clear water bottle with him, most likely to fill up. Her gaze followed him to the fountain in the corner of the hall.

A distant buzzing noise sounded, making the table vibrate.

"Is that lover boy again, Jules?" April said as Juliette picked up her vibrating phone and laughed.

"Wouldn't you like to know?" she replied, turning her phone over now.

April looked at Sade's confused face. "Juliette has a secret boyfriend. From what she lets us know, other than being tall, dark, and handsome, he's also a freshman at a university in Canada."

Sade tried not to look too taken aback. She wasn't sure if she was more surprised by the secret boyfriend or the university in Canada part. "How did you meet?" she asked.

"Summer camp," Juliette replied without hesitation. It felt as though she had rehearsed the answer before.

"In England?" Sade asked.

"Yes."

"Didn't know we had many summer camps in this country," Sade replied.

Juliette paused, narrowing her eyes a little, then smiled. "Yes, it was at Shakespeare camp. I was failing English, so my parents made me go. I was meant to go next summer too but I'm going back to Sri Lanka to visit my grandparents for a few weeks, so I guess Shakespeare can wait."

Sade nodded, considering her words. She found that over-explanations were often a sign of someone trying to compensate for the truth. After a moment's silence, she finally spoke again. "Is long distance hard? With you and your boyfriend?"

Juliette shrugged. "Not really, feels like he's always here."

Sade noticed something flicker behind April's otherwise unreadable eyes, before they returned to their usual cold brown hue.

"Speaking of boyfriends always being there for you, I'm going to kill mine when I find him. Can you believe he disappeared on me again? Something about his pointless lunchtime swim practice," April said.

"It's not pointless, April—practice is how we win nationals," Jude said as he returned with a now full bottle of water.

April gave Jude one of those looks that could definitely kill, but he seemed unfazed as he took a swig of his bottle. "I'm pretty sure Tweedledum is off swimming too, which speaking of . . . As captain, why aren't *you* with the rest of the chlorine addicts?" she asked with a raised eyebrow. The mention of August reminded Sade of the photos and his lie.

Juliette laughed. "Isn't it obvious?" Her eyes panned over to Sade and then back to Jude.

Jude's face turned a deeper shade of crimson but his confident smile didn't falter. "I have no idea what you're talking about, Jules."

"Sure," she replied. "Anyway, I need to get going, have to get some things from my locker before the warning bell," Juliette said, standing. "April, Sephy—you coming?"

April picked up her pink Telfar bag and grabbed her phone from the table. "I have some time to kill."

Persephone looked up for the first time since lunch began. "Yeah, sure," she replied, sounding very unlike herself. Not that Sade really knew Persephone all that well anyway, but she was definitely unlike the version of her that she had recently become acquainted with.

Sade felt the elephant in the room breathing down her neck—the awkwardness of not being invited. She wondered if she had done something wrong, said something wrong, or maybe they no longer had use for her. It was probably her questioning Juliette on her boyfriend. She could tell she had touched a nerve. Why hadn't she stopped talking?

"Sade?" April said, giving her a peculiar look.

"Sorry—did you say something?" she asked.

If April was annoyed at having to repeat herself, it didn't show. Her expression was still this impossible cipher. "Did you want to tag along?" she asked.

Sade looked over at Persephone, who had her arms crossed and was staring her down, also unreadable.

"Sure," she finally replied, grabbing her bag too.

"Let's head off, then, lunch is almost over," April said, already turning to leave before Sade could stand.

She got up quickly but was stopped by a strong grip on her sleeve.

"Wait—" a deep voice came from behind her. She turned and found herself face-to-face with Jude Ripley. "Hey," he said.

"Hi," she replied, watching April, Persephone, and Juliette disappear through the crowd, before turning her focus back to him.

"I, uh—this is going to sound weird," he started. Everything about his face was exaggerated. From his strong jaw to the near-white of his hair to his eyes. He looked like a doll, something she could so easily break. "But I was wondering if I know you from somewhere?" he finished.

Sade's eyebrows rose. "Where would you know me from?" she asked, her heart beginning to thrum incessantly in her chest.

"I don't know . . . maybe my dreams?"

Sade blinked at him. "Does that usually work?"

"Does what usually work?"

"That pickup line—do people usually like that?"

He laughed. "Honestly? No. But I hoped you would. A guy can dream, right?"

"Apparently, you dream a lot," she said.

"It keeps the imagination alive," he replied.

"I bet it does," she said.

"I was serious though. I feel like I've met you before . . ." He paused, eyes narrowing.

Her expression glitched, smile faltering as she watched him carefully. Waiting for him to finish his sentence.

"Although," he continued. "I don't think I'd forget your face if I had . . . so maybe I haven't," he said.

She relaxed her shoulders and shrugged in a nonchalant manner, as though she couldn't feel her heartbeat in her throat.

"Maybe," Sade said, glancing at the exit, where she could no longer see the girls, her nails involuntarily digging into her palms.

"I can walk you? I know where they went," Jude said, probably noticing the direction of her gaze.

She paused, taking Jude Ripley in, in all his charm offensive–glory, before speaking. "Thank you," she said, to which he smiled wider, like he had won something in this exchange.

As they walked out of the lunchroom together and down the halls, Sade could feel eyes on her. Students taking her in with shocked expressions. Envy, anger, and curiosity melding together and flowing from person to person.

"You were homeschooled, right?" he asked suddenly, after a few moments of quiet as they walked.

"I was," she said.

"What changed your mind?"

It was a question packed with a lot of assumptions about her homelife and circumstances. What made him think it was ever her choice?

But she couldn't blame him. All she had known of boarding school was from

133

the depictions seen in movies and shows, and despite some things being true, most were not.

"My father died, and I was the only one left in the house. It was either go and live with family in America or come here. I chose the latter."

"Oh . . . I'm sorry to hear about that, your dad, I mean," he said.

Sade looked at him, searching for signs of who Jude was, for signs of pity or regret. Neither were there.

"It's okay," she said.

"I lost my dad too, a few years ago—it helps knowing he's watching over me, and I'm sure your dad is proud wherever he's watching you from," Jude said.

Sade almost laughed. If anything, *she* was watching her father, every time she so much as glanced down at her shoes.

"I'm sorry to hear about your dad," she replied, instead of saying what she really felt. That her dad would be anything but proud.

He never wanted her to go to school, kept his tight grip on her for her entire life until his paranoia gave him a heart attack and sent him to death's door prematurely.

"Don't apologize, it was years ago," Jude said, coming to a stop now. "Just wanted you to know that you aren't alone in that. Not many people get it. How losing someone changes you."

It felt misplaced, but Sade tried to stop herself from smiling. The knife in her chest twisting painfully did the trick, instead making her eyes glaze over and her bones ache. She knew grief too well for someone of her age. Death was at first an unwelcome guest and slowly transformed into a bitter companion.

"Anyway, the girls are over there," he said, gesturing to the locker where the three stood talking. April was twirling her hair, Juliette riffling through her locker, and Persephone laughing at something one of them just said.

"Thanks for walking me," Sade said, unfurling her hands and feeling the sting from the marks her nails had left.

"Anytime," he said.

She turned to leave but he stopped her once again.

"Are you free on Friday after school? I have the regional swim competition and I get post-match jitters and always feel better when I grab coffee afterward," he said.

She looked at him for a few moments. "Are you asking me out for coffee?"

He shrugged. "You tell me."

"I'm not really interested in dating anyone right now," she said.

Something in his expression dampened, like that was not the answer he expected nor the answer he was used to.

"Who said anything about dating? I just wanted to grab coffee. I can even invite August to prove how much of a date it is not," he said.

Sade raised an eyebrow. "I thought we weren't allowed off campus during the week. Where will we have coffee?"

"There's a café on campus, only open for fourth years, but I'm friendly with the owner, so she'll let you in," he said with a shrug.

Sade regarded him closely, silently debating about it in her mind before nodding. "Okay," she said.

"Okay," he replied with a smile.

The warning bell would be ringing any moment now.

"I'm going to go," she said.

He nodded.

"See you on Friday?" he asked as he stepped back.

"Yes, see you *and* August on Friday!" she replied, pleased to see his face drop again at the mention of August. Then she turned toward the lockers where the unholy trio still stood, now staring at her.

Juliette wore a smile, Persephone looked displeased, and April, the usual undecipherable expression.

The warning bell finally rang, but before Sade could go up to the three girls, they were already walking away from her.

Students started to crowd the halls, hurriedly rushing to post-lunch registration, leaving her both surrounded and alone.

She felt the buzz of her phone in her pocket and took it out.

B: Is it true???

S: Is what true?

B: You and Judas

Sade sighed. Apparently, there were eyes in the walls.

S: What is it with the biblical names, first the Unholy Trinity and now Judas?

B: You're avoiding . . . It is true isn't it!

S: No.

B: The hallways never lie

S: We're just getting coffee

B: AHA!

S: Since when was getting coffee a crime?

B: Because getting coffee *is* a crime when it concerns Jude Ripley. It always begins like this. Judas sees a girl he likes, asks her out for a friendly coffee, and next thing you know, Paris.

S: Is Paris meant to be code for hooking up?

B: Yes.

S: Don't worry, I won't be going to Paris with Jude. Will be staying firmly put in England.

B: I'm sure the others said the same thing. But he always uses the same move, coffee, dinner dates, and then Paris. Always the same. And my friend, you fell for it.

THURSDAY
BAD OMENS

IT SHOULD HAVE BEEN CLEAR to Sade the moment the magpie had excreted all over her school sweater that morning that the rest of the day would be filled with more misfortune.

After all, the unfortunate sweater incident was what lead to having to change into her spare uniform, which she had actually not been given yet and had to request directly from Miss Blackburn herself, who she was almost certain purposely took her time in getting to Sade, which then resulted in her very first late detention ever.

It was almost past the two-week mark since Sade joined the boarding school, and it seemed that teachers were finally growing tired of her inability to learn all the school's rules and traditions in the ten days since she arrived.

Her bad fortune did not end there. During her Mandarin lesson, she had forgotten all the words and sentences she had so effortlessly been able to recite the week prior.

In her history class, she had somehow forgotten about the pop quiz that the teacher was so adamant on giving every Thursday, barely scraping a pass. Then, as if it couldn't get any worse, in English, her ink pen exploded and managed to ruin not only her pencil case but also drenched Persephone's notebook in the sticky blue tar-like substance.

At this point, Sade was close to pulling a Francis and walking out of the classroom without further explanation so her classmates—especially Persephone, who was looking at her now with a look of concern and pity—didn't have to see her completely break down over spilled ink.

It was as though she had walked under an invisible ladder and stroked a black cat all while whispering the number thirteen under her breath in her sleep, triggering this onslaught of never-ending bad luck.

As she attempted to wash the ink off her hands, she thought about how her luck had always been a fraught thing, and unless she somehow triggered these bad omens each night, it was not the magpie that morning or any other English superstition.

She was the bad omen.

When she got back to class after cleaning what she could of the ink from her palms, her classmates had already been dismissed and were packing up their things as the bell rang sharply from the speaker.

"Sade," she heard Mr. Michaelides call and she figured it was another detention, this time for her incompetence when it came to handling school supplies that even four-year-olds were able to handle without much hassle. Or some other thing that would further prove to her how crappy the day truly was.

She turned to him, preparing herself mentally for more humiliation.

"Sorry for the delay on the CCTV situation. I have been so busy with preparing mock exams, it completely slipped my mind. But I have access to the CCTV room at the reception and can take you there now if you haven't got another class?"

Oh.

She'd nearly forgotten the CCTV footage, then felt bad for being so preoccupied by trivial things that in the big picture didn't matter as much as Elizabeth.

"I have a free period," she said hurriedly as she gathered her things.

"Okay, good. Let's head off, then, see if we can catch the culprit," he replied with a smile. "You can wait for me outside; I just need to send a quick email before we go."

When Sade walked out of the classroom, she was both surprised and unsurprised to see Persephone there.

Unsurprised because, after all, Persephone's locker was outside this classroom, but surprised too because Sade had assumed that Persephone would be gone by now.

But there she was, by her locker, pushing her stuff inside.

Sade wondered if she should say something or just pretend that she somehow didn't see her. After yesterday, when the girls had seemed to leave her behind, she wasn't sure if she had been officially disinvited from their daily lunch gatherings or no longer interesting enough to wait around for. One minute it seemed they were all happy to have her there. Then the next it was like she was missing something and the joke was all on her.

But then again, this could also be her anxiety talking.

"A picture would last longer, you know?" Persephone said as she closed the locker and turned to Sade with a raised eyebrow and that not-smile smile she gave sometimes.

"What?" Sade asked, feeling embarrassed for being caught staring—which she definitely wasn't doing. She was merely noticing. Noticing the fact that Persephone was still there, in the usual spot she always was after class, where they'd strike up a friendly conversation. Always seeming to be waiting for someone.

Noticing was different from staring.

Persephone shook her head, her smile crooked as amusement danced on her lips. "Just pulling your leg," she said.

"Do you often pull people's leg?" Sade asked.

Persephone shrugged. "Only the people I like, I guess."

"So you like me?" she asked playfully.

It was so hard to tell with Persephone, and besides, it wasn't like they'd known each other long.

But she guessed she liked Persephone too.

"We eat lunch together every day, and I try to refrain from eating lunch with people I dislike . . . though, unfortunately, due to the company some of my friends keep, that isn't always possible," Persephone said, a note of disgust in her tone.

She wondered if this was how friends were made in boarding school. After all, it seemed that after eating lunch with Elizabeth and Baz once, they were happy to invite her into their circle. Maybe lunch was a ritual with more importance than she had previously thought. This they didn't teach in movies and books.

"I see," Sade responded.

Persephone stared at her silently, as she often did, in the way she did when she was considering something. Then her mouth opened to speak but instead of the smooth, steady gentleness of her voice, Sade instead heard something deeper and not as pleasant.

"Ready to go, Sade?" the voice said.

Sade turned to Mr. Michaelides, who was standing behind her now with his usual friendly smile.

Sade nodded.

"I need to hand in my comp sci coding homework now but I'll see you at lunch?" Persephone asked, barely acknowledging Mr. Michaelides's presence. Apparently, Sade hadn't lost the favor of the unholy girls yet.

"Yes, I'll see you," she replied.

And then, without another word or glance their way, Persephone turned and walked down the hallway, disappearing through the double doors.

WHEN THEY GOT INTO THE CCTV room, the security guard loaded up the footage from Friday and began rewinding the Turing entrance footage slowly. Mr. Michaelides squinted while Sade hovered beside him, her heart in her throat.

This was it.

The footage approached the time Sade had last seen the hooded figure on the screen, and she waited with bated breath.

But as the video wound backward and the shadows on the stone floor of the building morphed into different shapes with the passing of time, the video remained void of any human activity.

As the time came, and went, the video remained the same. Empty. No hooded figure holding Elizabeth's music box.

Nothing.

"The footage is clear," the security guard said.

Sade's heart stopped.

This can't be, she thought. *Something must be wrong.* The wrong date. The wrong time. Somehow the *wrong* footage.

But as she scanned the details on the screen, everything from the time stamp to the date were as they should be.

What was going on?

This was starting to freak her out more than it had before. Either whoever took the box knew she was looking for them and were now covering their tracks, or . . . she imagined it all.

But that wasn't possible. It happened. She was here and she saw the person in the black hood exit Turing House. She saw them—

"Sade?" Mr. Michaelides said, pulling her out of her sea of conspiracies.

"Hmm?" she said.

"It's good news. There's no sign of a thief leaving Turing House, and I can't imagine someone in your own house would take something of yours—they're your friends, surely. I'd suggest checking your room again for that box," he said.

Sade blinked at the paused screen. The invisible black cat perched on her shoulder, purring as more bad omens spilled and polluted her day.

"I guess so," she said. "Thanks for checking."

"No problem," Mr. Michaelides said.

Did she imagine it all?

Were the tricks her brain liked to play bleeding into other areas of her life, muddying reality to the point where the truth and the lie were no longer discernible?

You should never have come. The hiss in her brain persisted, right on cue. Always there to remind her that she would never escape herself.

She numbly exited the security office, thoughts all over the place, as Mr. Michaelides continued speaking. He might've asked her a question, might've even said goodbye but got no response.

Something was very wrong here.

She thought about everything that had occurred in the past ten days. The stolen music box, the doctored footage, the email from Elizabeth's dead great-aunt.

Someone was watching.

Someone had to know Sade and Baz weren't giving up on Elizabeth.

Her phone buzzed with a message, startling her.

It was just Baz.

B: Kwame—my source from rowing practice—finally got the ghost email, I'll show it to you after school

There was at least some good news.

S: Should I meet you at Seacole? she texted back.

B: Yes, I'll bring the biscuits

THE REST OF THE DAY went by in a blur.

Sade's mind was stuck in the security room, on the CCTV screen, rewinding and rewinding it. Her brain was feeding from the sea of conspiracies she had created.

She wasn't sure how long it took her to get to Seacole. She didn't even realize she had been walking until she was in front of the building.

Unlike on Sunday, she could see some students filtering into the building, but much like Sunday, when she entered the common room, it was still a lot quieter than Turing's was at this time.

There was a student seated on an armchair in the corner reading a book and two others doing some kind of puzzle.

Baz was in Seacole's mascot room, just off the common room—home to Seacole's mascot, a lizard called Aristotle. He'd texted her his location, and at first she'd questioned his choice in meeting place but upon seeing him seated in front of an old-looking computer next to the mascot's cage understood his choice in coming here.

"Hi," Sade said as she closed the door behind her, taking in the old-looking computer Baz was sitting at—the absence of a guinea pig in his hands or lap. "Where's Muffin?"

"Sleeping in, she was up all night—pretty sure my roommate, Spencer, either knows about her existence now or suspects we have some kind of infestation," he said, wiggling the computer's mouse.

"Hopefully, the latter," she replied, settling in next to him.

He squinted at the screen before turning it toward her. "Here's the email that was sent to the school."

Sade moved in closer, scanning the words on the screen.

FROM: Julie.Wang@bmail.com
TO: G.Webber@ANA.org.uk
SUBJECT: RE: Elizabeth Wang—Leave of Absence

Greetings, I hope this email finds you well.

This is Julie Wang, Elizabeth Wang's great-aunt. My apologies for not getting in touch sooner. I'm afraid I do not have consistent access to my phone or emails at the moment.

I am emailing to let you know that we would like to withdraw Elizabeth from school for the rest of the term. She came to me early on Tuesday morning, however due to the sensitive nature of Elizabeth's well-being, we weren't able to make her mother aware until yesterday. As you can imagine, it is a difficult matter to discuss. I have now had a discussion with her mother, and we have decided that due to Elizabeth's health, she is not able to attend school for the foreseeable future. I am sorry for any inconvenience caused in Elizabeth's absence.

Yours sincerely,
Julie

She kept going over that.

I have now had a discussion with her mother . . .

How did the email ghost know that Elizabeth's mum could be confused or unreliable if telephoned by the school about Julie?

"Kwame was able to source the IP address, and the email came from nearby—not Birmingham, where Aunt Julie lived and Elizabeth is supposed to be. He couldn't get me an exact location; he explained that IP only traces geolocations, but I think this still tells us a lot. That the email probably came from inside the school—"

"Which means that whoever sent it goes here," Sade finished.

"Exactly," Baz said.

Sade blinked at the screen. Dread pricked across her arms and legs as though her whole body had been asleep, and the blood flow was only just starting again.

"What a truly shitty day this has been. Only good thing has been that I got my phone back. They managed to repair it," he said, gesturing to the phone, which was plugged into the wall. It seemed to be steadily rebooting itself, now at 30 percent. The

142

phone oddly looked how she expected Baz's phone to look. The screen was cracked all over and he had a froggy phone case.

"Try not to drop it in tea again," Sade said.

"I'll try, but no promises," he replied. "At least I'll be able to see my old messages with Elizabeth. I haven't gone this long without speaking to her. It's weird."

"I can imagine," Sade said, though there was no need for imagination; she knew the feeling well.

WHEN SADE GOT BACK TO Turing, dinner had already come and gone—not that she was all that hungry with the day she'd had. She'd spent the last few hours in the room with Baz poking holes in the email and trying to think of a plan C. But it felt like they were stuck in quicksand: The more they tried to make a connection, the faster the ground swallowed them up.

The dread she'd been feeling the entire day followed her all the way to the dormitory. Up the French lift, and dragging behind her as she approached her room.

It was hard to believe that someone had been here, taken the music box, and erased the footage she'd seen on the CCTV. She just couldn't work out why.

The sense of unease crept around her as she got out her key and unlocked the door. She turned the light switch on and took in the room, her eyes trained on Elizabeth's side.

The state of the room matched the state of this whole situation.

And like the room, it felt like this mess was Sade's fault.

Her eyes moved over to her own corner of the room. She could feel the tug of the universe's puppet strings.

So much that she didn't even flinch when she saw the music box again.

Lying on her bed, as it had been the week prior, waiting for her once again.

She shrugged off her bag and numbly walked over to her bed. She reached forward, taking the box she'd been so certain was stolen into her hands and opening it.

The small Elizabeth figurine twirled and the music played, and she lifted the next compartment and the small figurine folded in on itself.

This time, though, the box was filled with nothing but jewelry. Expensive earrings, gold necklaces, a Rolex.

Instead, the box had become a treasure chest buried and waiting under its mark.

Sade couldn't help but laugh.

Who'd steal a box filled with seemingly worthless things and replace the same box with expensive jewelry?

Someone who clearly felt the notes Elizabeth had left were priceless in comparison.

Sade felt her heart scramble in her chest.

This time around, she didn't waste any time. She got her phone out and took pictures of the box, closing it and opening it, hearing the torturous sound of the nursery rhyme stopping and starting again. She sent all the photos to Baz before the box decided to scurry off again.

This time she had proof of its existence.

She closed the first lid and the twirling figurine appeared once again, Sade squinting now as the figure twirled and twirled.

The girl was different. She had blonde hair, not Elizabeth's dark brown.

But that wasn't the only difference.

The engraving behind, the one that had read, *For my dear Elizabeth—TG* . . .

It was gone.

Her phone buzzed with a message from Baz.

Sade watched the box as the blonde girl twirled around.

B: Is that the music box you were talking about?

She didn't have to look any closer.

It wasn't.

The boxes had been switched.

S: No, it seems to be fake. The original box had notes in it. This one has jewelry.

She hesitated before sending the next message.

S: I'm not sure why, but I think someone is planting things.

And if someone was planting things, pulling strings, sending emails from *inside* the school, Sade felt a gut-wrench that whatever had happened to Elizabeth was bad.

Sade thought back to the CCTV room. The doctored footage. Who had she told about the music box other than Mr. Michaelides?

The answer clicked in her mind suddenly, and she tossed her phone onto the bed, going over to her wardrobe now.

It was time she finally paid August a visit.

17

THURSDAY
THE SMOKING GUN

"BACK SO SOON, NEW GIRL?" August's voice echoed in the large pool room.

He was in Speedos, as he had been the first time she met him. The same smug expression was on his face as he stared her down, though this time she was wearing proper swim attire—her one-piece swimsuit, swim shorts, goggles, and swim cap.

"Yup," she said as she walked toward the steps nearest to August, sitting.

She watched him float, moving gently from side to side.

Drifting with the same ease with which he lied.

"Thought you didn't swim anymore?" he asked.

She had said that, and it had been a lie. A lie she believed at the time but a lie nonetheless.

Swimming was an addiction they didn't make patches for. It was something she needed to do to feel whole.

She tried denying it, but she'd felt off lately and maybe this was part of why. She needed the water as much as she needed oxygen.

"Well, now I do," she replied tightly, forcing a smile to make herself appear less agitated than she was. She would need to play along with his game, just for a few minutes, to get him comfortable before she cornered him. That was her plan.

August smiled at her. "Well, I'm glad. I always wanted a late-night swimming buddy," he said.

"Why's that?" she asked.

He splashed her, spraying water all over her torso and shocking her system. "I get to do that," he said as he swam away.

She feigned anger as she climbed down the steps of the pool, jumping in and swimming quickly toward him, splashing him back.

He looked shocked for a moment and then he placed his hands on her shoulders and pulled her underwater, getting her whole head and face wet now.

Once she surfaced, she could hear his laughter loudly as it bounced off the tiled walls.

"You're an asshole, Augustus," she said as she wiped her face.

"And you're way too slow, new girl," he said.

"No, I'm not—" she started, but he had already splashed her again.

"You're dead," she said matter-of-factly after a moment's silence. August smirked, racing toward the deep end.

It was weird how much water changed her mood, without her wanting it to. It was like a pool full of serotonin, flooding into her and making her anxieties about the world disappear for a few moments at a time.

It had been such a long time since she'd been able to swim like this, without such an unbearable guilty weight on her back. Even last time she was here, in Newton, the weight had been there. But now, she felt light somehow.

As light as a drowning corpse.

As she swam, and dived under the gentle blanket of chlorine, the blood and the lifeless body she saw floating barely fazed her. Unlike last week, when it had triggered her anxiety, this time, it was yet another companion in the water alongside August.

That was the magic of being submerged.

"Want to play another game, new girl?" August's voice sang out in a sultry whisper.

Sade stopped floating, the magic dissipating.

"What kind of game?" she replied.

"Lengths again?" he suggested.

She moved her arms anticlockwise in a semicircle, allowing herself to float back.

"How about we play a game of truth instead," she said, her voice bouncing off the walls and rippling along the surface of the pool.

He raised an eyebrow, looking intrigued, as he moved toward her.

"How does one play *truth*?" he asked with a sly smile.

"Well, I ask you a question like: Why did you lie about knowing Elizabeth Wang? And you, hopefully, reply with the truth." This wiped the smile from August's face in an instant.

"What?" he asked.

"I found some pictures of you guys in our room on the day of the vigil. Pictures of the two of you together."

August nodded slowly, breaking eye contact. "Why are you only mentioning this now?"

"I found the pictures after the vigil had ended and I didn't want you to think I was accusing you of something . . . but I guess there's no good way of saying, 'Hey, did you actually know my missing roommate even though you told me you didn't?' Without it sounding like an accusation."

"There isn't," August agreed.

Sade stared him dead in the eyes, trying to read him. "Well, did you?"

"Did I what?" August asked. He knew what she meant. He was avoiding answering her.

"Did you know Elizabeth?" she repeated. What she really wanted to ask, though, was, "What really happened to her?" and "Is she okay?" and all the questions that came behind that: "Were you guys dating?" and "Did you send that email?" and "Did you break into my room and steal that box?" and "Why? Why any of this?"

But she figured that these all did, in fact, sound like actual accusations, and making him think she suspected him of anything would only make him close up and lie again.

"I guess so," he said.

"You guess so?" she prodded.

"I guess I did know Elizabeth. But I also didn't. Not really."

The wind seemed to knock out of Sade when he said that. *Why would he lie if he wasn't guilty of something?*

"I know what it looks like . . . that I lied, but I promise I didn't know her. We used to hook up now and then, but who doesn't at ANA? Everyone's hooking up with someone. And it happened so long ago, more than a year ago. I haven't spoken to her since the last time," August said, looking and sounding embarrassed. "We weren't *together* or anything, it was casual. I'm pretty sure I wasn't the only guy either . . . so unless hooking up a few times suddenly makes me an Elizabeth Wang expert, I didn't know her."

The implication hung over them.

There were other guys.

TG?

The memory of the photos she'd found flashed behind her eyes. Elizabeth didn't seem to keep photos of these other guys she apparently hooked up with, so why August?

"Why would she keep photos of you guys?"

August shrugged. "I don't know. Maybe she had a crush on me or something. As I said, I'm not an expert."

She thought about the photo of the two of them huddled close, how intimate it had seemed.

Or maybe she had mistaken it for intimacy.

Who was she to know for sure anyway? Intimacy wasn't something she was exactly an expert in.

"How did you guys meet?" she questioned, feeling her theory crumble beneath her.

If August truly didn't lie, then who else could have known about the box? Or could have taken it for that matter?

"She was April's roommate in first and some of second year. We'd sometimes exchange a few words here and there when April wasn't around—it was mostly awkward, at first anyway. And then one day, we just stopped talking—"

"I think I get the gist," Sade said, not wanting that visual.

August cracked an earnest smile. "You're the one who asked for details."

"I guess that one's on me. I will never ask you anything again," she replied.

August laughed.

Sade still felt on edge as she watched him, not knowing whether to believe his words or not.

"Why are you asking anyway? Didn't her mum or something say she went back home?"

Sade nodded. "Yeah . . . I guess I was just curious, that's all." The box, the hooded figure, Elizabeth swam through her mind.

"Well, you know what they say about curiosity, new girl."

It killed the cat, she thought.

Sade furrowed her eyebrows at him. "Are you wishing me dead?"

He laughed again. "No," he said, swimming closer. Sade's heart pulsed in her chest as he moved quickly toward her like a shark ready to attack.

Blood encircling them both. "Curiosity makes your head too big and your head's already massive," he finished with a grin.

Sade splashed him in the face as payback for the insult.

"If my head is big, it just means I'm very smart."

"Whatever you need to tell yourself to help you sleep at night," he replied.

FRIDAY

AFTER SCHOOL ON FRIDAY, SADE found Persephone waiting for her by the reception area like she'd said she'd be, ready to walk with her to Juliette's lacrosse game.

Sade had only realized at lunch, when Juliette mentioned the game again, that it was at the same time as Jude's swim meet, and she had still not worked out how she would excuse herself from the group and rush off to meet him and August. But she had decided that would be future Sade's problem to figure out.

"Is Mars nice this time of year?" Persephone asked.

Sade hadn't realized Persephone had been standing in front of her. "What?" Sade asked.

"You didn't seem to be on Earth when I called you, which I've noticed is a common thing with you, always off someplace else . . . so I figured it was Mars," Persephone said.

"Sorry, I didn't notice . . . ," Sade began.

"I'm joking," Persephone said with a raised eyebrow and her signature almost-smile. "Come on, let's head off. Jules will kill us if we're late."

"Where's April?" she asked.

Persephone shrugged. "She said she'd meet us there, had to take care of something."

Sade nodded, and they started making their way to the big field where lacrosse games were apparently held when the weather was good. Despite the deep October chill in the air, this was, indeed, considered good weather for England in autumn, so outside it was.

When they arrived, people were already gathered in clusters on the seats, waiting for the game to start. The girls from ANA's lacrosse team were dressed in black sports skirts and black jerseys with their positions and numbers in bold white text.

The rival team was dressed in almost identical skirts and jerseys, although theirs were maroon, and they had their school crest etched onto the fronts of the jerseys.

Sade squinted at the crest, taking in the details. An all-too-familiar black bird was in the center of it. A wave of déjà vu knocked into her, making her feel unsettled.

"What school is that?" she asked Persephone.

"Uh, Nightingale Academy, I believe; they're from London—I've heard they're not that great, so, hopefully, we have a shot—" she started, cut off by April breathlessly saying, "I'm here, I'm here." She was panting a little, like she had run from wherever it was she had been.

"Took you long enough. Were you giving birth?"

April rolled her eyes. "Obviously not, just had to do something first," she said, finally catching her breath.

Her usually flawless hair was the messiest Sade had seen it, strands sticking out in different directions. Her makeup wasn't perfect either. It seemed that the sweat from running had melted it off slightly.

Persephone made a disgusted face. "Was that something you were doing with Francis?" she asked.

"A lady never tells," April said, waving her off. Sade noticed that April's habitually manicured hands were partially stained black with what seemed to be pen ink or paint.

Persephone's expression got significantly more repulsed.

The referee's whistle sounded loudly, followed by the deep yell of the coach on the field. "Game's about to begin, quiet down!"

"Let's go find some seats," April said.

The three found space in the middle row, not too close or too far from the action.

April put a giant pair of sunglasses on and crossed her legs, watching intently with Persephone as if this were a fashion show and April were Anna Wintour.

Juliette flew across the field, her lacrosse stick gripped in her hand and her eyes on the ball, ready to play.

April leaned in toward Persephone and whispered, "She's got this," to which Persephone nodded in return, nervously chewing her lip.

A small smile appeared on April's face, and it seemed like her guard was slowly lowering. Sade had never seen April look so pleasant.

It was nice how supportive they were.

Juliette seemed nervous on the field as she got into position opposite a student from the rival team.

It reminded Sade of how she always felt before one of her swim meets. This fear would fill her that losing would be the end of the world and that she'd let her family and her coach down. Winning felt like it was all that mattered some days. But as she often reminded herself, swimming wasn't all there was to life. At times, when swimming was hard, floating was good enough.

The game began and Sade watched as the girls charged toward one another, the ball passed along from stick to stick. It was so small it was hard sometimes for her to see who exactly had it.

In the end the match came to a draw, which led to a sudden-death overtime, meaning the first team to score a goal would be declared the winner.

She held her breath as the ball zigzagged across the field and came close to the goal so many times. Then at the last minute, a girl from team ANA retrieved the ball and hit it so fast the goalie didn't have time to process until the ball was already punching the net.

"Winning team, Alfred Nobel Academy!"

Cheers sounded around the field as the ANA girls huddled close, jumping and screaming. Persephone leaped up and cheered, and Sade realized then that they had been holding hands. Her hand must have accidentally found its way over to Persephone's in the tension of the match.

Sade let go, her palms embarrassingly clammy from the anxiety the anticipation had brought. She watched the girls from the other team, disappointment on their faces.

She knew the feeling well.

After all, Hussein girls were winners. Anything but a gold trophy was seen as blasphemy in their household.

Sade locked eyes with one of the girls on the field, who seemed to have been watching her for a little while.

Sade smiled cautiously, then looked away, shrugging off the weird feeling the staring gave her.

"You were amazing out there!" she heard Persephone shout as Juliette ran and hugged her.

"I thought you guys were about to lose for a moment there, that would have been unfortunate—I'm wearing my lucky boots, and it would mean I got my favorite pair of Garavani's muddy for no reason," April said with a smile, eyes blocked by the massive sunglasses on her face.

"Thanks for your contribution to our winning goal, April," Juliette said with a laugh, wrapping her arm around April's waist and resting her head on April's shoulder. "I was so sick with nerves before the game, still kind of feel sick now to be honest, but I'm glad we managed to win without me throwing up."

"If you throw up on my cardigan, I will murder you, Jules. This is cashmere," April warned, sounding disgusted. Juliette only hugged her tighter.

Like with Elizabeth and Baz, Sade almost felt like a ghost around the girls. Standing here silently in this private moment. Gate-crashing something intimate and small.

"Congrats on the win," Sade said.

The girls turned to look at her, a slight look of surprise on Persephone's face like she had forgotten that Sade was standing there.

"Thank you for coming! I'm sure you were bored out of your mind. I know sports games aren't as exciting to watch as they are to play," Juliette said.

Sade shook her head. "I wasn't bored at all. I used to watch lacrosse games all the time growing up, and I actually used to compete in sports myself."

"Lacrosse?" Persephone asked suddenly.

"I was a swimmer," Sade replied, to which Persephone said nothing, just stared at her.

Juliette looked between the two, a slow grin forming. "You know Persephone's last two ex-girlfriends were swimmers—" she started, only to be elbowed hard by Persephone.

Sade raised an eyebrow, confused. "That's nice. Did they swim for ANA?"

"One did, the other the rival team, St. Lucy's," Juliette replied, earning a dagger from Persephone.

"This game of matchmaker is getting tiresome. Are we leaving or what?" April asked, looking and sounding bored.

"Hey," a voice interrupted.

It was a girl from the other team. The one who had given Sade that weird glance earlier. And here she was again, looking at her strangely.

"Yes?" April replied, arms folded.

"Not you—her," the girl said, nodding at Sade. This caused the group to turn to Sade once again.

"Hi?" Sade said slowly.

"Sorry to interrupt, I just—Do I know you? I feel like I know you," the girl said.

"I don't think so—" Sade began, but the girl shook her head.

"I swear I've seen you before. At a party maybe or . . . I don't know, something," the girl continued, her eyebrows squished together as though she were trying to figure out a complex maths equation.

Sade forced a smile.

"I honestly didn't have much of a life before boarding school. I was homeschooled, so I'm probably not the person you're thinking of. I'm sorry . . . ," Sade said.

The girl looked taken aback. "Oh, I'm sorry. I just could have sworn—"

"She said she doesn't know you, okay? So get lost," April replied harshly, lowering her glasses dismissively.

The girl nodded, face hardening. "I didn't mean to offend anyone or anything. I just thought—"

"You thought wrong," Sade said.

The girl nodded slowly, gaze still glued to Sade. "I did. I'm sorry. I'll go now. Congrats on the win," the girl said before turning and walking away.

Sade felt bad. She didn't have to snap at her like that. There was no crime in asking a question.

She looked on, watching the girl join her team again before glancing back once and then quickly turning away when she caught Sade's eye again.

"That was unnecessary, April," Persephone said.

"What was, Sephy?" April asked, blinking fast as though she wasn't present for what had just happened.

"The way you spoke to that girl."

April fell silent, either quietly considering Persephone's words or thinking nothing at all.

Sade noticed this subtle tension between Persephone and April at times. The former always calling out the latter, the way they seemed to be the best of friends and total strangers at the same time.

April finally spoke. "I'm sorry, okay? You know I get cranky when I haven't eaten anything. Speaking of, are we going back to Persephone's to celebrate?" April asked.

"I thought we were going to yours?" Juliette said.

April shrugged. "Change of plans, my room is a mess."

Sade watched as the girls of Nightingale Academy disappeared back onto their school bus, unblinking until her eyes pricked. She finally blinked and wiped them before any tears could form.

"What do you say, Sade, want to join us?" Juliette asked, pulling Sade from her thoughts.

"I uh, have plans already . . . sorry," she said.

"No need to apologize; we can hang out anytime," Juliette said while wrapping a beautiful cerulean-colored scarf around her neck. "We should probably get going, though. It smells like rain."

Sade looked up at the sky. The clouds looked dark and heavy, much like her soul, ready to pour all its wet, icy contents onto the school grounds.

Her aunt used to say that the rain had the ability to wash away your sins. It was funny, living in England most of her life, she'd have thought all that rain would have already done the job by now.

"Mars, I'm guessing," Persephone said to Sade, forcing her gaze to move from the sky.

"What?" Sade asked.

"The planet you're always on, I assume that's where you have plans, right?" If Mars was the Spitz Center, where Jude's swim meet was currently happening, then sure.

Sade nodded. "Yes, Mars," she said, and Persephone did her sort-of smile at her.

"Have fun," she replied, lingering a minute before opening her umbrella and walking past Sade, probably to join April and Juliette, who had already started toward the entrance of the school building.

She wasn't sure what compelled her, but she found herself speaking before she could think. "Want me to bring you anything back? From Mars, I mean," Sade asked, turning to face Persephone, who had slowed her walking.

There was a pause before Persephone yelled back her reply. "Something sweet."

• • •

153

THE SPITZ CENTER LOOKED NEARLY identical to the pools one might see in an Olympic park, only the Spitz pool was slightly bigger. It made the already impressive swimming hall in the Newton building look like an insignificant pond in comparison.

By the time Sade arrived, the swim meet had nearly finished.

There were a few gaps in the seats dotted around the pool, so she made her way over to an empty one next to a familiar figure.

"Not swimming today?" she asked as she sat down and crossed her legs.

August, who had been leaning forward concentrating on the pool, seemed to jump at the sound of her voice. "Oh, hey, new girl," he said, then shook his head. "Francis really wanted to swim, and so Jude swapped us out last minute."

Sade looked at the pool, where the boys were lined up on the edge ready to take their places.

"I've told you before, my name is not new girl," she said, nudging him.

There was silence and then the referee raised a pistol to the sky and fired a blank shot in the air, which rang out with a resounding bang, bouncing and echoing. The boys dived into the pool and began to zip through the water like sharks. The suddenness of it was startling and exciting all at once.

"Sorry—Sade," he corrected himself, eyes still glued to the water. She noted the grave look on his face. Disappointment.

He wanted to swim today.

He trained every night, desperate. Trained probably more than Francis and Jude combined.

Sade still wasn't sure if she trusted August. He'd explained himself last night, but she couldn't shake the feeling that he was holding something back, and she hadn't decided if this made him bad or good yet.

Sade noticed his bouncing leg and nail-bitten fingers.

He didn't just want to swim today, it seemed like he needed to.

"Why did Jude swap you guys?" she asked, treading carefully.

August shrugged. "A favor, I guess. Francis really wanted this—he hasn't been able to compete since the incident last year . . . so I guess Jude was giving him another chance."

"What incident?" Sade asked.

August finally looked at her. "Oh nothing, it's not really something I should be mentioning anyway. I guess Francis should just be glad he's the headmaster's stepson is all; some of us need squeaky-clean records," he said with a tight expression, then looked back at the pool, slipping into another silence.

"Okay," Sade replied, still wondering what this incident was.

She could hear people cheering from the stands, but unlike the lacrosse field, the hall was packed with students. She could even see Headmaster Webber in the corner laughing with one of the other teachers.

In the movies, it was always American football players who made people react in this way.

It seemed that at ANA, swimmers ran the school.

Sade could see Jude in the water. At first, she wasn't sure it was him, since the swim caps and the goggles made it pretty hard to tell the boys apart. But she saw the white-blond of his hair sticking out slightly from beneath the cap and she was almost certain that no other boy at the school had the same almost-white hair that he did, in the way that no other ANA boy had the same pink afro as Baz.

Her eyes widened as she watched how fast Jude was, how his arms cut through the water like knives, and how jealous this ability to effortlessly do so made her feel.

"He's amazing, right?" August mumbled.

Sade nodded. "I didn't know he could swim like that," she said.

"He's like a water god, ranks in the top three in our age category in England— Coach thinks Jude could compete in the big leagues in two years," August said.

As the swimmers reached the final length, tensions were high, but it seemed that no one was surprised when Jude came in first. She was starting to understand why people seemed to worship him.

He stepped out of the pool, water spilling and dripping from him as he confidently removed his cap and shook out the water that had managed to get inside. The coach slapped him on the back and Jude went to shake a stranger's hand.

"Who's that?" Sade asked.

"A scout," August said, his voice lifeless.

"There were scouts today?" she asked.

August's eyes looked a little glassy as he nodded. "I'll get them next time; it's okay. Francis and Jude are fourth years, they needed this more. Besides, Francis has been here practicing all day; he worked hard for this." It sounded like he was trying to convince himself more than her.

Sade watched as Francis took off his cap, revealing the bright red of his hair as he walked toward the sides, a smile on his face despite coming in fourth place.

Not even enough to win a medal. The sound of her coach's voice found its way into her head. It was accompanied by another thought.

"Francis was here all day?" she asked.

August nodded. "Yeah."

She wondered where April had been then, if not with her boyfriend.

Jude suddenly appeared, with a grin on his face, where August and Sade were seated. "You came," he said to her.

Did he think I wouldn't?

She nodded. "I did."

"I'm glad," he said, staring down at her for a few awkward moments. August cleared his throat and Jude finally spoke again. "Well, I'm gonna go and get crowned winner, then I'll get changed but I'll be right back."

"I'll be here. August is good company," she said.

Jude slapped August on the shoulder and then leaned in. "Keep out of trouble, Auggie," he said. To which August replied with a tight smile and then Jude was gone.

August's demeanor seemed different toward Jude today, and Sade guessed it was probably the sting of the last-minute swap. Though something about this felt deeper.

"So I hear we have a date after this," she said, wanting to lighten the mood, make things less awkward and quiet. She didn't trust August fully, but seeing him look so devastated made it difficult to sit and do nothing.

"Ah yes, Jude told me about the not-date date that I'm being dragged along to."

"You didn't have to say yes to him, you know."

August laughed and looked at her properly this time. His expression was as unreadable as his sister's. "Have you met Jude Ripley? You always say yes."

THE CAFÉ WAS SMALL AND tucked away in one of the many hidden corners of the massive landscape that was Alfred Nobel Academy.

It barely had any seating, sold a total of four drinks, a handful of sweets, and, strangely, a collection of trinkets, and was owned by a woman who looked like she was in her early forties and hated life and people.

"Two of the usual for myself and Auggie, and for the lady . . ." Jude looked at Sade, awaiting her order.

"I think I'll need longer to decide. I don't mind paying for myself since this is not a date," Sade replied.

"Who said I was going to pay for you in the first place?" Jude asked, an eyebrow raised playfully.

"Just in case you were deciding to be a gentleman, I thought I'd forewarn you," she replied.

"You're mistaken. August is the gentleman. I'm anything but," he said to her with a sly grin, before patting August on the back and nodding toward the seats. "We'll be over there when you're ready."

She looked up at the menu, stuck between English breakfast tea and a latte. She decided to do what she usually did when she came to a crossroad.

Her eyes flickered between the two.

Ip dip do, the cat's got the flu, the dog's got the chicken pox . . . out goes you. Her eyes landed on the tea.

The latte it was.

"Could I get the Bunsen Brew," Sade said. The drinks seemed to all be named after more scientists, like most things at the school.

"Is that all?" the woman asked as Sade got out her wallet.

She looked at the selections of sweets and candies and then the trinkets. They were mostly things like postcards and key rings. She spotted one that was shaped like the Eiffel Tower.

It reminded her of the last real family holiday she'd had. The last holiday where things weren't so broken. When her mother was still alive. When she wasn't constantly haunted by nightmares, memories, and ghostly figures in the dark.

It was a trip to France, and at the hotel they could see the historic landmark from their window. She remembered going up a long elevator to the top of the tower on one of the days of the trip. It had just been them. No overbearing father in sight.

All right, you two, hold on and watch carefully. At night, the tower sparkles and you can see the whole city from up here—you don't want to miss it!

"Just these two, please," Sade replied, grabbing a Mars bar as well as one of the key rings.

There was a slight tremor in her fingers as she took out some cash from her purse.

THE NOT-DATE DATE WAS A lot less awkward than Sade had expected.

August seemed to loosen up a lot more once he had some coffee in his system, and the three talked about swimming and school, then argued about random TV shows for almost three hours before the café had to close, and the lady kicked them out.

They then spent another half hour by the reception, continuing their argument about whether SpongeBob was really the villain of his own show—to which Sade argued that he was. After all, despite following the different characters, the show was ultimately through SpongeBob's eyes—he showed the audience what he wanted them to see.

"That's bollocks; he's a kind and caring sponge. What did he ever do to you?" August asked.

Sade shrugged. "I don't trust him. Too happy."

Jude laughed. "You only trust sad people, then?"

"No one's that happy!" she replied.

"Well, as much as I love telling you how wrong you are, new girl, I have to go. I need to practice," August said.

Sade rolled her eyes.

"I might join you, Auggie—give me a moment, though," Jude said.

August nodded, looking between the two before holding his hand up to wave. "See you later, Sade," he said.

"See you," she replied.

Then he was walking away from them both.

Jude placed his hands in his pockets. "That was fun," he said.

"It was okay. I've had better dates," Sade replied.

Jude smiled. "I thought this wasn't a date."

"It wasn't."

"Did you want it to be?" he asked.

She narrowed her eyes a little. What game was he playing? "Did you?" she asked.

He paused, not offering a response at first, instead simply watching her. Perhaps trying to figure out what game she was also playing. "I did," he finally said, stepping closer. "But as you aren't looking to see anyone right now, I guess I'll have to wait and see when my charming personality will finally win you over."

Jude definitely thought highly of himself. And why wouldn't he? People treated him as though he were a god. Even his best friend. It was like he had the whole school under his spell.

Fortunately, his spells would not work on her. He was anything but a god.

"Good luck with that," she said.

"I don't need luck," he said.

"And why's that?"

He stared at her once more, stepping backward now, then shrugged. "You'll see," he said ominously.

Before going back to her dorm, she made a small detour to Curie House, asked for the room she required from a passing stranger in the common room, and made her way up. The house felt like the inside of an old English lady's cottage, with florals and quilts and a warm, soapy smell.

Sade finally found the door she needed: room 301.

Persephone's room.

She quietly crept toward the door and left her scrawled note on top of the Mars bar she had gotten earlier.

Something sweet.

And then she left the house and made her way back to her own.

The sky was almost pitch-black as she crossed the path that led back to the black-stoned building. Walking inside, she was immediately greeted by the sound of one million conversations floating around the house. People were still hanging out in the common room and in the dining hall. Some in corridors and others locked away in their rooms, as she would soon be.

She stepped inside the elevator and then out of it once it got to the third floor.

When her door came into view, she was surprised to see the slumped figure next to it. Familiar pink tufts of hair were secured under a green froggy hat.

"Baz?" Sade asked.

He looked up at her, standing immediately. The first thing she noticed about his face was how wet it was. The next thing, his expression.

He looked . . . angry.

"Where have you been? I've been texting you all afternoon."

"I'm sorry. I was hanging out with some . . . friends—Did something happen?" The next thing Sade noticed was that the tears weren't dry. They were new. He had been crying for a while now.

"It's E-Elizabeth," he said, voice wavering. "Th-they—"

"What happened, did they find her?" Sade almost said *body*. She had to stop herself from saying it out loud.

That Elizabeth was a body. Not a living, breathing person. A lifeless thing.

She braced herself for the news, knowing from his expression alone that it couldn't be good.

He shook his head. "Th-they took her things—her mum, she took everything."

"What?" Sade asked, confused now.

"It's all gone. Headmaster Webber and Miss Blackburn wouldn't listen to me—I tried telling them the email was fake. I told them about Julie being dead, I told them about the GPS thing on my phone, I told them everything. B-but they i-ignored me. They shipped everything back to Ireland." He was crying as he was telling her this, stumbling over his words.

Sade listened silently, then got her key and opened the door. As if to confirm what she already knew to be true.

Elizabeth's side of the room was stripped bare.

Remnants of Elizabeth once found in objects scattered all over the room were now gone. As if they were wiping the slate clean of Elizabeth.

"Baz, what did you mean, *the GPS thing on your phone?*" Sade asked, her mind whirring.

She didn't remember anything about a GPS on his phone.

Baz sniffed. "I tried messaging you—my phone finished restoring, and it sent me a bunch of missed alerts. Do you know of the app Friendly Links—"

"Yes?" Sade said, her heart in her throat. She'd never had any use for it, but it was one of those apps, like the calculator app or the weather app, that always came with a new phone. It was used for sharing locations with friends or, more often than not, locating your phone when you lost it.

"I'd forgotten Elizabeth used it before. She shared her location with me during the summer we went on vacation together. I'd lost my phone so she set up this GPS thing—anyway, it seems she never turned it off," Baz said, taking out his phone and showing her the screen. Through the cracked glass she could see the notifications Baz had gotten, and there was one with an update on Elizabeth's last location.

"The Friendly Links GPS is more specific than getting an IP address, which would most likely give us the general school area—this app gives us a specific region where her phone would've been last," he says, clicking onto the notification. "The app also lets you send messages when it signals your location. Elizabeth sent me five sandwich emojis," he said.

She remembered what Elizabeth had said about it, how a sandwich was their code for when something was wrong.

"I tried to check what her current location was, but there's no signal. The last time her location could be traced was Monday night. The night she was last seen. It says here that Elizabeth's phone was last in this area of the school grounds."

The map was unlabeled and showed their current location in relation to where Elizabeth's phone last sent a signal.

Sade felt a chill settle inside as realization struck.

According to this app, Elizabeth's last known location was near the beginning of the path that led to the dorms. Somewhere between the Newton Sports Center and Hawking House. Just after Jemison House, before the path split off to the staff quarters.

"If Elizabeth had gone past the staff quarters, CCTV would have tracked her movements. Yet the police couldn't find any sign of her on the school grounds that night," Baz said, lowering his voice like there was someone listening in. "There are camera-blind spots all over the school; it's how people are able to get away with a lot of things. But for Elizabeth to get that far along the path . . . she would have missed all the blind spots, which means either there's a secret blind spot in that area I don't know about that she used in order to go past the staff quarters and leave the school at night undetected, or—"

Sade interjected, finishing his sentence with a sick feeling inside. "Or Elizabeth never left the school grounds. Someone got to her first."

Baz looked green, like he could throw up.

He was finally considering the terrible thing you *never* want to consider in situations like this.

"I have a feeling that same someone probably sent the email too," he said, still refusing to state the unthinkable thing that was now the elephant in the room. The possibility that Elizabeth was gone for good. "The police searched the school for a whole week; wouldn't they find *something* . . . DNA or a sign of a struggle or something of Elizabeth's—her phone, anything she had on her?" He sounded helpless.

"Police miss things like this all the time, and seeing how little they seemed to care in the first place, it's no wonder they'd miss stuff," Sade said, her voice heavy.

Baz nodded, then went quiet for a few pensive moments. "What if the school is in on it? What if they did something to Elizabeth?" Baz said, looking and sounding paranoid.

"What?" Sade replied.

"They've constantly shut me down since last week. What if they didn't want to explore other possibilities because *they're* the ones behind it all? I mean, they sent her things back to Ireland, isn't that weird? If they think she's in Birmingham, why send her stuff back home? What if Webber and Blackburn wanted Elizabeth to leave for some reason and she didn't comply, and so they kidnapped her in the middle of the night and have her chopped up in one of Webber's storage cabinets?"

Sade blinked at him. A schoolwide conspiracy involving teachers wanting to hurt their students on purpose?

He'd clearly been watching too many true-crime dramas. Though he did have a point about Elizabeth's things . . .

He sighed, still looking teary and lost. "I know, it's ridiculous; there'd probably be a smell. But I don't know what else to think. It feels like we have nothing."

This definitely wasn't nothing. They didn't have any concrete answers yet, but this was, indeed, *something*.

If someone had done something to Elizabeth on campus, there had to be something, a clue that might give them something else to go on—maybe not a smell, but something else.

After all, she imagined there were limited ways someone could hide heinous crimes at a school. She hated to think it, but if there was *a body*, disposing of it would be difficult to do at a boarding school.

She didn't say this out loud, of course.

Sade thought about all the information they had already. The GPS, the email, the missing music box, the doctored footage.

"We need our smoking gun," Sade said.

Baz's eyebrows furrowed. "We can't bring guns to campus . . ."

Sade shook her head. "I don't mean a literal one. It's a metaphor. You know a gun has been fired because there's smoke left behind?"

Baz still looked confused. He wasn't getting it.

"What I mean is, we need something irrefutable, something that'll force the teachers to take us seriously. I think if we focus in on the area Elizabeth was last seen, and we retrace her steps from that night, we might be able to find it. We start with the easiest place, Newton, and then we work our way into the hardest. Hawking."

"How will we get entry into Hawking long enough to investigate?" Baz asked.

Sade's plans whirred in her mind like rotating files on a hard drive.

"Leave that to me."

I SLEEP, I DROWN & DISAPPEAR[2]

Dear Diary,

A few weeks ago I think I died.
But no one's found my body
yet. So I'm not sure if I actually did.
Or if it's another lie
I've told myself.

---

[2] An anagram

PART II

A NIGHTMARE SCREAM

"They say terrible things are done in darkness, but terrible things are also done in a light too blinding for anyone else to look at directly."

—*Dear Senthuran*, Akwaeke Emezi

18

SUNDAY

THE INVITE

AS THE POET ROBERT FROST once said: "Life—it goes on."

This was also true of quaint boarding schools in England.

Days passed, the sudden disappearance of a student was swept under the Louis De Poortere rug, and people moved on.

Most people anyway.

Unlike the other students at Alfred Nobel Academy, Sade had spent the weekend with Basil, ignoring her homework and instead trying to put herself into the mind of a missing girl. They needed to know what happened that night, where Elizabeth had gone, and where she was now.

They started with the facts. (1) Elizabeth had to have left the room sometime after curfew, when Sade had fallen asleep (so anywhere from ten p.m. onward). (2) Seeing as there was no back door in Turing and the front entrance had CCTV surveillance, Elizabeth could have escaped from one of the two windows in the hallways of Turing that had a fire escape or (less likely) used the window in her dorm room and the pipes along the walls as a makeshift ladder. The latter option would probably result in a lot of broken bones, so the former was the most possible scenario. (3) The statue of the school's founder, John Fisher, located at the entrance of the pathway leading to the dorms, was fitted with cameras. As Elizabeth wasn't picked up by any of the school's surveillance, it was highly likely she didn't go past that area.

Which raised the question, how would Elizabeth—or anyone—have left the school without being caught on any cameras?

They mapped out their search, and then, on Sunday evening, found themselves outside on the cold, wet school grounds searching for the metaphorical pluming smoke of a gun.

Having searched the expanse of the Newton Sports Center, walking the path Elizabeth most likely took, and tracing the perimeter together, they split up to check each floor separately. Sade ventured through the familiar swimming area, passing by the construction site, through to the pool she often found herself in, and back again. Like Baz, she found nothing useful.

She wasn't sure if it was the lack of results or the perpetual gloomy weather, but it was hard to stay positive.

"What are we looking for?" Baz asked after their failed mission in Newton. "It feels like we're just searching for the sake of it; what are we even searching for?"

It was a good question. What were they searching for? What was their smoking gun?

It was meant to be anything that could help them figure out what happened that night, but it wasn't exactly helpful to have their scope be *everything*. And yet, they had no other choice.

"What about her phone?" Sade suggested.

"What do you mean?"

"That should be our focus for when we get into Hawking. Her phone was last in this area; maybe she dropped it or maybe someone took it."

"That's a lot of maybes," Baz replied quietly. "How are we even getting into Hawking? You said you'd handle it, but Hawking House literally has fourth years who guard the front doors like one of Hades's three-headed hounds."

"Don't worry, I'm working on it. I'll get us in this week," Sade replied, which didn't seem to give Baz much reassurance.

Despite her enigmatic ways, she did have a plan. One that she'd been working on for some time. She just needed a few more days.

Baz looked away from her, pensively staring down at the cobblestoned path that led back to their dorms.

"Do you think she's alive?" he asked, surprising Sade. It was the first time he was asking the burning question out loud. "I ask because there's something so sinister about this. I feel it."

Sade didn't want to answer, partly because she wasn't sure her opinion would actually help anyone in this situation, so instead, she said: "Let's just continue trying to find our next lead—looking for Elizabeth's phone and getting into Hawking House. We should also try other places that Elizabeth frequented? Like the greenhouse. Could you get us in?"

"I tried getting into the greenhouse already; the biology teacher isn't the most pleasant person. She wouldn't let me up there a few days ago, but I'll try again."

"Great, so that's two places on our list. Hawking and the greenhouse," Sade said.

Baz just nodded silently.

By the time Monday rolled around, it was clear that Baz and Sade seemed to be the only people left in the world who were still hung up on Elizabeth.

For all everyone else knew, Elizabeth Wang had dropped out. A brief mystery, and now yesterday's news. Alfred Nobel Academy had moved on to its next big event: the Annual Owens' Halloween Party (doubling as their joint Seventeenth Birthday Party).

As usual, the world didn't stop and shift on its axis or consider personal grief.

As usual, life—it went on.

Sade received the invite on Monday evening, the envelope shoved underneath her dorm room door like a secret.

The paper was an ominous bloodred color.

She picked it up, examining it carefully. Searched for any signs of what knowledge the envelope held. Got nothing.

For a moment, she thought it was another clue. Something planted by whoever had switched the music boxes.

Sade opened the envelope and took out the blank white card inside, which unfolded to reveal a crimson-red pop-up Japanese maple tree.

The text on the page was handwritten and read:

> *You are invited to attend the 17th Birthday Party of August Patrick*
> *Owens and April Piper Owens.*
>
> *When: Saturday, 31st October—7:00 p.m.*
> *Where: The Hawking House Common Room*
> *Dress: A costume of your choosing*
> *(bad costumes will be turned away at the door)*

Sade looked up from the card and down at the floor she had picked it up from, noticing the shadow of someone lingering outside. She felt her heart pause for a moment and then jump when a sharp knock sounded.

"It's Juliette!" a friendly, familiar voice called out.

When she opened the door, Juliette was there, holding a stack of red envelopes.

"Hi," Sade said.

"Hey," Juliette replied with a wide smile. "Just wanted to stop by and see how you were doing. You disappeared on us on Friday . . . ," she said, voice trailing off.

Sade looked between the red envelope in her hand and the stack of them in Juliette's.

"It's April and August's Halloween party invite—designed by April herself. She's really into calligraphy."

"Oh, thank you."

Juliette raised an eyebrow. "You look confused."

"I'm not . . . I just, I've never been to one of these before."

"A Halloween party?" Juliette asked.

"A party in general," Sade replied.

"Do they not let you party in homeschool?" Juliette asked with surprise, her head tilted.

"There's not really anyone to uhm . . . party with," she said. Which wasn't entirely true.

Homeschoolers did have parties, but she figured this was the easiest answer she could give.

Juliette's mouth formed an O and she nodded, like it all made sense now.

"Well, it's fun, I promise. We're *all* really excited for you to come!" she said. Though Juliette seemed to be the kind of person who would find a lot of things that weren't necessarily enjoyable, fun.

"Can I bring a plus-one?" Sade asked.

Juliette frowned and said nothing at first. Then after a moment she spoke. "Boyfriend? Girlfriend? Significant other?"

Sade shook her head. "Just a friend."

"Hmm . . . in that case, I'm sure *April* won't mind," she replied in a way that made her think Juliette was hinting that there was someone else who possibly would mind if she was bringing someone other than her platonic, pink-haired friend named after a plant.

"Thanks . . . I'll see you tomorrow?" Sade said, taking a step back from the doorway.

"Yes, I'll see you," Juliette said, her smile appearing once again as she began to turn. "Oh, and Persephone told me to send her thanks."

"For what?"

Juliette shrugged. "Something about chocolate."

It wasn't until after Juliette went to deliver other invites that Sade remembered the note she had left on Friday after she had returned from her not-date with Jude and August.

Something sweet.

She took her phone out and messaged Baz right away.

S: I think I have our ticket to Hawking House

WEDNESDAY

THE SCHOOL WAS ABUZZ ALL week with conversations about what costumes every-one would be wearing, combined with the desperation for a red invite.

According to Baz, an invite to the Annual Owens' Halloween Party was as coveted as an invite to the Met Gala.

And all week, Sade witnessed the lengths people were willing to go to for April's approval.

At lunch on Wednesday, April spent most of the time at a table by the back of the hall interviewing possible last-minute attendees. The queue for her much sought-after party invites was longer than the lunch queue itself.

"Can she do that?" Sade asked no one in particular as she watched April wielding her power over the awestruck students at Alfred Nobel Academy who worshipped her very existence.

Baz was right. If this party was like ANA's own Met Gala, then April was definitely Anna Wintour.

They even had the same cold expression and hard-to-reach eyes.

"This is nothing. She used to make our nannies cry when we were kids. My sister doesn't really have a soul, so I actually think this is a huge improvement in terms of char-acter development. No one is crying yet. I count that as a win," August said with a smile.

Just as he did, a girl burst into tears and ran in the opposite direction from April's table.

"I guess I spoke too soon," August muttered.

"Did I miss anything?" Persephone asked as she joined the table.

"Just April tormenting the student body," August said, sounding bored.

"So another day ending in *y*?" Persephone asked, taking a bite out of her apple and staring at Sade as she did so.

"Precisely," August said. It was only the three of them at the table today. Sade had to admit, she preferred it. It felt quieter. Nicer.

"What are you guys wearing to the party?" she asked, trying to gauge what sort of thing was deemed acceptable at an event like this. It seemed like there would be unspoken rules about the customs of this sort of party that she'd need to learn to avoid embarrassing herself.

"Whatever April says I should wear," August replied, his answer annoyingly unhelpful.

Sade looked at Persephone expectantly. "I'm not going," Persephone said.

Sade tried not to look too taken aback. She'd assumed it was something they'd all attend, either by choice or by April's will. It was their best friend's birthday, after all.

"Oh . . . is there a reason?" Sade asked.

Persephone blinked at her. "I don't like parties."

That was understandable. They were loud and filled with sweaty bodies and bright lights—or so Sade assumed.

The rest of lunch was spent in silence, Sade watching April for most of it. And wondering to herself how it was that someone her age already seemed so sure of herself and had convinced others of this too.

After school, she found herself in Seacole House, seated on the floor of Baz's room looking at an old blueprint of Hawking House. It wasn't entirely accurate, seeing as it was a blueprint Sade'd found online from the 1980s, but at least it gave them somewhere to start.

She could tell Baz's determination was dwindling, though he wouldn't admit it. Admitting it would be giving up on Elizabeth.

So he trudged along.

The only thing seeming to keep his spirits high was the Owens soiree. It was not the priority but definitely a nice added bonus.

"I managed to finally get keys to the greenhouse," Baz said. "I asked Ms. Thistle to take us up there instead of the biology teacher. Told her I was assisting Elizabeth with something a few weeks ago and realized I left my scarf there. Thistle said she'd take us up. I know the police already searched the area, so it probably won't amount to much, but at least we can try," he said with a shrug.

"Can we go before dinner?" Sade asked, looking at the clock. Four p.m. They had time. And they needed to do something. Soon.

Baz looked at her gratefully. "Of course."

"Great, I'll just need to grab a cardigan. It gets cold up there."

ABOUT TWENTY MINUTES LATER, THEY were climbing the steps up to the roof of the science building with Ms. Thistle, who was going on about weekend plans at a local farm festival. While Sade had no interest in it at all, and was mostly focused on the matter at hand, Baz was asking all sorts of questions about the festival and its animal contestants.

"Here you are," Ms. Thistle said, unlocking the door to the roof and opening it wide.

The chill from the higher altitude wrapped around them as the cold air blew in through the door.

"All right then, go and look for your scarf; I'll be here waiting. I'm not meant to allow you two up here, so you only have five minutes," Ms. Thistle said.

"Thanks, Miss T," Baz said, giving her a smile as he stepped through, and Sade followed along.

Something felt weird about being back up here. She wasn't sure if it was the Elizabeth of it all or the change in altitude. Seeing the school from up here was dizzying.

She was admittedly a bit disappointed to find the greenhouse so empty and quiet. A part of her had hoped that Elizabeth had been hiding out here all along. But that would've been too good to be true.

Baz turned to Sade and spoke in a low whisper. "I'll search the left side of the greenhouse and you search the right."

Sade nodded and the two split up, going to their respective corners.

She scanned the rows and rows of plants, once again taking in the vibrant colors of all the strange-looking plants Elizabeth had introduced to her. She recognized the cheese-looking one as the monstera plant.

"Anything?" Baz called.

She shook her head. "Nothing."

They swapped sides, Sade on the left and Baz on the right. They ducked under the tables, moved plants around, desperation creeping in as the greenhouse seemed to shrink around them.

The greenhouse, like Newton, provided nothing new.

"Have you found it?" Ms. Thistle's jolly voice called out.

Baz let out a sigh, his breath coming out in wisps of smokelike air from the cold.

"No—nothing here," he yelled back. "Nothing here at all," he muttered to himself, staring down vacantly at one of the monstera plants.

"Okay! Well, let's get down from here quickly. I'm freezing to death with this cold!" Ms. Thistle said.

After moments of no movement, Sade tugged at Baz's arm. "Let's go," she said.

He shook his head.

"Ms. Thistle will probably drag us out soon—or worse, she might go to the staff quarters and get Miss Blackburn to."

Instead of moving with her toward the entrance of the greenhouse, he poked his finger into the mud surrounding the plant. She furrowed her eyebrows in confusion. What on earth was he doing?

He looked at her, as though he could hear her thoughts.

"The soil is wet," he said simply.

She blinked at him, confused.

"Someone's been watering the plants," he continued.

Sade remembered what Elizabeth had said on that first day during the tour.

I try to water this one every seven days, otherwise no one else will . . . Without me, most of these plants would shrivel up and die.

"So we found something after all," she said.

A FEW MINUTES LATER, THEY were in the classroom of the biology teacher, Mrs. Choi, who had been marking tests.

"Can I help you, Basil?" Mrs. Choi asked, looking a bit miffed at the sudden disturbance.

"I just wanted to ask about the greenhouse—"

"Basil, I already told you, I can't authorize access—"

"Yes, I know. It's something else," he said. Sade glanced down at his finger, still dirty from the soil.

"What is it?"

"I'm doing a project for class about the life cycle of plants . . . And I was wondering how often the plants in the greenhouse get watered?"

"Last I checked, Basil, you weren't taking a science for your A levels," she said with pursed lips.

"It's for German class," he said.

Mrs. Choi didn't look convinced by him but sighed loudly, pushing herself from her seat and walking out of the classroom into the hallway. "Follow me," she said.

They both followed her over to a science notice board in the corridor, where a chart hung.

"Here's the frequency with which we water the plants, or rather the caretaker does. Since a lot of the plants are low maintenance, the caretaker waters them about once a month—as you can see, the last time was—"

"Three weeks ago," Baz said, sounding exasperated.

"Exactly. Is that all you need?" Mrs. Choi asked, clearly wanting to go back to marking already.

Baz nodded. "Yes, thank you so much."

"No problem," she said, giving him a strange look as he stared hypnotically at the board, before walking away.

Once she was out of earshot, Baz took a picture of the board and then turned to Sade.

"The plants have been watered recently," he said, eyes wide and face brighter than before.

"Elizabeth? But how—" Sade began.

Baz shook his head. "I don't know, but whatever is going on, we need to get ahead of them now. We need to check if there are cameras capturing who's been in and out of there. And, if it is Elizabeth—that she's still here, in the school, we need to figure out why. If there's something she's hiding from . . . ," he said.

Sade thought about her own failed CCTV attempts. It was unlikely that Mr. Michaelides would listen to her again or that there would be another teacher willing to entertain the seemingly far-fetched theories they had.

They didn't know that it was Elizabeth for sure. It could be anyone doing this, after all. It seemed Mrs. Choi didn't even know Elizabeth frequented the greenhouse. It was possible Elizabeth wasn't the only student with access.

But they had something else to go on, however small. There was hope in that. Even if they had to be cautious.

"I think we should be careful about jumping to conclusions without solid footing. We probably only have one real chance to take everything to the teachers and the school, so we need to make sure our leads are solid before approaching Blackburn or Webber again. I say we wait and see what else we find in Hawking House on Saturday."

Baz nodded, then finally smiled for what felt like the first time in days. "Still can't believe we're going to an *Owens* party," he said. "I feel like I was born for this specific event, like my entire life has been building up to it."

Sade smiled. She'd finally done something good in the world. Fulfilled Baz's apparent lifelong dream.

"Have you known the Owens twins your entire life?" she asked.

"No, met them at school two years ago," he said.

As they exited the science building, the sky had already begun to darken in standard English autumn fashion, and Sade kept thinking about the wet soil.

Had it been Elizabeth?

The only thing that seemed to make sense anymore was that Elizabeth's ghost was haunting the school now in the same way the dead still haunted Sade.

You should never have come, the ghost girl said once more.

Too bad. I'm here and I'm not leaving until I fix things, Sade mentally retorted back.

"It's cake and custard night in Turing. Do you think Jessica will notice if I come over for a slice?" Baz asked, pulling Sade out of the conspiracies still floating around in her mind.

Sade's eyebrows furrowed.

"Doesn't Seacole have a cake and custard night?"

He nodded. "Yeah, but I swear it just doesn't taste the same. Sometimes I think the house cook is making our food with spite in his heart."

Sade couldn't argue there; she'd eaten at Seacole once and the food did have a bitter quality.

"Jessica will most definitely notice, but I can help you hide under the table when she's around," Sade said.

Baz looked elated. "What would I do without you, Watson?" Baz asked as they strolled through the quad toward Turing.

"I imagine you'd be a lot hungrier," Sade replied.

19

FRIDAY
THE FRIEND ZONE

IT WAS THE DAY BEFORE the party and Sade was sitting on the carpet in Baz's room pouring food into Muffin's bowl as Baz cradled the guinea pig in his arms.

The stolen guinea pig had become well-adapted to her new home in the cage next to Baz's laundry basket. And somehow Baz had continued to not get caught by the house prefect of Seacole.

It seemed that not every house was burdened with a Jessica.

Baz let Muffin slip from his arms and wriggle over to the bowl of food Sade had poured, before pushing himself up and grabbing a box of hair dye, a bowl, and an applicator from his desk.

"I want to go on the record and say that I have never bleached anyone's hair before," Sade said, taking the supplies from his hands as Baz took a seat on his desk chair.

He turned and looked up at her. "I trust you."

Sade nervously looked down at the pack of dye and then at his smiling face. "Well, if I accidentally incinerate all your hair, it's your loss—or rather hair loss . . . Don't say I didn't warn you," she said, muttering the last part.

"I could pull off being bald, I think."

"That's the spirit," Sade said as she started to section his hair and apply the bleach one inch from his scalp as Google had told her to.

Soon Baz's hair was almost all covered in the white substance.

She was going to definitely miss the fluorescent pink of his hair, but it was apparently necessary for his Halloween costume to work.

"How come you don't get in trouble for dyeing your hair? Blackburn kept having a go at me on my first day for not wearing my uniform, so I figured it would be a bigger deal," she asked as she slathered more bleach on his head. Alfred Nobel Academy seemed so hung up on the correct uniform being worn at all times but didn't seem to care about the color or style of the students' hair. It seemed counterproductive.

"It's because of The Great Hair Debate," Baz replied.

"The what?"

"The Great Hair Debate. Back in 2007, the head girl at the time, Afia Owusu, had argued that self-expression was important for creating a healthy school environment and so the school met the students of ANA halfway. The school got to keep the uniforms, but we can do anything we like to our hair."

That was a very interesting piece of trivia.

"I didn't know head girls and boys had that much power," she said.

He nodded. "They do. If I had a chance of even being nominated, I'd run merely to change the school lunches to bangers and mash day every day."

Sade laughed. "That's definitely the most pressing issue affecting students today," she said, moving away from him and over to the little bathroom in the corner to clean up.

"I agree, I personally learn better when I've had a sausage."

She walked back into the room, only catching the end of his sentence. He smiled, waggling his eyebrows, and she laughed.

As they waited for the bleach to take effect, Sade lay back on Baz's bed and stared up at the ceiling. The room was mostly silent, apart from the sound coming from Baz's tapping on the buttons of his Nintendo Switch and Muffin moving about on the carpet.

"Hey, Baz?" she said after a few moments of quiet.

"Yeah?" he asked. She looked over at him. His hair was beginning to turn into a very ugly orange.

"Is there anywhere I can do my hair nearby, like in town? I wanted to take out my braids."

"Sharna Brown in Curie House does hair."

Sade was surprised by that. She didn't know who this Sharna Brown was, but she didn't expect to hear there was a student who did hair in the first place.

"Do I just go to her and ask?"

"Pretty much," Baz said.

Sade hadn't decided what hairstyle she'd do next—whether it would be braids like she always did or something else. Something different.

She would have to see.

Half an hour later, Baz's hair was now an ugly yellow color.

They'd moved to his bathroom to wash the bleach from his curls. Then Baz began to comb through the now-blond hair, pausing when a chunk of hair slid out with ease with the comb.

"Oh fuck," he said.

"What?"

"My hair is falling out!" he said.

"Hey! I warned you that I'm not a hairdresser—besides, I thought you can pull off anything?"

"I know I said I could pull off being bald, but I lied. I'll look like Dwayne Johnson."

Sade pulled at a strand of his hair and it stayed in place. "See, there's hope. I won't let you become the Rock, I promise."

"Pinkie swear?" he asked, holding up his little finger.

Sade interlocked their pinkies together. "I pinkie swear."

An hour later, Baz was now a yellowy blond and still had most of his hair intact. As he dried it with the blow-dryer, Sade put Muffin back in her cage in the corner.

The sound of the door swinging open scared them both as Baz's roommate grumpily ambled in.

His roommate was a guy named Spencer Pham, whom Sade recognized from her psychology classes. He was tall, had long dark hair, and was what some might call handsome.

"Hi, Spence," Baz yelled over the sound of the blow-dryer.

"Fuck off," Spencer said as he threw his bag down on the bed, grabbed a pack of what seemed to be cigarettes, opened their dorm room window, and climbed onto the roof without another word.

"He seems nice," Sade said, pushing Muffin's cage farther back toward the wall.

Baz switched the dryer off and his now-blond hair was back to its usual curly state. He grabbed a hairband from his dresser and tied his hair up in one single bunch, making his head resemble an apple.

He looked happy—happier than he had been this time last week.

She wasn't sure if it was because the week was over or because of the party tomorrow evening or simply because he was newly blond. Regardless, Sade had done good, had made Baz happy. For once in her life, her presence didn't cause abundant pain and misery.

"Spencer's great," Baz said, as though Spencer hadn't just told him to F off.

Sade could see smoke outside their window swirling about, creating a temporary fog. "He's definitely . . . something," she said, getting up and grabbing her bag.

Baz swiveled around in his chair, a pack of Jammie Dodgers now in his hands as he shoved a biscuit into his mouth. Sade was beginning to realize that her friend had a Jammie Dodgers addiction. He seemed to always have some on hand: in morning assemblies, when they'd hang out in the Turing common room, and in his bedroom. Stashes of the jam-filled biscuit were all over the place.

But she figured this addiction didn't hurt anyone, and who was she to judge? After all, she had a more severe addiction to being enveloped in cold chlorine water.

Speaking of . . .

"I'm going to go, but text me if you need anything," she said.

He nodded. "Thanks for making me blond."

"It was my pleasure," Sade replied. She felt she still needed to adjust to his new look; it wasn't that it didn't suit him, but that it made him look more serious than he was.

The sound of the window being opened again caught her attention as Baz's roommate slipped through it. The boy, Spencer, stared at them both, eyes lingering on Baz's hair, taking him in. And then with no further comment, he walked into the bathroom and closed the door behind him.

"I think that's my cue," Sade said.

"I'm meeting you at Turing before the party, right? Can I get dressed in your room?" Baz asked. Sade thought being in Elizabeth's room would be triggering for him, but he seemed to like being there. Like it was as close as he could get to being near her at the moment.

So she nodded. "Of course."

"See you tomorrow, Barbara," Baz said.

"See you then, Kenneth," she replied.

As was now the norm before she left, they did the usual choreography with their hands, their handshake nearly perfected.

Then Sade waved and bid him her final goodbye.

As she stepped out of Seacole with her bag and swim kit in tow and into the somber evening, the crisp, icy autumn chill enveloped her, causing her legs to grow stiff and painful as the cold entered her bones.

She quickly made her way down the stone path leading to the Newton building, where she had spent most of her evenings before curfew this week.

Going down into the basement of the building, she passed the new pool still under construction, glancing at its bare bones as she walked past. She wondered when it would be ready for use.

The withdrawal from the water crept up on her all day, and she craved the release found in the way the water gently stroked her bare arms as she glided across it.

No matter what had transpired each day, the pool always made her worries disappear.

As usual, August was there and as usual they swam together—him trying to become the best, and her giving in to the worst version of herself. Over and over.

"What a waste," August said after nearly a full hour of swimming together. The water dripped off him as he exited the pool, drying his face with a towel.

"What is?" she asked, climbing out with him.

He looked at her and said with a serious expression: "You are."

"Didn't peg you as a misogynist, Augustus."

August chuckled lowly. "I'm not—if anyone loves girls it's me, trust me—I just meant that you're so good at this, at swimming, I mean . . . I don't know. I'll stop bringing it up when I get a valid explanation for why you don't compete."

She placed a hand on his shoulder, patting his skin gently. "You can keep bringing it up, then, Auggie, I don't mind."

His eyes narrowed at her. "Don't call me that. You make me sound like a toddler," he said.

Sade began walking back to the changing rooms, August beside her.

"You let Jude call you that," she pointed out.

August went quiet for a few moments, the sound of their feet hitting the wet tiles, then he finally said, "It's different."

Sade wanted to ask why but decided against it. "Okay, Augustus," she replied simply.

Silence followed for another beat and August said: "Are you seriously not going to give me a reason?"

"Maybe one day. We'll see," she said with a shrug and a tight-lipped smile.

"I bet I can change your mind," he said, halting his movements and stopping in front of her, blocking her way.

She raised an eyebrow. "How?"

"Follow me," he replied with an enigmatic expression.

She was hesitant at first, watching as he turned the opposite way, expecting her to follow.

Slowly, she followed him out the main doors and through the long hallway. It was much cooler here than in the pool room. She suddenly felt exposed in her swimsuit.

"Okay, if anyone asks, you never saw this," August said, standing in front of another door this time.

Sade shifted back a little. "You didn't bring me here to kill me, right?" she asked.

He gave her a dimpled smile and shook his head. "You have trust issues, new girl."

She folded her arms. "I call it being smart and not blindly following a strange boy into a room."

He nodded. "Fair enough, but I can bet on my signed Michael Phelps poster *and* on my sister's life that you would probably be able to beat me up if it came to it."

"Ever the feminist, Augustus," Sade replied.

He smiled. "As I said, I love girls."

Despite her concerns about the sketchiness of it all, Sade followed him into the dark room.

August immediately reached out for the light and the room finally came to life before her.

It was the other swimming pool, the one Elizabeth had mentioned was under construction. It was twice as big as the one they frequently used in the evenings.

August spread his arms out.

"Welcome to a swimmer's haven," he said, voice bouncing off the walls and echoing loudly.

The space was huge and fancy-looking, despite still being filled with machinery. Concrete mix had been messily spilled and covered some of the floor. She made a mental note to be careful not to slip in it and fall into the gaping, unfilled pool.

While the pool they practiced in had plain white tiles all over, giving it a very sterile dentist-office-like appearance, this one was filled with color and character. The walls were made with different-colored tiles. One wall had a replica of Katsushika Hokusai's *Under the Wave off Kanagawa* in tile form, like a mosaic. The other walls had plain green-and-white tiling that looked oddly familiar.

Sade scanned the pool. It was completely devoid of water, empty and cavernous. Just concrete and unfinished tiling. Something about seeing it deconstructed in this way, like the pool's own anatomy was exposed, was so weird.

Is this what surgeons feel when they see a beating heart for the first time?

"It's beautiful," Sade said.

"I know, right," August said, looking at her with the Owens Twins' signature impenetrable stare. "We are still thinking of what to name the space. The whole team has been voting on who to name it after. I suggested Phelps, of course, but Francis keeps trying to push the Adam Peaty agenda. Who would you name it after?" August asked.

Sade thought about all the swimmers she looked up to. "Probably Simone Manuel," she said.

"Great choice," August replied.

"When are they opening this up for use?" she asked.

"I'm not entirely sure. They've been building it for well over a year now—it was meant to be finished ages ago, but they paused the whole project for a few months. It should almost be done now. I'm glad you're impressed."

"It is really nice. Not sure how it would persuade me to join the team, though."

"Well, I figured you'd see this new swimming pool and realize that only a tasteless person would turn down the opportunity to use it."

"Can I not just use the pool any time I want, though, like I already do?" she asked, folding her arms.

He smiled. "Ah, you see, that's the thing. The reason this pool is being built is so the swim team can have a separate practice room from the general student body. It will be accessed by a special key card and everything. And so, unfortunately for you, new girl, you will miss out," he finished with a playful shrug and an evil smile.

She hated to admit it, but he got her there.

"Having second thoughts?" he asked, grinning now.

"I'm sure my good friend Augustus will let me in with his key card, if need be," Sade said.

He laughed and it echoed around the room as he elbowed her lightly. "Not a chance."

"Wow, and I thought you were a good person, a gentleman."

His smile faltered slightly and he went silent for a few moments, and then he finally replied: "Most of the time."

AFTER RETURNING TO THE CHANGING rooms, getting dressed, and saying good-bye to August, it was almost time for curfew—aka, almost time to get scolded by the house prefect of Turing.

Walking out of the Newton building always felt so different from walking in.

Sade felt renewed, like she was finally invincible. It was a feeling she wished would last forever. Only she'd arrive back at Turing, take the lift up to her dorm room, and feel that heaviness return as she slid into bed and into the eerie quiet of the half-empty room.

But today, something was different when she got to her floor.

Today, there was a note and something round wrapped in plastic with a bow left in front of her door. She knelt down and picked them both up.

An apple.

Something sweeter—P

Sade couldn't help but smile. The sound of someone clearing their throat nearby barely fazed her.

"Shouldn't you be in your room already?" Jessica asked, arms folded and face squeezed into an expression of deep disappointment.

"Sorry—I was just about to—"

Jessica held up her hand, then gave Sade a slip of paper, only slightly bigger than the one already folded in her palm.

"This is your third strike, so I have to write you up," Jessica said.

She can't be serious, Sade thought. But seeing as it was Jessica, something told her she was.

"Okay," Sade said, strangely only mildly irritated by Jessica today.

After being dismissed, she walked into her cold, quiet room. But unlike other nights when the emptiness and silence of the room weighed her down, not even Jessica or the empty, quiet space could take full effect.

She got some water from the bathroom and sprinkled it onto Elizabeth's forget-me-not plant gift, giving it life.

As she lay down to die for the night once again, it dawned on her why it was that tonight felt different from other nights.

She had been at Alfred Nobel Academy for three weeks now.

In that short time, she had somehow gotten something she never thought would be possible for someone like herself.

Friends.

20

SATURDAY
ALL HALLOWS' EVE

SATURDAY MARKED THE BIGGEST EVENT in the Alfred Nobel Academy calendar year.

The Annual Owens' Halloween Party—what was previously organized by the school as just a Halloween dinner that took place in one of the halls in the main building and that all students were eligible to attend. But with the arrival of the Owens twins, the occasion soon became exclusively theirs.

Overnight, the school had been decked with ghoulish decorations, large fire-breathing pumpkins, and Halloween-themed bunting. Students roamed the campus dressed as everything from ghosts to superheroes to obscure versions of characters from television shows and film.

It seemed as though Wednesday Addams herself had thrown up all over the school, turning the whole place into something dark and wonderful.

Sade had woken up early, eaten the apple Persephone had left her the previous night for breakfast, and then spent the whole morning and some of the afternoon taking out her braids for the first time in weeks, washing her hair and braiding it down into something that could fit under the wig she would be wearing later for her costume.

By the time she had done all that it was already three.

She had a few hours left until the party, with Baz due to arrive about thirty minutes before it started.

Therefore, she had about an hour to fit in some reading for class.

She grabbed her psychology textbook, notebook, and laptop; pulled on her bonnet to cover her hair; and left to go to the library.

Turing was louder than it usually was on a Saturday afternoon. Students, dressed in their various disguises, packed the common room and foyer.

It seemed that everyone was out today, the spirit of Halloween infecting them all, even those not invited to the party, and the library was no different. Black glittering skulls adorned the shelves, fake bones and spiderwebs dangled from the tall ceilings, and googly eyeballs stuck to the figures in the stained glass windows, making them a lot less ethereal-looking and more ridiculous.

Sade went over to her usual table at the back, hoping it was available. The table could fit multiple students—up to six at least, but Sade preferred having it to herself. She believed the table to be lucky and needed all the luck it could give her to get through the rest of the term in one piece.

Not that she thought the table was *magic* or anything, but she had found that ever since she had begun working at that specific table, the work wasn't as hard to digest. She'd certainly had less rational things happen to her before.

When she rounded the corner, though, she felt disappointment hit her as the table was occupied by someone already.

It took her a few moments of staring to realize the person was Persephone. At her table, a book open, and her face resting in her palm.

It was weird that Sade hadn't recognized her at first, given that she saw her on a regular basis. Sade realized that not only was this the first time she had seen Persephone on a weekend, but it was also the first time she had seen her out of uniform—which probably explained how long it took to figure out it was her in the first place.

Persephone didn't seem to be dressed as a character of any kind, and yet her non-uniform felt like a costume all the same. She wore a thick lace choker around her neck, a black corseted waistcoat, washed-out jeans, and spiky platform boots.

Intimidating as ever.

"Hey," Sade said, which made Persephone look up from the book she was reading.

Sade squinted at the title: *Passing.* By Nella Larsen.

"Hi," Persephone said, blinking at her. "Did you want to use this space?"

"Yeah—but it's fine, you were here first."

"I don't mind you joining. I'm not working or anything," Persephone replied.

"Oh—thank you," Sade said, taking a seat across from Persephone.

She placed her psychology books on the table and rummaged through them before she found the right one, opening it up to what the class had been studying a week before she arrived at Alfred Nobel. She was almost caught up in one subject that wasn't English at least.

Persephone went back to her book and Sade focused on hers.

She began reading the section on classical conditioning and the case study by Pavlov but was finding it hard to concentrate.

There was something awkward about studying in the presence of others. It felt like they'd judge your methods and finally see through you. See that you were mediocre and not as smart as they might've thought. And right then, Sade couldn't seem to focus on the words on the page. Her mind wandered off, concerned with things that had nothing to do with Ivan Pavlov or his dog.

Her gaze drifted once again to Persephone and her book, and Sade was surprised to find Persephone's eyes no longer on the text in front of her but on Sade.

She'd been watching her.

"You zone out a lot, I've noticed," Persephone said.

"Sorry—Were you calling me?" Sade asked.

Persephone shook her head, leaning back this time. "It's been an hour and you've been staring at the same page the entire time. No notes written, just this expression . . . like you're . . . dreaming," Persephone said.

The very reason Sade didn't like studying around others.

"Psychology's boring," Sade said with a shrug.

"You do it other times too," Persephone said.

Sade raised an eyebrow. "Have you been watching me?"

Persephone silently stared at her, her lips slowly tugging upward into a smile.

Sade liked it when she smiled.

"Maybe," Persephone answered.

Sade didn't really know how to reply to that. "Aren't you meant to be reading a book?" she asked, noticing now that the book was no longer in front of Persephone.

"I finished it," Persephone said. "It wasn't a long book." So she was reading Sade instead. "I was actually about to leave; it's about four and I'd like to avoid the fanfare as much as possible." Persephone stood up, a tote bag slung over her shoulder. Sade assumed she meant the Halloween party and all the chaos that came with it.

"Are you really not a fan of Halloween?" Sade asked.

Persephone shook her head. "I love Halloween. It's my favorite holiday. It's the social-gathering aspect I'm not a fan of. I'm going back to my room to marathon all the Halloweentown movies."

The evening Persephone had planned sounded . . . lonely.

"I'd invite you to join me, but I take it you're still going to April's party?" she continued.

Sade nodded slowly. "I am—I came here to distract myself from overthinking about the party and also try to do some work before I had to get ready. I'm a little nervous about it, though. I almost don't want to go."

"There's no reason to be nervous. There are worse parties you could be attending." Something shifted in Persephone's expression as she said that.

"Like what?" Sade asked.

"Like my mother's art galas—a bunch of stuffy old people trying to one-up one another for hours on end; it's exhausting," Persephone replied.

"That does sound exhausting. I can see why you don't like parties," Sade said.

"It helps when you know at least one person there. April used to always come to my mum's parties with her parents, so it was never as bad as I'm making it sound. Just very boring. It was always nice having her there, though—at least I wasn't alone."

Sade felt her stomach twist at the mention of that word.

Alone.

"Have you and April known each other long?" Sade asked, swallowing the lump forming in her throat.

Persephone nodded. "For as long as I can remember. We met Jules here in first year, but even though I didn't grow up with her, I'd do anything for them both."

Sade had assumed they'd all met at the boarding school or even that Juliette had been the childhood friend of April's given how easygoing their relationship seemed. There was sometimes this intensity she felt between Persephone and April, and she had assumed it was their lack of closeness. But it wasn't that at all.

They knew each other too well.

As well as siblings could.

Animosity wasn't always a negative thing; it was sometimes just a symptom of caring for someone deeply.

"Even attend a party for them?" Sade asked lightheartedly in response, just as the sound of screaming students and loud laughter from outside the library reverberated around the building, making the shelves vibrate as more students escaped buildings and stormed around the campus.

"Well, I better be off before it gets worse. Last year on Halloween, I heard that a guy climbed on the roof of the main building and then proceeded to urinate over any-one underneath—I don't want to be his next victim if he decides to strike again this year," Persephone said, recounting this story with a disturbed expression but never quite meeting Sade's gaze.

It felt as though she was either ignoring the question or had momentarily forgotten what was asked. "I'll see you later?"

Sade nodded, and Persephone left.

Leaving Sade at the table, alone.

THE PARTY WAS STARTING SOON.

Baz had arrived, his hair slicked down with copious amounts of hair gel.

In preparation for her own transformation, Sade had fastened a blonde wig to her head, put on layers and layers of brightly colored makeup, and spent most of the time attempting to squeeze into the pink dress she had ordered.

By the time she was done, she had concluded that whoever decided latex was a suitable material for clothes needed to be jailed for their crimes against humanity.

As she stared at herself in the mirror, she couldn't help but wonder what Elizabeth would have worn. It was likely that, like Persephone, she wouldn't even show up to an event like this. Then again, who knew what Elizabeth would really think. Not even Baz seemed to know.

He walked back into her room after going to Seacole House to check on Muffin.

His appearance almost scared her, he looked so unlike himself—which was kind of the point. Baz looked like a frat boy had possessed him. She imagined she looked just as scary.

They were dressed as Barbie and Ken—Baz's idea.

It seemed they would both be suffering, all in the spirit of Halloween.

"You look like you would be friends with the boys at Eton," Sade said.

Baz smiled. "Thank you, and you look like a character from *Made in Chelsea* called Kitty or something."

Sade found his comment ironic, given that she had actually grown up in an area not so far from Chelsea. She was more herself than she had been in a long time, and it was almost comedic that her Halloween costume was not so much a costume after all.

"Well, my middle name, Kehinde, does begin with a *K* . . . so close enough," she said.

She walked over to her laptop and pulled up the school website. She'd been scouring it before Baz came back, specifically, the pictures detailing the updated rooms and amenities in Hawking House.

"I got some pictures of the communal areas in Hawking House. Ideally, it would've been great to have access to the non-communal areas, but we need to make do with what we have." Sade's voice came out more confident than she felt. "The main goal is to figure out what Elizabeth might have done that night. The last time her phone sent out a signal was in that area, so obviously our goal is to find her phone . . . Alongside trying to figure out where she might have gone if she went into Hawking. We want to look for anything weird or suspicious."

"Like the equivalent of the greenhouse's wet soil," Baz said.

"Exactly, we're looking for wet soil," she responded. "Right, let's do this, I guess," Sade said, shutting the laptop closed.

"Ready to attend your first-ever party, Barbara?" he asked as she joined arms with him.

She was terrified.

"Never felt more ready, Kenneth," Sade replied, masking her lie with a confident smile.

As they left, Sade took one look back at the forget-me-not plant Elizabeth had given her. It was now placed in the center of the room by the windowsill. The only thing left of Elizabeth.

It felt as though the plant was watching her as she turned off the lights and closed the door.

Leaving it and Elizabeth in darkness.

HAWKING HOUSE WAS GIGANTIC.

That was the first thing Sade noticed when they arrived at the dormitory building.

She had seen the house countless times before, of course, but had never really *looked* at it. The white-stoned exterior seemed to have regular upkeep, the bushes on the patio of the house trimmed and frequently maintained. Very different from the moss-covered and unkept exterior of Turing. It seemed like Hawking House's care-taker actually cared.

At the door, a student dressed as the devil checked off their names on an official-looking list like a bouncer at a nightclub, before letting them inside.

The common room was also massive. It was triple the size of Turing's and a lot more lavish. With Chesterfield couches, oil paintings, and marble flooring, it was clear to her at least that this house was one the school favored.

It made sense, seeing as most of the swimmers on the boys' team were assigned to Hawking. She wouldn't be surprised if the golden boys of the school got more privileges than just that.

As she entered the crowded common room with Baz, she was surprised to find teachers dotted around the area, watching the students mingle as the music vibrated through the air.

The students didn't seem all that bothered by their presence. Possibly because this kind of surveillance was the norm for them. Even Baz seemed unfazed.

Sade didn't know what she had expected, but she certainly hadn't anticipated see-ing teachers dressed in their own costumes. They stood by the snack tables, supervis-ing the drinks as well as the students.

It felt more like a strange, twisted version of prom as opposed to a high school party in which anything could happen.

"We can split up and do a search of the sections of this floor. You do the common room, I'll check the halls and try the non-communal areas too," Sade whispered.

Baz nodded. "Sounds good."

"I'm going to quickly go over to April to give her my gift; do you see her anywhere?" she said to Baz as she scanned the room, gripping the small gift in her hand. It was hard to tell who was who in the garish costumes.

Baz shook his head. "Maybe she's arriving later?" he said.

"Or maybe she wants to make a grand entrance," Sade said jokingly, just as the music suddenly changed and an upbeat tempo began to play, followed by a booming sound as white fog erupted in the room, making the students step back in shock and the teachers forward in alarm.

From the fog, April emerged with Francis as the opening notes from "You're the One That I Want" from the musical *Grease* began to play.

As the fog dissipated, their costumes came into full view. April was dressed in a skintight black jumpsuit and a pink bomber jacket. Her hair was curled and she was wearing a grin that almost seemed menacing.

Next to her, Francis wore a black leather jacket, with his usual weird gloves. His red hair was slicked back and styled in an old-fashioned manner.

"You were right," Baz whispered.

It seemed that her week of being invited to join April's intimate circle was educational after all.

Cheers erupted around the room as April welcomed everyone to *her* birthday party. Sade spotted August in the corner as April gave her speech, waving the fog away from his face and attempting to cough discreetly.

He wore a black Spider-Man suit and an expression that told her that he was most definitely not looped in to the whole fog and dramatic surprise entrance business.

April's monologue soon came to an end and Sade saw this as her chance to give her the present.

"Hi, Basil," an unfamiliar deep voice said.

Sade turned to look at the owner of the voice, a stranger dressed in a purple coat. She couldn't tell if he was meant to be the singer Prince or Willy Wonka.

"Hi, Kwame," Baz replied, eyes glued to the tall dark stranger in front of them. For some reason, his name sounded familiar to her, but she wasn't sure why.

"You're blond," Kwame said.

"I am," Baz replied.

The guy, Kwame, looked between Baz and Sade and then back to Baz like he was piecing something together. A brief look of disappointment crossed his face.

Sade realized where she'd heard the name before. This was the Kwame whom Elizabeth had teased Baz about. The same Kwame who had helped him get into the email from Elizabeth's "great-aunt."

"You're Barbie and Ken, I'm guessing?" Kwame asked, a soft, sad smile crossing his face.

What he was really asking: *Did you guys come here together?*

Baz nodded, not possessing the ability to read minds the way she could, so Sade had to intercept.

"No—I mean, yes, we are Barbie and Ken but not *Barbie and Ken* . . . if that makes any sense?" she asked.

Kwame blinked at her. "No, it doesn't," he said.

"I mean we're just friends, Baz and I. Two peas in a pod. Platonic buds," she said.

Sade could feel Baz staring at her, probably wondering what the hell she was on.

"Oh," Kwame said, face brightening a little.

Sade patted Baz on the shoulder. "I'm going to go and give April her gift. I'll report my findings later."

Baz still looked confused, eyes darting back and forth between Sade and Kwame, but nodded anyway. "Yes, I'll uhm, see you later."

Sade mouthed: "Have fun," then she smiled at him and moved away, leaving the two boys alone.

April was in the corner, Francis's arms wrapped around her. Sade saw Francis giving April a fond expression as she spoke animatedly to the people already handing her their own gifts.

Sade looked down at the wrapped box in her hand before walking toward the corner April was in, careful not to go too fast and slip. The shoes she was wearing weren't exactly user friendly.

As she moved through the crowd, slowly, she felt herself being pulled back by something—or rather someone.

She turned to see who was gripping her arm and found Captain America staring back at her.

The costumed stranger removed his mask, revealing the smiling face of Jude Ripley. He eyed her costume, looking her up and down like she was a meal. She felt herself instinctively recoil.

"Wow," he finally said.

She crossed her arms. "What?"

He shook his head, eyes meeting hers now. "Nothing. Just that I almost didn't recognize you—I mean, you usually look nice and everything, but wow," he said.

"Thanks," she said. "I'm meant to be Barbie—like the doll."

He nodded, like it made sense to him now. "Where's your Ken?"

Sade gestured to Baz in the corner, laughing with Kwame.

Jude eyed Baz for a few moments and then turned back to Sade. "I could take him."

"What?" Sade said.

"In a duel for your affection, I could take him."

Sade laughed in his face. "Are we in the eighteenth century or something?"

"We could be if Ken over there isn't scared," he replied.

Sade rolled her eyes. "Well, the first thing you should know is, he's just a friend, and second, his name isn't Ken, it's Basil."

Jude's eyebrows furrowed. "Like the plant?"

"Exactly," Sade replied.

Jude hummed, considering it. "I guess he won't mind then if I steal you away to play a round of foosball in the game room."

"You're inviting me to play a game?" she asked.

"Yes."

"What's in it for me?"

"Well, if you win . . . I take you out on a date, and if I win, I take you out on a date," he said, raising his eyebrows suggestively.

"That doesn't sound like fair odds," she said, feeling her stomach twist into tightly wound knots, making her nauseated.

The way he looked at her . . . it made her feel itchy.

Jude shrugged. "Life isn't fair, I guess."

She stared at him for a moment and then she said, "How about if I win, I get something else."

"Like what?"

"A secret," she said.

"A secret?"

She nodded, serious. "Yes."

He looked up, considering it, before looking back down at her. His icy-blue eyes pierced through her like they usually did. "Okay, then, I'll give you a secret—if you win, that is."

Sade glanced at April in the corner, still surrounded by her devoted followers. The gift and the investigation could wait.

"Deal?" he asked, holding out his hand.

"Deal," she said, choosing not to shake it.

• • •

A SMALL CROWD GATHERED TO watch them play in the adjoining game room.

It was slightly nerve-racking. She'd only played foosball a handful of times, and there were the watchful eyes of the bodies around her.

Even August made an appearance, sitting on the sidelines, watching the pair get ready.

Sade heard Jude mutter something to some of the boys on the side, resulting in slaps on his back and a fist bump from one of them.

Juliette grabbed on to Sade's shoulders, pulling her attention away from him. "You have to win. Jude's ego is already unbearably high. You must crush it, Sade. Into a pulp." Given that Juliette was dressed as Cruella de Vil, her words seemed to match the costume.

"I can hear you, Jules," Jude yelled.

Juliette ignored him, and instead gave Sade a thumbs-up, whispering, "You can do this!"

The two moved to their positions on either side of the foosball table. The referee—a student dressed as a Rubik's Cube—announced the game rules, blew a whistle, then yelled, "Start!"

It didn't take long before the game was in full action.

Sade could hear the crowd yelling, screaming their names. She could see Jude sweating and grinning, and she could feel the vibrations of the table as the handles spun and the miniature football players frantically moved about.

It felt like the game had only been going on for moments before she heard the whistle again, and the sound of Jude's teammates screaming and jumping up and down.

Jude held his hand out, like she imagined he did whenever he beat members of the opposition in swim meets. A truce.

"Did I mention I suck at games?" Sade said, still not taking his hand.

Jude smiled. "Didn't need to mention it; I saw it for myself."

"It was a fluke," she said.

"The game is the game," he replied, dropping his hand now.

The game is the game, she repeated inside.

Sade was about to come back at him with a witty retort but stopped when she noticed August slip out of the room. He was looking down at his shoes with a strange expression on his face.

He seemed off tonight.

Her attention was brought back to Jude when she felt him lean in and whisper in her ear, "I'll pick you up tomorrow at five for our date." His voice felt like one million tiny insects were latching on to her limbs and tracing their tiny tentacle-like legs across her arms and back. And then he was gone, off to celebrate with the boys on the other side of the game room.

She felt Juliette pat her on the back. "We'll get him next time," she said.

Sade nodded. "Definitely," she said, gaze going back to the door leading to the main room, where August had walked through. "By the way, do you know where April is? I want to give her this gift."

Juliette eyed the gift, taking it from Sade and shaking it lightly. "A pen?" she said.

Sade was surprised at her ability to guess so quickly. "How'd you know?"

"Years of practice," she said with a smile. "April will like it; she's always writing poems and stuff. I'll show you where she is."

Sade didn't know April wrote poetry. She'd bought the pen because it was one of the only things that could ship in time before today. At least April would have some use for it.

Juliette linked her arm through Sade's and led her out of the game room, through the crowd, and over to April.

"Hello! You look pretty!" April said, sounding the happiest Sade had ever heard her. Then she whispered: "This isn't apple juice." Which immediately cleared things up.

"Hi—thank you!" Sade replied, trying to match her energy, relieved she wouldn't be evicted from the party at least. "I got you a gift."

April's eyes widened and she took the gift, shook it, and smiled. "A pen!"

It was scary how they casually did that.

"Where's French?" Juliette asked.

"He went to find Jude, probably something about swim practice, as usual," April said with a shrug, taking a sip from the cup, eyes widening and moving to focus past where Juliette and Sade were standing and at something behind them.

"Oh my god!" April said.

Juliette turned and did a high-pitched squeal, which only prompted Sade to look at what the two of them were reacting to.

Or apparently who.

April bolted toward the person, hugging them tight. Sade tried to figure out who it was, but it wasn't until April stepped back that she realized.

Persephone.

Sade went still, taking in the completely altered appearance of the girl she had only seen an hour before.

Her blonde hair was now bright red and sticking up in all directions. A miniature golden crown was fastened on top, and her makeup was bold and bright, with crimson-stained lips and with little hearts dotted across her face. She wore a fitted black-and-white suit and sparkly red heels.

"Holy shit, Sephy—you look amazing," Juliette said.

Sade felt her heartbeat quicken in her chest and attributed it to how warm the room was.

"Thanks, Jules—you don't look too bad yourself," Persephone said.

"Are you meant to be David Bowie?" Juliette asked.

"Close," Persephone said with a wicked smile.

"Queen of Hearts?" Sade asked, her voice embarrassingly high-pitched.

Persephone turned to look at Sade and her smile faltered, morphing into surprise as though she hadn't noticed her standing there before.

Sade could feel her skin warm as the other girl gave her a subtle once-over.

Persephone nodded, eyes meeting hers, making her heart go even more erratic. "The one and only."

"I thought you weren't coming," Juliette said innocently, mischief dancing in her eyes.

Persephone tore her eyes away from Sade finally and shrugged. "I didn't want to miss my best friend's seventeenth birthday."

Juliette side-eyed Sade and nodded. "Yeah . . . I'm sure that's the reason."

April placed her hand on her chest, completely ignoring Juliette's comment. "That's sweet enough to make me cry—but as you know, I got my tear ducts removed for my sixteenth birthday, so that, sadly, isn't possible."

Sade couldn't help but wonder if April was being sarcastic. But if she wasn't, it was clear that only one Owens had that procedure. August looked like someone who cried a healthy amount for the average human being.

"Is August around?" she asked, remembering the way he ducked out of the game room minutes before. She needed to focus on her priorities.

"He's probably in his room. He's been in a mood all day," April said, waving her off and taking another sip of her "apple juice."

"Oh—could you tell me what his room number is?" Sade asked.

The three girls looked at her now, silently. Like she had said something inappropriate.

"It's 320. Why?" April asked, an eyebrow arched.

"I was going to check on him—you know, house siblings, it's a two-way street sort of thing," Sade said, trying to sound casual despite feeling like she was suddenly being interrogated.

194

"Hm, that's nice . . . I don't think I've spoken to my house siblings in years. They were *so* annoying, always bothering me about one thing or the other."

"They're meant to, April. That's literally the purpose of the whole thing," Persephone said, tugging April's cup from her grip and taking a swig herself. Making a face when the *juice* hit the back of her throat.

April rolled her eyes. "Whatever—Sade, if you do find my miserable twin, tell him I'm cutting the cake with or without him."

Sade nodded, deciding she wasn't going to repeat that to August. "Will do," she said, giving them a final smile—and Persephone a final glance.

THE SOUND OF "GREASED LIGHTNIN' " blared in the distance as Sade stalked the dark, well-kept halls of Hawking House.

At first, accessing the non-communal areas seemed to be much easier than it looked. The halls were mostly empty, so she could slip between them like an invisible thing. She wandered around the first years' floor for a while, looking for clues, finding none. She did the same on the second floor and was just as unlucky.

However, when she got to the third floor, she finally ran into a problem.

"Hey! You're not meant to be up here," a gruff voice called from behind her as she moved about the third-year corridor.

She turned to find two tall boys dressed like gladiators. One had black hair with waves, and a serious expression. The other, with strawberry-blond curls, just looked confused.

Baz was right about Hades's hounds.

"I'm looking for my friend," Sade said, swallowing hard.

"Which friend?" one of the gladiators asked.

"August . . . he's my house brother," she replied, though they didn't look all that convinced.

"What's his room number, then?" the same gladiator asked, his arms folded, eyebrow raised.

"Three-twenty," Sade said confidently, as though she visited him all the time.

The gladiators looked at each other and then, to Sade's relief, they nodded.

"All right then," the strawberry-blond gladiator said. Without another word, they turned and left her alone.

Out of fear of more hounds, Sade decided to end her search in the non-communal areas as she didn't have any more excuses left.

She found August's room and knocked loudly on his door, waiting for a beat and listening for the sound of movement behind the door. She knocked again, this time hearing a groan followed by footsteps, before the door was yanked open to reveal a pissed-off-looking August.

"I told you, I don't know where he—Sade?" August's annoyance immediately dissolved as he saw it was her, surprise evident on his face.

"Hi," she said.

"I didn't mean to yell at you—I mean, I wasn't yelling at *you*—I thought you were Francis, but anyway, I'm sorry. Hi, come in," August said, stepping to the side and letting Sade into his room. "Sorry about the mess," he said as he shoved things in corners. His costume was half on and his regular clothes were strewn about.

His erratic movements reminded her of Elizabeth on that first day when she'd shown her to their dorm room.

"Is everything okay? You seemed a bit off downstairs—April said you weren't having the best day."

August shook his head. "Of course she'd put it like that. You know, this morning I told her I'd rather practice than show up to a party of people I don't particularly want to be around right now. Know what she does? She calls Maxine and tells on me, so I'm forced to be April's puppet. I'm sure she'll notice that I have no plans of returning to the party soon and tell on me once again."

Sade felt bad for essentially alerting April to the fact that she couldn't see August around.

"Who's Maxine?" Sade asked.

"Our mother," he said bitterly.

Sade's eyebrows went up at that. She'd never called her parents by their first names. She knew it was something people did . . . but still it took her by surprise.

The name *Maxine Owens* sounded familiar. *Wasn't that the designer jewelry brand?*

"Oh . . . well, that sucks. I'm sorry you aren't enjoying your birthday."

He took a seat on his desk chair and looked up at her. "It's okay. Honestly, I'm not really a big fan of our birthday anyway. Never was. It was always April's to celebrate and mine to witness."

Sade nodded awkwardly, not wanting to overstep, but also wanting to provide some comfort.

She looked around his room, taking in the space. He had two massive posters of Michael Phelps hanging near his bed, along with a Phelps quote: "eat, sleep and swim"; a large wardrobe; and a desk. She paused when she realized there was no second bed, just one double pushed to the side.

"No roommate?"

August shook his head. "His room is through there; we just share a bathroom," he said, pointing at a wooden sliding door.

"Wait . . . so you essentially have your own room," she said slowly, in awe at the inequality of it all.

"Yup," he said.

"You lucky bastards. You know us peasants have to share a room half the size of this! Are you guys bribing the school board or something?"

"Perks of Hawking House, I guess," he said with a smile.

"I'm not buying it," Sade said. "I think you guys are up to something."

"I promise, there's nothing sketchy going on. We're just God's chosen ones."

She shook her head. "That's bollocks and you know it."

He laughed at that, and she smiled. "Aha! I knew you were capable of that," she said.

"Of what?"

"Smiling. You haven't done that at all since I've seen you today; you were *really* bringing down the mood."

He huffed, pretending to be offended. "Wow. You're a delight."

"I know," Sade said, walking closer to the beanbag nearby, but accidentally tripping over a discarded hoodie on the floor. "Oh, sorry—" She stopped just as she saw the print on the back of the hoodie.

It looked familiar.

Black with an abstract print—which she could now see was definitely the outline of a fish.

It was just like the hoodie from the CCTV.

She hadn't been able to make out any other details on the footage, but August's hoodie had *Owens* written on it as well as the number 23.

"It's okay—I really should stop leaving my clothes everywhere," he said.

Sade continued to stare at it. "It's a nice hoodie."

"I guess so. It was a gift in first year when I made the swim team."

Sade looked up. "All of you guys got it?"

He nodded. "Yep, everyone. Girls' team, boys' team. I wear it mostly as makeshift pj's. Nowadays, we mainly wear the varsity jackets from our sponsors—Webber gets aggy if we don't. I used to be really proud of it all, being on the team, having the hoodie and the jacket, but being a reserve isn't anything to celebrate these days."

Sade took a seat on the beanbag and crossed her legs. "I think it's pretty cool, actually—being a reserve. And I think you'll be a really good captain someday."

August said nothing at first, then he shrugged. "Maybe."

"I got you a birthday present, by the way," she said, remembering the other box she brought, now tucked away in her purse. She took it out and tossed it to an intrigued-looking August.

He shook it, but unlike April and Juliette, didn't seem to know what it was.

He opened it carefully, eyes widening when he saw the contents of the box. "No way," he said, lifting out the goggles inside.

She had noticed that despite being an *Owens*, August for some reason didn't have a pair of his own Swedish goggles, which, while being weird for an elite swimmer, made sense with the person she understood August to be. He didn't seem all that fussed about trends or high-tech things.

She'd chosen the swimming goggles she'd always used. The best.

"Thank you," he said, eyes glassy.

"Maybe now you'll be as good as I am," she said.

He laughed again. It was music to her ears.

"You're mean, Hussein," he said.

"But fair," she replied.

His smile only seemed to widen and his expression told her that his birthday was no longer quite the awful occasion he had anticipated it would be.

He got up, placing the goggles back in the box and putting it inside his wardrobe somewhere. "I'm going to grab some water. Even though you're mean, I don't mind getting you a drink. Any requests?" he asked.

"Juice is fine," she said.

He nodded. "Will be back soon, just going to the vending machines."

Her mouth hung open. "You guys have vending machines?"

"Of course," he said as he walked to the door, adding as he left: "And an indoor Jacuzzi!"

The boys of Hawking had to have some dirt on Headmaster Webber at the very least, and while Sade couldn't prove it, her gut feeling rarely failed her.

She sat in the quiet room for a few moments before the buzzing started.

August had left his phone behind. It continued to buzz again and again until it fell off the table and onto the floor, knocking his key card off with it.

She uncrossed her legs, reaching forward to pick them both up. But when she glimpsed the screen, her focus halted as the phone buzzed in her hands.

Notifications from some group chat were popping up.

New message from purple dragon: apple juice and vodka aren't a good mix, what was Jack thinking?

New message from green lion: the ratio is way off but gets results

Sade tried to select the message, her curiosity getting the better of her, but August's password stopped her.

As the notifications piled on, the messages stopped showing up individually.

You have 12 unread messages from The Fishermen.

"What the—" she whispered as the buzzing persisted.

The Fishermen . . .

"Missed me?" August's voice rang out from behind her. She dropped the phone back onto the table and quickly readjusted herself on the beanbag.

"No, was more than happy staying here alone reading your list of due assignments on the wall," she said, her heart pounding unevenly in her chest.

"I hope what you read didn't bore you to death," he replied.

Her mind went back to the phone again. Something didn't feel right about it . . .

"Not at all," she replied, standing and taking her phone out of the pocket in her purse. Somehow, she'd already been at the party for a whole hour and hadn't yet done what she'd come here for. "I should go, actually; I promised a friend I'd help him with something."

August looked a little disappointed, but nodded. "Here's your juice for the road," he said.

She accepted the juice box with one hand, keeping the Hawking House key card in the other.

"Thank you, Augustus. Want me to bring you cake from your party?"

He shook his head. "I'm good. I think I'm just going to go for a swim," he said.

"Have fun, fish boy," she said.

He laughed. "I won't lie; I suddenly prefer the name Augustus."

"Too bad," she replied. "I think fish boy suits you really well."

WHEN SADE RETURNED TO THE common room, Baz was nowhere to be found, so she texted him.

S: I almost got caught by some of Hades's Hounds upstairs so didn't really get to explore much of the non-communal areas, also it's way too crowded in here to search properly, but I think I have a plan b for getting into Hawking when everyone's gone—where are you?

Her phone vibrated instantly with a message from the blond in question.

B: Yeah, I tried searching in the game room but there were too many bodies—also I'm near the front section, I lost my ken scarf somewhere

The *front* was relative to where you were positioned in the room.

She scanned the room for his blond mop of hair, but unlike when his hair was bright pink, blond wasn't exactly a unique and easy color to find in this crowd.

"Barbara!" she heard a voice call, and immediately turned to find herself face-to-face with a giddy-looking Baz.

"Did you find your scarf?" Sade asked.

"Nope, still missing. I last saw it somewhere here—I hope the Turing Thieves didn't take it. I'm really fond of that scarf," Baz said solemnly. "How did you manage to escape the hounds without being skinned alive?"

"I told them I was going to August's room, which I actually was," she replied.

Baz raised an eyebrow. "I thought your fling was with Jude?"

"My *fling* is with no one. I was simply hanging out with my house brother, who also happens to be the birthday boy," she replied. "Where is your fling anyway? Kwame, right?"

Baz laughed. "Fling? Kwame doesn't even like me like that."

"Oh yeah? Why did he come up to us earlier, then?" she asked.

"He wanted help with the German homework. Typical jock uses loner boy for help and nothing else."

Sade blinked at him. "Baz."

"Yes?" he replied.

"You suck at German."

"Way to kick a boy when he's down."

She laughed, placing her hands on his shoulders. "*No.* I mean *you really* suck at German. You're the one who always tells me that your teacher begged you to choose a different subject. And the fact that he says this in front of your entire German class . . ."

"Yes, my teacher is a Debbie Downer, what about it?"

It was so obvious, and yet her oblivious blond friend couldn't see it. "Kwame asked you for help in German . . ."

He nodded, realization slowly hitting him. "Oh."

"Yeah." Sade smiled.

"I'll be right back . . . ," he replied, then walked away without another word.

Sade decided to wait on the sidelines while Baz went to find Kwame.

The party was still in full swing.

In the corner by the entrance, she spotted a basket with a small sign above it labeled: LOST AND FOUND. Peeking out seemed to be a small silk cream scarf. One that looked a lot like Basil's Ken scarf.

She walked over to it, and up close there was no doubt in her mind that this was, indeed, the missing scarf. At least they found something tonight after all.

She plucked the scarf out of the basket of long-forgotten items beneath. A treasure trove of lost souls. Some seemed to be years old, with scratches and dust residue. Others clearly newer. Like the shiny metal yo-yo, the beat up purse with the engraving *we're all mad here!*, and . . . a four-leaf clover necklace with the name *Connor* engraved into it.

It reminded her of all the four-leaf clover stickers all over Elizabeth's boots.

I like the stickers, on your shoes, Sade had told her.

They're meant to bring good luck, Elizabeth had replied.

She felt a pang inside.

Her gaze went back to the wonderland purse and she wondered if Persephone had stayed at the party.

A part of Sade hoped she hadn't, so that she could continue blaming her overactive nervous system on the heat in the room and definitely not the unholy blonde—or at least for tonight, as a result of her costume, the unholy redhead.

She pulled her focus from the lost and found basket and looked around the room for signs of Baz.

As her eyes wandered, she spotted a different redhead: Francis. He was outside talking to Jude, looking all worked up about something yet again. She watched him push Jude backward, clearly drunk or on something, only to be dragged back by someone else.

There was a teacher nearby, too busy eating a bowl of Pringles to notice the commotion outside.

"I did it; let's get out of here," Baz said, breathless, as he found Sade again. He took her arm and started walking through the crowd, managing to swipe a box of sweets on the way out. Meanwhile, Sade barely had time to throw her juice box away.

"Did what?" she asked as she followed him.

"I kissed Kwame. And now we must leave before he finds me and asks more questions."

"You what?!" Sade asked as they stepped out into the night.

Baz rubbed his eyes and sighed. "I'm going to avoid him forever now. I'm quitting the rowing team and I might finally make my German teacher happy by quitting that too—"

"What are you going on about? Did Kwame reject you?" she asked, feeling bad for encouraging Baz to go after him. She had been so sure, though.

Baz shook his head. "No, I didn't give him the chance to. Just ran out of there. But it's fine; there's no need to know right now. Even if I embarrassed myself in there, I can simply blame it on the apple juice," he said.

Every day she spent with him, she realized more and more that her new friend was the strangest person she'd ever had the pleasure of meeting.

"You are ridiculous, Basil dos Santos," she said as they walked the path back to Seacole.

"No, I'm Irish," he replied simply.

Once back in Seacole House, Baz made Sade tea and the pair sat in the quiet common room to debrief.

The only sound came from wrappers as Baz worked his way through the stolen sweets.

Sade held up the key card she'd swiped from August's room. The one she hoped would open all entrances of Hawking, seeing as he was the deputy head boy.

"How'd you get that?"

Theft and subtle manipulation, she wanted to say, but instead answered with: "I found it on the ground, and I figured it would be much easier going into Hawking with this on a quieter day when there aren't as many *hounds* around," she said. The lie slipped out so easily, as they always did. She was unsure what Baz would make of her stealing the key from someone.

Then again, he did steal both sweets and an entire live animal from the science labs . . .

"That was lucky," he said, and for some reason it sounded sarcastic, like he could see through the lie. Though it was most likely just her guilty conscience. "How about we go tomorrow morning or afternoon? Sniff out the areas we couldn't today."

"I can't do the afternoon," she said. "I kind of have a date."

Baz paused his eating. "With who? August?" he asked.

She cleared her throat awkwardly before speaking. "Jude, actually."

His eyes widened. "No fucking way—"

"It is the result of me losing a bet; it's not that serious."

Baz sat back, leaning against the wall with a sly smile. "Sure. Morning, then, since you're busy in the afternoon."

She nodded. "Morning works—"

"I wonder if he'll take you to London—that's usually his first move before Paris."

"What?"

"Judas," he replied.

Sade sighed. "I thought we'd moved on from that already."

"I haven't. Not sure that I ever will," he said.

"Anyway, yes, morning. We can meet up at around ten?"

"Works for me," Baz said, still sporting an impish grin as he popped a few sweets from the box in his mouth. Then he placed it on the ground and reached out to the shelving unit nearby for a board game.

"Want to play?" he asked.

She still had some time to kill, since curfews were much later on weekends and, with the Owens party, it seemed today's curfew was even later still. She nodded.

As he set up a game of Connect 4, Sade disappeared into herself. Her thoughts jumped from point to point, from the key she'd stolen, to the date with Jude, to all the things she'd set out to do that hadn't yet been done. Time kept slipping from her grasp, moving on so quickly she could barely keep up.

"All done. I'm yellow, you're red," Baz said, positioning the game between them.

The person going first was decided by rock, paper, scissors.

"Best out of three," Sade said.

He nodded and then held his fist out.

After she covered his "rock" twice with her "paper," the universe decided that Sade would go first.

She inserted her first disc into one of the slots, hearing the familiar sound of the clacking plastic.

"I never understood the logic behind rock, paper, scissors—I feel like, surely a rock could break through paper, especially if it's one of those ones with really jagged edges. Also, scissors cutting through paper doesn't mean the paper is defeated; you aren't broken by a single tear or cut; what message are we sending to children—"

"Basil, it's your turn," she said.

They played two rounds of Connect 4 before moving on to Snakes and Ladders, then Ludo, followed by whatever else Baz could find in the shelves of the Seacole common room (which admittedly wasn't much).

By the time they had played each game in the Seacole common room twice, Baz had lost every single round.

"These games are rigged!" Baz announced while accusatorily pointing at the Connect 4.

"They're not rigged," Sade replied.

"Says you—you've won every single round. It's either rigged or you're using witchcraft."

"Definitely the latter," she said, wriggling her fingers.

Baz squinted at her. "One more round," he said.

"It's almost curfew . . ."

"Just one, I need to win just one."

Sade looked from the clock to the desperation on Baz's face.

"Okay," she said, setting up the game once again. As she moved the pieces back into place, she could feel Baz's gaze resting on her.

As expected, Baz lost once again.

"Okay, so the game isn't rigged. I just suck," he finally declared, now willing to admit defeat.

It wasn't so much that he sucked at games, but that Sade was really good at them.

With all that time locked away inside, she'd had time to practice, and an equally capable opponent to practice with.

And so, she became good at them. Though, maybe good was an understatement.

"You'll improve with time," she said smugly.

He wore a scowl as he packed away the pieces into the box.

"I wish we'd worked out that inscription on the music box. The one with the initials addressed to Elizabeth," he said suddenly.

Sade nodded. "Same, though it's not like we could do much with it now. We don't even have proof it ever existed."

"Maybe it doesn't have to exist. When we were getting ready for the Hawking plan, I was thinking about whether we should be focusing more on the inscription. For all we know, the inscription person could be the same person who sent the email and they might also be the person who knows what happened to Elizabeth that night. Maybe it's our other wet soil."

Sade considered this.

Sometimes to look forward, you have to look back.

"We should do it tomorrow," Baz said suddenly.

"Do what?"

"Find TG. Figure out which students share the same initials in the school records and take it from there."

It was so simple and yet she hadn't considered doing it before.

Sade thought again about Elizabeth's last known movements. That the GPS app had shown she'd been between Hawking House and Newton . . . but still close to the staff quarters.

"Not just students," she said. "Everyone. Teachers too."

21

SUNDAY

THE TEDDY EQUATION

THERE WAS SOMETHING ABOUT SUNDAYS that made Sade feel on edge.

A weird, unsettling feeling that something wasn't quite right.

Perhaps it was the empty promise of a new week.

Or maybe it was that at home, tragedy always seemed to strike on Sundays. Her mum died on a Sunday, and her father would often return home from business trips on Sundays, bringing with him his unpleasant air. Perhaps it was that.

And now it seemed the dread that was always there had been made worse by everything that had happened.

The Sunday morning after the Halloween party, a sharp knock sounded on her door and for a split moment, Sade's mind convinced her that Elizabeth had returned. In those fleeting seconds, before the rational side of her brain took over, her heart felt as though it was ready to burst out of her chest and wither away, the hairs on her arms stood upright, and sweat lightly formed on the top layer of her skin.

Then, when she questioned why she was so scared in the first place, the physical symptoms of her perpetual anxiety subsided and she was able to think clearly once again.

Except when she opened the door, there was no one there. Just a bouquet of sunflowers and a note tucked between the petals.

> *I look forward to seeing you this afternoon—JR*
> *PS. Don't ask where we're going—it's a secret*

She had almost forgotten about the game she had lost yesterday, and the date Jude had promised.

Almost because it had been all she could think about last night.

It wasn't like she *had* to go on the date with Jude; the game was not legally binding. But going would help her figure him out. In the spirit of *keeping your friends close* and all.

She placed the sunflowers next to the forget-me-not plant and lay back down on her mattress, staring up at the ceiling and trying to empty her brain long enough before she had to get up and meet Baz for their *mission* in half an hour.

The plan, they'd decided in the end, was to try snooping through Hawking again, if and only if they were unsuccessful with what Sade was calling *Operation Thistle*: which involved distracting Ms. Thistle so that they could look at all the student and teacher files kept in cabinets in reception.

Anyone with the initials *TG* would be a suspect.

Sade just hoped that any new discovery wouldn't lead to more unsolvable questions. They needed something to take to Webber and Blackburn, to convince them that this was not a closed case—that Elizabeth was not in Birmingham, and could very well be in danger, or . . .

Her phone suddenly buzzed with a message from Baz.

B: There's been a slight Muffin-Roommate domestic, will have to meet you at the main entrance

S: Okay, see you soon, she replied, deciding not to ask any questions.

Her brain was spiraling already as it was. Anxiety jumbled her thoughts into a distorted mosaic of noise. *Jude. Jam. Thistle. TG. Jam. Jude. Elizabeth. TG. TG. TG.*

When Sade closed her eyes, she could still see the engraving on the box.

For my dear Elizabeth—TG

Who was TG?

They were going to find out.

"DREADFUL WEATHER TODAY, ISN'T IT?" Ms. Thistle said as Sade approached the reception desk.

Sade shrugged. "I quite like the rain."

Ms. Thistle looked appalled. "I can never relate to autumn enthusiasts; I'd much rather be in a hot, tropical country than freezing in the middle of nowhere, but alas."

Sade smiled. Ms. Thistle was like a ray of sunshine; everything she did and said could trigger light in even the darkest of places.

"Anyway, enough about the weather. Did you need something, dear? I have been busy all morning trying to get through the paperwork I missed yesterday, what with all the noise and ruckus caused by that party."

"Uhm, yes . . . I was wondering if you had any heating pads. I hit my knee pretty badly last night. I thought I could sleep it off, but it's just gotten worse."

Ms. Thistle glanced down at Sade's perfectly healthy knee and then back up at her face, which she was trying to pull into a convincing grimace. She wasn't sure it was working.

If Ms. Thistle could see through her lie, she didn't show it. "Oh dear," Ms. Thistle said with a frown that looked genuine. "Have you gone to see the nurse?"

She shook her head. "I didn't know where it was."

Also a lie.

The nurse's office was on the other side of the school. It probably would've taken her just as long to get there as it did to get to the reception area.

"The heating pads are in the nurse's office . . . Should I call over the nurse to examine your knee? I can have her bring heating pads with her."

Sade shook her head. "No, it's honestly not that bad. I just wanted something to help with the pain really."

Ms. Thistle's frown only got deeper. "We usually make sure students are examined first before we give out anything like that—"

"It's my uterus," Sade said abruptly, interrupting Ms. Thistle. "Not my knee. I'm on my period."

This made Ms. Thistle's eyebrows go up in surprise. "Oh," she said.

Sade tried to look embarrassed at having to admit she was on her period. Though there was nothing embarrassing about it, she knew it was one of the rare things that made people get all flustered and stop asking questions. "I'm having really bad cramps, and—"

"Say no more," Ms. Thistle said, waving her off. She pushed herself out of the chair. "I'll be back with some heating pads. Could you watch my desk in the meantime?"

Sade gave her a smile. "Of course, Ms. Thistle. Thank you for understanding."

Ms. Thistle returned her smile, patting her on the shoulder. "It's really no problem, dear. You aren't the first student to come to me with a *private issue*, and you certainly won't be the last. I'll be right back."

Sade watched her hurriedly amble down the hallway. She waited until she turned the corner before she took her phone out.

S: She's gone

Baz emerged from the entrance doors, sliding in quietly with the guinea pig cage in hand.

"We have about fifteen minutes before she gets back, I reckon," he said, placing the cage on the counter. "I'll stand watch while you search the cabinets."

Sade nodded, looking behind her for any sign of teachers or security lurking before walking to the receptionist's area and over to a wall filled with rows and rows of cabinets.

"Which one is it?" she asked.

"The gray ones on the far right," he replied in a hushed tone.

She didn't question how he knew this, the same way she didn't question other strange things Baz did. Instead, she quickly made her way over to the pair of gray cabinets, one for students and another for teachers.

She started with the teachers, which didn't take long as there were fewer of them than there were students.

From a quick scan, she determined there were no teachers with the desired initials, so she moved on to the students.

She noticed the small label stuck on top of the second set of cabinets with STUDENTS 1–4 and an arrow pointing downward, where more tiny labels denoted the year each file was from.

Sade pulled open the first years' drawer and found rows and rows of folders of different colors, each color corresponding to a house, all placed in alphabetical order. She moved quickly, scanning the files for the initials of each pupil. She found two TGs: Theresa Gorman and Truman Grant. After a moment, though, she realized that the likelihood of TG being a first year was zero, seeing as they would have only just started at ANA mere weeks ago.

She lingered over Tommy Hilthorpe (TH) and Samantha George (SG), then closed the drawer.

She opened the third years' drawer now, scanning the files and noting familiar names from students she'd spoken to in class or had heard about in passing but didn't know personally.

Sade spotted her file under *H*. It was a solid black color—the color of Turing House's tie—and labeled *Sade K. Hussein*.

She looked up at the clock on the wall. She had about seven and a half minutes to get through them all.

"Found anything yet?" Baz said.

She quickly pulled her file out of the drawer, flipping it open.

"Not yet," Sade replied as she read the first page in her open file.

SADE KEHINDE HUSSEIN
CURRENTLY NO LIVING IMMEDIATE RELATIVES
MOTHER—SUICIDE
FATHER—CAUSE OF DEATH UNDISCLOSED
EMERGENCY CONTACT: YINKA HUSSEIN (UNCLE)

"Sade, we have three minutes, give or take," Baz said, pulling her eyes away from the file.

How had that much time passed already? She stuffed her file back into the drawer and quickly looked over the rest of the names.

Still no luck.

It wasn't until the fourth drawer that she finally struck gold.

Buried in the blue-colored Hawking House fourth years' files was finally a single student with the initials she required.

Theodore Grenolde.

Sade took out his file quickly and skimmed through it.

He was a member of the boys' lacrosse team. A mostly A-grade student with the exception of English, which he was failing. He was applying to several of the top universities in the country and . . . he was the newly elected president of the school's biology club.

"I think I found something!" she said, trying to keep her voice low. Near the back of the fourth years' cabinet she could see the name *Jude Ripley* peeking out.

"We haven't got time, take what we need. I'll return them later."

"Hold on!" she said, pushing the drawer closed. "Okay, I'm done."

She walked out of the receptionist's area a few moments later with the blue file. Baz grabbed ahold of it and placed it discreetly under his arm.

"I have to go before Thistle returns. I'll meet you back at your room."

Sade nodded, not even getting the chance to respond before Baz was off, rushing away with the cage in his hand and out of the entrance.

"Sorry I took so long," Ms. Thistle said, rounding the corner in a hurry, sounding breathless. "They really should move the nurse's office to a more convenient location."

She handed Sade a heating pad and a little labeled pouch with two paracetamols. "There you go. Make sure you rest up."

"Thanks, Ms. Thistle," Sade said, trying not to feel too guilty for lying and making her walk all the way to the other side of the school.

When she got out of the main building and headed down the path to Turing, she made a quick detour over to one of the side paths where no cameras would catch her movements.

Once she was there, she lifted up her sweater and pulled out the other folder she had managed to procure.

The name of the student the folder belonged to was in bold text:

JUDE RIPLEY

. . .

BAZ WAS WAITING FOR HER when she arrived at Turing.

He was seated outside her door, with the file open in his lap and the cage next to his thigh.

"Hey, any wet soil yet?" she asked as she got her key out. She opened her door and Baz followed her in.

"Lots of it, filled with earthworms and dirt," Baz said. "Did you know Teddy was Elizabeth's nemesis?"

"Teddy?" Sade questioned.

"Theodore Grenolde," Baz said. "Or Teddy, as most people call him."

"Her nemesis, how? I didn't know people had nemeses in real life."

"Teddy is the reason she got demoted from her role as biology president. He wanted her spot and ratted her out to Mrs. Choi. I should have suspected him from the start, but honestly, he's rather forgettable, really boring if you meet him in real life."

It was interesting. TG had to be this guy—it was too coincidental otherwise.

"But if they were enemies, why would he gift her a music box?" Sade questioned. She thought about what August had said about Elizabeth seeing other guys too. "Do you think there was more to their mutual hatred than just competition? Maybe they dated. Did she ever talk about him before they became enemies in a way that might suggest that she liked him?" she asked.

Baz shrugged. "Honestly, I don't know. It seems that Elizabeth kept a lot of that part of her life secret from me, so my guess is as good as yours. But I guess we can confront Teddy with this, see what he knows. Biology club usually meets during lunch on Mondays and Wednesdays, so we can find him tomorrow and confront him them," Baz said.

Sade nodded. This lead felt like it was going somewhere. "Sounds like a good plan," she said.

Just then Sade heard the sound of heavy scuffling followed by small squeaks.

"Muffin's awake," Baz said. "Better go and feed her before a repeat of earlier happens."

She figured this had something to do with the Muffin-Roommate domestic he described. "What happened earlier?" she asked as Baz moved toward the door.

"Muffin was hungry and tried to eat my roommate Spencer's favorite teddy bear. She managed to rip an ear off and Spencer went ballistic and threatened to flush Muffin down the toilet. Literally held her over the loo and yelled in her face."

Sade's eyes involuntarily widened. As usual, what came out of Basil's mouth was never what she expected.

"Don't worry; it's all good now. I sewed the ear back on and Spencer apologized to Muffin."

That didn't sound like the Spencer she had met the other day.

"That's weirdly nice of him . . . Do you think he'll tell on you for having Muffin in the room?"

Baz shook his head. "I don't think so; he's not the snitching kind."

Sade nodded slowly.

Muffin squeaked louder, prompting Baz to move closer to the door.

"I'd do our secret handshake, but as you know, that requires both hands and mine are full," he said, gesturing to his hands with his chin. Then his face moved into a creepy sort of sly smile. "Have fun today. Let me know how Paris goes."

She rolled her eyes in an exaggerated fashion. "Will do," she said, and then added in a more serious tone, "but just in case things go badly and I need to escape, could you make sure to be by the phone?"

Baz nodded, the smile settling into a softer line on his face. "Of course," he said.

She said goodbye to both of them, watching Baz enter the lift and disappear before she closed her door behind her and began riffling through her things, searching for appropriate "date-wear." She still couldn't believe that she had agreed to this. It was probably a bad idea.

It is most definitely a bad idea, the voice in her head replied. Followed by the usual predictable line:

You should never have come.

The hissing voice inside continued to ring, sending her threats and warnings in the form of menacing whispers.

She laid out a few options, trying to figure out an outfit that could serve most situations, since Jude was keeping her in the dark about where they would be going.

Each option seemed suitable for a variety of occasions. Apart from anything that required long-distance travel.

She just hoped that wherever Jude was taking her, it wasn't Paris.

22

SUNDAY
NEXT STOP, PARIS

JUDE ARRIVED PROMPTLY AT FIVE p.m., as promised, knocking sharply on her door.

Sade was greeted by his familiar blue eyes and pale face. He was dressed differently than she had thought he would when he wasn't in uniform. Still dapper, but a lot more casual than she had anticipated. Like he was trying to throw her off his *rich f-boy player* scent. He seemed like the sort of guy who would wear an Armani suit to the grocery store.

She was relieved at her own wardrobe choices. She'd decided to go for a maxi dress, leather boots, and a jacket—her hair was now out of her usual braids and tied up in a low bun. Whatever he was planning, she seemed to be appropriately dressed for it.

"Hi," she said.

"You look . . . beautiful," he said, staring at her, taking her in slowly.

She was aware of this fact. It was something people didn't like girls to admit to knowing, but she had always been aware that she was beautiful. A lot of people were. Beautiful, that is.

And a lot of beautiful people had rotten souls. Her mother had warned her of this.

"Thank you. You don't look so awful yourself," she replied, which made him laugh.

"Thank you. Your compliments will get you very far, Hussein."

It was nearly dinnertime in Turing House. Sade hadn't anticipated just how many people would be out of their rooms and waiting to be called into the dining hall. As she walked down the hallways and stairs with the golden boy of Alfred Nobel Academy, she could feel their eyes and their daggers prickling her back.

"Didn't know you were famous," he said to her as they exited the house.

She rolled her eyes. "Yeah, I happen to be the tall, annoying, blond captain of the boys' swim team, so people pretty much treat me like I'm the second coming of Christ."

"Wow, you sound like a piece of work," he said.

"Truly, I am," she replied.

Sade followed Jude along the pathway that led to the main building. Instead of going to the office to sign out, Jude continued walking toward the main gate onto the road.

"Shouldn't we sign out?" she asked.

She had read in the school handbook that leaving the school grounds without signing out or stating your whereabouts could result in a suspension or even expulsion.

"I already signed us out," he said. "Fourth-year privileges mean that I can pretty much go wherever I please on the weekends as long as I have parental consent and I'm back by curfew."

She wondered what other privileges fourth years got—she hadn't read that part of the handbook yet.

"I'll be right back," he said to her before walking up to the security guard that Sade had seen on her first day here. Jude said something to him before slipping him a few notes and returning to her.

"Ready?" he asked.

Sade's eyebrows furrowed. "Did you just . . . *pay* the security guard?"

"Yes," Jude said.

"Why?"

"In case we're late getting back, he'll let us in," he said.

"Why would we be late getting back?" she asked, subtly trying to get him to reveal where they'd be going.

"Trains back from London can be unreliable," he replied with a shrug.

This didn't make her feel any less anxious. If Jude thought withholding information was romantic in any way, it really wasn't. It was just creepy and annoying.

Half an hour later, they were at the train station.

Jude paid for two train tickets and handed Sade her own.

"Where are we going?" she finally asked him as they scanned their tickets and walked onto platform three.

He gave her a sly smile and said: "Paris."

She slowed her pace for a moment. "What?"

"I'm joking. You should see the look on your face," he said with a grin. "You've been at ANA for more than a week. I know you probably heard the rumors about me by now."

She raised an eyebrow. "I don't think I have. What are they?" she asked, the lie slipping out with ease.

"That I'm not that great at relationships, I guess."

"Not that great, how?"

He heaved a sigh as they stopped walking and Sade looked up at him with a questioning expression.

"I don't like to waste time. I usually know pretty early on if someone is right for me, and when they aren't, I end things."

"What has Paris got to do with that?" she said.

He shrugs. "People think I take girls there to give them some fantasy before breaking up with them, but I take people there because I like Paris. It's easy to get to know someone in Paris," he said.

"Why didn't you take me to Paris, then?" Sade asked.

"I didn't want you to think I was playing games," he said, looking directly into her eyes. "I didn't take you there, because I think you're different . . . worthy of more than just Paris."

Sade took a minute to consider his words. "You know, you essentially told me I'm not like other girls, which is not the compliment guys think it is. Makes me think you *are* playing games actually."

He nodded, then as the train to London pulled in, he spoke again. "Noted. Next time, I'll take you to Paris. Just like all the other girls."

The train came to a stop and Sade frowned. "Don't. I hate Paris," she said brusquely, before stepping onto the train and into the first carriage.

THE TRAIN RIDE TO LONDON was silent. Jude was quiet and Sade focused on the passing scenes outside the train window instead of the voice in her head that told her to run.

She considered texting Baz already but wasn't sure how that would help at all. It wasn't like she could tell him where she would be yet.

London was a big place, hard to pinpoint her every move like she could at school.

Then again . . . maybe she could.

She opened up the Friendly Links GPS app and scrolled to Baz's name in her contacts list before pressing Share Location. This way Baz would know where she was regardless. It made her feel like she could finally relax a bit more.

It was raining when they got to King's Cross. Jude took out his umbrella and held it over her head.

"Thank you," she said.

"What can I say, I'm a gentleman," he replied.

"I thought you said you weren't one?"

"You must have misheard me," he said, grinning. Then he led her to one of the black cabs outside the station and opened the door.

"You still haven't told me where we're going, by the way," she said as she climbed into the large taxi.

The car door slammed shut and the cabdriver asked: "Where to?"

And Jude looked at Sade with a mischievous glint in his eye and then replied, "The Victoria and Albert Museum."

When they arrived, the museum was closed.

"It's closed," Sade said, looking at the big sign outside the building. Things always shut early on Sundays. She could have reminded him of this if he'd told her where they were going earlier.

"One moment," Jude said, stepping forward and taking out his phone. He got on a call and she heard him tell the person on the phone that he was here, and a moment later, a security guard arrived and opened the gate.

"Welcome back, Mr. Ripley. Here's the key—*don't* lose this one, please," he said, handing Jude a large brass key.

"Of course," Jude said, holding up his pinkie. "I promise."

The security guard looked like he didn't believe him, as though it was a routine between them now.

"Make sure to lock up, and—"

"Don't touch anything, yes, I know," Jude replied.

"Have fun," the security guard said, this time to Sade.

Different my ass, she thought. It was clear he brought other girls here too. Baz was right about Jude's playboy tendencies. And since she was on to him, she could play with him too.

She gave the security guard a smile that he didn't return; he just walked away, leaving the two at the entrance of the museum.

"Did he just . . . give you the keys to the Victoria and Albert Museum?" she asked as they walked through the gates.

"Yes."

She was pretty sure this was illegal. "Why?"

Jude smiled. "If I told you, you wouldn't believe me, and also . . . I'd have to kill you."

She raised an eyebrow. "You can try; I'm an orange belt in judo," she told him.

He didn't seem fazed by this at all. It was like he was used to his dates threatening him. "You'll have to pin me down sometime," he replied suggestively.

She rolled her eyes, about to tell him that he was clearly a masochist but stopped herself as she stepped into the museum, awestruck. She could hear his shoes as he moved to stand next to her, looking around at the interior too.

It was mostly dark inside, and yet she could see it all so clearly. The marble pillars, the high ceilings, the stone, and the green-and-blue spindly piece that hung from the ceiling like one of Elizabeth's strange plants. She hadn't been to the V&A since she was six. She hadn't been to a museum at all in so many years. She'd almost forgotten how entrancing they were.

They walked toward the only lit exhibition in the corner, their footsteps echoing as they approached the portraits fixed to the walls and the stone statues of naked figures around the room.

It felt like they were the last two people in the whole world.

"It's beautiful, isn't it?" he said. "The museum after dark."

It is, she thought, locking eyes with the girl in the oil painting before her. An amused expression played across her face.

The silence and the darkness made Sade concentrate more on what was around her. It made everything heightened and the paintings even more haunting. Paintings meant to depict something pleasant turned strangely morbid in the dark. The painting of a child in front of her seemed to flicker and distort, and she swore she could see beads of tears on the brims of the child's faintly drawn eyelashes.

It reminded her of the fact that childhood was meant to be like a painting. Colorful brushstrokes clouding your memories of the events and people, nothing particularly traumatizing or morbid for the brain to take note of. So, memories become intricately painted canvas portraits to hang in the museum of your mind and trigger nostalgia for a time you could barely recall.

That's what childhood was *meant* to be.

But hers felt nothing like this painting. There was nothing beautiful or forgettable about her memories.

She looked at the painting again as it flickered back. This time, there was no sign of tears or misery in the child's expression.

Just joy. And the safety net of the child's own mother's arms behind it.

She nodded finally, her own eyes glassy as she replied, "It is beautiful."

THE PAIR SPENT ANOTHER TWO hours in the museum, observing the art and then eating pastries in the closed Victoria and Albert café. Jude seemed to also have some kind of arrangement with the staff members there, tipping them as they left.

By the time they got back to Alfred Nobel, it was already nine and Sade was exhausted.

As they walked along the path to the school, Jude stopped abruptly, checking his phone.

She peered at the screen, seeing the notifications lighting up. She wondered if he had been texting other girls while they were out. She wouldn't be surprised, given his reputation.

"I know a secret pathway," he said, putting his phone away now.

"Why do we need one? I thought the guard was going to let us in."

"This way is faster, and less of a headache if the matron catches us, trust me," he replied, basically ignoring her question.

She didn't trust him, but still she followed him to a side path with stairs that seemed to lead to a tunnel. In the tunnel there was a gate, and he pushed in numbers on the old-fashioned metal keypad. The gate opened.

Before she knew it, they were climbing more steps again. This time, the steps brought them up to the quad area behind the main building.

"See," he said as they came up from the tunnel.

Sade was still processing the fact that they had literally come from a tunnel underground outside and were somehow now inside, minutes later.

"The tunnel is only used by teachers and security at the school, and sometimes when we have away meets, Coach takes us under the tunnel to make leaving and entering the school more efficient."

Sade nodded. "And I'm guessing you have the password to the gates because you paid the security guard to tell it to you."

"Yes. The password is changed every week, so I asked him for it."

"For a price," Sade replied.

He smiled at her, like the casual displays of his wealth were fun to him.

"Yes. For a price—although I'm not sure many people at this school could charm the security as well as I can."

"Is that what you did at the museum too? Charmed him with money?"

Jude nodded. "Something like that."

"Stop talking in riddles."

"I'm not."

"You are. I want a straight answer. How much does it cost to go into a museum after its closing?"

Jude stared at her for some time and then he finally spoke clearly.

"It's not as much as you might think, not when your mother is a countess anyway," he said.

Sade raised an eyebrow. "Countess?"

"Told you, you wouldn't believe me if I told you."

"No, I believe you; it's just, wow." She laughed.

"What?"

"Nothing. Really. I just didn't know counts and countesses were still a thing."

"They very much are, and my mother takes the title as seriously as she does the abandonment of her children," he replied.

"How Victorian," she said.

Jude insisted on walking Sade back to Turing House, and she let him. When they finally arrived in front of the near-black building, he placed one of his hands in his pocket, using the other to run his hand through his hair as he looked at her.

On his forearm she spotted a tattoo she hadn't seen before, usually hidden by his uniform. It seemed to be a badly drawn fish and underneath, *JR*.

"Interesting tattoo," she said pointedly.

He looked down at his tattoo like he'd forgotten it was there, then just smiled at her. "Did you have a good time today?" he asked.

"It was nice," she said.

"Just nice?" he replied, stepping closer.

She nodded and he leaned in close. "I'll need to do better next time, then."

"How are you so sure there'll be a next time?" she asked, edging back a little.

He shrugged and Sade remembered what August said about Jude.

Have you met Jude Ripley? You always say yes.

"Go out with me again next week," he said, his face so near to hers she swore she could see into the dark depths of his soul.

Go out with me. It wasn't a question.

"I'll think about it," she said.

Jude tried to look unaffected by the semi-rejection. "Okay," he said, "good night."

Without another word, he walked away, back down the path they had come from. She watched after him for a few moments, finally exhaling, not realizing how much anxious breath she'd been holding in, and then turned toward the entrance of her dorm, tapping her key card to unlock the door.

IT WAS MUCH QUIETER THAN it had been when she left. Curfew was approaching, and the residents of Turing knew better than to test Jessica's patience.

She made her way up to her floor using the stairs instead of the French lift, which seemed to be temporarily out of order.

When she finally got to the third floor, she let herself catch her breath before turning into the hall where her room was.

When she reached her door, she noticed a package outside with a label stuck on the side. The mail days, when students at Alfred Nobel would receive their official post for the week, happened on Fridays, not Sundays.

Unlike her fellow dorm neighbors who would squeal at the sight of a care package from their mothers or a gift card from their nannies, Sade never received any official mail.

Could it be that a distant relative had sent something? It was highly unlikely, given how much her extended family hated her, but still she felt a jolt of hope inside when she saw it.

She got closer and went to reach for it, stopping when she saw the name on the label, printed in large capitalized text.

ELIZABETH WANG.

SUNDAY
THE LIGHT BULB MOMENT

SADE HAD ALREADY CROSSED SO many lines since she arrived at the school.

She had gone through her missing roommate's things, broken into the CCTV office, and extracted confidential student files.

As she sat with the unopened package on her bed, she wondered, *How far is too far?*

Had she already crossed the threshold of what was redeemable, or was there still hope? It was hard to tell.

The package was light and had patterns of sea animals dotted all around, from octopuses to seahorses.

Before she could think up any more reasons not to, her fingers began to lift the tape around the package, the brown wrapping paper slowly unfurling as her heart hammered away.

When she was done undressing it, she held it up, surprised at its contents.

Light bulbs.

Specifically, a box of UV light bulbs.

That was it?

Sade opened the box the light bulbs were in, hoping to find something—anything else that might give her more of a clue as to what this meant.

But it truly was just light bulbs.

How disappointing.

At least with the music box, when she'd snooped then, she got an inkling of something. The invite she never got to decode, the written notes in Elizabeth's handwriting, and, of course, the engraving.

All this box produced were bulbs and sea-related wrapping paper.

She'd hoped the universe had been kind and sent something useful, like the contents of the original box. But, instead, she got *this*.

As Sade took in the nothingness, her mind snapped back to earlier with Jude's weird fish tattoo, then to the music box and Elizabeth's notes, and then to the party.

To being in August's room . . . notifications with the weird usernames that came from the group chat with the even weirder name.

The Fishermen.

She hadn't put it together before, why it had given her pause in August's room when she saw the name of the group.

What were the odds that the same Fishermen Elizabeth had scrawled on the notes in the music box had anything to do with all this? *Fishermen* wasn't that common of a word in day-to-day conversations.

Yes, it could be a coincidence.

But Sade didn't believe in coincidences.

MONDAY

"I HAVE A RANDOM QUESTION," Sade said.

It was Monday morning and she was seated opposite Baz, eating breakfast in the Turing dining hall.

He'd been eating breakfast at Turing since last week, without fail.

"Ask away," he said.

"Is it normal to receive packs of bulbs?" Then she lowered her voice a little. "I got a package last night addressed to Elizabeth with light bulbs in it."

His eyebrows knitted together. "I mean, the school can be quite liberal with supplies. I get a package of things every few weeks like tissue and bulbs and whatnot. Maybe it was dropped off for Elizabeth out of habit."

She nodded.

It made sense, and yet she wasn't sure that was all there was to it.

"Are you going to eat all that?" Sade asked as she watched Baz attempt to fashion some structure out of his toast and hash browns.

"Of course," he said, sounding somewhat offended.

"We only have"—she checked her phone—"twenty minutes left if we want to be on time for class. And I still have to get my stuff."

"You clearly have no faith in my abilities," he replied as he took a bite of the toast on the top of the pyramid he had built.

"Basil, what on earth are you doing here?" a voice suddenly asked.

Baz looked up at Jessica, toast hanging from his mouth and his hand gripping the pot of baked beans he had been dipping the toast in.

"Eating," he replied, his voice muffled as he chewed.

"I've told you countless times that you can't eat here."

"And I've told you to show me the rule book where it says that," he replied.

Jessica disliked Baz more than she disliked Sade, and Sade suspected that he had been kicked out of Turing plenty of times in the past, long before Sade even arrived at ANA.

"If I catch you here again during breakfast, I'm going to report you to Headmaster Webber and request that you face suspension," she said, voice as pinched as her expression.

Then she walked off, ready to torture more poor souls so early in the morning.

Baz continued eating his food, unaffected by Jessica's threats.

When they were finished with breakfast, Sade went up to grab her things from her room while Baz waited outside for her. She threw random textbooks and folders into her bag, almost knocking over the light bulbs on her table.

"You should just pack before breakfast," Baz said as they hurried out of Turing.

It would make her life easier, but then that would require her to be an organized human being. Something she once was, but since starting boarding school, had seemed to have lost.

"I'll see you at the science block at lunch for mission *TG*?" he said, mouthing the last part as he walked away from her to his own classes.

Mission TG was to ambush Theodore Grenolde and hopefully finally find out how all these pieces fit together.

"See you," she replied with a nod, waving as he walked through the doors and left her outside.

She had English first period and headed to A block, walking into Mr. Michaelides's class, where she took her usual seat.

Mr. Michaelides was writing the learning objectives as students slowly piled into the small classroom. For once, she was one of the first to arrive, though she wasn't quite sure how she'd managed that.

She watched the door for a moment, then pulled out the text they were reading this week—*A Streetcar Named Desire*.

"Hi," Persephone's voice rang clearly. Sade looked up instantly as Persephone took the seat next to hers.

The last time she'd seen her was at the Halloween party, two days ago, dressed as the Queen of Hearts. Persephone still had streaks of temporary red dye in her hair, making her usual bleached hair look more like a strawberry blonde.

"Hey," Sade replied.

Mr. Michaelides's voice boomed over everyone. "I'm going to be reshuffling the class a little today so you can analyze the text with a partner you're not so used to speaking to." This prompted groans and loud sighs. "Exchanging new ideas is a good thing!" Mr. Michaelides continued brightly.

"I guess I'll see you at lunch, seeing as Mr. M is probably splitting us up," Persephone said jovially.

"Yes, though I might be late today; I've got biology club."

Persephone raised an eyebrow. "You're interested in biology?"

Not in the slightest, she thought.

"Trying something new."

Persephone nodded, standing up from her seat. "Well, I hope you have fun . . . trying new things."

And then she smiled at her and Sade wondered if Persephone knew that she had the most infectious smile in the entire world.

Maybe even the universe.

BIOLOGY CLUB TOOK PLACE AT the beginning of lunch and welcomed all parties interested in the pursuit of biological knowledge.

Or at least that's what Theodore Grenolde said when he addressed the newcomers to the club.

Today Sade and Baz were those people.

"Grab your lab coats, gloves, and goggles and make sure that if you're handling any of the animals, you do so with care. We recently had a guinea pig and hamster debacle that resulted in the loss of one of our beloved guinea pigs," Theodore said.

Sade knew the guinea pig in question was very much alive, living out her best life in Baz's dorm room. But of course, she wouldn't say anything about that to the biology club president.

Baz had a complete poker face, like he wasn't the culprit.

"I'm going to split you all into groups. Half of us will be doing some experiments on plants and the others will be tending to the hamsters at the back. Those of you lucky enough to be in group two, be careful with the hamsters. They're dreadful little creatures; all they do is shit themselves and then die. Mrs. Choi has warned about not letting any more premature deaths or missing rodents happen."

Teddy began sorting them all, assigning them to either group one or two.

Ones were to be with Teddy, experimenting on plants, and twos were to go with his assistant—a pale girl named Lauren, who had a pink tie—to be with the animals. Sade counted down the order as he sorted, trying to determine what number she'd be given.

The odds were again never in her favor.

Before she could subtly shuffle down and maneuver herself so that she could be sorted correctly, Theodore was already standing next to her, glaring at Baz.

Teddy wore a grimace as he looked at Baz. "I'm changing the order: You'll be in group two," he said.

"Hey, how is that fair?" Baz said.

"It's fair because I'm the president and I make the rules and my rules state that if I don't want the best friend of my sworn enemy in my group, then I don't have to have him there."

Sade couldn't believe he was serious about this enemy thing. It made him look even more suspicious.

Teddy assigned Sade to his group, then moved on to the remaining lot still waiting to be sorted.

Baz muttered something under his breath about Teddy being a dictator, once he was out of earshot.

"What now?" Baz asked.

"I'll try to see what I can get out of him, then we'll confront him after the club finishes."

Baz nodded and went over to the other side of the group, with the rest of the twos, making sure to return Teddy's death glare.

Sade followed Teddy and the group over to a table with a bunch of leaves on them.

While he explained something Sade did not have the brain capacity to understand, she studied him.

He was a medium-height, lanky boy with thick brown hair and freckles all over his face.

Beneath his lab coat, she could see his blue-and-black Hawking House tie.

Was it possible that he was one of the *other guys* Elizabeth had been talking to? Is that why they were enemies?

"These plants secrete pheromones, which are special chemicals that they use to communicate with other plants—"

"Is that like the love hormone in humans?" Sade asked.

Teddy's head snapped up and he looked at her directly. "Kind of—the hormone you're talking about is oxytocin, but we do produce pheromones. Anyway, back to the plant pheromones—"

"So we're like plants?" someone else asked.

"That's a complicated question, yes and no. Depends on what you believe, I guess, but there's evidence that suggests that humans did evolve from—"

"My sister has pheromones—" another first year said.

"Please stop interrupting me. I can answer all your questions one by one, but you're going to have to let me finish first," Teddy said, clearly growing annoyed with the group he selected for himself.

A second year raised their hand and Teddy sighed, nodding at them.

"Can I join the other group?" they asked.

Teddy nodded, defeated. "Go ahead," he said.

They smiled and pulled off their gloves, rushing over to the group on the other side of the classroom.

"Any more questions? Specifically about plants, please," he asked.

Sade raised her hand this time.

"Your question . . . ? Sorry, I didn't catch your name," Theodore asked.

"Sade," she said.

"Yes, Sade, what is your question?"

"It's to do with skullcap plants. Mrs. Choi said there were some in the greenhouse."

Teddy looked grateful for a science-related question and so he nodded.

"Yes, what about them?"

"I heard they're very hard to keep alive in comparison to the other plants in the greenhouse, such as the monsteras—why is that?" she asked.

"Well, I imagine they need to be watered as frequently—I won't lie, though, I'm not so well versed in the goings-on of the plants in the greenhouse; I haven't really been up there," he said.

"Oh, that's strange," Sade said.

"What's strange?" Teddy replied with a raised eyebrow.

"I went up to the greenhouse a few days ago with Mrs. Choi and it seemed that the plants had been recently watered and tended to. Mrs. Choi said that the president of the biology club takes care of them, so I figured you'd know about them," Sade said, lying through her teeth.

She wasn't quite sure what she was hoping for in this line of questioning. To have her intuition pick up on his guilt? To maybe see his reaction, see if he looked surprised or confused or maybe something else entirely?

But instead, Teddy's lip curled and he looked . . . annoyed. It was clear that he knew that it was Elizabeth whom Mrs. Choi would have been referring to.

"Mrs. Choi is mistaken, *this* president doesn't," he replied without hesitation, then proceeded to grab a bottle of some solution. "I take it that's the end of the questions now; time for more important and relevant things. Such as testing the pH of the surface of this plant," he announced, not looking at Sade again.

Soon biology club was over, only lasting about twenty minutes.

Sade walked over to Baz, who was in the corner of the lab talking to one of the hamsters.

"I didn't get much out of him. He's quite prickly," she said, pushing her goggles up to rest on her head as Baz placed the hamster back in its cage.

"I'd use a *different* adjective to describe him, but yeah, Teddy isn't the easiest to speak to. I've only interacted with him in passing, but Elizabeth said he's a giant a-hole most of the time."

Sade nodded in agreement, then turned to analyze Teddy once again.

He was by the front of the class explaining some science-y thing with the most condescending tone she'd heard—after maybe Jessica.

When she'd initially imagined TG, she imagined a faceless person with a menacing grin. Not a nerd with a god complex.

"Let's confront him before lunch is over. I'm starving," Baz said.

"**WHAT DO YOU WANT, BASIL?**" Teddy asked when they approached him.

"A truce," Baz said.

Sade tried not to look surprised. She had no idea where this was going.

"A truce?" Teddy questioned.

Baz nodded. "Yes, I don't think you need to hate me because you hated Elizabeth. I know you always disliked her because she got crowned as president instead of you—"

Theodore scoffed. "That's not why I dislike her."

"That's what she always told me," Baz said with an innocent shrug. Which made Teddy's face redden and his eyes blaze with a subtle anger.

Baz was good at this. Good at finding his buttons and pushing them.

"Of course she'd tell you that. She has no idea what integrity looks like—" Teddy said, but Baz cut him off.

"So what is the reason, then? Were you guys ever friends? Or has it always been this way—hate at first sight, if you will."

Teddy sighed. "The science expo," he said.

Baz looked as confused as Sade felt. "What?" he asked.

"You know, the international science expo—happens twice a year. You are her best friend; I assumed you'd know about its existence."

"Oh, is it that science convention thing in Scotland or something?" Baz asked.

Teddy rolled his eyes. "Yeah, that science convention thing in Scotland or something," he mimicked.

"What's that got to do with you and Elizabeth?" Sade asked, speaking up for the first time in the exchange.

Teddy looked at her, surprised, like he hadn't noticed her there before. "It has everything to do with her. I was meant to go there and showcase my project in my second year, but Mrs. Choi picked Elizabeth instead of me. That was okay; I like a little healthy competition. Then came third year. I spent months working on my project, and Elizabeth destroyed it—"

"How do you know she destroyed it?" Sade asked.

"She apologized. She'd conveniently, 'accidentally' knocked it off the table."

"That must have made you very angry," Sade said.

"Only for a little while; karma came to her in the end."

Sade saw Baz's face harden. "What's that meant to mean?"

Teddy shrugged with a smile. "You don't see her here anymore, do you?"

Sade felt her heart go still in her chest.

Was Teddy admitting to something? Should she take out her phone to record this conversation—or rather this confession?

"Wh-what did you do to her? Are you the reason she's missing? Did you take her?" Sade said.

Now Teddy looked confused.

"Sorry?" he said.

"What do you mean about karma?" Baz asked, his voice low as he stepped closer to Theodore.

Teddy's Adam's apple bobbed in his throat as he stared Baz in the eye. Sade could see his fingers vibrating by his side.

She was scared for Teddy's answer.

Was she right about TG all along? Teddy had hurt Elizabeth because of some trivial academic rivalry?

"I told Mrs. Choi that she killed the class hamster and she got demoted from president, which meant she was disqualified from this year's science expo so I got to go."

"Oh," Baz said.

Sade's muscles were still tense, but her heart started beating steadily once again.

"What did you mean by taking her and her being missing. I thought she dropped out?"

Sade shook her head quickly. "I was just . . . uhm . . . joking," she said weakly.

Teddy looked irritated. "You're not funny."

"That was all it was, then, between you guys?" Baz asked. "Did you see her at all on the Monday she . . . left?"

Teddy shook his head. "I wasn't even on the school grounds that week. I was at the expo."

"Do you have proof of that?" Baz asked.

"Is this an interrogation or something?"

Baz smiled. "Yes, proof, please."

Teddy stared at them both for several moments and for whatever reason, obliged. He took his phone out of his pocket, tapped the screen a few times, and then presented a picture of himself standing in front of a banner that read 53RD SCIENCE EXPOSITION GLASGOW, holding a giant bronze trophy. On top of the picture was the date it was taken. That Monday afternoon, three weeks ago. Like he'd said.

"Happy?" he asked.

TG wasn't Teddy Grenolde.

"Delighted," Baz said.

"I only came in third place, sadly, so you can go and tell Elizabeth and have her rub that in my face. But at least I got a trophy. She's never placed in the top five," he said smugly.

Sade looked at him, disturbed.

"I'm sure Elizabeth will lose plenty of sleep over your *third place* trophy," Baz replied sarcastically.

Teddy's face screwed up a little and then he gave Baz a clearly forced smile. "A plant-themed name like yours, wasted on such an unremarkable human being."

"I could say the same about you, Teddy, nothing cute or snuggly about you."

Theodore smiled. "You're funny."

"I know," Baz replied.

Sade couldn't tell if the pair were friends or enemies now. Perhaps both.

"Are you two done wasting my time now? I need to clean up before the end of lunch."

"We're leaving," Baz said, backing away. "Don't get too excited."

"I'll try not to throw a party," Teddy replied, scowling at them both.

As they discarded their lab coats and exited the biology room, Sade heard Teddy shout: "Don't come back to my club again, Basil."

"I love you too," Baz yelled back.

Once they were out of the science building, Baz looked at Sade wearily. "Well, that was yet another dead end," he said. "He isn't TG, which means that TG might not be the initials of a name."

"What else could they be?"

"I'm not sure," Baz said, running a hand through his blond curls. "I just know that I no longer feel hungry. Will you be okay at lunch without me? I think I'm going to go and lie down in the nurse's office."

Sade nodded. "Want me to accompany you?" she asked.

He shook his head. "I'm good—we should meet up after school, though. We can watch a movie to take the edge off from everything."

"Sounds good, what movie?"

"*Shrek*, that movie always makes life feel less like shit."

"*Shrek* it is," Sade replied.

Baz gave her a thumbs-up, walking backward now. "I'll see you later?"

"See you," she said, waving at him.

As she walked over to the lunch hall, her mind was still with Teddy. Specifically, his initials.

What else could the engraving *TG* mean?

TG.

The Fishermen.

What did it all mean?

Maybe she needed to ask people who would know things Baz might not. People with encyclopedic knowledge of the goings-on of the school.

People like the *Unholy Trinity*.

THE LUNCH HALL WAS STILL filled with students when Sade arrived, but she also didn't have much of an appetite.

She spotted the back of Persephone's strawberry-blonde head and approached the table where the unholy trio sat, noting how empty the table was now.

"Hello," she said, taking a seat.

She barely got any acknowledgment, with Juliette too busy on her phone—most likely texting her secret boyfriend—and April busy with fixing her hair.

Persephone replied on behalf of them. "Hey, how was biology?"

"You take biology?" April asked, now paying attention and looking a little disgusted.

"No, I just tried out the lunchtime club they run," she replied.

"That's worse," April muttered, going back to fixing her hair.

Sade just smiled at that.

"I have to take biology; it can be really interesting sometimes," Juliette said.

"In what world?" April asked.

While Juliette started listing all the fascinating aspects of the subject, Sade glanced up at the large clock on the wall. There was only ten minutes left of lunch.

She didn't have long.

"Have you guys ever heard the phrase *the Fishermen* around the school? Is it some kind of ANA lingo or something?" Sade asked, cutting Juliette off midsentence.

Juliette looked at Sade and then paused before shaking her head. "I can't say it rings any bells."

"Same," April replied while tapping on her phone. Sade wasn't convinced she had even heard the question.

Persephone, on the other hand, had clearly heard her. Persephone's fork clattered on the ceramic plate, and her expression instantly shifted.

"Persephone?" Sade asked.

Persephone blinked like she was snapping out of something. "No, I haven't heard of it either," she said, looking away from Sade now.

She was hiding something; otherwise, why act like that? Why act like the phrase had electrocuted her?

The warning bell sounded and April finally put her phone down. "I need to get something from my locker before class. You guys coming?"

"Sure," Juliette said. Persephone stood with her, still avoiding Sade's gaze.

"How about you, Sade?" Juliette asked.

"I have to meet a friend," she lied.

Juliette nodded and waved, and before she knew it, Sade was alone at the table.

Her brain was turning over a new question.

Why was Persephone lying?

AS EXPECTED, PERSEPHONE WAS IN the library after school, working in her usual corner.

Sade was supposed to meet Baz for the movie, but first she had something she had to take care of.

S: Meet me at the library, she messaged Baz.

"Hi," Sade whispered, taking a seat in front of Persephone.

"Hey," Persephone whispered back.

"We need to talk about the Fishermen."

Persephone shot her a look. "I told you I don't know what or who that is."

Sade looked at her, tracing her face for signs she was telling the truth.

"I don't believe you."

Persephone stayed quiet for a few moments. Her face slowly twisted into a frown. Then she shut her textbook and grabbed Sade's hand, pulling her up from the chair and walking toward the stairwell.

Once through the library door, she let go of Sade's hand and crossed her arms.

"You can't go around asking people questions and then calling them liars. It's a shitty thing to do."

"I'm sorry," Sade said, taken aback by Persephone's sudden forwardness.

Persephone looked at her, expression softening a little. "Okay."

"It's just . . . I was worried about my old roommate. Elizabeth. She'd mentioned that word in passing, *the Fishermen*, and it just seemed odd. I also heard August say it once and thought it was too much of a coincidence."

Persephone folded her arms. "Didn't your roommate leave?"

Sade nodded. "Yes, but . . ." She wasn't sure whether she should be honest. "Something feels weird about the way she left."

"I thought you barely knew her?"

"Yeah, I didn't, not really."

"So why are you putting so much effort into this girl?"

Sade couldn't explain it, not fully.

"We didn't know each other, but we were friendly—sort of. She was nice to me even though she didn't have to be. And I feel like something weird happened with her before she . . . left. And I'm trying to figure out what."

Persephone nodded. "She used to be April's roommate, you know. Your friend."

I know, Sade almost said, but didn't.

"What happened?"

Persephone shrugged. "I don't know all the details. But I know they hung out and then Elizabeth moved out and they stopped talking altogether. Juliette thinks it's the August thing, but I don't think April is that petty."

"The August thing?" Sade asked, wondering if it was about them hooking up. It seemed likely, but seeing how vague August was about it, and how Baz hadn't known, she'd assumed it was a secret.

"Yeah, August and Elizabeth. They were apparently dating for most of first and second year. Jules thinks April got upset about them sneaking around. Who knows what really happened. All I know is, April kicked Elizabeth out of their room and Elizabeth moved into the dorms toward the end of second year."

They were . . . *dating*. For nearly two years. Not hooking up casually like August had implied.

She was in such a state of shock she barely registered her phone buzzing in her hands. She looked down at the screen, expecting a message from Baz, but instead her notifications showed her a preview of a photo attachment from Jude.

J: You were swimming in my dreams last night

It took her a moment to realize that Persephone was also distracted, staring down at the phone with Sade. Sade felt her face warm and she quickly pocketed her phone.

Before she could comment on the August and Elizabeth revelation, Persephone was speaking again. "I take it the rumors are true, then. About you and Jude," she said, her voice steady but her eyes telling a different story.

"There's no me and Jude, we're just . . . hanging out," Sade said, which made it sound like there was definitely a her and Jude.

Persephone's eyes looked bright and angry and a little sad all at once. "You should stay away from him. He's a player and he will only hurt you."

"You seem to hold rumors to the same standard as truth," Sade replied.

"Well, rumors are just well-disguised truths, more often than not. I'd believe the rumor," Persephone said in a snippy tone.

"So you think I'm lying about Jude?" Sade asked, feeling defensive.

Who was Persephone to accuse her of lying anyway? Thinking she knew everything when she didn't.

"Didn't say that."

"You implied it, with your whole spiel about rumors being some version of the truth. You should learn to think for yourself and not go around spewing baseless accusations."

Persephone's eyes dimmed and narrowed, as though Sade had blown out the light source as she spoke. "Everything I know about him isn't because of some silly made-up rumor a first year started. I know this because Jude used to date April and he broke her. If it were up to me, we'd never hang around him, but Jude is August's best friend and August is April's brother and April is my best friend. She won't like that you're dating him either. You should delete his number, pull away from him. He's not company you wish to keep. Trust me."

Jude and April dated? That wasn't something she expected to hear either.

And now Persephone was asking Sade to stay away from him because of their bad blood. April had probably heard these *rumors* and asked Persephone to warn her off. Persephone was merely April's messenger.

"I can look after myself, thank you," Sade said.

Persephone's arms dropped to her sides and she gave Sade a look she had never given her before.

It was a look of both disdain and fear.

"Good luck with that," Persephone said sharply, before turning and pushing the door back into the library so hard Sade thought the hinges would fly off.

Sade breathed a sigh and followed after a moment, noticing Baz now seated on the table she was at before, holding a bag filled with snacks for their film night.

Persephone's things were still there, but there was no sign of Persephone.

"Did I miss something?" Baz asked. He must have seen Persephone storm out.

Sade shook her head.

Another lie.

She needed that distraction more than ever now. "*Shrek* awaits us," she said, forcing herself to smile.

"Is it weird that I kind of see what Fiona sees in him?" Baz asked as they made their way out of the library.

"Yes, very weird," she replied.

24

TUESDAY

FRIEND OR FOE

FOR THE FIRST TIME IN days, Sade didn't sit at the lunch table with Persephone and her friends. Nor did she sit next to Persephone in English.

The revelations in the library's stairwell had made things tense and awkward, and Sade was pretty sure she was no longer welcome in their group.

Instead, she spent lunch with Baz in the Seacole common room.

Baz lay flat on his back and Sade sat on the sofa, doing her Mandarin homework last minute.

"What is it called when you want to sleep for a year instead of constantly worrying whether your best friend is alive or dead?"

"Sounds like a healthy response to me," Sade replied.

Baz sighed quietly, exhaustion stretching his voice. "I wish there was a pill for this. Maybe Jude will have something to help me feel numb enough to sleep properly again."

Sade looked up at the mention of Jude. "What do you mean by that?"

"Judas, he sells pills," Baz replied.

Sade tilted her head. "He's a drug dealer?"

"Mm, or a pharmacist, whatever you want to call it. I've never gotten anything from him before. Was too scared I'd get hooked on something—you've seen my Jammie Dodgers issue."

Sade's mind was whirring a little. Jude. A drug dealer.

"You look shocked. Didn't you know? I thought it'd be common knowledge, but I guess because you're new . . ." Baz's voice began to filter away as Sade considered what that meant.

Sade shook her head. "I didn't know . . ."

"Well, now you do. Maybe you can be his mafia wife or something—" Baz started, but was cut off by Sade lobbing a cushion at his face.

After a few moments of silence, Sade spoke again. "Don't do it."

"Do what?"

"Pills."

Baz's eyebrows raised in surprise.

"I won't; don't worry."

Sade nodded, satisfied with his answer, and went back to looking over the vocabulary on the page.

"Sade," Baz said suddenly and quietly.

"Yeah?" she said, glancing up.

Baz covered his eyes with his arm.

"Between the email ghost, the music box, the lack of concrete evidence for anything, and no grown-up believing a word I say . . . I wonder if there's even a point in trying anymore. I know saying that makes me a shit best friend and I will probably never forgive myself for this, but I don't know if I can carry on."

"Carry on with what?"

There was a moment's silence before he spoke again. "Everything," he said. "Just everything."

Sade watched him quietly, unsure of what to say. She could see water slip down the side of his face, heading toward his ear. Tears.

"Ignore me; I'm just tired," he said with a sniff.

"Want to go and sleep?" she asked. Baz nodded silently.

Sade pushed her worksheets into her bag and pushed herself out of the seat.

"I'll leave you to it. Message me if you need anything," she said, moving to leave but stopped by something trapping her leg.

Baz's hands were wrapped around her ankle.

She looked down in alarm.

"I'm sorry," he said with a sniff.

Sade felt her chest tighten at the words.

I'm sorry.

It wasn't like she always had this reaction to the word; it was the way he said it. Baz's voice sounded like it was buried under so much. Under the weight of knowing he'd failed.

"You don't need to apologize, just rest. We'll speak later."

He nodded, letting go of her ankle. "Okay."

Sade left Baz and walked out of Seacole to the quiet confines of her dorm.

Outside her room was another bouquet of bright yellow sunflowers. The argument with Persephone played in her mind.

You should stay away from him . . . he will only hurt you.

Jude used to date April and he broke her.

She already knew whom it was from before she read the card.

Finished thinking about it?—JR

She entered the room, placing the flowers and the card next to the other flowers he'd sent her on Sunday.

Then she picked up her phone to send a text.

S: You're getting rather good at this stalking thing, she messaged.

Her phone buzzed immediately.

J: I take it you're charmed by my efforts?

She waited two minutes before answering.

S: Not the word I'd use, but sure

He messaged back after three—catching on quickly to her game.

J: That a yes?

Four minutes.

S: Only because I like sunflowers

Five.

J: Sure, that's the reason

J: The café on campus—Tomorrow after school

Six.

S: Sounds good.

Seven.

J: See you then. He wanted the final word.

Sade let him have it.

She'd win this game of theirs in other ways.

IT WAS AROUND DINNERTIME WHEN it became apparent that (1) Sade wasn't hungry and (2) being in her room was causing her more harm than good.

With the argument she'd had with Persephone still playing on her mind and the conversation with Baz earlier, she found she needed to be somewhere else.

As usual, she chose the pool.

Newton was close to empty at this time. Almost everyone was inside their own dorm buildings, eating and socializing.

And as usual, her swimming companion was already in the pool doing laps.

Sade stepped out, watching him cut through the water like a human shark, deter-

mined and focused. Like herself, August sought out the water as his private companion. Practicing alone instead of with the rest of his team.

She took a seat on the side of the pool, skin prickling as her feet lowered into the
warm, chlorinated water.

When he finally came up for air, he spotted her right away. A slow smile crept onto
his face as he swam toward her. "Greetings, new girl."

She wanted to reply, *Hi, liar*. But she decided not to; she had to be smart about this.
If Persephone was right and August was lying about dating Elizabeth, she was scared
of what else he was lying about.

"I've been here for almost four weeks now. Will you ever let go of that nickname?"
she replied, pushing herself into the water and feeling her thoughts dissipate.

He shook his head. "Nope." He splashed her.

"That's a shame. I guess I will keep calling you Augustus, then," she replied, matching his energy by splashing him back. The water completely went over his head, surprising him.

She noticed he was wearing the goggles she had given him for his birthday. They
suited him.

His eyes seemed to narrow, a thirst for vengeance swimming in them, and before
she knew it, he was grabbing her shoulders and dunking her under the water.

Despite the shock of it, she managed to hold her breath in time and proceeded to
kick him underwater, which wasn't as effective as she would've liked.

Being in water was like being in outer space. Moving about in it felt like defying gravity—her movements slow and soft, instead of quick and hard like she wanted
them to be.

When they finally came up for air, his goggles were pushed up and he was laughing, moving closer to her. Then, he kissed her.

By the time she'd registered what was happening, her hands had moved faster than
her mind and she was pushing him away. Hard.

August's eyes were wide and filled with regret. "I'm so sorry—"

Sade shook her head and recoiled. "I'm g-gonna go," she said, moving to the steps
and climbing out of the pool quickly.

"Sade—" August called out, but she was already gone.

Inside the changing rooms, she could feel her heart banging in her chest and her
brain clawing.

You should never have come, the voice hissed.

Sade felt her fingers trembling as she quickly pulled on clothes over her wet
swimsuit, not bothering to shower or change. She needed to get out of there.

You should never have come. She rushed out of the doors of Newton, the cold, wet air instantly sticking to her.

When she got to Turing, the foyer was loud and bright, and people were piled in the dining room and the common area.

She got into the lift, pressing the button to the third floor a few times before the doors wrenched closed and the small, boxed space finally began to ascend. She felt gross. The wet swimsuit made her skin feel wrinkled and itchy. She needed a shower. Needed to get everything off her.

She got out of the lift and turned into the hallway, running toward her door, while rummaging frantically in her backpack for her key. She was so engrossed she didn't realize there was a person standing at her door until she literally bumped into them.

"Sorry—" she said, her breath hitching as she found herself looking at Persephone.

Persephone stared at her strangely. "I didn't see you at lunch today," she said.

Sade didn't think she wanted her there.

"Which I obviously don't blame you for, given what happened yesterday and all. I wanted to say I'm sorry. I didn't mean to sound controlling. Jules says that I need to work on how intense I get . . ." Persephone's voice trailed off, a weird look still on her face.

Sade shook her head. "No need to apologize. I shouldn't have reacted that way either."

Silence filled the space, the awkwardness still plaguing the hall.

"Truce?" Sade finally asked, holding out her hand.

Persephone placed her hand in Sade's and shook it. "Truce."

"Was that all?" Sade asked, still itching to shower.

Persephone shook her head. "I wanted to talk to you about the thing you mentioned yesterday. *The Fishermen.*" She said the last part in a whisper.

Sade nodded, her heart still rattling away behind her rib cage. "Want to come inside?"

"Yeah sure," Persephone said as Sade opened the door with her key, trying to ignore her shaky fingers.

She flicked the lights on, feeling the cold air graze her skin as she slipped her shoes off and took a seat on the bed. Her swimsuit still stuck to her under her clothes, but she didn't want to change or do anything before she'd heard what Persephone was going to say.

Persephone stood in front of her, as though she was awaiting instruction.

"*The Fishermen,*" Sade said. "What about it?"

"Where exactly did *you* hear that name? Was it from August, like you said?" Persephone asked.

Sade wondered if she should disclose the truth about how she really came across it, through the music box first with Elizabeth's scribbled notes and then August's phone. Given that Persephone was so close to the twins, it seemed like too big a risk. But she and Baz had seemingly exhausted all their avenues and she needed answers.

She also figured telling Persephone the truth was only fair. She wanted Persephone to be forthright, so she needed to lead by example.

"I saw the name pop up on August's phone . . . some kind of group chat. I thought it was weird because Elizabeth had mentioned it before," she said, only bending the truth a little.

"Did Elizabeth say anything else?"

Sade shook her head. "It was very vague."

"And you think this Fishermen thing might be connected to why Elizabeth left?"

Sade looked at her for a few moments. She looked sincere, like she cared about this and genuinely wanted to help.

"I do."

Persephone nodded. Sade could see the cogs working in her brain as she considered this information.

"I didn't lie before, about not knowing what it meant. But I can see that finding out what happened to your roommate means a lot to you and I think I can help." Her voice was even, her face serious. "But I'll need something in order to help you."

"What is it?"

"I need you to get into August's phone."

Sade's eyebrows shot up. "What?"

"There's this cloning app, all you need to do is unlock his phone and have the Bluetooth do the rest. It will completely clone everything on August's phone—hopefully, that'll show you what the Fishermen are and maybe help you figure out what was going on with Elizabeth."

That was . . . genius.

"Won't he notice if his phone is missing?"

"You wouldn't be taking it for long; you'll just need it long enough to download an app that will transfer all his data onto another device."

Sade nodded. It didn't sound too difficult.

"Why are you helping me all of a sudden?" she asked.

Persephone looked at her as she usually did. Like she could see through her completely. "Because I always help my friends," she said simply.

And something told Sade that she was telling the truth.

WEDNESDAY

"READY TO ORDER?" JUDE ASKED her after school, at the on-campus café.

She had been zoning out through the day and barely even registered meeting up with Jude and coming here.

Focus, the devil inside hissed.

"Let me look at their menu," she said, picking up the small laminated page.

"Are you okay?" he asked.

"Yeah, why?" she replied.

"You seem off today," he said with a shrug. "Did you not like the flowers?"

She'd received a big bouquet of roses this morning. Her room looked like a funeral parlor. She'd thrown so many flowers away the bin was overflowing with them.

She shook her head. "Can I ask you a question?"

He leaned back in his chair. "Sure. But I get to ask you something in return."

"Okay," she said, leaning in close. "Did you used to date April?"

His smile faltered. "Where'd you hear that?"

"Around. Did you date or were you just hooking up?" she asked, wanting a clear answer.

"That's two questions." He was deflecting.

"Okay then, answer my first one."

His fingers tapped on the table. And then he leaned in, elbows in front of him now. "Are we dating?" he asked.

"What?" Sade said.

"Me and you. Are we dating?"

Sade blinked at him. He had completely ignored her question.

When she didn't answer, he continued on. "I like you a lot, and I feel like I want to get to know you more. Despite what you think you know about me, I don't date multiple girls at once. So my question is, do you want to go steady?"

Something about that question was unsettling.

"Going steady, is this the 1930s?"

He grinned. "What can I say? I'm a traditional guy."

"You still didn't answer my question," she said, increasingly annoyed.

"What was it again?" he asked, feigning ignorance. Something in his expression shifted.

Persephone was telling the truth. That much was confirmed by his body language and deflection.

She had just about had it with boys who thought they could do whatever they liked because they knew how to charm and gaslight.

She imagined that everything else Persephone had said had to be true too.

Sade got up suddenly, and the smile on Jude's face faltered.

"I'll see you around, Jude," she said, and then she walked out of the café without another word.

THURSDAY

DIVING

SADE WAS CONVINCED THAT SOME teachers found the torture of their students enjoyable.

It was the only explanation as to why Mr. Michaelides had given them the task of working on this project in small groups and had decided that for some reason she should be grouped with Francis.

At least the other person in their group was Persephone.

Francis looked smug as he sauntered over to the table where Sade sat, pulling out a chair, spinning it around so it was backward, and sitting down.

"This should be the easiest A that I will ever get. Thanks for your service, ladies," Francis said, his voice teasing.

"You are literally a fourth year, retaking third-year English in order to graduate on time. If I were you, I'd pay close attention and avoid having to continue retaking this class well into your twenties," Persephone said, and Sade had to force herself to bite back a laugh.

"At least I won't be well into my thirties still bitter, single, and miserable like you, dear Seph," Francis replied.

"Fuck you, Francis," Persephone said.

"In your dreams," he replied.

Sade wondered how April let her boyfriend talk to her best friend like that. She also wondered how April even dated someone like that, but she guessed that it was one of those things she'd never understand.

"Do you think you girls will be good without me for a bit? I need to go outside for a smoke," Francis said, taking the cigarette from its permanent position on his ear and placing it in his mouth.

"You're going to do whatever the hell you want anyway, so why pretend to care what we think?" Persephone muttered.

"You know me well, Sephy. See you guys in a bit," Francis replied before getting up and walking right past a very confused Mr. Michaelides.

"Uh, Mr. Webber—I mean, Francis—where are you going?" Mr. Michaelides asked.

Francis barely looked at him as he gave off his flippant reply. "Need a smoke, helps with my nerves."

"I think you really shouldn't—" Mr. Michaelides began but was cut off by the redheaded boy.

"My father said it's cool; don't worry—see you soon, Mr. M," Francis said, and then without another word left the class swiftly like it was nothing.

Sade knew he was the headmaster's stepson, but surely even that had its limits?

Mr. Michaelides just stared at the door after him, defeated.

Sade decided to focus on the project and not on the lack of consequences it seemed there were for the well-connected at the school.

Their project was to make a poster timeline of the books they had already studied and would be studying, placing each book in its historical period and writing down a significant event relating to the period in question.

As expected, Francis didn't return for the rest of the lesson. Sade was beginning to understand why he was retaking the class in the first place.

"Projects are due on the Monday after half term!" Mr. Michaelides yelled over the sound of people exiting and disappearing into their own worlds and conversations. Another reason why teachers were sadists. Most of them had set homework for the one-week half-term break next week.

"Have you gotten the phone yet?" Persephone asked Sade as she opened her locker and placed her bag inside before shutting it closed.

Sade shook her head. "I'm working on it."

"Let me know when you do," Persephone said. "See you at lunch?"

Sade nodded. "See you."

Then she watched Persephone walk away, off to her government and politics class.

Sade's next class was a free study period, so she went to the classroom where students with frees were meant to get registered. When she arrived, she was surprised to see August standing outside, leaning against the wall, on his phone.

She slowed down, and August finally looked up.

"Hi," he said. Deep regret and embarrassment played across his face.

She eyed the phone in his hand. "Hey," she replied stiffly.

She hadn't seen him since Tuesday, when he'd kissed her in the pool. She imagined that was probably why he was here, given the guilt radiating off him like a bad stench in a cartoon.

"Are you free?" he asked.

"Kind of, I have a free period, was just going to catch up on work. Do you have a free period too?" she asked, despite knowing he didn't. She'd never seen him in this class. Though, it was possible that he managed to persuade the teacher to let him spend his frees elsewhere.

He shook his head. "I came to see you. I uh—I just wanted to apologize for what happened on Tuesday. I should never have done that, and I'm so sorry if I crossed a line or made you feel uncomfortable in any way. You're a good friend to me and I'm just . . . I'm sorry."

She didn't say anything at first. It wasn't that he had rendered her speechless, but that she just didn't know if she had an adequate answer to give him.

She could say *It's fine*, but it wasn't. It wasn't fine. She wasn't sure if she could trust him again, especially after finding out—again—that he had been lying to her even after she'd confronted him.

"How did you know this was my next class?" she asked instead.

He didn't seem to anticipate that question and looked even more embarrassed now. "Perks of being the deputy head boy, I guess. I saw your file and looked up your schedule. Told my teacher that I had deputy head boy duties to do, and so he let me miss the first ten minutes of class."

Sade raised an eyebrow. "Ten minutes? That's the amount of time you thought it would take to win me over?" She was only half-joking.

"No, but I figured asking for any more time would make him suspicious," he replied. She nodded.

He looked distraught, like he was seconds away from getting on his knees and groveling.

She could use this to her advantage.

"Are you free tonight?" she asked him.

"Why?"

"I think I will try out for the swim team after all—but for one of the reserve spots. I'll need help practicing. So will you help me?"

August's eyes lit up at the mention of this. "Of course." He looked relieved, like he was glad he had his friend and late-night swimming partner back.

Sade felt something close to relief. She was finally a step closer to getting her answers.

● ● ●

AUGUST WAS AT THE POOL already when she arrived after dinner.

He hadn't yet noticed her. He was doing laps, with his usual razor-sharp focus, the water being the only thing in the world that really mattered to him.

They were almost too similar in that regard.

She took this as a chance to move quietly into the boys' changing rooms while he was distracted.

The good thing about Newton being mostly unoccupied at this time was that it meant that it was easy to find August's things, as he had the only locker in use. The lockers, ironically, didn't have locks on them.

Despite the myth of the Turing Thieves, it didn't seem the school was all that fussed about safety protocols.

She opened the locker door and took out August's black backpack, placing it by the sinks. She unzipped the smaller pocket and the larger zip on the bag and began riffling through it, searching for the item she needed.

She felt the smooth glass screen before she saw it, taking it out to examine.

His phone required a passcode to open.

In the distance she could still hear the sound of water splashing as August swam and she tried her first combination.

His birthday. *3110.*

The phone vibrated in her palm.

2 attempts left.

What else could it be?

What else might he care about enough?

The splashing persisted in the distance and Sade tried her second guess.

2323. The number on his jersey, twice.

The phone vibrated once again.

1 attempt left.

She sighed.

She tried to remember conversations they'd had. Things she had spotted in his room that could indicate what he truly cared about. They said eyes were windows to the soul, but then again, so were bedroom walls.

And then, she finally got it.

"Please let this be right," she whispered as she typed in her final attempt.

2004. The year Michael Phelps had his historic series of wins at the Olympics in Athens.

The phone unlocked.

She was in.

FRIDAY
KISS AND TELL

IT WAS THE FINAL WEEKDAY before the half-term break, and the halls of Alfred Nobel Academy were filled with excited students ready to leave the school and go on ski trips or on Caribbean cruises with their families.

Sade wouldn't be going back home. The next week would be spent at the boarding school with the rest of the students who couldn't make it home for whatever reason or who had families they didn't particularly want to see or who, like herself, were orphans.

Or like Baz, who decided that having his mother scrutinize him all week was something he was happy to miss. She was glad that she'd at least have him by her side during the break.

She hypothesized that the real reason Baz didn't want to go home was Elizabeth. He didn't want to face Elizabeth's mum or have to lie to her about everything being fine. Hiding out here was safer. At least they could hide together.

It also gave her a chance to keep trying to find answers, especially from August's phone.

"I've had to resort to plan B in the whole Kwame debacle," Baz told her as they walked to lunch.

"What was plan A?"

"I told you, hide and drop out."

She laughed. "Oh yes. How could I forget. I'm guessing that didn't pan out?"

He nodded. "It's too late to drop out of German, and I can't miss any more rowing practice; otherwise, coach *will* break into my dorm and skin me alive."

"So what is the plan B, then?" she asked him.

"Pretend it never happened," he said, and just as Sade was about to ask how that would even work, a voice interrupted.

"Hey," Persephone said. They both turned to her, stopping in their tracks.

"Hi," Sade replied.

Baz was a little awestruck.

"I got your delivery," Persephone said, looking at Sade. The delivery being the copy of August's phone's data. "I'm gonna go through it this evening—you can join me if you'd like?"

"Yeah, I'd like that," Sade said.

Baz thrust his hand forward toward Persephone. "Basil dos Santos, I'm a big fan of your work—I was in the audience when you won that spelling bee in first year with the word *misogynism.*"

Persephone stared at him, unblinking. And then after a few awkward seconds of nothing, she said, "Thanks."

It was clear she didn't know how to process Baz. Partly because of the amount of unfiltered enthusiasm he brought to most conversations but also Sade imagined, his now blue hair. She looked like she was experiencing some kind of sensory overload.

"Is it okay if Baz sits with us at lunch?" Sade asked. Baz didn't always eat in the dining hall, but when he did, she felt bad for abandoning him and letting him eat alone.

"I'm sure April wouldn't mind," Persephone replied.

When they entered the lunch hall together, Sade was surprised to see their usual table was full of strangers. It looked like the strangers were all boys from the swim team.

She'd been thankful that August and Jude hadn't been spending that much time at their table recently due to their rigorous swim practices, but for some reason, today they were both there.

She hadn't spoken to Jude since their non-date, but she immediately felt his eyes on her as she sat down.

She could hear Baz introducing himself to Juliette, who was complimenting his hair color.

Sade started eating her baby carrots, her anxious brain having already gnawed away at her appetite.

She always had this feeling that something bad would happen, and often this feeling would amount to nothing—just her brain playing games.

But sometimes this feeling would accompany a real anxiety-inducing event.

Almost as if the universe could hear her inner turmoil and decided it wanted to test the bounds of how much more anxiety she could take, Sade suddenly heard and felt a bang as Jude got up on their table and yelled "HEY!" across the room.

It caused everyone in the crowded dining hall to quiet.

"I have an announcement to make," he said, looking directly at her.

Oh. No. Sade thought.

All eyes were on him now.

"I like someone a lot. And I think she likes me too but needs me to prove my commitment, and so here I am. Committing."

There were low gasps and Sade wanted to shrink back into the shadows and disappear. But she couldn't, even if she wanted to; it would only draw even more attention to herself.

"I'm not used to not getting my way. I'm the captain, I steer the ship, but this girl, she challenges me and I want everyone to know that I like Sade Hussein and she's the only girl for me."

What the hell is he doing? she thought as all eyes shifted to her now. She was still holding a carrot, frozen like a massive spotlight had been directed on her and the brightness and intensity of its glare were making her sweat as the heat melted her skin.

"Anyway, that's my announcement. You may all resume dining," Jude said with a grin and then jumped down from the table once again. But of course, people couldn't simply go back to eating. Not after a bombshell like that was casually dropped.

The school's apparent resident playboy wanted to play no more.

Sade slowly looked up, all eyes around the table trained on her.

August looked shocked. Francis looked shocked. They all looked shocked. Well, everyone but April.

April didn't seem even remotely interested in what had just transpired.

"Gotta go, guys; we've got swim practice," Jude said, placing his hands on August's shoulders.

August soundlessly got up, tearing his eyes away from Sade and walking off with Jude, who had this weird, knowing smile on his face as he walked out of the lunch hall.

The other strangers followed behind like puppets, clapping Jude on the back and laughing.

Sade finally looked at Persephone, who looked more betrayed than shocked . . . *Close to tears*, Sade thought.

She wished Jude hadn't done that.

Whenever she'd watch a movie or read a book where a boy would make a huge declaration of love like that, she never found it romantic. The opposite, she found it disturbing. Almost like the girl was cornered, forced to go along with the master's puppet show in order to not upset him.

The table was still silent.

"Well, that was . . . something," April said with a bored expression on her face.

Persephone suddenly stood up, and they all looked at her as she silently walked out of the lunch hall.

"What the hell just happened—is lunchtime like this every day?" Baz asked, watching the exit Persephone left through.

"I'm gonna go and check on her," Juliette said softly before getting up and giving Sade an awkward smile and leaving the hall too.

Sade felt like the worst person in the entire world.

"I'm sorry, April," she finally said, unsure of what else to say.

"What for?" April asked, sipping her Diet Coke with a perplexed expression on her face.

"I, uhm, know you dated Jude and I didn't mean to step on your toes or anything—"

April waved her off. "Who cares? You can date whoever you like—I'm with Francis. I'm not mad or anything."

This surprised Sade.

Persephone had said April *would* mind.

But April was here, apparently unbothered by what just happened.

Maybe it was never about April at all.

Sade felt her emotions spiral, jumping from anger to confusion all in a matter of seconds.

It was Persephone all along.

Why would she tell her to stay away? What was she trying to tell her?

Only Persephone could answer these questions.

She had to go directly to the source.

SADE MADE HER WAY OVER to Curie House just before dinner started.

It was raining heavily outside, so most students were indoors, protected against the brewing storm. She felt as though she was responsible for how severe the weather had gotten, like her current irritation was fueling the dark clouds. Urging them to fill more and more until they burst open onto Alfred Nobel Academy and drowned them all.

When she got to Curie, she immediately made her way up to Persephone's room, knocking sharply on the door once she got there and waiting.

For a few moments no answer came.

It wasn't until she raised her hand to knock again that Persephone finally pulled open the door.

"We need to talk," Sade said.

Persephone simply nodded, letting her into the room.

Like Sade's room, Persephone's had two single beds. Persephone's side was filled with all-black décor, everything neatly put away, and she had several posters on her walls, including posters of the periodic table and one of Paramore from their *RIOT!* era hung up over her bed.

Persephone closed the door and turned slowly back to the room.

"What's your deal?" Sade asked. But she didn't want an answer just yet. "You attack me at the library, saying how April would hate if I hung out with Jude, when April doesn't even care. Truthfully, I think you care for some reason. And you lied to me. So I ask, what is your deal, because I swear I have had it with people this week—"

Sade stopped when she noticed Persephone's eyes were filled with tears now.

She didn't want to make her cry. She just wanted answers.

Persephone wiped her face and for the first time since Sade walked in, she spoke.

"He's a rapist," she said, quietly.

So quiet that Sade almost didn't catch it.

"What?" she asked, as a reflex, though she had heard her clearly. Sade's heart stopped.

"Jude. He's a rapist."

I SLEEP, I DROWN & DISAPPEAR[3]

Dear Diary,

Months ago, on April 9, I think I died.
Not to be paranoid or anything, it's just I'm pretty sure
I did.
It'll explain the flies that have been gathering around my rotting
flesh. It'll explain the weird ache in my chest,
and the lack of a beating heart. It'll explain why
I've found it hard to sleep in months. Why on the morning of April 10,
I stepped into the shower to try and wash the previous night away
but haven't been clean since . . .

---

[3]An anagram

250

BEST-LAID PLANS

THERE WAS A SILENCE THAT followed those words, those four words that would change everything.

"Jude. He's a rapist."

Persephone's face was wet and looked how Sade felt inside. Like everything was so twisted and dark.

Like a curious child whispering "Bloody Mary" in the mirror, hoping that their home was haunting enough to conjure a damned guest in the glass. Saying those words, *finally saying them*, conjured her own damned thing. It was all so visible now.

It was clear that Persephone had never said those words aloud before, and the heaviness of it was now as plain as day.

Sade wanted to say so many things to her, to ask so many questions, but she didn't know how. And so she settled for: "I'm so sorry."

Persephone wiped her face again and turned away from her.

"I started going through the things on August's phone before you came," she said, ignoring Sade's apology.

"What did you find?" Sade asked, playing along with Persephone—not asking the question she wanted to ask but couldn't. *What did he do to you?*

"His camera roll is abysmal, as are his text messages. He only takes pictures of *nature settings* and his only messages are to April and his mum, which is kind of suspicious, and it made me think he probably had hidden apps . . . I went through the apps, searching for what he might be concealing, and it didn't take long for me to finally find where the Fishermen hide," Persephone replied, and Sade came closer as Persephone showed her the phone screen identical to August's.

"Here it is. It's a boys' group chat. I haven't seen much of it yet, but there's this app they're using, disguised as the calculator app, and they have nicknames and they post really vile things about girls at the school. I'm pretty sure there are pictures and videos too, but they have been password protected. I had a guess at some of the passwords from context clues and it seems that each one is opened with the nickname they have for the girl in question."

Sade felt her insides twist, imaginary insects scattering across and crawling on her skin.

As she scrolled, she saw so many names. So many boys.

She wondered which of them was August and recoiled at the thought.

"There was something else . . . ," Persephone said, scrolling to a more recent update.

The cactus: Did you guys see Jack at lunch, standing on that table like an idiot and declaring that he is whipped for new girl?

Jack the Ripper: I can assure you, I'm not whipped. It's all part of the game, lads.

The kettle: What game?

The kettle: Has this got anything to do with your birthday?

Jack the Ripper: Maybe . . . New girl is frigid as hell—I didn't even get any action on our dates. Gonna give her something to help with the nerves. Hopefully she won't remember being so frigid in the end.

Persephone watched her, as the realization of who Jack the Ripper was and who he was talking about sank in.

She was New Girl, and Jude Ripley was the Ripper.

She felt numb.

"It happened at the end of first year," Persephone said, finally breaking the silence. Her voice soft and timid, but steady. "There was a party, and I was roped into going. April hadn't started dating him yet, but I knew she liked him a lot. He had just joined the school that year, and to her he was this shiny, new, mysterious puzzle she wanted to rip apart and decipher. I didn't know how to tell her that he made me feel uncomfortable. Gut feelings aren't exactly scientific.

"He had this way of watching you, singling you out, making you feel so special. And April loved being worshipped, I guess. Me, not so much." Persephone blinked and more tears escaped. "He'd always make seemingly innocent advances. Brushing up against me, telling me I looked beautiful even when I told him to stop . . . and that night he offered me a drink. I declined and he did not like that. Sometime later that night, once he'd obviously had a few drinks and there weren't many people around, he cornered me and told me that *one day* he'd get me, finally turn me straight. I used to gaslight myself. Because he *technically* didn't go further than the threat; it was all just something that played out in my head. But I felt powerless, and that feeling never really went away. Especially when

April started dating him. He was always there, this constant reminder of that night. And he's still here, always here, and I can't do anything about it."

Persephone had been living with this tucked away inside, unable to tell anyone, until now.

"I'd heard sometime after that there had been girls he'd hooked up with at Hawking parties who weren't okay afterward. Said that after . . . they couldn't remember a thing about the night or about being with Jude."

"You didn't tell a teacher about this or your parents or—"

Persephone shook her head, tears bleeding from her eyes and down her face. "It's just speculation. A bunch of rumors. Who would believe me? Or the girls?"

A pang of guilt shot through Sade.

She suddenly remembered how Persephone's face had darkened when Sade had accused her of lying and believing too much in rumors.

Sade wanted to wipe her tears away. Make sure he never made her cry again.

"They need to be stopped," Sade said. "All of them."

28

MONDAY

CRACKING THE CODE

THE SCHOOL GROUNDS FELT HOLLOW.

The students not on vacation drifted about without direction, like lost souls trapped between the veil.

Sade felt more ghoulish than usual with the absence of most of the student body and the growing sense of foreboding on campus. She found herself sleepwalking two nights in a row—which wasn't all that unusual—but what *was* weird was her waking up each time perched by the edge of Elizabeth's bed.

Other than her troubled sleep, she had spent the weekend with Persephone—who wouldn't be going home either—moving between Sade's room, the library, and Persephone's room in Curie House and going through the Fishermen group chat, Sade trying to figure out the link the Fishermen could have to Elizabeth, and Persephone trying to figure out which username corresponded to which boy at the school (with little luck) as well as working on the beginning of the group project that Francis had decided to skip out on. He found a better use of his time at the Owens ski resort in Switzerland for the week.

Now it was Monday, and Sade was tired of staring at computer screens. But unfortunately, as foretold by Batman, crime never sleeps and apparently neither did she.

As she lay on her bed in her ever-quiet room, she heard the sound.

It was an unusual . . . beeping noise . . .

She sat up and watched the door suspiciously as the beeping continued. Then, suddenly, it stopped and a black envelope slid under her door.

She reached down to pick it up. The envelope was thick and had a silver fish engraved onto it.

Sade's body went still.

It looked like the same envelope from the music box. The one with the code.

She tore it open and turned the card over to where the message was. Again, it was in Morse code. Was that what the beeping outside was too?

Sade ripped open the door, wanting to catch the deliverer of the envelope, but the hallway was empty.

She scanned the area, running out to see if anyone had gotten into the lift or to hear the sound of footsteps clattering down the stairs, but there was nothing but silence.

It was as if the person had either slipped into the dorm room opposite hers, room 314, or had completely disappeared.

Strange.

She went back into her room, pulled the card out, and began scanning the message.

For Sade

.-. .- - ... / - .... .- - / .... --.- ..- . .- .-.. / -.... . -.-. --- -- . / .- /
-- . .- .-.. / -.... - / .- / --.- ..- --- - . / -.... -.-- / - .... . /
.-.. . --. . -. -.. .- .-. -.-- / .--- --- .... -. / ..-. .. ..-. .- --..-- /
--- ..- .-. / ..-. --- ..- -. -.. . .-. --..-- / - .... . / --- .-. .. --. .. -. .- .-.. /
..-. .. ..-. -- .- -. . / .... .. -- ... . .-.. ..-. .-.-.- / .-. . -- . -- -... . .-. /
.... / .-- --- .-. -.. ... / .-- .. ..-.. -.-- --..-- /
.. -. - . .-. -. .- .-.. .. --.. . / - .... . -- --..-- / .- ... / -.-- --- ..- / .- .-. . /
-. --- .-- / .--. .- .-. - / --- ..-. / - .... . / .... .. --. .... . .-. / .-. .- -. -.- ... /
--- ..-. / - .... . / .-- --- .-. .-.. -.. . .-.-.- / -... .. .- .-. / .... - . .- -.. . /
--. ..- ... - .- -- --..-- / .. / .- -- / .-. . .-. .- .. . .- .... . -. / .---- /
.. -. ..-. --- .-. -- / -.-- --- ..- / - .... . .- - / -.-- --- ..- .-. / ..... .- ...-. /
-.... . -. / .... . .-.. .-.. ... . . - .-. . . -.-. / .- .... / --- -. . / --- ..-. / - .... . /
.-. ..- ..- -.-. .-. -.-- .-.- / ..-. . .-- / - ---- / .. . - - . -. .-. . .-. / .- /
..... .- .-- -. -.-. .. -. . --. / .... --- --. .. . .-. .- .-. / ..-. .. --. -. ... /
- ..... / - -.. . . .- .- . ...- .... / -.... . ... -. -. . . ... / .. .. -. . .- ...- .- .-. .-.-.- /
.-- . / .-.. -.. --- --- -.-. / ..-. . --- .-. .-. .-. -.. / - ---- / ....- .... .. -. . .-. .-.-.- /
-. .-- --- ..- --..-- / .- -. . . -.. / .-. .- . -- . -- -... . .-. . . .- .-. --..-- / -.. . --- -. . . .-. -. . . /
... --.- .. ..- . . .-.. ..- . .-. .-.- / -..... - - ...-. --

Dear esteemed guest, I am pleased to inform you that you have been selected as one of the lucky few to attend a Hawking Soiree.

Please find the details behind this invite.

We look forward to having you, and remember, don't squeal. -TFM

TFM. The Fishermen. This must have been the message Elizabeth got too.

And then, Sade remembered the rat outside their dorm room door that first day. Had Elizabeth squealed?

She swallowed, feeling that same sinking in her chest.

On the back of the invite was a date, a time, and random numbers written in black ink. She turned it back around and stared at the code and the message hidden behind it.

Sade heard the sound of her phone buzzing in her pocket and had to force herself to pull her eyes away from the message to look at it.

J: You might receive something today—don't be alarmed, it's just my birthday invite

Jude hadn't messaged or spoken to her since his grand display on Friday. It was like he was waiting for her to make the first move.

But it seemed that he had grown tired of waiting.

S: Message received.

J: It's a hawking tradition, the morse code. I hope you weren't too freaked out by that. We have morse code everywhere in Hawking—the wallpaper in the common room has the school motto written over and over again in code. It's pretty cool right?

A Hawking tradition. That phrase sounded so sinister.

She remembered what Baz had said about the Hawking parties on her first day at the school, and she wondered if this was one of their many strange traditions.

S: Very, she replied, hoping the sarcasm wasn't discernible through text.

She clicked off their chat and went to the one she now had with Persephone.

S: I need your help

Immediately, the three dots popped up before Persephone's response, Be right there, appeared on the screen.

Her phone buzzed again, another message from Jude.

J: So, do you accept the invitation?

Sade stared at his words, wondering why it was that Elizabeth had one of these invitations. Jude had said it was his birthday, so maybe Elizabeth's invite was from his birthday the previous year . . . but that still didn't answer her question. In fact, it posed more.

How did Elizabeth know Jude well enough to be invited to his party? August maybe, since they were dating?

And most important, why was she so interested in *the Fishermen*?

PERSEPHONE SETTLED ON SADE'S BED, staring at the invite with a look of concentration.

"This is a Hawking party invite," she said as soon as she saw it. "Aka, wannabe frat party that mostly happens whenever we have a break or half term," she continued. Sade remembered Elizabeth also referring to frat-like parties. "You get this black invite, and you go to the location they tell you to."

"Jude said it was his birthday invite."

Persephone looked up at her. "It probably is. The Hawking boys will use any chance to throw a party. April goes to them all the time. Or at least she used to . . . not sure if she still does anymore . . ."

Persephone got out her phone and typed in the coordinates from the back of the invite, nodding when she saw them. "I thought so," she said.

"What?" Sade asked.

"The coordinates are for the house Jude's mother bought him. April would always tell me how he never went home, even during the summer and winter breaks. Apparently, his mum can't stand him . . . and I honestly don't blame her. You should decline the invite," Persephone said.

"What?" Sade said.

"You should decline it. Nothing good comes from a Hawking party, and besides, you saw the messages in the group chat—Jude bets on you showing up."

Sade understood where Persephone was coming from, understood the danger. But she also knew that they needed to be stopped.

"What if we use the invite, though?"

"Use it how?" Persephone asked.

"To go to the party and catch Jude. I can be on the phone to you the whole time, and you can record the conversation. I can get him to admit to what he's doing and we can show someone, stop these parties from happening—stop everything that happens there," Sade said. *Stop these monsters from hurting people. And work out whether this all had something to do with Elizabeth too.*

Persephone didn't look too pleased at the idea.

But this was something Sade wanted to do. Something she had to do.

It was only a matter of time before someone else got hurt.

"We can have a code word for danger and plan ahead so that I'm not trapped there."

"I don't know about this . . . ," Persephone said. "What if he catches you or you can't escape on time or—"

"I'll be careful," Sade assured her. Some risks were worth taking.

You should never have come. The hissing voice returned, as expected.

Applying to ANA was one of those risks.

Persephone was quiet for a few moments, but then she finally nodded. "But we need to plan properly, okay? We can't fuck this up, even a little bit," she said, staring at Sade earnestly, concern in her deep brown eyes.

She realized she had been quiet for too long and forced herself to resurface. "Okay," she said.

Then the door to her room suddenly opened and Baz was standing there with a bag of popcorn in his arms. Sade had forgotten that she had agreed to watch *Shrek 2* with him.

He still hadn't been sleeping and Shrek seemed to be the only antidote to his downward spiral.

"Do you not know how to knock?" Persephone asked.

Baz looked surprised to see her there. "Was I interrupting something?"

"No," Sade said, just as Persephone replied, "Yes."

Baz pushed his hand out for Persephone to shake. "We met the other day—"

"Yes, I remember you," Persephone said, not touching his hand. "Parsley, right?"

"Basil," he corrected.

Persephone blinked at him.

"I'll join you in the movie room in just a moment, Baz," Sade interjected, sensing that this conversation needed a change in direction.

Baz looked between them, eyebrows furrowed like he suspected more was going on here.

But instead of inquiring further, he just nodded. "See you," he replied, leaving the dorm room now.

Persephone looked a little annoyed.

"You can join us if you'd like?" Sade said.

Persephone shook her head. "I'll see you later, after you're done with the movie. We'll plan this whole disaster then," she said, then got up from the bed and left the room without another word.

Leaving Sade alone, with a new quiet hope brimming.

29

WEDNESDAY
RED-HANDED

THERE WERE THREE DAYS UNTIL the Hawking party and Sade was in the library, trying to catch up with her Mandarin classes and homework.

This was proving to be difficult, however, given that she was sitting across the table from Baz and Kwame.

After the initial weirdness at the party and the general avoidance, the two boys seemed to have moved on from it all and were hanging out more—especially during the half-term break.

Baz was "tutoring" Kwame in German, despite being terrible at it, and Kwame was clearly pretending not to know anything.

"What does this mean?" Kwame asked for the nth time.

Baz squinted at the page, probably trying to figure it out himself. "I think . . . it means, pineapple juice?"

Kwame's expression told Sade that it definitely did not mean that, but he nodded anyway.

Between the German being spoken out loud and the Mandarin that Sade was trying to read, it had been near impossible to focus for the past hour.

"I think that's all I can manage today. I've gotta go prep for my uni interviews," Kwame said.

"Oh, right. You got that interview at the Oxford summer camp, for physics, right?" Baz asked.

Kwame nodded. "Hoping to apply in fourth year. With any luck, I might be able to become a broke PhD student in a few years like my brother," he replied jokingly.

Baz had told her that Kwame was one of the few scholarship students at ANA, like Elizabeth.

"Anyway, thanks for the help, B," Kwame said with a smile, grabbing his workbook and standing up now.

Baz nodded, returning his smile. "Entschuldigung! That means anytime."

Sade was pretty certain that wasn't what it meant at all.

Kwame looked like he was holding back laughter. "Ah, you learn something new every day." Then he scratched his head, suddenly looking nervous. "We should hang out more, you know outside the library . . . if you are ever free."

Baz nodded. "I'm happy to tutor you wherever," he said.

Sade sighed loudly.

"Yeah . . . sounds good. I'll let you know when I need help again," Kwame said, seeming a little disappointed.

"See you around!" Baz said as Kwame walked away.

Once Kwame was out of earshot, Sade lightly hit him on the shoulder.

"Ow," Baz said.

"What was that?"

"What was what?"

"Kwame literally asked you out and you rejected him."

"He didn't . . . ," Baz started, then his eyes went wide. "No. He didn't."

"Yes, yes, he did."

Baz placed his head in his hands. "Why do people always speak in code around me? It makes it very difficult to understand them."

"I'm honestly trying to root for you, so next time don't reject him so I can root for you both."

"Okay, Tyra Banks," Baz said, rolling his eyes. "I do think if Kwame was interested, he'd just say it. He's a straightforward kind of guy."

"Maybe it's hard to be straightforward when it pertains to affairs of the heart," Sade said.

"Why are you speaking like that?" he said with an eyebrow raised.

"Like what?"

"Like Jane Austen; it's weird."

She just smiled. "If you thinkest so."

Baz shook his head at her as he got up from the chair. "I'm gonna go to the vending machine to get some M&M's. Want anything?" he asked.

She shook her head and then he was off.

A moment later, someone else slid into Baz's seat.

Jude.

"Hello," he said.

"Hi," Sade replied, feeling tense. It was her first time seeing him since Friday. The first time since she'd found out what the Fishermen were.

He leaned in close and she resisted the urge to punch him squarely in the jaw. Instead, she stayed still, trying to seem as neutral as possible.

"I know what you're planning, and it won't work," he said softly.

"What?" Sade asked, her heart in her throat. Was it possible that Jude knew about them stealing data from August's phone, or them learning about the group chat . . . or even their plan to record and expose him at the party?

His smile looked menacing. It felt like he knew *everything*.

"I know you're getting me a surprise gift, and I'm telling you now that I'll probably figure it out, so you might as well just let me know what it is."

Sade's heart paused and she felt a slow relief spread. "Unfortunately, I can't do that," she replied.

"That's too bad," he said. "Should I pick you up on Saturday? You can give it to me then." He said this in a way that made her skin crawl, and he was looking at her in a way that made her want to be invisible.

"No," she blurted out, then quickly added, "I mean, I'm fine to find my own way there . . . part of the surprise and all."

He nodded, not looking the least bit suspicious. "Okay," he said, looking up as Baz approached the table with a large bag of M&M's and a juice box.

"See you later, beautiful," the blue-eyed boy said before pushing himself up and walking away, disappearing into the bookshelves.

Sade felt like she could finally breathe again. She hadn't realized she had been holding her breath for so long and now her rib cage hurt.

Baz sat back down. "What was that about?" he asked.

"The party on Saturday," she said.

Baz's eyebrows shot up. "You're going to a Hawking party and you didn't tell me?!"

"It's Jude's birthday, so I'm not sure if it counts . . ."

"Any occasion thrown by a Hawking boy is a Hawking party," Baz said, wide-eyed.

"Well, I guess I'm going to a Hawking party," she replied awkwardly, feeling bad that she couldn't invite him.

Under different circumstances she might've—especially with the Elizabeth connection to all this—but with the plan that she and Persephone had put together, it was important for her to go in alone.

"Wow, the life you lead. Sometimes I'm convinced you have this secret identity and I have no idea who you truly are."

THE HALLS OF TURING WERE quieter than ever. It served as a constant reminder that while most of the student body were away with their families, she was here, alone, always.

With her mind full and her chest heavy, she realized she couldn't do any quality work today, so she decided to go back to her room to shower, watch reruns of *The Great British Bake Off*, then, hopefully, sleep instead of being awake and having the anticipation and worry gnaw at her brain constantly.

She dumped her bag onto her bed and went over to her laptop to load up the show before she went to shower.

As she moved her mouse pad, a notification appeared on her computer's screen.

She had a new email on her school account. She never really got emails—other than the occasional spam from shopping sites, but even then, those usually went straight to her junk folder.

She took a seat, clicking twice on the notification button.

The email opened up, and she froze when the message appeared.

Stop digging. You'll only get hurt.

Her mind zeroed in on the first two words. *Stop digging.*

She felt a cold flush throughout her body and she looked around her room, like the sender would be standing right behind her if she turned.

She then looked back down at her screen. The email came from what seemed to be a burner address. Someone hiding behind a screen, like a coward.

She reached out to her keyboard with shaky fingers and typed back a reply.

WHO IS THIS? Sade messaged.

Seconds later, her notification bar pinged with a new email.

YOUR EMAIL COULD NOT BE DELIVERED, THIS EMAIL ADDRESS IS NO LONGER VALID.

Who sent that email?

Her mind went back to the library.

I know what you're planning, and it won't work.

She felt her heart shudder in her chest, her throat closing slowly.

Was this Jude? Did he know about her plans? Was he threatening her now?

She felt like there were eyes in the walls. Watching her every move. Waiting to see what she did next.

She wanted to show this to Persephone, see what she thought about it. But she knew that if Persephone learned about this threat, she'd abandon the plan completely. She'd say it was too dangerous.

But this wasn't about Sade. It was bigger than her.

There was no turning back.

Not now that she was so close.

I SLEEP, I DROWN & DISAPPEAR[4]

Dear Diary,

A few years ago, I thought I died,
but I've been told that was a lie, so I guess
I'm a liar.
I'm still stumbling around that dark room, searching for that switch.
I don't sleep anymore, and my heart hasn't beaten in years.

---

[4] An anagram

30

SATURDAY
THE HAWK

IT WAS THE DAY OF the Hawking party and Sade hadn't slept.

Her anxiety had kept her up, her brain tormenting her with thoughts and worries about the present, past, and future. The clawing in her mind had been persistent, the hissing voice and the relatively empty room haunting her until the sun came up.

Relative because *she* was still always there.

The girl from the shadows.

She was always there at night, but no longer brought Sade any comfort. Just stared at her, all judgmental and sad.

Though burdensome, being kept up by her existential thoughts worked out in her favor, seeing as she had to be awake early for her hair appointment in Curie House with Sharna Brown. The third year was not only a skilled hairstylist but was also apparently a master at the flute.

It had been a while since Sade had done her hair, and something about cheating on her regular hairstylist was a little exhilarating, she had to admit.

When Sade arrived, Sharna already had the extensions pulled and laid out on her bed. Sharna's roommate was still sleeping and Sharna had a chair in the center of the room facing the window. Sharna, like a good portion of the student body, had returned from her holiday last night, in time for school to resume on Monday. It was why she could only do Sade's hair now.

"You can sit over there. Waist-length faux locs, right?" Sharna asked with a yawn. It was seven a.m. and not even the birds were chirping yet.

Sade nodded, taking a seat. "Yeah."

Six and a half hours later, Sharna's roommate was awake and watching some movie on her bed and Sharna was dipping the ends of Sade's extensions into a bowl of steaming-hot water to seal them.

Sharna gave Sade a hand mirror to examine her hair and Sade smiled up at her. She swore people who could do hair were practically magicians.

"Thank you," she said.

"It's all right. That'll be eighty."

Sade paid her, then was on her way.

It was just turning two and there were still many hours until the party started. She messaged Persephone that she was done and went over to her dorm room to go over the plan. Everything had to go off without a hitch.

It was dangerous—Persephone reminded her of this much every time they spoke about it—but Sade knew it was likely all they could do for now. It was their only option to help expose what these boys were doing and also her only way of finding out how Elizabeth was connected to all this.

When she knocked on Persephone's door, Persephone answered and gave her the strangest of looks.

"Hello," Sade said with a smile.

Persephone didn't smile back. Just stared at her.

Is it possible she knows about the email and wants to call this whole thing off?

Sade felt her smile falter a little.

After a moment of prolonged awkward staring, she finally spoke.

"Your hair looks nice," Persephone said.

Sade's eyebrows shot up. "Oh . . . thanks, yours too," she replied, even though Persephone's hair was always the same. Short, curled, and blonde.

Persephone stepped aside, finally letting a warm-faced Sade in, and then immediately got to work, taking out the sheet of paper they had been using to track the timeline of events tonight.

It was simple really.

The plan was split into pre-party things, such as getting permission to leave the school grounds and making sure the audio would be high quality and ready for use.

The other half of the plan was the party walk-through. They would leave ANA early, and Persephone would meet a dodgy guy she knew from her mother's rich-lady circles who would drop off a car for her. They would drive to Jude's house. Sade's audio would be connected to Persephone's phone via an app, and Sade would say the safe words (Jane Austen) if she was in danger.

She would attempt to get Jude to tell her what he'd done with the girls in the past: Had he drugged them? Was Elizabeth involved? Sade wanted to get him to confess to everything, so they had concrete proof.

It was clear that Persephone still thought this idea was very ill-conceived, but she also knew that Sade was determined to do this and so she was forced to oblige.

"Let's get ready," Persephone said, packing her small bag of equipment and a change of clothes.

Sade nodded, pulling out her floor-length silver party dress and heels to change into. She'd decided to wear an oversized blazer over her dress so that she'd have large pockets to place things in, such as the phone she'd be using to record. Among other things.

Sade felt her nerves rattle through her, her skin cold and prickly with goose bumps. *I can do this. It's all going to be okay*, she thought.

There was no room for error here; everything had to go exactly as she'd planned.

THE PARTY WAS ALREADY IN full swing by the time Sade arrived.

There were people spilling out of the main entrance of the large house that some might call a mansion. A pair was kissing by the bushes, and music blared from the open door, knocking her back a little as she approached the entry point. There was a bouncer who checked her invitation before letting her in.

The inside of Jude's home was exactly as she had imagined it. White walls, marble everything, crystal chandeliers all around. It was almost blinding.

"New girl!" August yelled, approaching her with a smile.

She flinched, both upon seeing August and also hearing the name. The very nickname the boys in the group chat had given her. The group chat that August was so clearly a part of.

She hadn't seen him in days, purposely avoiding the pool.

"Hi," she replied, grimacing when he hugged her.

His voice was so kind and gentle, and she had thought he was too.

It may have been an unfair assessment given that she didn't know the full extent of August's involvement in the chat, but seeing as he was Jude's best friend and he had lied about being involved with Elizabeth, how could she have expected him to be any different?

Even if he didn't do the vile things Jude did, he had to know about them. Didn't that make him just as bad?

"Jude's been looking all over for you. I didn't know you guys were dating," he said, his words slurring. Then he dramatically clutched his chest when she didn't confirm or deny this fact. "Et tu, Sade?" he quoted in mock betrayal. "Wouldn't have kissed you if I knew you were spoken for."

Her stomach turned and she tried not to make a face. The version of herself who thought August was a harmless guy who occasionally spoke like a grandfather would have asked him what century he was from. *Poorly quoting Julius Caesar and using such old-people speak like "spoken for"? You are truly an old man, August,* she'd have said.

But now everything he said just sounded slimy and calculated.

"Oh, where did you see him last?" she asked, not acknowledging his statement.

"He was by the pool, I think?" August said, pointing in the opposite direction.

Sade nodded. "Thanks, I'll go and let him know I'm here."

She gave him a tight smile and told him she'd see him after. Then she went to the kitchen counter, where a guy dressed in what seemed to be a butler uniform was serving drinks to a house full of mostly minors, girls she recognized from school but didn't share any classes with. He looked like he was in university and had to be at least nineteen.

She asked for two drinks—nonalcoholic—and went outside to find Jude.

As August had informed her, Jude was there doing a bad interpretation of the Macarena. He had on a crown that said BIRTHDAY BOY and he was grinning from ear to ear.

He spotted her, looking happy to see her, and his eyebrows shot up. "Sade!" he said, walking over to her and grabbing her by the waist. She could smell his hot beer breath and it made her feel sick.

"Happy birthday," she said softly, trying not to look as grossed out as she felt.

"Where's my present?" he asked.

"I'll give it to you later," she said, which only made him smile more.

Then he finally let go of her and she gave him one of the drinks she'd gotten.

He took it and downed it in one go before chucking the plastic cup into the vibrant blue pool, now a wasteland filled with the casualties of the night so far: someone's underwear and a bunch of red Solo cups.

"Hey, hey, we should play a game," Jude said to everyone and no one.

The small crowd outside seemed excited by the prospect of that.

"Strip poker!" someone yelled.

"Seven minutes in heaven!" another screamed.

But Jude had already decided what he wanted.

"We're playing Never Have I Ever . . . ," he said, eyeing Sade. This made his drunk party guests very excited. Likely because they got to pretend they were playing a game when really it was just another excuse to get even more wasted.

Sade always hated being around drunk people. She nursed her apple juice in her hands and wondered how long this night would be.

"Want to lose another game, Hussein?" Jude asked in her ear, his hot, wet breath prickling her skin, his words more slurred than August's.

"I do a like a challenge," she said in response, which made his eyes brighten and glow.

He thought he had won already.

THE GAME CONSISTED OF THREE rounds of Never Have I Ever, where she was forced to listen to the drunken details of strange sexploits and semi-illegal goings-on the guests had been a part of.

Jude held his hand up. "My turn . . . never have I ever . . . given a guy blue balls after a first date," he finished with a wide smile, his words slurring a little. It was clear he'd already had too much to drink.

Sade felt dread building up inside as he turned to her with a snarky expression. "Drink up, new girl," he said, leaning in to whisper.

She narrowed her eyes at him, wanting to get up and move away from him—or even better, punch him in his entitled face. But she couldn't. Not if she wanted this plan to work.

So she forced herself to smile and take a sip of her juice.

Laughter filled the room as people caught on to the meaning behind his words.

"This one is such a *tease*, I love it," Jude said, wrapping his arm around her tightly and taking another swig of the drink in his hand.

After the game, he invited her up to his room as expected.

And as planned, Sade played along, following him to a quieter place in the house. She was relieved to still see some people lurking around upstairs. At least it wouldn't be completely deserted.

Jude kept stumbling as they walked, like he could barely carry his own weight.

Good, Sade thought.

At his bedroom door, Sade discreetly brought out her phone and pressed the red button on the audio recording app, waiting to make sure that it was connected. Persephone messaged her a thumbs-up and Sade placed the phone in her pocket.

She felt her nervous system begin to flare up.

"Don't worry; we won't do anything you won't want to do," he said quietly.

She nodded and followed him in.

Once inside the spacious room, she immediately took in the windows and the exits.

"Planning your escape?" he asked her with a sly smile as he went over to a mini fridge and got out two glasses.

She shook her head quickly. "N-no, I, uhm, your room is really nice. I was just looking around." His room looked like something that someone else had put together—more like a hotel suite than a bedroom. Everything was beige and untouched, almost like no one lived here at all. She spotted a small, framed photograph of Jude with a slightly older-looking lady in the corner. "Did she pick out your room's color scheme? Your mum," she said, feeling too hot. So she took off her oversized blazer and draped it on the chair behind her.

He shook his head, walking to her with the two glasses of whatever he'd poured out. "The countess has things she cares about more than the décor of her son's room. I hired someone."

He offered her a glass, but she didn't take it. "It's nonalcoholic. You're Muslim, right?"

She nodded, taking the glass. "Yeah, I am." She inspected the mysterious blue liquid, raising it up to her nostrils to see if she could smell anything.

"It's just blue lemonade; it won't poison you," he said with a grin.

She tried to return the smile but couldn't bring herself to. Her hands were shaky, like the rest of her body.

"How does that work anyway? You dating and whatnot. Isn't it against the rules or something? Not trying to be offensive—I'm Catholic."

She shrugged, still inspecting the drink. "Well, first of all, I'm not dating anyone, am I? And second, I think that's a rather personal question. Seeing as I'm not the spokesperson for everyone and that we aren't monoliths, I can't really answer that, I'm afraid."

Jude nodded. "Interesting," he said with a smile on his face. He took a swig of his drink, eyeing her as he did. "Drink up."

She stared down at the drink in her cup and then slowly lifted it to her lips, pretending to take a sip.

"You look really good tonight," he said.

"And I don't other nights?" Sade asked.

"Unfortunately, I don't see you most nights," he replied, his eyes dancing around her dress and her body, landing on her drink finally.

He was going to get suspicious if she didn't keep drinking, so she took another pretend sip.

"That's a shame," she said.

Jude nodded as he sipped more of what she assumed was beer. Then he stumbled closer to her, gripping her waist with his hands. He was swaying a little, clearly struggling to keep his knees from buckling.

"So . . . what's my birthday present?" he asked, looking at her suggestively.

"I'll give it to you soon," she replied. "Hey, is that a hammock?"

He nodded without looking in the direction of the hammock, instead moving even closer, his hands lowering.

"You should kiss me," he said.

She forced a laugh. "Is that a question?"

"No," he said, one of his hands crawling up and down her arm, then making its way over to her lower back.

"What are you doing?" she asked. Her heart was hammering away.

"Just trying to have fun," he said, his face mere millimeters away from hers.

"Well . . . ," she started, reaching into the pocket of her jacket draped behind her.

And then she did something that was not part of Persephone's plan.

She turned the recording off.

She cocked her head at him and nodded. "I can have fun."

Jude smiled almost menacingly as Sade pressed her hand to his chest and pushed him backward in the direction of the hammock.

He stumbled and she continued forward.

"What are you doing . . . ?" he asked, eyebrows wagging. Then he turned to look at what was behind him and seemed pleased. "Ah, so you're a swing kind of girl, then?" he asked as she gave him one final push and he fell into the hammock with a grunt.

Sade shrugged, watching him as he tried to maneuver himself into a reclining position with great effort. The drink in his hand spilled a little with each labored movement.

"You look like you're struggling there," Sade said, folding her arms.

"I'm . . . uh," Jude began, then seemed to lose track of his thoughts before finding them again. ". . . I'm okay, I'm just . . . ," Jude began.

"Woozy? Dizzy? Out of control?" Sade offered.

Jude nodded. "I guess so," he said, rubbing his eyes.

Sade watched him as he downed the rest of the drink, before chucking it onto the ground and spreading his arms out toward her.

"Come lie with me. I need warmth," he said.

"I'm good here. I'm sure you'll manage," Sade replied.

He snorted, rolling his eyes. "Do you ever get tired of the act?"

"What act?" Sade asked.

"You know . . . pretending you don't want me? Pretending to be a Goody Two-shoes . . . I know about you and August. Can't I get some action too?"

Her and August? It was clear Jude was talking out of his ass.

"It's not an act; maybe I just don't want you," Sade said.

Jude laughed, shaking the hammock as he tried to push himself up again.

Sade stepped back instinctively as he quickly tried to balance himself. He looked up at her with a sly smile but just as quickly his expression shifted, his eyes squinting and his mouth twisting.

"You know, sometimes you look . . . strange. It scares me," Jude said, staring at her intently. "Like . . . someone . . . someone familiar."

Sade didn't say anything, just watched him watching her. When he attempted to stand again, she held out her hand and shook the hammock, watching him fall back.

"You're drunk," Sade said.

"Why's the ground shaking . . . ," Jude said as he tried to steady himself.

"It's not a nice feeling, is it?" she asked, swallowing as her voice shook a little.

Jude didn't answer the question, just sat back up and looked at her again.

"The *real* fun hasn't started yet, though," Sade said, feeling her eyes burn. "The real fun is the next morning when you don't remember a thing . . . Oh wait, that isn't fun. It's confusing and scary. It's violating. It's worse than anything you could imagine."

Jude stared at her, really, *really* stared at her, and it seemed he was hit by several things all at once.

Nausea. More dizziness and above all, the clarity that came with recognition.

Jude's eyes were wide, his eyebrows raised. He tried to stand again. "Jamila?" he questioned, and Sade felt her burning eyes sweat as she blinked. Ready to push the hammock once more and stop him from coming near her.

She shook her head.

"No, not Jamila. Sade," she replied.

31

SATURDAY
DEATH'S DOOR

SADE LEFT THE PARTY AS quickly as she could.

Someone shoved a lavish gift bag in her arms as she exited. The cold from the night enveloped her as she shivered and sprinted toward the car Persephone was waiting in.

Except, Persephone wasn't in the car.

Sade felt her stomach drop and she turned, looking for signs of her friend.

"Where are you?" she whispered as she walked to the other side, the cold air making her breath appear in intricate swirls of gray-white.

"Persephone?" she asked the wind, but no one answered.

She turned back toward the house, getting the sick feeling that Persephone had gone inside.

The last thing Sade wanted to do was return to the party, but she felt her legs carry her toward the door she had just rushed from. The bouncer was nowhere to be seen and the music had somehow gotten louder and more overwhelming.

You should never have come. For once Sade agreed.

"Sade!" Persephone said, rushing out from the foyer. Her eyes were wide and terrified.

"The app must've switched off or malfunctioned or something. I didn't hear you say the safe words but I couldn't risk it so I had to go inside—"

"I'm fine," Sade said, her teeth starting to chatter together, matching the subtle quaking of her arms and legs.

"Are you sure? You're shaking! I was so worried. I kept thinking something had happened, that you'd been hurt or—"

"Persephone, I'm fine!" Sade said, which finally made Persephone pause and take a breath.

"You're fine," she said.

They walked back toward the car and Sade waited to get inside before she told

Persephone that their mission failed. That instead, Jude had tried to come on to her and she fled as soon as she could.

But she didn't get to because—

"Persephone . . ."

"Yeah?"

"I think . . . I left my blazer and my phone in Jude's room."

ENTERING THE HOUSE AGAIN FELT like she was in some twisted *Groundhog Day* reboot and kept finding herself in the same place.

She kept her head down and walked as quickly as she could to the stairs, climbing them fast and almost bumping into two girls making out on the stairwell.

Downstairs, she could hear people yelling, "Fight! Fight! Fight!" while "If U Seek Amy" blasted from the speakers.

She hoped Jude wasn't in his room upon her return. She hadn't exactly left on the greatest of terms. Best-case scenario for her would be that he was somewhere else passed out. Away from her for good.

She cringed as she placed her hand on his bedroom door, looking around her to make sure no one could see her, then she said, "Hello?" hoping no one answered from inside.

Luckily for her, there was no reply. The room was seemingly empty.

She slid through the door, closing it behind her gently, before tiptoeing toward the chair where her blazer lay.

"Thank God," she whispered, then turned around, wanting to make her swift exit.

Only, the sight of something stopped her in her tracks.

There was someone on Jude's bed.

Lying there, sprawled out and unmoving.

She stepped closer to the person, her breathing turning shallow as she approached. She froze once she was close enough to identify the face.

"J-Jude?" she said, her heart hammering as she examined his still form. His face was this slightly pale blue color now and was decorated with body glitter. "J-Jude," she said again, nudging his shin with her heel.

But there was no reply.

And how could there be?

Dead people couldn't talk.

I SLEEP, I DROWN & DISAPPEAR[5]

Dear Diary,

   I'm glad
   he's dead.

---

[5] An anagram

PART III

CLIPPED WINGS

"That one may smile, and smile, and be a villain."

—*Hamlet*, Act 1, Scene 5, William Shakespeare

32

SATURDAY

ESCAPE

JUDE'S WASN'T THE FIRST DEAD body Sade had seen.

The first had been her mother's, in the bathtub when she was ten.

The tap was still running, water spilling over the edge of the tub and onto the floor, seeping into the cracks in the tiles and tickling Sade's toes when she stood in it.

"Mama?" she whispered, stepping toward the bathtub, wondering why her mother looked like this. Why she looked so . . . still.

"Mama, wake up!" Sade said louder, but her mother didn't stir.

She poked her mother hard and jumped back when her body slipped into the water silently, as though she were a rag doll and not a person.

"Mama!" she screamed at the top of her lungs, knowing now that her mum was some- place else and this person was not her.

She didn't quite understand at first that what she was seeing was a dead body.

Didn't initially get why her mum's head lolled to the side like it was empty.

Although her father fed her lies about what happened to her mother, Sade later figured out that this was what death looked like. And she knew now, without a doubt, that Jude was dead.

I have to get out of here, she thought immediately, her chest tight as she looked around, searching for a quick escape without having to be seen by others at the party again. She spotted the balcony at the back of the room, grabbed her blazer without another thought, and rushed toward it.

Sade sprang through the doors of the balcony, running down the connected spiral staircase while trying hard to move quickly and not break any bones.

She didn't realize she was crying until she got back into the car and Persephone looked at her strangely.

"Did you get the—" Persephone began, but cut herself off. "What happened?" she asked, her eyes filled with worry.

Sade said nothing at first, too shocked to speak.

"Sade?" Persephone whispered, looking so concerned.

Sade finally looked up, her breath shaky as she attempted to speak. "H-he's dead."

Persephone's eyebrows shot up. "Who?"

"J-Jude—I found him in his room and he was d-dead," she said, more tears escaping.

"Are you sure?" Persephone asked.

Sade nodded. *Without a doubt.*

"Fuck."

Fuck indeed.

They sat in silence for a few minutes, Persephone staring at the party with a blank expression on her face.

And then without warning, she pushed her key into the ignition and started the engine.

"Where are we going?" Sade asked, putting her seat belt on.

"I don't know, but you shouldn't go back to school in this state, and besides, it's way past curfew. Going back would just be trouble," she replied, and pulled out of the side road by Jude's house, driving off into the night.

33

SATURDAY
THE WORST OF TIMES

THEY ENDED UP IN A B&B nearby.

The B&B was quaint and wooden, and the receptionist at the front didn't seem all too fazed by their presence despite how late it was.

"Could we get a room for the night?" Persephone asked, taking out her wallet.

"Queen-sized bed okay for you both?" the receptionist asked, chewing gum and typing something loudly on her keyboard.

"Twin beds," Persephone said, with a forced charming smile.

"We only have a double and a queen, sweetheart," the woman said.

"We'll take the queen," Sade replied.

"All right, here are your keys—breakfast is at six and ends at ten, checkout is at twelve. Any questions, just press one for reception. Hope you have a nice stay," she said, then hit the space bar on her keyboard, going back to whatever she had been watching before they interrupted.

Their room was on the first floor. It was medium sized with many florals—floral bedsheets, floral wallpaper, floral carpets—and it made Sade feel a little sick.

Then again, it could be the whole *seeing a dead body* thing.

Persephone shrugged off her jacket and put it on the dresser in the corner. Sade attempted to remove her heels, which was very difficult to do. Especially since her hands hadn't stopped shaking.

"Let me help," Persephone said, bending down in front of her and unhooking the metal attachment that held the straps together before slowly unraveling them. "There, all done."

"Thanks . . . ," Sade said, finally slipping the shoes off and placing them in the corner.

She sat on the bed and watched as Persephone took her own shoes off, before eventually zoning out and disappearing into the wall and its many floral patterns, her mind running through the events of the night at a dizzying speed.

His face was so blue and still and dead. Jude was dead. She had failed.

She always failed.

"Hey, you okay?" Persephone asked, standing in front of Sade now.

Sade shook her head. "He's dead."

"I know."

"What do we do? What if I was the last person to see him? What if people think I *killed* him—"

"You didn't," Persephone said, talking her down. "That's what matters. You didn't kill him. You'll be fine. They'll find who did this and everything will be okay. We do need an alibi, though, since we signed out of school last night, but we can sort that out in the morning."

Persephone sat next to her and turned the TV on, putting on the same soap the receptionist downstairs was watching.

Sade looked at the goody bag in her hand and opened it up to see if there was any water.

There wasn't.

Instead, she found a new diamond-encrusted watch and four cupcakes with Jude's face on them.

The non-blue, non-dead version of his face, that is.

"Want a cupcake?" Sade asked.

Persephone nodded. "I'm starving."

The pair ate the cupcakes in silence. Sade tried to pay attention to the soap and not on her brain's many worries about what might happen when someone discovered the body.

After a while, Persephone suggested they go to bed.

"I can sleep on the floor," Persephone said. "If that would make you comfortable."

Sade shook her head.

She never did like sleeping alone.

Especially during thunderstorms, she'd climb into her mother's bed and sleep next to her until the sun came up and the storm subsided.

"You can sleep next to me, I don't bite," Sade said, which made Persephone laugh.

"You sure? Your canines look quite sharp."

"I promise," she replied.

Persephone took off the top layers of her clothes and climbed into the bed. Sade joined her but kept her dress on, since she wasn't wearing much underneath and didn't want things to be weird.

"Oh fuck," Persephone suddenly said.

"What?"

"Forgot to turn everything off, hold on," she said, jumping up and turning off the TV and lights so that they were in complete darkness.

Sade felt the bed move as Persephone returned. The two of them lay in silence and Sade missed the sound of the TV and how it helped quiet her head, even a little.

She wasn't sure how much time had passed, but she assumed Persephone had managed to get to sleep and it was just her awake in this suite. But then she heard Persephone shudder a breath.

"Sade . . . ," she said softly. "Can I admit something? I just need to say it, and I know it will make me a bad person or whatever, but I need to say it."

"Go on," Sade said back.

"When you told me he was dead, I felt . . . relieved. I know I'm not meant to wish death on anyone, but I am. I'm relieved he died."

Sade didn't say anything in response to that. She just lay there silently.

Neither of them said anything more for the rest of the night.

At some point Sade slept, but her sleep was constantly disrupted by nightmares of her mum and of Jude and of Elizabeth and all the other people who were just gone from her life.

When she woke in the morning, she was horrified to find that she had somehow shifted onto Persephone and was holding her like a koala would a tree.

It wasn't until they were back in the car on the way to drop it off that Sade apologized.

"No need to apologize. I thought it was . . . nice, though you kept whispering *I'm sorry* under your breath, and it was kind of like ASMR to me."

Sade felt her face grow warm.

"I'm sorry," she repeated. "It won't happen again."

"I had no idea you were planning on us sharing a bed again, but no objections from me—as I said, it was like ASMR."

THE JOURNEY BACK TO ANA was quiet and heavy.

She'd considered suggesting that they not return to campus. That they go on the run. Escape any consequence of last night. For all they knew, the police might already be at the school, waiting for the partygoers to return. But not returning might be worse for them both. Might make them look even guiltier.

The car felt like a pressure cooker, ready to explode at any moment. There were so many things to worry about, but no solutions to fix the problems that had been created. So silence filled the car until the air felt so thick Sade couldn't breathe.

Persephone had to drop the car off in town, then they took the bus back to the school in more silence, Sade waiting for Persephone to say something first.

It wasn't until they'd gotten through the school gates that she finally did.

"Wait," Persephone said, placing her hand on Sade's arm to stop her from walking on down the path.

"Yeah?" Sade said.

"Are you okay?" she asked.

No. She wasn't. She hadn't been for years, but it just kept getting worse. She tried to fix things, but she ended up making a bigger mess of everything.

"I'm fine," she said.

Persephone looked at her like she knew it was complete bull but didn't press her on it.

"Okay, well, I want to say something because a shit fest is about to happen. They're going to find the body, if they haven't already. And I need you to stay calm for when that happens. I was thinking all night and this morning, and I think we're going to be fine. People won't want to tell on themselves, plus there were so many people at that party. It'll be impossible for the school to figure out just how many and who exactly was there. I'm sure you didn't even keep track of the guests last night, right?"

Sade nodded.

"So just act normal and we wait to see what information comes."

Sade wasn't sure she knew what normal was anymore. Her normal looked very different depending on the day. Sometimes her normal involved constant panic attacks throughout the day. Sometimes it was low moods and a lack of energy, and other times her normal was feeling haunted by the dead.

A few minutes later, they found themselves in the reception area signing themselves back in.

"Where are you two coming in from?" Ms. Thistle asked as Sade signed her name. She looked up, glancing at Persephone's equally taken-aback expression, unsure of how to answer the question.

"There's been an *incident*, so just for precaution's sake Headmaster Webber has asked me to note down the whereabouts of everyone who signs back in today," Ms. Thistle continued.

"We were visiting my family," Persephone said, deciding on their alibi, it seemed.

Ms. Thistle eyed Sade's sparkly dress and the remnants of dried mascara on her cheeks.

"It was my great-uncle's ninety-seventh birthday," Persephone said before Ms. Thistle could question them anymore.

Ms. Thistle nodded. "Oh wow, ninety-seven. You know, when he gets to one hundred, he'll get a letter from the King."

"I didn't know that," Persephone said. "Will make sure to tell him."

Ms. Thistle smiled and Sade returned her smile, trying not to let the fear and the inner turmoil show on her expression.

They then walked away from the reception, back outside where the fresh air pushed welcome oxygen into her lungs again and she felt like she could breathe easier.

"Your great-uncle's birthday?" Sade questioned as they began making their way back to the dorms.

"Yes, it wasn't a complete lie. He was ninety-seven when he died last year," Persephone said.

Sade's eyes widened. "Can't the school call your parents to check your alibi and find out that is a lie?"

"Don't worry about that," Persephone said.

"What do you mean, don't worry? I *am* worried, and I am scared."

Persephone placed her hands on Sade's shoulders, forcing Sade to look at her. "Listen, worrying isn't going to help us. Focus on the present, not the future, or the past. We'll be fine."

She wasn't sure if Persephone's method of telling herself that everything would be fine quite worked for her.

Things were rarely fine in her life.

More often things were big, earth-shattering, and anxiety-inducing.

Persephone squeezed her shoulders lightly and gave her usual almost-smile, her septum piercing dangling above her stretched lips.

"I'm going to go and prepare for school tomorrow. You should go and lie down and try not to think or catastrophize so hard."

"Catastrophizing is kind of my thing," Sade replied weakly.

"I can tell," Persephone said. "But freaking out won't help us. We need to stay one step ahead of this whole mess."

After walking Sade to Turing, Persephone headed to her dorm, leaving Sade to catastrophize alone.

Inside Turing, she could hear students walking around the halls, suitcases being dragged and excited voices catching up after the week away, talking about whatever European country their parents had taken them to for the break.

Two girls passed by her, whispering to each other.

"*Did you hear about the Hawking party?*" one asked as Sade got into the lift.

"*Yeah ... I heard that police were swarming the place—apparently someone died.*"

It felt like a storm was brewing.

As the lift ascended, Sade could feel her soul weighing it down. Soon everyone would find out and the storm she felt coming would wreak havoc through the halls.

And she wasn't sure if she could survive this tempest.

IF SHE DIDN'T SWIM TONIGHT, she felt that she could die.

Despite avoiding the pool all week in an attempt to avoid August, she decided that she would rather risk running into him.

Of course, this wasn't rational, but anxiety was rarely rational.

When she arrived, she was pleased to find the pool empty. She relished the cold warmth and let herself fall back, close her eyes, and float.

But closing her eyes was a mistake.

Despite her night of sleeplessness, she had underestimated how tired she truly was. She didn't feel the way her body began to sink. Or the chlorine filling her nostrils and her mouth as she sank slowly to the bottom.

By the time she realized she had dozed off, she was already under.

Her eyes widened as she kicked and fought to resurface, but she was choking on water the way a fish would choke on air.

She finally came up again, breathing hard and coughing. When she recovered, she contemplated leaving, seeing as her tiredness had almost drowned her, but she paused when she noticed something in the water.

Her eyebrows furrowed as she swam closer to it. To the dark mass that seemed to ripple on the surface.

She hesitated before holding her breath and going back under. She swam closer to it, gasping. Instead of the body that sometimes haunted her in the pool, this one was different.

IT WAS JUDE. STARING UP at her. Blue face. Wide eyes. Floating and staring up at her.

She knew it wasn't real. It never was.

And yet that didn't stop her from crying.

I SLEEP, I DROWN & DISAPPEAR[6]

"I'm sorry, I just thought—"
"You're a liar. No one will believe you."
◀◀
"I'm so—"
▶▶
"You're a liar. No one will believe—"
◀◀
"You're a liar."
◀◀
"Liar."
◀◀
"Liar."
◀◀
"Liar."

Dear Diary,

I can't remember—
I can't remember anything.
So maybe he's right.
Maybe I am.

---

[6] Are you watching closely?

34

MONDAY

THE WRITING ON THE WALL

RUMORS OF JUDE'S DEATH SPREAD through the school like a wildfire.

By breakfast on Monday morning, most people had heard of the party and the events that supposedly took place.

"*I heard he OD'd,*" one girl hypothesized as Sade ate her cereal.

"*Well, Lori Stevens told me that he didn't actually die and he's in a coma in the hospital,*" another said.

"People are saying he faked it, and that the body they found was his evil twin brother, Jameson," Baz said as they walked to the emergency assembly Headmaster Webber had called.

But Sade knew he was dead. She had seen him with her own eyes, unmoving. His body as lifeless as a painting.

At the assembly, they took their seats and watched as the teachers whispered at the back of the hall. Everyone was talking, inventing theories.

Headmaster Webber stepped forward with a grave expression on his face.

He tapped the microphone, which made an uncomfortable sound, but it didn't stop the noise, so he finally sighed and yelled, "SILENCE!"

His voice blared from every speaker in the room, causing an awful screeching sound and making the entire room shake.

"Thank you," he said in a softer voice now. Though an edge of something else remained trapped in his tone.

It sounded like anger.

"As you all may have already heard, this weekend there was an incident at an off-campus party. I'm very sorry to say that one of our students, Jude Ripley, lost his life at this party."

Gasps sounded from around the room, and voices began rising across the hall.

"This is a tragedy—and what I believe should have been an avoidable event. We are working with the Ripleys as well as the local police to investigate what happened to Mr. Ripley, so you will see police around the campus again. Anyone who was at the party or who has any information is asked to come forward immediately. Jude was a huge part of Alfred Nobel, a student who excelled in every part of his school life. He will be much missed."

Sade heard someone blow their nose and another person sniffle.

"Going forward, we will be strictly monitoring everyone's whereabouts to ensure the safety of every student. The school will be placed on a complete and total lockdown. No student goes out and no one comes in. Your parents and guardians have all been informed of this decision. This will be implemented until further notice."

The last part of his speech was cut off by an outcry of rage at this decision.

"*They can't keep us here against our will, can they? We have rights!*" a boy yelled.

People looked confused and irritated, unsure of why the school was doing this. Why it seemed that they were being punished when only a small, privileged minority had gone to the party.

But it was very clear what the school meant by this.

The students would be prisoners now that the king had fallen.

"We also expect that those who attended the party will come forward to face the consequences peacefully. You have until the end of the day tomorrow as we start our own formal investigation into every person at this school and their whereabouts on Saturday night. You are all dismissed," Headmaster Webber said finally before stepping down from the podium.

It was happening.

Sade spotted Persephone in the corner of the hall, her arms crossed and her face unreadable. Then as though she could feel Sade's eyes on her, she suddenly looked back and locked eyes with Sade. Their lie simmered in between them.

Persephone's once impenetrable expression was now loud and clear.

We are fucked.

THE REST OF THE DAY dragged by at a snail's pace and was filled with even more dread.

At lunch, April, Francis, and August hadn't bothered showing up and Sade wasn't sure if she had even seen them during the emergency meeting this morning.

It was just herself, Persephone, Juliette, and Baz at the lunch table.

Jules had cried, calling Jude a poor guy who deserved better, and all the while, Persephone said nothing and ate her food in silence.

But Sade knew what she was thinking.

"It's funny in a fucked-up way how obvious it is that the school cares more about their white golden boy than Elizabeth. She brings in no money and so they don't have to make a fuss. It's hilarious, so fucking funny," Baz said as they walked down the path by the quad. He wasn't laughing; he looked close to tears.

"Whiteness prevails as always," she said, feeling sad for Baz, but mostly for Elizabeth.

"I want to sleep and forget this year even happened," he said.

Since his failed attempts at finding information to help reopen the Elizabeth investigation, Baz had been sleeping more, yet he still looked like he wasn't sleeping at all.

"No, we're going swimming," Sade replied. "I promise it's nice."

She'd come up with the idea of dragging Baz along with her to the pool the night before when she saw Jude floating in the water. She was scared to go back alone and needed a new swimming partner, and Baz reluctantly agreed to try it.

"I don't see how splashing around in the pool could be helpful right now, but I'll keep an open mind."

Thirty minutes later, Baz had managed to splash Sade and cover her entire face with water. She gave him a death glare. The two had been in the pool for at least fifteen minutes and Baz went from a reluctant participant to a water menace in the matter of five.

They were so preoccupied by the water and the razor-sharp focus of getting the other back for their water crimes that she didn't notice August until he said, "Hi," forcing her to stop and float toward where he was standing.

"Hey," she said.

August looked wrecked. His usually tidy uniform was more disheveled than even Francis's tended to be, his eyes looked red, and his shoelaces were untied and dragging as he walked. She could tell that he had also come to the pool to get away from the gossip about his best friend's death and looked almost . . . disappointed at the sight of Sade and Basil.

August nodded at them and then without another word he left again, the double doors slamming hard as he disappeared behind them.

SADE FINALLY GOT BACK TO her room just before dinnertime. Baz had to go to rowing practice, but even though she was scared of being at the pool alone, she couldn't bring herself to leave the water.

So she stayed a little while longer in the pool until her skin was raw and wrinkled.

It had been a long day, and while she wanted to pretend this weekend never happened, she couldn't. She needed to meet with Persephone and figure out what they were going to do.

She couldn't keep living like this, constantly looking over her shoulder. Afraid that at any moment she would be interrogated by the police and not know what to do or say.

When she turned on the light in her room, the bulb's flicker indicated that it needed to be changed.

She remembered the pack of light bulbs that Elizabeth had received and retrieved them from the drawer in the table, unscrewing the light bulb that was now useless. With her phone's flashlight, she opened one of the packs and fitted a bulb into the socket, screwing it until it sat firmly in place.

Except when she turned the light on again, the usual warm yellow glow from the previous bulb was replaced by a weird, dewy blue light. The UV, she realized. And then she looked across the room.

Elizabeth's side was suddenly illuminated with drawings and writings.

Sade walked toward the walls slowly, trying to make sense of what she was seeing. Her eyes danced around. There were drawings of Elizabeth and Baz, a haiku about birds . . . Every single blank space was covered: Elizabeth's thoughts, moods, worries played out across the wall.

But as she moved once more, Sade's heart stopped.

The Fishermen are rapists, it said on the wall. It was written over and over again. She felt herself go cold.

Sade imagined Elizabeth at night, writing the same words over and over. As if Elizabeth needed the reminder that these things were real and happening. She saw at the bottom of the wall that Elizabeth's handwriting seeped into illegible ramblings, the signs of her hand growing weak as she wrote.

The world went still, knocked off its axis.

This was why Elizabeth had gone missing. It had to be. Something happened with the Fishermen. It was all connected.

Sade's eyes followed more and more scribbles repeating those same four words.

The Fishermen are rapists.

It felt like if Elizabeth had run out of ink, she might have used blood next. Needing to let the walls of the school know who and what its occupants were.

And when the sentence stopped and a new wall began, Elizabeth had started to name names.

Green Goose—Lance Pilar—Mendel House

Gray Sheep—Corbin Shephard—Hawking House

Jinja Spice—Jerome Maxwell—Einstein House

Sade stared at the names, making sense of the pattern in front of her.

Jack the Ripper—Jude Ripley—Hawking House

Elizabeth had known about the chat. She'd known about the Fishermen. And this was where she'd kept everything she'd found.

The Net—Password: JohnFishersMen

Was she going to expose them? Expose the Fishermen?

She recalled Elizabeth's face from that day she went missing. Scared, determined.

She was going to do something that day. Sade could feel it but she hadn't known what. Until now.

She felt a sinking inside as the puzzle pieces finally began to fit.

Someone had found out and stopped Elizabeth.

She thought about the email from Elizabeth's dead great-aunt, the phone GPS signal dying, the dead rat, everything.

Then she stared at the sickening words on the wall once again.

What did they do to her?

35

MONDAY
SHOW-AND-TELL

S: We need to talk, meet me in Turing when you're done with rowing practice

SHE PAUSED BEFORE SENDING BAZ a follow-up message.

S: It's about Elizabeth

Then she sped-walked to Curie House to find Persephone.

When she knocked on her room door, though, Persephone wasn't the one who answered.

Instead, it was some girl with dark skin and a shaved head, who Sade realized was probably Persephone's roommate, Maribel.

Maribel must have sensed Sade's confusion, because she immediately said:

"Persephone's at dinner; she left a while ago, so she should be up soon. I was just about to leave anyway; the room is all yours."

Sade nodded. "Thanks."

Maribel stepped aside, letting Sade in.

Sade hovered awkwardly as Maribel tossed her clothes about, clearly searching for something. It was hard to make out the floor on Maribel's side of the room, completely covered by textbooks and clothes and shoes. A big contrast to Persephone's neat and alphabetized side.

Persephone's décor gave Sade the feeling she was getting a rare glance into her mind. Sade noticed the posters hanging above the bed again, this time her brain paying attention to one poster that said, *Hello, World!* And next to that was another one, with the famous *Hamlet* lines "To be, or not to be" and the expected skull image beneath it. Next to those was a shelf filled with stacks of books.

Sade turned her attention to Persephone's desk, the clone phone resting there. Her mind flashed back to Elizabeth's walls.

While Maribel was still turned away, she picked up the phone.

Unlocking it, she went onto the hidden group chat app. The notifications had stacked up, the messages constant. She clicked onto the files, opening one labeled

The Net. She had seen it before, when they initially gained access to the app, but like everything else, it had been password protected.

Until now.

Sade opened *The Net* folder, typing in the password she had seen earlier.

JohnFishersMen

And then she watched as the pictures began to load. Some were open, and others required a further password.

She clicked on the first one that showed up.

It was a picture of some boys she didn't recognize in a lavish-looking room, posing with wineglasses and smiles. At the top of the screen, she saw the date the picture was taken. Five years ago. These boys had likely already graduated.

She clicked out of it as more downloaded, scrolling to more recent photos. The boys here she recognized from the swim meet she'd gone to and others from just moving about the halls. She recognized some of the girls too. The pictures seemed innocent as Sade scrolled through; just people—Alfred Nobel students—partying in fancy dresses and suits. There were pictures in some kind of beach house, everyone in swimwear. The photos spanned years.

Hawking parties.

Sade clicked on another picture, watching it load, until—

April.

Wearing a black minidress, surrounded by a group of laughing people.

She swiped through to another photo and April was there yet again, in the same position. This time a banner was visible in the background.

WE ARE THE CHAMPIONS

This must have been after a meet.

Maybe a party to celebrate their win.

But Sade remembered what Persephone had said—it had been seared into her brain:

There had been girls he'd hooked up with at Hawking parties who weren't okay afterward. Said that after . . . they couldn't remember a thing about the night or about being with Jude.

Could it be that Hawking parties were thrown not for "fun," but for the so-called *Fishermen* to target girls. To invite them, then spike drinks? To do what they wanted with them?

Sade felt sick.

She looked back down at the photos, scrolling backward now, landing on another photo of April, this time with August, smiling and holding wineglasses up to the camera.

Was it possible that April knew about the Fishermen? About what they did and the purpose the Hawking parties served? She was August's twin sister, after all.

She must have known something.

Sade got the idea then to search for August's nickname in the list of names in the directory, stopping when she found the most obvious one. *KingPhelps.*

Tapping on his name brought her to a list of the times he was mentioned in the chat. She scanned the list, eyebrows furrowing at one of the messages that seemed to have a password-protected image attached . . .

"Are you her girlfriend?" Maribel asked suddenly, and Sade almost dropped the phone.

"What?" Sade spluttered.

Maribel turned back to her and looked her up and down. "You're her type, so I figured—" she said, interrupted by a knock. "Who is it?" she yelled, walking over to the door and pulling it open.

"Sorry, forgot my keys . . . ," Persephone said, walking in, pausing when she noticed Sade. "Oh hi," she said, staring at her. Sade pocketed the phone quickly.

"I'm going to go now. Nice meeting you, Sade," Maribel said with a wink before grabbing a bag from her bed and leaving the room promptly.

"Hey," Sade replied.

"Is everything okay? I hope Maribel didn't bother you much or anything. She's nosy as fuck, but nice enough that it never warrants me requesting a room transfer."

"No, she was nice. It's just . . . there's something you need to see."

"HOLY FUCK."

Persephone had been staring at the walls in Sade's room for a while now.

"I think Elizabeth knew who the Fishermen were and had been trying to find a way to expose them. I don't know if it's every name on the chat, but it looks like she had enough information to show someone. She figured out the code names, which name matched which student. I think we should show someone right now. Someone like Ms. Thistle, she'd listen surely," Sade said.

Persephone looked pensive. "I think we should first confirm who is involved and how. The evidence needs to be airtight, especially with Headmaster *Gaslight* in charge and everything that has happened with Jude at the moment. Let's look at everything together again. I should have brought the clone phone," she said. "I can run back—"

"I have it," Sade replied, taking it out of her pocket. "I swiped it as we were leaving."

Persephone looked relieved as she took the phone into her hands and clicked onto the app. "I think the code names are related to the passwords to some of the locked pictures. Give me the name of a random boy and I'll guess who the girl he's dealing with might be, based on what I know from gossip circles."

Sade was surprised that Persephone knew much gossip, given that she seemed way more interested in her books than anything else.

"Curious Fox is . . . Liam Carter," Sade said, reading from the notes on the wall.

Persephone typed it in and then opened up one of the password-protected photos he had sent. She entered his name in the username bar and the name of a girl.

After a moment's silence, she finally looked up. "It worked."

Persephone tested it out on another guy, and while it took her a few tries of guessing the girls he might be referencing, she finally got it on the fifth go.

Both photos seemed to be of the respective girls. Both were private pictures they had sent to the boys, likely assuming they'd stay private. But here they were, on this group chat being shared and saved and discussed.

One boy wrote:

The things I could do to her.

And another:

Maybe she should come to the next Hawking party, I bet we could have some fun

And those were the least awful messages of the bunch.

Some of the things they wrote were so deplorable, Sade wondered how people like this even existed.

Sade glanced at Persephone, noticing how pale she looked now. This was probably triggering for her.

"Are you okay? We can stop for now. I know it must be hard to see . . ."

Persephone shook her head. "I'm fine. It's just—this is worse than I thought somehow . . . ," she said quietly, looking sick to her stomach. "So many boys, people you wouldn't even think would do things like this . . ." She looked up at Sade. "How do you think your roommate is connected? Do you think she left the school because she couldn't handle being in the same classes as these boys— because honestly, I relate to her at this point. Not sure that I've felt safe here for a long while."

"I don't think Elizabeth left on her own volition," Sade said. Then she thought back to August, or *KingPhelps* as he liked to call himself. The messages he'd sent, and that password-protected photo.

Persephone looked at her, confused. "What do you mean by that?"

She wasn't sure how the theories she and Baz had been playing with would sound to someone else. But at this point, she had nothing to lose if Persephone thought she was losing her mind.

"You know that email, the one the school got about Elizabeth leaving?"

Persephone shook her head. "I just heard she went to stay with family."

"Yes, well, the school was told about that via email. That Elizabeth was with her great-aunt Julie. The only problem is, her great-aunt Julie is dead."

Persephone's eyebrows shot up.

"That isn't the only weird thing. Basil, Elizabeth's best friend, had that Friendly Links GPS app that lets you share your location with friends. The last time Elizabeth's phone was picked up by a signal was around the Hawking House area. Usually, if someone turns off the link, it shows a message. But with Elizabeth, the signal just got lost that night. Like her phone had been switched off or destroyed."

"Okay, that *is* weird, and scary. Do you think someone from the group found her and did something?"

Sade nodded. "I think so. Worst part is Webber wouldn't even listen to us. A student is missing and all he can do is tell Baz that he's imagining things."

"Sounds like typical Webber to me. The only time he seems even relatively interested in student life is when it involves sponsors or a championship," Persephone said.

The sound of rapping at the door made Sade jump suddenly.

"It's open," she yelled, knowing from the sound of his knocks alone who it was. A wet, breathless Baz trudged in.

"I g-got your message, wh-what happened?" he asked, teeth chattering. It was raining outside, and he wasn't wearing a coat nor his school sweater. The white dress shirt clung to him as he shivered. He then seemed to notice the weird hue to the room, and the wall of writing. "What's all this?"

Sade didn't really know where to start.

But still, she told him everything.

BAZ WAS SILENT AS SADE explained it all.

Partly, she imagined, from the presence of Persephone in the room, but mostly because of the nature of what Sade was disclosing.

"I think Elizabeth was going to out the Fishermen, and they stopped her before she could," she finished.

Baz stared up at the walls, his expression blank. He was so still, Sade was scared she'd broken him, but then he sneezed loudly, confirming he was still functioning. "Fucking hell," he finally said.

After several moments of silence, Baz looked up at the ceiling. "You said the UV bulbs were sent to you. Who sent them?"

Sade had been wondering the same thing.

"I don't know," she said. It felt too eerie to be a coincidence. "But at least now we have this," she continued. "Do you think this would be enough for them to finally listen about Elizabeth?" Sade asked, wanting to give him time to process but also being acutely aware that there really wasn't any time at all. "It has to be, right?" she asked.

"You should simply make them listen, not ask for Webber's permission," Persephone said.

Sade and Baz turned to her.

"How?" he asked.

"We don't give them a chance to turn this information away—we let everyone see and decide for themselves. Surely that would force the school to open the investigation back up. Especially if you tell them about the GPS thing. That feels like an unquestionable lead to investigating everyone mentioned in the chat, the Hawking House parties, and conducting a much more thorough search of the premises."

No wonder Persephone was deputy head girl. She was clearly a genius.

"That could work," Baz said, nodding determinedly.

It felt like there was forward movement once again. New hope brewing.

"Was Hawking House the only place the GPS picked up?" Persephone asked.

Baz shook his head, taking out his phone to show her the page displaying the area of Elizabeth's last-known movements. "She was around this area in general."

Persephone took the phone, her eyebrows furrowed as she scanned the screen.

"Hmm, that's strange . . . ," she said.

"What is?" Baz asked.

Persephone pointed to the dot on the screen that represented Elizabeth's last signal. "I use this app quite often even though their interface is terrible. You can zoom in here and it gives you more specific information. Can you see the little letters there? The red W symbol? It's a compass that shows the direction her phone was facing." Sade squinted, seeing it now. The little compass letters. N, E, S, W. Or *Never Eat Soggy Waffles*, as her tutor used to say.

"It seems that Elizabeth was entering Newton, not Hawking House."

"Why would she go to Newton?" Baz asked.

Sade's thoughts whirred as a single name came to mind.

"August," she said. "She was meeting August."

TUESDAY
ALARM BELLS

THE NEXT MORNING, ANOTHER EMERGENCY assembly was held.

This time, though, Headmaster Webber was accompanied by men in police uniforms.

Sade recognized one of them as the one she'd spoken to when Elizabeth went missing.

Students took their seats and Headmaster Webber waited for everyone to quiet down before making his announcement.

"Good morning, we won't be keeping you long, just a few updates. It is with great shock that I have to announce that Jude Ripley's sad and untimely death is now being treated as a murder."

The hall erupted with noise. Outrage, disbelief, upset.

Jude wasn't just dead.

He had been killed.

Sade felt Baz squeeze her hand.

"We urge that those of you who were in attendance at the party or might have any information about the case to come forward as soon as possible. The police will be conducting interviews with Jude's close friends and acquaintances, as well as his year group. Thank you to those who have already come forward. It is greatly appreciated. "

Sade wondered how many people had come forward so far. She chewed on her lip nervously. Were there pictures from that night? She should have checked the clone phone.

Her thoughts were interrupted by a loud squeaking noise and a thud as the doors to the auditorium opened and August Owens appeared, looking even more like a hot mess than he had previously.

"Sorry," August said, his voice echoing as he slumped into one of the back seats casually, then took out his phone as though he didn't care that he was extremely late for an assembly.

Webber continued to speak and Sade continued to stare at August.

The boy who did nothing but lie.

"It seems that Elizabeth was entering Newton, not Hawking House."

"Why would she go to Newton?"

"August," she said. "She was meeting August."

Baz's eyes were glazed over. "Do you think he did something to her? We should tell Webber that it was him, they can investigate him—"

"We have to be smart," Persephone interrupted. "We don't know that it's him she was meeting. We have one shot at this. I say we focus on exposing the Fishermen and then directing the school toward Elizabeth in this equation."

"I hate him," Baz muttered, bringing Sade out of the memory from yesterday. He was looking back at August too. "Elizabeth was going to expose him and he probably got his family to disappear her. His dad works for the government; it's the type of thing he could probably do."

Sade heard someone clear their throat and looked up to find Miss Blackburn standing at the side and watching them with her finger on her lips, signaling that they were making too much noise.

"In other news," Headmaster Webber continued. "There will be a memorial for Jude tomorrow in the Newton Sports Center, where we will be unveiling the new pool and remembering Jude, his talents, and all the good he did."

Sade spotted Persephone seated in between April and Juliette, her face tight.

Sade wanted to whisper about the memorial to Baz but was aware that Miss Blackburn was probably still watching and so she refrained from doing so. She looked at the cold matron once again, noticing now that her gaze was not on Sade nor the audience, but on the headmaster. Her eyes squinted at him and she had a look of distaste on her face, as though she too couldn't stand him.

Once dismissed, Sade didn't move to get up immediately. Instead, she waited for the rest of the students to clear out before making any movement. Lingering at the last row, she pretended to search for something in her bag as the police spoke in hushed tones to Headmaster Webber near the front of the room, though because of the room's size, their voices still echoed enough for her to pick up their words.

"We're trying to keep this under wraps from the media. It wouldn't be good for our school or even the students if paparazzi were swarming outside," Webber said.

"We understand. But our priority is the wishes of the victim's parents, the safety of the students, as well as the ongoing investigation. We can't control what the media picks up."

"Yes, but you must understand that a drug scandal could ruin—"

"Again, we respect and understand that. But we have to investigate it. The boy was found with a myriad of drugs in his system, including Rohypnol—"

"Sade, are you coming?" Baz asked from the top of the steps by the exit.

Sade looked up at him. He had been joined by Persephone, who looked distracted.

Sade nodded. "Yes, be right there."

As they walked out together, Sade's heart was still ringing loudly, the conversation she'd just eavesdropped on replaying in her mind on a loop.

"They really need to stop having those pointless emergency assemblies. I feel myself literally losing years of my life," Baz said.

"When I'm head girl, I'll campaign against them," Persephone replied.

"Persephone, you saint," Baz said, looping his arm through hers.

Sade remained silent, trying to make her heart slow again but finding it increasingly hard to do so. Not when the enormous weight of her actions was pressing down on her. She felt like the entire sky would swallow her whole.

Soon they'd piece it all together and find out what really happened to Jude.

It's only a matter of time.

WEDNESDAY
MEMORIAL

THE NEXT DAY THERE WAS a memorial for Jude in the Newton Sports Center.

With Jude being the golden boy of the academy, the turnout was as expected. It felt like everyone in the school was crammed into the natatorium. And it seemed like the tears being shed were real.

Such a stark difference to the vigil held for Elizabeth all those weeks ago.

Sade considered not attending but worried it would look suspicious. Instead, she gritted her teeth and joined the rest of the student body in the morbid display. Baz had decided he didn't mind looking like the killer and instead stayed behind in Seacole with Muffin.

The service began with a speech by the coach of the boys' swim team, who broke down crying after every other word—mostly, it seemed, because he knew that the swim team was screwed in the finals without Jude.

Next up was Headmaster Webber, who also seemed tearful, which Sade suspected was because of the family's major donations to the school. The countess's money was something he would dearly miss.

The school choir—which Sade hadn't known existed—sang "This Little Light of Mine."

During the song, Sade kept her eyes firmly planted on the ground of the pool area, wishing she could tune out this song about Jude being some kind of divine light in the world.

As she focused on the floor, she spotted a weird smushed green sticker in between the tiled lines of the ground surrounding the pool. It kind of looked like a four-leaf clover.

Applause interrupted her thoughts, forcing her head up as the song ended and the choir bowed. After they left, it was announced that there would be more speeches from staff and students, including August, who seemed to have tidied himself up somewhat.

"Jude was not only a brilliant captain, but also my best friend and my brother. He will be dearly missed," August began, his voice devoid of any emotion. "While the police are working to find who did this, we are keeping spirits high with the unveiling of the new swimming pool." He pressed a button and the electric cover over the pool began to retract like a convertible car's roof. The pool was filled and rose petals that spelled out Jude's name floated on the top. "I present to you, the Ripley Swimming Pool." Loud cheers sounded all over the hall, rippling and echoing as people celebrated the life of a monster.

Sade didn't join them.

Behind August stood all the boys on the swim team, dressed in their varsity jackets. She spotted Francis, right behind August, looking messier than he normally did.

The swim team boys all stepped forward one by one, dropping their swim goggles into the pool, fragmenting the rose petal pattern.

More cheers sounded.

Once the show was over, August moved away from the pool, his eyes locking on Sade as he stepped back. At first, she thought she was imagining it, but something about the look felt like it was specifically for her.

"I want to get drunk," April announced to the group as the memorial came to an end. She seemed to not care at all that her ex-boyfriend was dead and that her brother was clearly mourning in some strange way.

Even Juliette was crying. She hadn't stopped since the memorial began.

"Honestly. Me too," Persephone said. "I could use fifty drinks right now."

"We can use Sade's room. She's the only one of us without an annoying roommate," April said, raising an eyebrow at Sade as if awaiting confirmation without asking her first.

Sade nodded. "Yeah, sure," she said, then remembered the walls and the light bulb situation. "I'll just go back and clean up my room real quick. I should be done in thirty minutes-ish?"

"I'll join you—to help clean," Persephone said.

April smiled, linking her arms through Juliette's, who was still sniffling. "Great, I'll go and grab my stash. See you guys in a bit," April said, then turned to leave with Juliette.

"What a shit show," Persephone said once they were out of Newton and away from the mourning people.

Sade agreed. All these celebrations around Jude made her angry. She almost envied Baz for not having to witness that. "I need to switch out the light bulbs before April and Juliette come over," she said.

"You haven't switched them out yet? Isn't the UV light distracting?"

Sade shrugged. "My lights are mostly off anyway, and even then, the UV light doesn't bother me much."

The longer she spent with the walls, the more she felt she understood Elizabeth. A patchwork of her mind. It seemed the writing started off as something she did out of boredom, with doodles and quotes from her favorite songs. A space that was then overtaken by the Fishermen and everything she'd found out.

Once they got to Turing, Sade and Persephone rode up to the fourth floor. She wanted to see if Jessica might have a spare light bulb before she needed to look elsewhere.

To her luck, when she knocked on the door, the nosy house prefect opened, her face pinched as she saw it was Sade on the other side. Jessica glanced at Persephone and seemed surprised to see her there.

"Hi, Jessica, I was wondering if I could get a spare light bulb? Mine stopped working this morning."

Jessica sighed. "For future reference, you can get them from the storage cupboards downstairs. But luckily I have a few spares; hang on a second," she said, moving into her room and then reappearing moments later with two boxes. "Anything else?"

Jessica was being so . . . nice . . . It was weird.

"No, that's everything," Sade said, and Jessica nodded, said goodbye, and closed the door in her face.

"You know, she's never usually that kind to me. It must be because you're here," Sade said as they got back in the lift.

Persephone looked at her. "Why, though?"

Sade pressed the third-floor button and nodded down at Persephone's deputy head girl badge.

"Maybe that. Jessica seems to respect authority."

"If only being deputy head girl meant anything. It's a pretend role, really. The head girl and boy are the only positions with any power, and unfortunately, our current head girl, Katarina Plum, is more interested in being neutral and apolitical than doing anything that actually matters. If I was head girl, I could definitely do something about the Fishermen," Persephone said as they got out of the lift and turned the corner to Sade's room.

Sade was about to say something about Persephone running for head girl when she saw what was on the ground.

Persephone slowed her walking, then stepped back. "Is that a—" Persephone began, but Sade interrupted with an abrupt "Yes," her heart in her throat now.

Placed outside her door was the body of a dead rat.

Rats that squeal become a meal. That's what the invite had said.

"I think I'm going to be sick," Persephone said, her face screwed up.

Sade felt like she was experiencing some kind of twisted déjà vu. The dead rat outside the door on her first day. Was she now the rat that someone believed had squealed?

She felt shaky as she moved toward it.

This was a message. The same message that Elizabeth had received.

Her mind automatically went to August. "I'll remove it quickly before April and Juliette arrive," she said, opening her room door and stepping over the dead rat. She searched the room for a plastic bag, her heart still hammering away, her vision wavering.

Sade finally found an old Waitrose bag stuffed into one of the drawers and used it to pick up the dead rat from the floor. She could feel its limp body through the bag. How soft and hard it felt at the same time.

She tossed it quickly in the nearest bin, looking up at Persephone, who genuinely looked green.

She quickly switched the bulbs, and hadn't even started to process what to do next, when April and Juliette arrived.

April put on a playlist of songs that didn't seem to really match the vibe of the post-memorial haze they were in. The only good thing that had come from this whole situation was that their classes had been canceled until Friday. At least Sade didn't have to concentrate on classes while also figuring out everything with the Fishermen.

The rat's dead eyes were seared into her brain. Elizabeth had been involved in this—the Fishermen—and she'd received a rat just before she disappeared. What would happen to Sade now that she'd received the same? Would she mysteriously vanish at night? Or something worse?

She didn't want to be alone tonight and almost wondered if Persephone would say yes if she asked her to stay.

Persephone was seated in the corner with a wineglass by her feet; April had her legs stretched out and was leaning back on the floor, staring up at the ceiling like she was in a blissful daze; and Juliette was lying on Sade's bed.

Sade was next to Persephone, drinking the Capri Sun that April had gotten for her, knowing she couldn't drink with them, which was surprisingly nice of her.

"Hey, Sade, do you have any paracetamol? I have this killer headache," Juliette asked.

"It's in my top drawer," she replied, just as her phone buzzed with a message from August.

A: csn yiu come to the pooL pls?

S: Are you okay?

A: im sooooo okay

August was drunk or high; she wasn't sure.

It was good timing because she'd been wanting to speak to him. It might've seemed careless of her to consider going alone, but she wasn't scared of August.

"Uhm, guys, I'll be right back," she said, pushing herself up and slipping into her shoes.

"Is everything okay?" Persephone asked her.

Sade nodded. "Just need to check on something."

WHEN SHE GOT TO NEWTON, August was there in the Ripley pool. Fully clothed in the suit he had worn to the memorial, he was floating in the pool with a large bottle of merlot in one hand, rose petals surrounding his body.

"Hey," she called out, but he didn't seem to hear her at first. "August?" she tried again, stepping closer to the edge of the pool.

This time he looked up. And then he gave her a weird smile. "Hello, girl 1,465 that my best friend was fucking," he replied. Then he followed this up with, "Just kidding—he said you were prudish."

Sade felt her heart go still. This August didn't sound like the August she had spent the last five weeks getting to know. Then again, that August was always a liar, so maybe this was the real him and he was just now showing her how ugly he could get.

August finally stood up in the shallow water, pulling the cork off the already half-empty bottle in his hand and downing the rest. Some of it spilled down his suit, staining it red, and trickling into the pool, producing droplets that looked so much like blood.

"Are you okay?" she asked as he chucked the bottle to one side.

"I'm peachy, told you that already," he said, climbing out. His suit was completely drenched and heavy-looking as he trudged up the pool steps.

"Sorry, I was just worried about you," she lied. "You seem very different—"

"Do you mind if I ask you a question?" he asked, looming toward her.

Sade felt uncomfortable as she moved back from his unfocused gaze. "Sure, go ahead," she said. She had questions of her own.

His eyes seemed red and angry. "Where'd you go that night? During the party?" he asked.

"What?" Sade replied, taken aback. Her heart was in her throat.

"You were at the party, right? Where'd you go? I remember seeing you one minute and then the next, you were gone. Like magic," he said with a wide smile.

"Uhm, I went home—"

He clicked his finger and grabbed his head. "Wait, I know where you were," he said, pointing his finger at her. "You were with him, right? Heck, I think you were the last person to see him before he, you know . . ." August bent his neck and made a cracking sound with his mouth.

"I don't think so," Sade said, stepping back again.

"No . . . no, I'm pretty certain it was you. I remember looking up and seeing you guys going into his room. Maybe you aren't as prudish as I thought. You guys have fun? Hmm? Did he show you a good time?"

"What are you implying, August?" Sade asked.

He laughed. "Oh, I think you know."

They stared at each other for a few moments before Sade sighed. "I'm gonna go," she said before turning around.

"Yeah, that's just like you, isn't it? Flee the scene of the crime quickly, right."

She didn't stop to humor him or wait to see the other ways his sharp tongue could cut her, just walked away. Her heart was banging at the walls of her chest, the persistent voice hissing inside.

It was hard to tell when a shift was coming that was big enough to rock your entire world, but when it arrived, it always seemed so obvious.

When Sade approached Turing, she didn't stop to think why there was the distant sound of sirens. She didn't question why it seemed that there was this hushed whispering when she entered, as people looked up as though something or someone was up there. When she stepped out of the lift and into the hallway, she noticed her door was open and hurried voices were coming from it.

She walked in quickly and was surprised to find Jessica accompanied by Miss Blackburn.

And a body on the floor.

Juliette. Her face deathly pale and her eyes closed.

This couldn't be happening. Not again. Sade could feel eyes on her.

Persephone's eyes.

She turned to them and Persephone was giving her a similar look to August's—a look wrapped in suspicion and anger.

April just looked blank, as usual.

"What happened?" Sade asked. But her question went unanswered because two paramedics came rushing in along with two first aiders from the school and asked everyone to step back.

The first paramedic went to check on Juliette, their movements quick as they assessed her breathing. Her eyes were only open slightly, as she seemed to fall in and out of consciousness.

The other spoke to Persephone about what had happened, asking whether she'd had anything to drink, and about her known medical history, then telling Miss Blackburn they'd need to take Juliette to the hospital.

"Can we follow her?" Persephone asked.

Miss Blackburn seemed slightly annoyed at Persephone interrupting her conversation with the paramedic and looked like she was about to say no.

"Please," Persephone said.

Miss Blackburn reluctantly nodded. "I'll have to get special permission for you all to leave the school," she said.

"Thank you," Persephone said.

THE THREE GIRLS SAT IN the waiting room.

Sade was between April and Persephone, April doodling something in a notebook and Persephone ignoring Sade.

She couldn't ask what had happened, but she suspected from the way Persephone was acting that they felt that she was to blame.

The nurse tending to Juliette stepped out and Persephone got up immediately. "Is she okay? Can we see her?"

"You can come and see her now. Your friend is going to be fine. We found traces of Rohypnol in her system, which made her pass out—"

"She was roofied?" Persephone asked, confused.

Sade felt her heart plummet in her chest.

"It would appear so, but she'll be fine. We should be able to discharge her tomorrow morning," the nurse finished.

"You can go and see her one by one, and then I need to get you all back to school before curfew," Miss Blackburn said.

Persephone went first. Sade watched the clock as the minutes passed. The ten minutes Persephone spent in the room felt more like ten years to Sade. Her leg kept bouncing, anxious energy bubbling inside.

The nurse called April as Persephone walked out, carrying on right past Sade and over to the bathroom at the end of the hall.

By the time Sade was called in, Persephone still hadn't returned. She got up and went into Juliette's room.

She felt like a fraud standing there. It wasn't as if she even knew Juliette properly. She was an intruder.

"Are you okay?" Sade asked.

Juliette nodded. "I'm fine, honestly, just really tired," she said with a smile.

Sade nodded, feeling guilt weigh on her even more. "Okay, well I'll leave you to it then . . . ," Sade said, stopping herself from apologizing because then she'd have to explain *why* she was apologizing.

A few moments later, she was leaving the room. She felt numb as she walked over to a nearby vending machine, hoping some juice might help her nerves settle. Only, she couldn't bring herself to raise her arm and tap in the number combination for the juice. Instead, she just stared into the vending machine's glass case, until her vision crisscrossed and blurred. She thought she heard a creaking sound from above. She blinked back tears and raised her head to the ceiling, watching as the flickering lights in the hallway got more and more irregular, as the ceiling plunged toward her, crushing her to dust.

The sky had finally fallen and killed her. Just like she thought it would.

What have I done? she thought, sniffing back tears. She didn't deserve to cry about this.

Juliette had Rohypnol in her system, and it was all her fault.

Everything was always her fault.

She was the bad omen people wore talismans like four-leaf clovers to protect themselves against.

She was the ladder you're not meant to walk under.

She was the black cat lingering and stalking your shadow.

She was all of it.

She was the problem.

ON THE DRIVE BACK, PERSEPHONE didn't look at Sade once. She probably hated her, and Sade couldn't blame her if so.

When they finally arrived at the school, Persephone hugged April and said goodbye, watching her walk off into Hawking as she claimed she needed Francis after the trauma of the day.

It was obvious that Persephone was stopping herself from rolling her eyes at that.

And then it was just Sade and Persephone left.

"Can I walk you to your room?" Persephone asked her quietly.

Sade nodded, noting her grave tone.

They walked in silence to Turing House, and in silence up to the third floor. And then when Persephone had finally walked Sade up to her room, she asked to come inside.

Coming back to the room always felt like returning to a crime scene, but even more so today.

The room felt cursed and heavy and silent.

When they walked in, Sade closed the door behind her and Persephone stood with her arms crossed, watching her.

"I'm sorry," Sade said.

Persephone didn't speak at first, but Sade could see her thinking. "What for?" Persephone asked.

Was this a game? Did she want Sade to spell out what she'd done?

"F-for what happened to Juliette, I'm so sorry. If I had known it was in there I would have warned her—"

"Why exactly was there Rohypnol in your room, Sade?" Persephone asked in an accusatory tone.

Sade didn't say anything. She couldn't bring herself to speak.

Persephone nodded, as though her silence was answer enough. "I'm gonna ask you some questions, and I hope that you can be honest with me," Persephone said.

Sade remained quiet.

"After Juliette took the paracetamol in your dresser, she started acting weird, loopier than usual, and then passed out. The nurse said what she took wasn't paracetamol. It was Rohypnol. At the end of the assembly yesterday, I heard the officer talk about how Jude had Rohypnol in his system, and so I'm going to ask you a very simple question, Sade. Did you do something to Jude?"

She suspected that Persephone was really asking: *Did you kill Jude?*

Sade felt the wind knock out of her. The ceiling started to crumble again, squashing her lungs flat.

This couldn't be happening, not now.

"I think you should leave," Sade said.

"I'm not going anywhere until I get a fucking answer," Persephone said, voice rising.

Sade could feel the scraping in her mind, the pain that split her open, the voice that haunted her trickling in.

She shook her head. "P-please, Persephone, I can't do this right now."

"I don't care; I need answers. I need to know if I'll be arrested for aiding and abetting. I need to know if I should stop planning for my future right now. I need to know if I should be calling my mum and her lawyers. I need to know, Sade, I need to know now."

Sade felt tears rest on her eyelashes, and she sniffed. "I'm so sorry," she said to Persephone.

"What for?" she asked, an edge to her voice.

Sade blinked and felt the heaviness disappear as tears trickled and meandered down her face, tickling her chin.

You should never have come!

She was in agreement. She should never have come here.

Persephone didn't deserve to suffer because of her.

Maybe it was time to explain.

Though once the truth was out there, Sade worried that no one would look at her the same. "I—I need a moment, it's a lot—"

Persephone nodded. "Take your time."

TWO YEARS AGO

THEY WERE WHAT SOME PEOPLE in Nigeria called ibeji.

Ibeji meaning two of the same.

Twins.

Sade Kehinde and Jamila Taiwo Hussein.

Taiwo the eldest and Kehinde the second in every way.

Her mum always said that twins were special. People made songs about twins. Prayed to the gods for them. Saw them as some kind of miracle invention.

Her aunt Mariam never quite agreed with the claim. She thought twins were a curse, split to purge the evil part of the soul. She used to pick them both up, inspect them closely with suspicion, and then she'd always frown at Sade and whisper, "You're the bad one."

It seemed Aunt Mariam wasn't the only one who thought so.

Parents lie and tell you that they love their children the same, but they don't. They always have a favorite.

Sometimes it's as subtle as a tighter hug or a lingering loving gaze. Other times it's as loud as her father striking her across the face and wishing out loud that she was dead.

Parents had their favorites, whether they wanted to admit it or not.

And Sade was definitely not her aunt's or her father's.

TWO YEARS BEFORE SHE ARRIVED at the pearly black gates of Alfred Nobel Academy, before the many tragedies that had followed her and led her to the boarding school, Sade resided in an idyllic town house in London with her father, twin sister, and the ghost of their late mother.

Her mother had died four years prior, and while the world forgot and moved on, the Husseins never could.

Her sister became consumed by schoolwork, using books as a distraction from her painful reality.

Her father became stricter and even more unkind.

And Sade became stuck in her own head.

She sometimes swore she could hear her mother's laughter echo around the house or the sound of her footsteps trudging up the stairs. She could still see her in the reflections of the glass cabinets, the mirrors and the windows, could smell her warm rose-scented perfume, feel her cold hands tucking her into bed each night and her gaze lingering on her as she slept.

But she knew none of that was real. She knew it was her grief conjuring up false realities.

It was strange losing someone like that. One day there, the next gone, leaving this empty space where her love could no longer go. Her death caused this permanent crack in the family, so visible it was hard to miss.

Things weren't perfect before her mother's passing. Far from it. But when she was still there, there was so much light that it eclipsed everything else—her father's open hatred of her, the fights her parents had that would occasionally turn physical, and the storm Sade always felt brewing inside her, making her feel like the whole world was so bleak and helpless.

She didn't know it at the time, that what she felt was something doctors called *depression* and that it apparently ran through the maternal side of her family. Consumed her great-grandmother Sola, taking her grandmother Taiwo next, and then her mum. What they failed to diagnose was whether these feelings came about because of both the chemicals in their brain as well as the pattern that was the men in their lives.

Sade's father had killed her mother, and slowly, he was killing her too.

In his grief, his grip on her freedom tightened. Jamila was certain it was because he was scared of losing more family, but Sade knew it was because he hated being out of control.

He never let them leave the town house. There was this constant surveillance, a paranoia that weakened his heart every day. If they wanted clothes, a maid would take a trip to the mall and fetch them. If they wanted exercise? Well, there was a gym, a coach, and a personal trainer available whenever they wanted. Education? Home tutors.

Sade felt like she couldn't breathe most of the time. She hadn't seen the outside of the house in so long. She hadn't even spoken to another kid her age, other than her sister, in years. It was like her father was punishing them for something.

"I hate him," Sade told Jamila one day when they were lying on the sun beds by

311

their special place, the large lake on the edge of the garden. "I hate him so much. I hate that he keeps us inside. I hate that he thinks he knows what's best and I hate that he let Mum die—"

"Don't say that," Jamila said quietly.

"Which part?" Sade asked.

Jamila sat up and looked at her. "All of it."

Sade laughed. "Are you taking his side now? After everything he's done, I thought you wanted freedom too—"

"Yeah well, I just feel like . . . he's not as bad as you make him out to be . . . He's just sad and scared."

Sade rolled her eyes. Of course *the favorite* would defend him.

"Did he buy your allegiance or something? Why are sticking up for him all of a sudden?" she said.

But when Jamila didn't reply, Sade frowned.

"Jam?"

Jamila sighed. "We talked and he agreed to let me go to this private school nearby. I start in a few weeks."

Sade's eyebrows shot up. "Oh my god, really?"

Jamila nodded, still not looking Sade in the eye.

"That's amazing!" Sade liked her tutors but she wanted companions her own age aside from her sister.

"It really is! They have a great lacrosse team I'm hoping to try out for and all these wonderful archaic buildings and a long history," Jamila said brightly.

Sade couldn't believe her father had had a change of heart. He seemed so dead set on them being trapped inside forever. "What made him change his mind about us never experiencing the perils of high school?"

"Uhm, I think it's just me, for now. He said I could go but you had to stay."

Sade's face twisted. "Why?"

Jamila shrugged. "I don't know, maybe it's because I'm older, but hopefully in a few months he'll see that it's not scary at all and he'll let you come—"

Sade almost laughed in disbelief. "I can't believe you. You got a 'get out of jail free' card and you took it. He never intends on us both living a life. Just you."

Jamila shook her head. "Don't take it the wrong way, Sade."

"How else am I meant to take it?"

Jamila said nothing.

Sade pushed herself up from the grass. "I'm going inside."

"Sade—"

"Leave me alone," Sade said, walking away quickly before her sister could see the tears starting to fall.

MONTHS HAD PASSED IN THE Hussein home, and Sade hadn't spoken to her sister since the argument in the garden. Not that Jamila hadn't tried.

Sade had just become very skilled at avoiding her.

She'd eat quickly at dinner to avoid having to hear about Jamila's perfect day at school. She'd avoid their special spot—the lake in the garden—knowing Jam would be there waiting for her. She'd listen out for when Jamila was hovering outside her door, hoping to talk things through.

Until one day Jamila no longer did.

Sade assumed her sister had given up on trying to mend their relationship after her betrayal, but when she noticed that Jamila was no longer coming down to dinner or going to school, she understood that wasn't the case. Something had happened.

"Your sister realized that school wasn't what she thought it to be," her father had said, when Sade finally asked him. He was seated in his armchair with his legs crossed, reading a large newspaper, seemingly unbothered by the fact that his older daughter was uncharacteristically absent.

After stopping school, Jamila was no longer tutored at home, and she rarely came out of her room. Yet this seemed to concern no one else but Sade.

Whenever she'd see glimpses of her sister, she noticed how different she looked. Bloodshot eyes, bones poking out through her skin, and the brightness she normally exuded turned down completely.

It was like something vital had been stripped away.

She probably got expelled for getting a bad grade or something, Sade reasoned with herself, even as her worries grew and her suspicions remained that something terrible had happened.

But that was the thing about sibling fights. The loser was the first to speak, the first to crack. And Sade loved to win.

To her relief, on a random Saturday after so long without speaking, Jamila finally broke.

Sade heard her sister's quiet footsteps approach her room again. This time, she didn't wait for Jamila to linger and then leave. This time she rushed up to her bedroom door and flung it open.

As expected, her sister stood on the other side. Sade almost gasped at the sight of her.

She looked so . . . different.

Sade stared at her distorted mirror—her pointed collarbones, her gaunt cheeks, her peeling skin. She felt for the first time in years that the person she saw staring back at her was a stranger. Jamila shifted her top slightly to cover the bones that were poking through her skin and offered Sade a fractured sort of smile.

Before Sade could say hi or anything, Jamila was speaking.

"Want to go to the mall?" Jam asked.

"What about Dad?" Sade said.

Jamila grinned and Sade could now see fragments of her sister in the face that was so pale and sickly. "He's on a business trip; don't worry."

Sade nodded. "Okay."

IT WAS STRANGE HOW SOMETHING as simple as a trip outside could fill her up with so much light, but it did.

They were seated in a café now after a day of shopping. Or well, a day of Sade shopping and Jamila observing quietly.

"Today was nice," Sade said, peeling the sticker on her cup out of habit.

"It was," Jamila agreed. "I'm glad you enjoyed it and that it made you happy. I sometimes worry that you have so much sadness inside and I have no way to fix it."

Sade was surprised at that. She didn't really think Jamila paid that much close attention to her. "You don't need to fix me, Jam. I'm doing okay."

Jamila gave her a sad smile. "Yeah, I know."

"Are you? Doing okay?" Sade asked.

Jamila paused before answering. "Today's been a lot better than most."

Sade wanted to ask what had happened, why she had been so different. But before she could, Jamila was talking again. "I'm sorry for leaving you behind," she said.

"It's okay," Sade said, even though it wasn't. But she wasn't angry anymore; she just wanted her sister back.

"It wasn't okay. I should have done more. But I guess you can't really change the past. I realize that now," Jamila replied with a distant look in her eye.

Sade noticed that she hadn't touched her coffee, the eggs Benedict they'd both gotten, or the cinnamon bun now on her plate. The old Jamila would never have passed up the opportunity to eat something sweet.

"You know what gets me through really tough times?" Sade said.

Jamila looked at her suddenly, as if she'd been startled out of her own thoughts.

"What?" she asked.

"I tell myself to keep swimming, and if I can't do that, if that's too hard, I simply float."

"Of course you would use a swimming metaphor."

Sade shrugged. "It works."

Jamila nodded. "I'll keep that in mind."

THAT NIGHT, JAMILA SLEPT NEXT to Sade. It had been years since they had done this, and Sade hadn't realized how much she missed it. Missed the warmth of someone beside her.

"Why is it that I feel the safest in the whole world when I'm next to you?" Sade whispered.

She could feel Jamila's smile. "Probably something about the womb. We did share that space for nine months; it was pretty intense."

"Yeah, it's probably that," Sade replied, and then she added quietly, "We should always do this."

"Do what?" Jamila asked, sounding tired.

"We should always sleep next to each other. I don't need my own room, I just need you."

Jamila was quiet for a while before she finally responded with a nod. "Yeah, we should."

In the morning, however, the space next to Sade was cold and Jamila was gone.

After their closeness yesterday, Sade felt a need to be near Jamila again. She went to her bedroom to find her. It was a Sunday, but even though their home classes stopped for the week, Sade knew Jamila loved studying; she checked the library, the living room, the garden where she'd sometimes see her reading, then wandered round the house once more, coldness sinking into her bones.

She went back to her room, but couldn't shake the feeling that she was missing something. And that's when she saw it.

A sticky note was on her mirror, written in her sister's distinctive cursive hand-writing.

I'm sorry.

Sade had a bad feeling about this.

She ran out, rushing through each room as she checked them off in her mind. The sticky note remained gripped in her hand. When she'd exhausted her options inside the house, she realized her only option now was out.

Dread gathered in a ball inside her as she checked the one place she'd been avoiding.

315

It was as if she instinctively knew to avoid it. To distract herself with the maze of the town house as she processed what she would soon know to be true.

The door to the back garden had been left wide open. The sky was blue-gray and spitting warm rain from its overwhelmed clouds, and Sade was still in her nightgown.

She gently placed her bare feet onto the ground, stepping out from the safety of the inside and the ignorance that came with it. She could feel the wet spikes of grass beneath her feet, tickling her toes as she stepped into the garden and toward the lake.

The garden was large enough that, from a distance, the lake and all its inhabitants were disguised, but once you stepped over the threshold, the clear rippling water filled with bright fish and old plants would come into view. Nothing could hide anymore. Not even the truth.

Closer now, the truth laid bare in the open, she felt the hairs on her arms rise and her heartbeat come to a stop.

There was something in the lake. Something bigger than any fish or plant she'd seen before. Something white and brown and *still*, so still. Something that wasn't *something* at all.

But *someone*.

Someone who looks—

She didn't finish that thought.

Instead, a switch went off in her mind and suddenly she was moving forward.

"Jamila?" she asked as she reached the edge of the lake.

No answer.

"Jamila!" she screamed.

Nothing.

The body—her sister—began sinking into the water, slowly disappearing beneath the grubby surface.

Sade could feel her airways constricting, could feel her vision crumbling, her limbs shaking. She needed to do something.

Before she knew it, she was throwing herself onto the edge of the bank, letting her body sink into the murky water with a loud splash. There was no time to think, only to swim, to stop nature from taking its cruel course before it was too late.

Sade swam like she never had before, frantically and without care for technique, her strokes uncertain and jittery as she reached out for her sister.

She grabbed Jamila's arm and then her torso, fighting to pull her up. But the more she tugged, the harder it got.

It was strange how small her sister was now. She was so small and frail in Sade's arms, like her bones, her organs, *everything* had been extracted out of her.

Jamila, please . . . , Sade wanted to say, to *scream*. But she couldn't. The thing about screaming underwater was that no matter how much you did it, your voice would be eaten up, stolen by the water.

She hadn't realized how far into the lake they'd both sunk until it began to hurt. She had been holding her breath for so long she felt her lungs ache.

She fought it as much as she could, but eventually she had to come up for air or she'd drown too. Though when she got to the surface again, she still couldn't breathe.

And it felt like she had already drowned.

THE POLICE RECOVERED JAMILA'S BODY.

She was placed in a white plastic body bag and removed from the lake quickly.

Sade had attempted to go back in but it was too late. Her sister was no longer there. Just a body that happened to wear the flesh mask of her sister's face.

The police asked her some questions, then they left her alone sitting in her wet nightgown on the damp grass.

Sade wasn't sure how long she had been sitting at the lakeside afterward. Everything seemed to happen in slow motion, until suddenly it was dark outside and her father was back from his trip.

"How could you let this happen?" he asked her, his eyes glassy and red. "You had one task, to look after your sister, always, and you failed her and now she's—"

"I'm sorry, I tried saving her—"

"You didn't try hard enough. Just . . . just go to your room. I don't want to see your face anymore."

That night, she didn't sleep.

She didn't cry either.

She didn't do anything.

She wondered if she was broken.

Why wouldn't she cry? Weren't you meant to cry?

But she almost felt nothing. Her mind was strangely quiet.

It was hard to process how you could go from laughing with someone one day to their laughs ceasing to exist altogether the next.

She didn't sleep or cry the next night either, or the night after that. She was exhausted, but she couldn't sleep.

She heard her father cry. It's all he seemed to do. She'd hear a string of curses in Yoruba, followed by prayers in Arabic.

"Why, God, must you take everything from me? Why? I have nothing left."

He repeated this on a loop, crying until his throat was raw.

She envied him. He wasn't broken like she was.

He wasn't heartless.

WEEKS AFTER HER SISTER'S DEATH, Sade saw her again.

She was standing in the corner of Sade's room, dressed in her white nightgown and staring at her blankly.

Sade felt her heart pulse as Jamila watched her, unblinking.

"J-Jamila?" she said into the dark, hoping this wasn't a sign that she had finally lost the plot.

Jamila didn't answer.

It was like she was a hologram projected from the depths of Sade's nightmares.

Assuming that this was the result of sleep deprivation or maybe a side effect of the expired milk she'd accidentally consumed with her tea, she turned away from the projection and forced herself to forget it was there.

But it wasn't long before she felt her bed dip, and the cold hands of her sister slip around her tightly.

Sade froze, too scared to breathe.

"I'm here now; you can sleep," Jamila whispered. This didn't bring much comfort. Not that the ghosts of dead siblings were known to.

Jamila held her tighter, and Sade found herself beginning to relax again. She would write this off as a weird dream. She had many of those, some of which made her sleep-walk all over the house. This was merely one of those occasions.

Jamila returned the next day, rose from the ashes in the corner of her bedroom, and held on to Sade tight as though scared that holding her any looser would make her slip away.

As though Sade was the dead one, not her.

After a week of Jamila's nightly visits, Sade finally asked the question that was racking her mind.

"What happened to you?" she whispered. Because she knew that Jamila's change didn't come from nothing.

Had someone done something?

Had someone hurt her so badly it was the final thing that pushed her over the edge?

"Please tell me who did this. I'll kill them, Jam. I'll find them, and I'll kill them."

But there was no answer. Jamila only squeezed her harder.

So while Sade couldn't cry like a normal person, she decided there was something she *could* do.

She would find out what happened.

THE NEXT DAY, SADE WENT into Jamila's bedroom.

It still smelled like her, citrusy and clean.

While Sade technically saw some version of her sister at night, she smelled nothing like the real Jamila.

Ghost Jamila smelled of dust and smoke, was cold and silent.

Something the real Jamila never was.

Going through Jamila's belongings felt strange, like she was invading her privacy somehow. But she decided that the cost of not knowing outweighed everything else, so she riffled through, looking for something, anything, to help her understand what had led to all this.

After a few moments of searching, she finally came across her sister's journal.

On the front of the journal was a collage of photos Jamila had pasted together. Sade's eyes lingered on the photo in the center. On the picture of the three of them: their mother and the two of them in Paris.

Inside were journal entries from over the years. These weren't daily, more so spread over months and only accounting for the really important things Jamila wanted to write about.

Like an entry she did on an ice-cream cake she had eaten that was particularly great.

It was kind of wholesome.

As the years went on, the journal entries got more frequent and a lot more intense.

I miss Mum a lot, the house feels colder without her, she wrote.

Sade flipped past more pages about her mum, things she didn't even know Jamila thought about. Notes on their mum's recipes she'd been trying to remember and perfect. Memories she was reflecting on. One page had even been covered in their mum's perfume with the words: *the sky has not yet fallen* written in purple ink in the center. It was clear that their mum's death had taken a toll on Jamila in ways Sade didn't think about. Jamila always seemed to wear a brave face about it, choosing to protect Sade instead. Like the perfect big sister she is. *Was.*

Sade felt tears prick her eyes. She quickly moved past those pages, knowing that she could spend forever thinking about her mum if she wasn't careful.

She flipped through pages of more of Jamila's thoughts.

And then she came across a page that surprised her.

Today I met a boy in my new school.

The next entry was about him too.

He always tells me how beautiful I am. I can't believe that someone so perfect likes me.

Jamila journaled about sneaking out to meet the boy. About wishing she could tell Sade about him, but Sade wasn't speaking to her.

Then for a while . . . the entries just stopped.

Sade flipped the pages, searching for more words in her sister's handwriting, only when she got to the back, she finally saw her writing again. Like Jamila meant to hide it.

The entries were long and short.

They seemed to be written in a more sporadic manner. Whereas her non-hidden entries were dated and in order, these were all over the place. Dates backward, entries in random order.

July 13

I haven't slept in what feels like a century. I can't sleep. I don't know if I ever will again. I bet he's fast asleep in that new boarding school. I bet this doesn't rot his brain and make him feel so twisted and ugly and wrong in his own skin. I bet he's okay.

May 8

I've developed an unhealthy habit. Scrolling the deep dark throes of online forums. I didn't start off searching for him. It was just a way to pass time, really. People post all sorts on there. They've even found missing persons from these posts alone. They post other things too . . . things I relate to now, I guess. So I thought, why not? Sade won't speak to me, but maybe someone who gets it might.

March 6

I think I was raped.

Sade felt something crack inside, as she read those words. It felt like her whole world was crumbling.

And then for the first time since the day at the lake, Sade cried.

WITH HER FACE STILL WET and her chest still burning, Sade strode into her father's office.

He was away on another business trip, so the house was quiet as it usually was these days.

They were never allowed in here—but she'd seen glimpses of the room before. All dark wood and prestigious awards and degrees hung about.

Her bones rattling, her skin hot with anger, Sade tore through her father's files, following a hunch she had.

She found the file she required in a locked cabinet under his oak desk, tucked away at the back, hidden from prying eyes.

Jamila Hussein the file read.

Her father kept files on everyone in his life. It was part of his business and life philosophy. Keep your enemies close and your family even closer.

All their doctor's notes, tutor reports, swimming progress charts and things Sade didn't dare to think about were locked away in this cabinet.

The key was hidden in plain sight, disguised on his desk as an ink quill.

Her fingers shaking, Sade opened Jamila's file. She scanned the pages, sniffing as the information was spelled out plainly on the page in formal text.

Jamila Hussein was removed from Nightingale Academy following an incident with a male classmate. A drug test found that Miss J. Hussein was sharing and allegedly distributing drugs to the male classmate, J. Ripley, who she accused of accosting her at a social gathering and forcing her to engage in nonconsensual relations.

Mr. J. Ripley's representatives have denied all accusations, and as Miss J. Hussein was the only one out of the two with positive drug test results, she was immediately removed from the institution.

There was an initial lawsuit drafted by Mr. J. Ripley's representatives, which was kindly voided and settled by Miss J. Hussein's representatives outside of court.

Sade finished reading the documents with one final clear thought in mind. She was going to find him.

THE PRESENT
WEDNESDAY

"MY SISTER MET JUDE AT the school she went to. They were dating, it seemed, and he invited her to a party. At the party, he drugged and assaulted her. And then she died. I blame him for it. He killed her. Not immediately or physically maybe, but in all the ways that mattered. He killed her."

Sade wiped her eyes. She hadn't let herself think about the details for such a long time—focused on the now of it all.

"My father deteriorated after that. Then about a month and a half ago he just dropped dead. Suddenly, I was an orphan. I had no family, and nothing more to really live for, and I just kept thinking about the guy who hurt her. I researched all I could about him. He was kicked out of the school after being caught selling drugs on school grounds, transferred to Alfred Nobel Academy, and all of a sudden he had a clean record, a fresh slate. I decided sometime last year that I was going to find him and make him pay for what he did. So I applied here in secret. I wanted Jude to feel as powerless as he made Jamila feel, and all the other girls I know he's hurt. I didn't want to kill him. I just wanted—"

"Retribution," Persephone finished.

Sade paused. "I guess so."

Persephone was silent.

She imagined Persephone no longer trusted her, nor wanted to work with or befriend someone who had lied to her for so long about so much. So it was a surprise when Persephone's expression softened and her crossed arms dropped to her sides.

"Can I give you a hug?" she asked.

Sade was stunned. "Y-yeah, sure," she said.

And Persephone stepped forward and wrapped her arms around her tightly. Sade felt a weight fall from her shoulders, and the scraping in her mind dulled, suddenly.

"You don't hate me," Sade whispered.

Persephone shook her head. "I'm mad at you for not telling me sooner, but I don't hate you."

Sade wasn't sure if Persephone was unwise or just way too trusting. Especially considering the implication of what she had just admitted.

That she may have killed Jude.

"Do you think they serve tea in prison?" Sade asked, hoping the somewhat morbid joke would lighten the mood. If Persephone had put two and two together, the police must be close to figuring out the connection too. Any day now she would be found and locked away forever.

Which maybe wasn't the worst thing, in the end. A part of her wondered whether this was all apt punishment for being unable to save her sister. The other part of her recognized that maybe this was always what she wanted. To be caught and punished. She wasn't a mastermind after all.

Her plan always had holes. She just didn't care to fill them.

Persephone pulled back and stared at her earnestly. "You're not going to prison," she said.

Sade smiled at her, resignation already filling her down to the bone. "I appreciate your positivity, but the police are going to trace the Rohypnol back to me eventually. It's just a matter of when."

Persephone shook her head. "I'm a realist. If you were screwed, I'd tell you. You're not going to prison, because the drugs didn't kill Jude."

Sade was confused now. She had heard the police talk about the Rohypnol. She had seen his body afflicted by death. Persephone herself had asked what she had done to him.

"I was listening to the police officers after the assembly. When you and Baz went off to classes, I sneaked back. I was hoping for some information so that we could get ahead of the police. I knew they'd had the autopsy results back. So yes, Jude was heavily drugged up—as he always is—but that only made them curious; it wasn't his actual cause of death."

"What killed him?" she asked.

"I'm not sure," Persephone replied. "But the important thing is, you didn't. I hope you stop beating yourself up over it. Even if you had killed him, I'd still have your back. Partners in crime and patriarchy smashing, always."

Sade felt a little tearful. "Thank you," she said simply. And Persephone gave her that almost smile that always made her insides glow.

"No problem. I'm really sorry about your sister and everything you both went through," she said. "People need to know the truth about Jude. The Fishermen won't get away with this."

Sade wanted to believe this, but it felt so hard to accuse a dead man of anything. Especially one as beloved as Jude Ripley.

"How? It feels like they already have," she said.

"I had an idea while we were in the hospital. I guess the anxiety of not knowing if my friend was going to live or die fueled my brain juices—I tend to work well under pressure," Persephone said, taking out the clone phone.

"We have all the information here. Right here, on this phone. And now we have Elizabeth's code system. We set up a website, and then we release the information, the texts, everything to everyone—I took a seminar on coding over the summer, and it shouldn't be too difficult to do."

Sade considered it carefully. Considered the idea of letting go of everything, letting the public know everything they knew. All this wouldn't tell them what had happened to Elizabeth or where she was now, but it would do something about the people who caused her disappearance in the first place. It was like throwing all their darts at the target and hoping for a bull's-eye.

"So, what do you say, Mars?"

Sade raised an eyebrow at the nickname. Mars. If she had a lighter complexion, it would show that her face was the very color of the planet.

"I think that could work."

I SLEEP, I DROWN & DISAPPEAR[7]

Dear Diary,

Decades have gone by since the night I thought I died.
Not much has changed.
I still can't breathe, my skin is still cold, my heart is still
frozen in time, and I'm bleeding out inside.

---

[7] An anagram

40

FRIDAY
NOT SO NOBLE

THE WEBSITE WENT LIVE DURING third period on Friday.

Sade and Persephone had spent the late evening of Wednesday and all of Thursday working on it.

Persephone had wanted to use school computers in blind spots, where it would be near impossible to trace the origins of the website. Sade wasn't so convinced this would protect their anonymity and instead suggested another idea.

Her idea found them in Baz's room in Seacole, watching Kwame work his magic on Sade's laptop. He randomized the IP to make it harder to track, then put up firewalls to protect the website from hackers. He also helped with pointers on how to manipulate the website and hijack other software such as the school's mainframe.

Sade liked that Kwame was a no-questions kind of guy. He felt trustworthy—though she could tell that Persephone was highly suspicious of the guy.

When Kwame left the room, they began transferring the data from the clone phone to the site, showcasing all the evidence they had gathered. Sade had enlisted Baz's help to make things go faster so that they could have the website ready before lunch rolled around on Friday afternoon. Alongside screenshots from the chat, they used Elizabeth's list from the wall, pairing all the usernames with the respective Fishermen and their yearbook photos.

And it had all culminated into this moment.

As planned, hundreds of phones went off at the same time across the school. Email and text chimes buzzed and pinged in synchrony as all the students received an anonymous message with the website's link. The website also took over the screens of the boards in each classroom and the digital boards around the school.

The text that flashed up on the website, NotSoNoble, read:

Hello, Alfred Nobel Academy, we have a problem.

The website had an automatic scrolling function, immediately flashing up the name of each boy from the Fishermen group chat and hyperlinks to screenshots of the things they had said and done.

None of the inappropriate photos of girls were released and any names or nicknames had been blanked out. The narrative was focused solely on the perpetrators, leaving no room for shaming the victims.

Sade was in her psychology class when the link was sent out. There was a rumble of voices, which bubbled over into outrage as people began opening the links.

Her psychology teacher, Mr. Lanister, had attempted to quiet the students, but found himself stopped, face red and alarmed as the website scrolled in front of him.

By the time lunch rolled around, Sade had watched several of the Fishermen boys called away, into Headmaster Webber's office, and by the end of the day, it seemed that almost everyone knew of the group and the website.

"Jerome Maxwell got pulled from my history class during fourth," Baz said quietly as the three sat at the usual table in the library after school.

"Lance Pilar was pulled from my class too," Persephone said. "Hopefully, by this time on Monday, we'll have a verdict from Webber on the Fishermen."

Sade hoped so too. It felt that almost everyone had seen the website now, and who the Fishermen really were. She had a good feeling about all this. Something she didn't have often.

BEFORE DINNER, SHE WENT FOR a celebratory swim. For the first time since Jamila's death, she could finally swim without seeing her body, or *any* body for that matter, in the pool with her.

She lay back, letting herself drift and relish having a clear mind for once. No clawing or the usual sense of impending doom she got.

Just quiet.

She could hear the sound of feet slapping on the tiles in the distance. Someone approaching the pool. And then, a voice.

"Haven't seen you in a few days," August said.

Sade's eyes opened and she stopped drifting, placing her feet firmly on the pool floor and swimming forward a little.

He was standing in his full uniform, looking more like the put-together version of himself she was used to seeing.

"Breaks are good," she said, climbing up the ladder to get out of the pool, wanting to be on equal ground.

He had this intense look in his eye, like he was glaring at her. "I guess so."

She grabbed on to the towel she kept on the side bench and wrapped it around herself. Sade wondered if he was here to confront her about the website.

326

Surprisingly, despite being Jude's best friend, he seemed to rarely speak in the group chat, so there wasn't as much on him that could be uploaded. Though this didn't make him innocent. When he did contribute, while small, his contribution had significant consequences.

So significant she had hoped he would come to the pool tonight so that she could look him in his lying face and ask him *why*.

"Are you planning on coming into the pool?" she asked.

He shook his head. "Just here to see you, really."

So they had similar motives it seemed.

"What about?"

He placed a hand in his pocket, and the intensity in his expression increased. He looked like he wanted to burn her. Which was interesting seeing as she wanted him to burn too for what he had done.

"Where were you the night Jude was killed?" August asked. "I saw you go into his room, twice."

Sade raised an eyebrow, trying to seem unfazed by the question, though feeling her heart skip and her chest become tight. "I have no idea what you're talking about," she said.

August laughed. "Don't lie to me, Hussein. Just answer the question."

Sade thought about what he said, but instead of answering, she decided to ask her own question now. "Why did you lie about dating Elizabeth?"

That seemed to catch him off guard. "I told you, we were just hooking up—"

"We both know that's a lie. I guess it's why I won't ask you why you sent that email pretending to be her great-aunt Julie or why you sent me that email warning me to stop digging. I know you'll just lie some more," she said, and he didn't even flinch at the mention of the emails. It was him, and he didn't care that she knew. "I'm assuming you've seen the website by now, so we also both know what you did. You sent that video of her to your friends. What sort of person does that?" she asked. "All you've done is lie to me. Where is Elizabeth now? What did you do to her?"

She felt sick to her stomach as she remembered that video of Elizabeth. The very personal one August had sent to the group chat, likely without her consent or knowledge.

August looked murderous. "You don't know what you're talking about."

"I don't? Enlighten me, then."

He didn't respond to that. "I know you're hiding something, and I'm going to prove it. I know you have something to do with Jude's death, and I will speak to any officer who asks to see me and tell them I saw you. Because I see you for who you are, Sade," August said darkly.

"And what is that, August?" she asked, with as much confidence as she could muster. "At least I'm not a coward like you. If you really had something on me, you'd have gone to the police already. But you can't, because you don't. A weak threat from a weak boy."

August scoffed but didn't say anything. She had rendered him speechless. Instead, he gave her a final glance before walking out of the natatorium. The doors slammed fiercely and the sound reverberated around the pool, leaving Sade with a sinking feeling inside.

She got the sense that the storm was brewing.

"HEY," SADE SAID WHEN BAZ opened his room door twenty minutes later.

Her skin was still wet and she was still feeling cold from the pool and the exchange she'd had with August.

"Hi," Baz said, surprise evident on his face.

She hadn't told him she was coming like she usually did. She hadn't planned on coming either; she just didn't want to be alone.

"Just came over to see if you wanted to have dinner together at Turing?" she asked.

He studied her face carefully for a few moments before nodding. "Yeah, of course, let me get some shoes on," he said before going back into his room and pulling out a pair of sneakers.

The room was quiet, and she could see the outline of Spencer lying in his own bed and typing away on his laptop. She found the distant clicking sound of the keyboard slightly jarring.

"Okay, let's go," Baz said, now ready.

They walked down the stairs of Seacole in silence, Sade breaking the quiet once they got to the foyer and out the doors.

"I've been monitoring the website with Persephone, by the way, a lot of traffic," she said.

Baz simply nodded silently. Something about his demeanor seemed a little off, but she didn't push.

"We're hoping that Webber does something by Monday."

Baz still said nothing, just walked with her along the path opposite to Seacole.

Before they got inside Turing, she pulled his arm, forcing him to stop walking. "Is everything okay?" she asked.

Baz looked at her and sighed. "I'm just a bit tired, to be honest. I feel like Elizabeth has been lost in all this. It all started with her, but she's still gone. Everything's still a mess."

Sade frowned a little. "This is connected to Elizabeth, though—she was working on exposing the Fishermen—"

"I know," he said, looking down at the ground. Sade felt torn. She hadn't told Baz about the video August had sent the group. Baz knew what the group chat was for, but she couldn't tell if he'd worked out yet just how Elizabeth might fit into all this and Sade didn't know how he'd react to knowing what August had shared of Elizabeth in there. She wasn't sure if Elizabeth would *want* Baz to know either. She'd clearly kept it from him for a reason.

"I get that exposing the Fishermen is important, but Elizabeth is important too. Shouldn't we be finding out who in the Fishermen chat knew that she knew about the group? Shouldn't we be reporting August or *someone* for whatever might've happened to her?"

"That's what we are doing," Sade said softly. "But like Persephone said, we have to be smart about this. I want to find out what happened to Elizabeth as much as you do—I promise, she hasn't been forgotten. We will solve this."

Baz nodded solemnly. "Okay," he said. She wasn't sure he was convinced by her reassurance, but if he wasn't he didn't show it. Instead, he smiled at her and looped his arm through hers. "Let's go inside. I'm starving."

THE DINNER HALL WAS FULL with Turing students, as it usually was at the peak time of dining hours.

Sade had been moving her food around the plate and thinking, instead of eating. She stared at the windows, noting how dark the clouds had gotten. The storm was brewing. She could feel it.

As though the universe was listening in to her thoughts, her phone buzzed loudly on the table.

P: Come to Franklin House, room 324. It's an emergency.

Her eyebrows furrowed. Wasn't Franklin April's house?

"Is everything okay?" Baz asked with a full mouth.

"I don't think so . . . I got this weird message from Persephone."

"What message?"

"An emergency at Franklin House."

Baz looked confused. "Isn't that April's house?"

Sade nodded. Her phone buzzed again.

"Do you need me to come?" he asked quickly.

P: Don't bring leaf-boy

Sade knew she meant Basil. Persephone seemed to struggle with remembering his name. When they'd met up on Thursday evening to input the data into the website, she kept referring to him as *Minty*.

"Uh no . . . I'm sure it's fine, probably about our English coursework or something."

Baz nodded. "Should I keep your lasagna for you?"

Sade shook her head. "You can have it. I'm not all that hungry anyway."

Baz looked pleased. With a wave, Sade was gone, now rushing through the cold, wet evening to Franklin House.

The Franklin House tie was pink, as was the interior. The walls were a light pink, almost peachy color and had a really unique wallpaper print pattern of the human heart. The floors were cherrywood and, similarly to Turing, a portrait of the house's namesake, Benjamin Franklin, hung in the entrance.

Only, this portrait had been vandalized. An X had been scrawled over Franklin's face and body in bright fuchsia spray paint. Next to this portrait now hung a painting of another famous scientist: Rosalind Franklin, her portrait intact.

A brass plate hung next to it with the engraving: THIS HOUSE WAS ORIGINALLY NAMED AFTER RENOWNED SCIENTIST AND MISOGYNIST BENJAMIN. WE REJECT THAT.

It was kind of cool, she had to admit.

Sade rushed up to room 324.

She moved to knock, but the door opened immediately and she almost hit Persephone in the face.

"Come in quickly," Persephone said, and closed the door behind her before Sade had even fully squeezed into the room.

"What happened?" she said, noticing the disturbed expression on Persephone's face, while looking around the room.

Juliette was crouched in the corner while April sat on the bed, a pale, corpse-like figure beneath the blanket.

Sade's stomach flipped.

Another body.

Then the slow, gentle rise and fall of the person's chest confirmed that they were still breathing.

Sade stepped forward, her heart lodged in her throat.

The person on the bed wasn't a stranger.

It was Elizabeth.

41

FRIDAY

THE RETURN

"I-IS TH-THAT—" SADE STARTED, A cold chill running through her.

"I can explain," April said.

But Sade could barely hear her voice over the sirens in her head.

How was this possible? Elizabeth, here, in April's room?

Elizabeth, here, *alive*.

"I found her here in Franklin," April said. "In the bunker in the house's basement . . ."

Sade's hearing kept fading and then sharpening and fading some more. Like her body was shutting down from the shock.

April went on, offering an explanation that seemed so far-fetched Sade didn't know what to make of it.

From what she could gauge from April's nervous rambling, the school, like many Victorian buildings that survived the Second World War, had tunnels and bunkers. Some of which the school and its inhabitants knew about and others that had to be discovered by chance.

April had found one of these bunkers in Franklin in first year.

April went down there sometimes for quiet and, coincidentally, this evening, she'd found Elizabeth there before dinner, barely conscious.

Sade glanced at Elizabeth again. The sight of her sent even more shock waves through her body.

She looked nothing like the girl she had met over a month ago. This girl looked so sickly pale and thin and unwell.

She reminded her of Jamila.

"I called Persephone for help and she called you and Jules, and now we're here. Elizabeth told me not to call any teachers, so I don't know what to do."

But how did Elizabeth survive down there with no food or water? Who put her there? How did she get there in the first place?

"We need to call an ambulance!" Persephone said, clearly frustrated.

"I second that. She looks like she's dead or dying," Juliette replied, looking sick.

"Elizabeth said she didn't want that—"

"When did Elizabeth tell you this?" Sade asked. "You said she's been unconscious."

"She was talking before," April said.

"And you only *just* found her a few minutes ago?"

"Yes."

Sade could tell there was a lie in this story; she just didn't know where.

"We need to call an ambulance, now. If she dies, we will all be at fault," Sade said.

Persephone immediately took out her phone and April looked betrayed.

"Hey, it's three against one. I'm calling," Persephone said.

"I'm gonna get a teacher," Juliette said, rushing out the door.

Minutes later, the first aid staff rushed in, alongside the house prefect and Sade's favorite matron, Miss Blackburn, who as usual did not look pleased to see her.

"Of course when there's a fire, I know you'll be involved, Miss Hussein. Please, everyone who doesn't sleep here, go out into the hallway and stay there."

Persephone and Sade shuffled out of the room, while Juliette went down to direct the ambulance.

"I need to tell Baz," Sade said, taking out her phone to call him.

It was hard to know what exactly to say.

Hey, they found Elizabeth but aren't sure she's going to make it.

Or:

Elizabeth is here on April's bed. She was apparently here this entire time in a World War II bunker.

Neither seemed particularly sensitive, nor did it seem alarming enough for the gravity of the situation.

"Hello?" Baz said, picking up after the first ring.

"You need to come to Franklin, room 324. They found Elizabeth. She's in April's room right now," she said, looking over to where April was seated on the plush chair in the corner of her room, staring off into the distance. She was perfectly poised, as though unaware of the commotion around her. Sade thought April was staring at her at first but realized soon after that she was staring at nothing, her face devoid of any emotion. Sade felt a flash of annoyance. April could at least pretend to care.

"Wh-what?" Baz's voice came through the receiver. "What do you mean they found her?"

"She's alive," Sade said, realizing that she didn't specify that before. Her voice cracked a little as she spoke.

"I'm coming," Baz said.

He didn't wait to hang up before she heard his footsteps and running. She heard him apologize after bumping into someone, it seemed.

She ended the call and slipped her phone back inside her pocket as the sound of loud voices came from the stairs.

"She's straight through there," Sade heard Juliette say as people in paramedic uniforms appeared around the corner.

Through the open window in April's room, Sade could hear the first crack of thunder as rain poured from the sky onto the campus.

The storm had begun.

SADE WATCHED AS THE PARAMEDICS carried Elizabeth's limp form out of April's room.

She looked how Jamila had looked when they lifted her out of the lake.

Dead.

Baz was there now, asking one of the first aid staff if he could go with her, to which Miss Blackburn interrupted with a blunt *no.*

"But—" Baz began, only to be silenced by her again.

"We need to let the paramedics concentrate. I understand that it hurts to see your friend in this state, but if you care about her well-being, you will let the professionals do their jobs efficiently."

Baz's eyes narrowed and he laughed sharply in a tone Sade had never heard before. "That's fucking rich coming from you," Baz said to Miss Blackburn.

Sade felt the world go still, her eyes almost popping out of their sockets.

"I beg your pardon, Mr. dos Santos?"

"I have been literally telling all of you that something was wrong for *weeks.* That Elizabeth was not okay. That she wasn't with her "great-aunt," but that she was still missing, and that I knew something bad happened to her. You kept sending me away, telling me I was making things up. Now look at her. I was the only one who cared—if anything, it is your fault this happened. We could have found her sooner if you had just listened to me," Baz said, tears streaming down his face, and his voice rising.

Miss Blackburn blinked at him slowly. Sade was sure that Baz was about to receive a suspension or worse.

But to her surprise, Miss Blackburn calmly replied, "We'll keep you and your friends updated on Elizabeth's progress," before turning away to talk with one of the first aiders.

Baz stood in silence for a few moments, his whole body shaking.

Sade reached up to grab his hand, pulling him backward. As if his limbs were jelly, Baz slid down next to her on the ground, his face wet as he sniffed and looked up at the sky.

"You three should head back to your dorms. We won't be getting any updates for a while," one first aider said, Miss Blackburn now leaving the area with the paramedics.

"When do you think we will be able to see her?" Sade asked.

"As soon as we know, we will tell you, okay?" the nurse replied, giving them a kind smile.

Nothing felt kind about keeping them in the dark, though. It felt cruel. Especially for Baz.

It had been five weeks since Elizabeth went missing. Since the police and the school had decided she wasn't worth looking for. Since he was forced to reckon with the fact that she might not be found.

And now, she was here. She always had been. Right under their noses.

Alive.

"Let's go," Baz said soberly, wiping his face and pushing himself up from the ground. "Hopefully, there will be an update in the morning."

MONDAY

SATURDAY AND SUNDAY WENT BY with no real update on Elizabeth.

It had been two entire days and the hospital was only keeping Elizabeth's immediate family in the know about the state she was in.

And by family they meant her mother, who, according to Baz, seemed too inconsolable to really relay much to him. She mentioned something about a head injury and a concussion, but it was hard to get much information out of her.

Other than that, Baz seemed to be doing better mentally knowing now that Elizabeth was at least alive.

The school held another emergency assembly on Monday morning.

Headmaster Webber's hair looked white from stress. Three emergency assemblies in one week had to be some kind of record. But unlike the other morning schoolwide meetings, today they were joined by a group of police officers who stood at the front next to Webber like his own personal bodyguards.

Sade figured it would be about Elizabeth, seeing as the student the school neglected so terribly had been found on its own premises. Though, strangely, she hadn't really heard anyone talking about Elizabeth and what happened on Friday. With the way the students of ANA loved to gossip, she was surprised that no one seemed to know yet.

It was as though it never happened.

"Over the weekend, I became aware of a certain website displaying intimate student details to the World Wide Web." Headmaster Webber began. "The school is working tirelessly to disable the website, but in the meantime, we urge the creators of NotSoNoble to come forward and allow us to put an end to this foolishness. If the perpetrators do so by the end of today, I can guarantee that the repercussions for their disruptive behavior will be less severe than if caught by our experts."

"So what you're saying is . . . Exposing the rapists we attend school with is a bad thing?" a girl from Franklin House asked loudly from the back.

This encouraged a rumble of voices, some protesting what she said but the vast majority in agreement with her.

"Now, I think it's important to be careful of the accusations we make." Headmaster Webber's voice had a cold edge to it. "This is again why that website is doing more harm than good. As soon as we are able to remove it from public servers, we can sort out this issue privately."

"He's spineless," Persephone said from her seat next to Sade. "Cares more about his pocket than what the website is saying."

Persephone had monitored the website's growth over the weekend. Each day the traffic only grew. And it was clear that if the school's so-called experts were able to, they would have taken the website down already.

More voices took over around the hall, but Headmaster Webber was determined to ignore them, continuing with his speech, his tone louder than before. "On another perilous matter, we are still gathering the names of all the attendees of the party that occurred last week. It is taking longer than desired due to the lack of transparency from students involved. But rest assured we will have a complete list very soon. Can the following students please stay behind after the assembly."

Sade held her breath as Webber read out a list.

She was surprised when he called April.

And even more surprised when her own name wasn't mentioned.

"Why do you think he's told them to stay behind?" Sade asked after they were dismissed.

She didn't try listening in on the conversation like before. She was too scared that Webber would see her and remember that he wanted to interrogate her too. She was out of there as fast as she could.

"I heard that he's been designating time slots in the day to interrogate them individually," Baz said, licorice dangling from his mouth.

"Webber wants to single people out. Air their names in public. Shame them into the truth," Persephone said. And then she continued quietly, "It's a good sign that he hasn't mentioned our names yet. They've gone through a good portion of the people who were at the party now. It seems they used student logs from that day, bitter friends ratting out those who managed to get an invite, as well as those stupid enough to come forward themselves. Even with all this, it's impossible for the school to know with certainty every single person who went. So if Webber does call one of us, we deny knowing anything. We stick to our alibi."

That was, if August didn't make good on his promise to report her and his suspicions of her.

Sade had always thought silence was the song of the guilty. An innocent person would try and prove that they were just that.

But Persephone had a point. Right now Sade looked incredibly guilty, and not drawing attention to herself was probably the best thing she could do.

SADE WAS IN LAST-PERIOD HISTORY when the call came for her in the form of a student with a pink slip, just like weeks before when she was called in and told about Elizabeth's disappearance.

"Headmaster Webber would like to see Sade Hussein," the student said to her history teacher, Miss Fuller.

All eyes were on her.

Sade felt her heart in her throat as she stood up slowly, unsure of whether she was being brought in for the website or the party.

Either way, her response would be the same. Silence.

"Is it true what they say about the Hawking parties?" the student who had pulled her from class suddenly asked.

Sade was confused. "What?"

"The Hawking party. Is it true that they give out Rolexes?" he clarified.

So she was being called in for the party.

She had finally been caught.

Like Persephone had said, the lack of indiscretion was meant to be about shaming people into submission. But instead, it inspired spectacle, a source of morbid entertainment for the students of ANA—like a public hanging in the Victorian age.

She felt sick.

"Can I quickly pop into the bathroom?" she asked. "I'll be fast."

The student nodded and led Sade to the nearest toilet. She rushed inside, feeling like she needed a moment to think.

She locked herself in a stall and closed her eyes, waiting for her hands to stop shaking.

She needed to calm down. Nothing bad had happened yet. She would be fine. She just needed to focus on something else and not on her spiraling thoughts.

So she opened her eyes and for a moment just focused on the graffitied walls of the bathroom stall. They were filled with random drawings of super Ss and hearts and writing about idle gossip around the school.

She felt her mind clearing as she focused on what illicit affairs random strangers were having and not on her own problems. Only, as her eyes shifted upward, something gave her pause.

Scratched into the door were random fishes surrounding text.

Michael O'Connell is a rapist.

Sade didn't know who that was, but seeing it was enough to make the sick feeling return.

Banging on the main door of the bathroom made her jump suddenly.

"Hurry up," she heard the student call out.

Sade quickly exited the stall, splashed some water on her face, and then followed the student over to Webber's office, her mind still on the graffiti and what it all meant.

As they rounded the corner to the hallway where the headmaster's office was, she saw Persephone outside looking bored, like she had been there for a while.

Was Persephone in trouble too?

Persephone sat up when she saw her. "What are you doing here?"

"I'm on the list . . . ," Sade replied.

The student who had brought her there knocked on Headmaster Webber's door twice.

Persephone's eyebrows furrowed. "No. I saw it. You're not," she said, just as two police officers stepped out from the office.

"Sade Hussein?" one of them asked upon seeing her.

What was going on?

Sade felt shaky as she nodded.

Then one of them moved in front of her, while the other grabbed her arm and placed it behind her back before forcing the other into the same position.

"You are under arrest on suspicion of murder. You do not have to say anything, but it may harm your defense if you do not mention when questioned something which you later rely on in court. Anything you do say may be given in evidence—"

"What's happening?" Persephone yelled, moving toward Sade, only to be blocked by the second officer.

"Please step back," he said.

Sade could feel her heart racing, her anxiety spiking as the officer's rough hands bound her arms together.

Miss Blackburn seemed to emerge from the shadows and Sade could hear her ask Persephone to let the officers do their job. It felt like she was underwater. Her senses were failing her, and she could barely hear anything over the noise in her head. Her vision blurred; she couldn't concentrate on anything else.

In the distance she thought she heard the school bell go off, indicating the end of the period as well as the school day. Students were leaving classrooms now, and soon they would be watching Sade get escorted by the officers off the school grounds.

Right on cue, the hallway filled with uniformed bodies.

She couldn't hear their voices yet, but she could feel their gazes start to burn into her skin.

Sade was moved out of the school entrance and into the back of the police car. As the car pulled out of the school gates, her senses began to return, one by one.

First her hearing with the loud, aching blare of the police-car siren.

Then her sight as red and blue lights spun and painted the ground.

The taste of blood from her anxious biting down on her tongue.

"The school will send a legal guardian and they will be present at the station if you wish them to be," one of the officers declared.

But Sade could barely hear him over the sound of the sirens and her dizzying thoughts.

It was now clear what was happening to her.

They thought she had killed Jude.

THE FIRST TIME SADE HAD seen a police interrogation room was on TV.

She had been watching one of those eighties cop shows with her sister and thought, *This can't be real.*

It seemed too dingy. Like a dramatized and exacerbated version of the truth.

And it wasn't real.

The interrogation room in the local police station was a lot worse. It was darker and there was mold on the ceiling. To make matters even more grim, there was this wet-dog smell that penetrated the room and her nostrils, making her anxiety-induced nausea even worse.

To make matters even more dire, Miss Blackburn had to be present in the room, as was the legal obligation for minors being interrogated. Thankfully, Miss Blackburn's presence next to Sade was like that of a shadow—she could almost pretend she wasn't there at all. Almost.

"Water?" one of the officers asked.

Sade shook her head.

He offered Miss Blackburn some too, but she also declined in her usual cold manner, clearly not pleased to be there, either. He took a seat with his own cup, placing it on one of the ringlets on the water-stained wooden table.

"I'm PC Park. We met a few weeks ago, and this is my colleague PC Stevens. We want to ask you a few questions, and for the sake of our records we will be taping this session." To make a point he tapped the tape recorder, which had a red button indicating that the session was being recorded. "The interview will be conducted by Officer Stevens. Please answer all questions as truthfully as you can. Anything said in here can be used against you in the court of law, are we clear?"

Sade nodded, the nausea building more.

"Right, let's start, then."

TRANSCRIPT OF INTERVIEW
Names and identification redacted

OFFICER: This interview is being recorded. I'm PC ▮▮▮▮▮ and I'm based at ▮▮▮▮▮▮. Please state your full name.
SH: ▮▮▮▮▮▮▮▮▮▮▮▮▮▮.
OFFICER: Is it okay to call you ▮▮▮▮▮▮ I don't think I can pronounce that.
SH: I'd prefer to be called by my name.
OFFICER: Okay, noted. Also present during this interview is OFFICER ▮▮▮▮. Let's get straight into it. It has been alleged that you were at a party hosted by the deceased, Jude Greggory Ripley, previous Saturday. Correct?

SH: Who said I was?

OFFICER: Unfortunately, we cannot disclose that information at present. Please answer the question, Miss ██████.

SH: I wasn't there.

OFFICER: Okay . . . we have been informed that you *were* at the party. It has also been alleged that you were dating Mr. Ripley and were seen in a heated argument, days prior to the party. Is this correct?

SH: No.

OFFICER: Which part?

SH: I wasn't dating him. We were acquainted and he had expressed that he was interested, but we were not dating.

OFFICER: So the multiple witnesses were lying, then?

SH: People lie.

OFFICER: Eyewitnesses also said they saw you going into Jude's bedroom with him. You were the last person seen with him at the party, and so you must understand our concern here.

SH: I don't actually. Understand your concern.

OFFICER: Okay. Well, let me provide more of an explanation. Witnesses say that you were dating the deceased. Witnesses saw you engaged in a heated argument only days before the party. Then at the party, witnesses say that you were in his bedroom minutes before he died. We also found DNA on the deceased that we'll bet will match yours, under his fingernails—which to us indicates some sign of struggle—as well as fibers of hair on his clothes. Can you now understand our concern and why we had to bring you in today, ██████

SH: My name is ████.

OFFICER: Sorry. ████, can you understand?

SH: No, I cannot understand.

OFFICER: Very well, then. You realize we have the right to keep you in custody, given that you refuse to answer our questions. If you gave us something to work with, we could all go home. It's as simple as tha—

THE DOOR OPENED AND ANOTHER officer peered through.

"Sorry to interrupt. We need to let the girl go. They've brought someone else in," the officer said.

Officer Stevens looked irritated. "The meeting just began and we have eyewitnesses and DNA—"

"Yes, well we have something else now. A new conflicting statement."

SADE WAS RELEASED SHORTLY AFTER, relieved to finally be out of that small room. Miss Blackburn went to fill out her release forms while Sade stood and wondered what had happened.

As soon as the thought passed, in the universe's usual brilliant timing, she saw police walk through the entrance of the station with an unhandcuffed August.

They briefly locked eyes before he went into a room and the door shut behind him. He looked . . . scared.

Sade could hear two familiar voices bickering outside, so she moved to the exit of the station, toward the commotion.

"Obviously this is the right station; it's literally the only one within a five-mile radius," Persephone said.

"If you say so." Baz.

"Hi, guys," Sade said, intruding on the conversation before Persephone attempted murder in front of the local police and had to be dragged into one of those disgusting interrogation rooms too.

They both turned to her, and Baz's eyes immediately widened and his mouth pulled into a smile. Persephone, who was leaning against a nearby wall, stood up quickly.

"Hi," they both said at the same time.

"How did you guys get here?" Sade asked, both surprised and relieved to see them.

"Persephone used her deputy head girl powers and got a teacher to drive us down here," Baz said.

"We weren't expecting you to be released so quickly. They said it could be hours . . . ," Persephone said, her face a little red.

"I ran straight from my German class when I heard. The school basically imploded when you got taken away and it has just been chaos. I'm really glad you're okay—Miss Thistle said you were taken to the station and so I kept thinking the worst. I'm just glad that the Scooby gang is back," Baz said, smile only growing wider.

"I told you not to call us that."

"The Three Musketeers?"

"They're all white men."

"Brown bitches?"

"I swear to god, Basil," Persephone said, just as Sade enveloped them both in a hug, shutting them up. They hugged her back and she felt her eyes water at the realization that she wasn't alone.

"This is very nice and everything, but I think Baz left out an important part of why we're here," Persephone said once the hug had gone on for long enough.

Sade stepped back.

"Oh yes, we also came because of Elizabeth. She's awake and is allowed visitors," he said.

Sade's eyes widened, more relief spreading. "That's amazing. Are you going to see her?" she asked, confused as to why he was here with her when his best friend was at the hospital, awake.

"Yes, I will. But she asked to see you first."

THE HOSPITAL FELT HAUNTED.

Lights flickered, shadows stitching up the walls as nurses and doctors and patients wandered the halls like zombies and ghouls, and the bone-chilling cold only increased the sense of impending doom Sade felt.

It was weird that there were so many books about haunted houses and schools when hospitals were just as haunted, maybe even more so. After all, it was here that so many people died or were in a state of constant near-death.

It didn't help that Elizabeth looked like a ghost right now, her face paler than Sade had ever seen it.

"Hello," Elizabeth had said when Sade walked into the room. "It's been a while," she added, her voice croaky and monotonous.

Sade had been surprised that Elizabeth wanted to see her first. They had only known each other for mere hours before her disappearance.

"Hi . . . you look well," Sade said.

"That's bullshit. I know I look like death," Elizabeth replied with a smile.

She looked so much happier here than when Sade had met her weeks ago.

"Yeah, well . . . I didn't want to say," Sade said, which made Elizabeth laugh gently.

"I heard you got arrested for murdering Jude Ripley," Elizabeth said, cutting right to the chase. "I'm glad they let you go."

"Why's that?" Sade asked.

"Because I know you didn't do it. I told them you didn't."

Sade's eyebrows furrowed. What was Elizabeth talking about? "You spoke to the police?"

"Yes, they interviewed me about what happened to me. And I told them everything, and now August is in custody. I'm not going to lie. I'm a bit annoyed that Jude is dead. It would have been nice to see them both put away."

Sade's mind was reeling.

She had so many questions. But the most pressing one:

"What *did* happen to you?" she asked.

And Elizabeth told her everything.

A YEAR AGO

ELIZABETH AND AUGUST HAD BEEN dating since first year, and yet now in second year, not much had changed since the early days of their courtship.

For one, their relationship was still a secret. And, two, Elizabeth suspected that it would always be a secret.

The Owens' choice in partners was political. Hooking up with someone was one thing, but dating was like a business merger, and August knew that dating Elizabeth would be a poor business choice.

So, for him, their relationship was something private and shameful.

For her, it felt embarrassing to be the object of someone's shame.

Elizabeth couldn't admit to Baz that it was happening. Even as the weeks stretched into months, which then stretched into a year. Baz would have told her she deserved better than to be someone's fling in the shadows, and he would have been right.

She did deserve better.

But Elizabeth foolishly believed that August thought of her as highly as she'd always seen him.

Foolish, indeed.

That was the problem with love. It created blind spots in your mind. Bloodred flags were blocked out by high levels of dopamine and the trick of a gentlemanly smile.

So Elizabeth didn't notice what she should have.

Like why the person who claimed to like her didn't want to be seen with her.

Explained away by family politics and social optics.

Like why August loved to take pictures of her, with or without her permission.

She explained that away too. He liked photography. She was his muse. How romantic.

Or why those pictures became videos. Private videos during private times. Videos she hadn't known he was taking until later.

Again, an explanation.

He must like her so much that he wanted to replay those private moments on a loop. She should be flattered.

Right?

So she let it go.

And when one of those pictures he'd taken had somehow spread around school, he had an explanation ready, as always.

"No one knows it's you; you're barely even in it!"

Elizabeth shook her head. "You're missing the point."

"What is the point, then?"

The point is . . . you didn't ask me and you should never have taken them. But she didn't say that.

"Why are the pictures from your phone now on the phones of nearly every student at the school? I could lose my scholarship if Webber finds out; this could follow me—"

"You're being dramatic, Liz. You know how ANA is. This will die down—"

"And you're still not getting the fucking point," Elizabeth said, tears now trickling down her face. "*How* did they leave your phone?"

August shook his head. "I don't have time for this; I need to practice."

"Just answer the question."

He sighed, avoiding her eyes now. "I don't know, okay! Maybe someone hacked my cloud, or I don't know . . . Jude has my phone sometimes, he could have seen it or something."

Elizabeth wiped her face roughly and stepped closer to August, her eyes squinting and her arms crossed. "You sent it to Jude, didn't you?" she said in a pitch so low it almost came out as a whisper.

August shook his head. "I didn't say that."

"Why mention him at all, then?"

"Because you wanted an answer. I was giving you an answer. I don't know why we are even together if you don't trust me," August said, the last part of his sentence almost knocking the wind out of her.

Was he trying to dump her? He couldn't be . . .

"Maybe we should take a break. When you're in a less accusatory mood, we can resume things," he said, picking up his backpack. "I'll see you around." Then he left Elizabeth, with a pit of guilt in her stomach as if this was all her fault.

Elizabeth's heart hurt, so she went where she always went to mend broken parts of her.

"Hey," Elizabeth said as she jumped down from the ladder leading to the bunker beneath Franklin House.

"Hi, how goes it?" April was seated on a plush chair nestled in the corner of the small space that the bunker allowed.

They had discovered the bunker in first year. Elizabeth had been sent down to the basement of Franklin to get supplies for the house prefect—who was too lazy to do it herself.

Given her immense knowledge of vegetation, seeing the green-covered patch in the basement shaped in a perfect square was all Elizabeth needed to know that there was an entrance to somewhere farther, hidden beneath the moss.

She brought April down with her to investigate, and they found the bunker underneath an old, rusty trapdoor.

April had slowly added small pieces of furniture into the nooks and crannies over the summer break.

And now it was the place they often went after school. Their own Narnia of sorts that no one else was allowed to know about. Not even Baz or April's friends. It was theirs alone.

Elizabeth sniffed, settling down on the beanbag planted in the corner.

April hadn't looked up at her until that moment, too busy painting her toes a fresh new coat. "Is everything okay?" she asked, concern on her face as she took in Elizabeth's disheveled appearance.

"It's nothing," Elizabeth said.

April narrowed her eyes at her.

"It's definitely something . . . ," April said. Then realization seemed to strike. "Ahh, it's my brother, isn't it? You know I told you hooking up with him was a bad idea." Her talent had always been reading Elizabeth's mind.

"It's not your brother," Elizabeth said, looking at the ground and not at April.

"Sure it isn't. Anyway, let me know if I need to beat him up. You know I will."

Elizabeth forced a laugh. "Yeah, yeah, I'll let you know."

It felt premature telling April about their break. She still hoped that by the end of the week they'd be back together again. All the bad words would be taken back and she could go back to pretending that she was okay being someone's secret. And the photos forgotten.

HOWEVER, THE BREAK WOULD BECOME permanent. Not just the state of their relationship but also the state of Elizabeth's heart. A crack was now inside her ventricles, causing permanent scarring.

It was funny how fast August moved on. Not a week after their fight, he was already seen cozying up to Mackenzie Peters—vice captain of the girls' swim team and daughter of Dutch billionaires.

A suitable candidate for an Owens to publicly court.

Annoyingly, August was right. Most of the students of ANA soon moved on from the illicit photo spreading around.

All but one.

She didn't notice at first the way he looked at her. But once she did, it was hard not to notice.

Jude Ripley's icy-blue gaze was a hard poison to shake.

"What are you looking at?" Baz had asked Elizabeth one day when she'd become distracted by some kind of secret staring contest she had going on with Jude.

She snapped out of it, quickly responding with: "Nothing, just daydreaming about dropping out again." And then she returned to staring at the food on her plate and not the hungry gaze of the blond third year.

Elizabeth figured that the best way to get back at August for his royal douchebaggery would be to entertain Jude, long enough for August to notice.

Bad idea.

Hooking up with Jude was very unlike hooking up with August.

For one, she wasn't in love with him.

And the other thing, she didn't mind that it was private with him. It wasn't something she wished the public to know of.

Especially *not* April.

She and Jude only ever kissed, with the very occasional PG dry hump. Based on his reputation, she figured that he would soon grow tired of her, but strangely enough, he seemed committed.

"I don't know how August could lose a girl like you," he had whispered to her sweetly on one occasion.

She laughed. "By being an asshole, that's how."

Jude's eyebrows shot up. "That's surprising. You know we call him *The Gentleman* on the team."

She did know that.

It was something August was pretty proud of. It fit in with the brand he had of the dapper charming guy.

He'd even send her presents using the name with a really gentlemanly old-timey note, like

347

For my one true love—TG

Or

For my dearest Elizabeth—TG

One time he sent her this beautiful, old-fashioned jewelry box. His mum was a jewelry designer, so he had it customized for her. All his gifts were old-fashioned; they matched him perfectly.

She used to tell him he was such an old man, and he used to smile and play up to it even more.

She hated how much she missed him. He didn't deserve to be missed.

But her heart was traitorous.

Elizabeth kissed Jude some more, hoping to forget August and his charming ways. But it was no good.

Love was a bitch.

THE INVITE ARRIVED SOMETIME AFTER she had begun her secret rendezvous with Jude Ripley.

It was as black as night with the letters written in Morse code and coordinates at the back telling her where to go.

She had heard of Hawking parties before in passing. Everyone was obsessed with them. These secret parties that only the elite of the elite at ANA got to attend. And now Elizabeth had a coveted place there.

It was winter break when the Hawking party occurred. Most students had left campus already, but she stayed because home was not a place she really enjoyed going back to these days. Not with her great-aunt gone and her mum's lack of acknowledgment of her death.

She didn't tell Baz about the party, per the instructions about *not squealing*, and she felt bad about it. But it was better than having to admit to him how she got the invite in the first place.

The party was at a town house in London, where a person at the door took her name and checked her invite before letting her inside.

Elizabeth had been to parties before. But never to one so lavish.

Being at a school with so many rich kids who flaunted their wealth at every turn was hard, since the thought of losing her scholarship took the fun out of nearly everything. She was never as carefree as the majority of the student body.

But maybe tonight she could be.

TIME SLIPPED AWAY SLOWLY, AND she hadn't had nearly as much fun as the rumors about Hawking parties suggested she would.

She knew no one there personally. They were all just popular rich kids, leagues ahead of her, who looked down on her. If April had at least been there, she wouldn't have felt so alone.

She'd walked into the kitchen at some point to grab a bottle of water, and the group of girls had stopped talking when they'd heard her moving about. They turned to her, looking right through her as though she was invisible, and then carried on with their conversations. She felt as insignificant as a ghost.

She was ready to go home when a familiar voice stopped her in her tracks.

"I hoped you'd show," Jude said, staring through her with his ever-penetrating gaze.

"I was actually planning on leaving," she admitted.

He didn't look offended. "I'll let you in on a secret—these parties are usually quite boring. But it's a shame, the only interesting person here is leaving. I even got you a drink."

She raised an eyebrow at that, then in the corner of her vision spotted August in the kitchen mixing a drink for himself.

She felt her chest squeeze at the sight of him, her heart betraying her once again.

"Want to go somewhere quiet to talk?" Jude whispered.

Elizabeth pulled her eyes away from August, settling now on the cold blue gaze in front of her. "Sure," she said, accepting the glass Jude had brought her before following him out of the room, eyes still trained on an unassuming August, who she was now beginning to realize didn't care for her at all.

"YOU'RE SO BEAUTIFUL," JUDE HAD said to her.

Wait, where am I? she thought.

She could barely see anything through the hazy fog of her vision.

And why did her bones feel so heavy? Was someone on top of her?

"Waas hapninng," she slurred, and it sounded like her speech was somehow happening in slow motion.

Large hands stroked her hair softly and she wanted to move them away, but her hands felt like one million weights were on them.

She tried to figure out where she was through her limited vision.

The room was small, and the bed beneath her was hard and cold.

Her skin was also cold.

Someone should turn up the heat, she thought. She wished she had something to cover her exposed torso and legs.

Her vision shifted and she could see the blur of a familiar face hovering above her.

"So beautiful," he said again.

She shivered some more, her face wet, tears oozing from her eyes like a wound had been opened.

"B-blanke-t-t," she managed. But it was too quiet to be heard over the sound of *him*.

Suddenly, light burst through the room and another familiar voice rang out.

"What the—" it said. "What are you doing?"

"Isn't it obvious?" Jude replied with a laugh, his voice distorted and terrifying.

She blinked, hoping her vision would focus. *Get up,* she tried to tell her brain. *Scream. Do something.*

But it was like she wasn't there. Her eyes could move, but the rest of her was frozen.

IT WAS MORNING WHEN SHE could move again.

She had this pounding headache and a throat so dry it made her feel like even drinking all the world's oceans wouldn't satisfy her.

She was in a room, alone.

A knock on the door made her jump. When it opened, a guy she didn't know popped his head through.

"Hey, we have to clear out before afternoon when the owners get back. Get dressed," he said, then left as swiftly as he entered.

Get dressed?

She looked down, surprised to see that she was barely wearing anything. A fractured memory shuddered through her.

The outline of a figure. "How could you do this?" he said. Betrayed. A door slamming. Indescribable cold.

What happened last night?

That was a question that would haunt her in the days that followed.

She returned to campus. Everyone seemed so enamored by the Hawking boys and their latest party.

But nothing felt glamorous about the hollowness that resided inside of her since the party nor the many gaps in her memory. She was almost certain she was losing it.

This feeling inspired several Google searches. She scoured the internet for answers that might help her understand the symptoms she was experiencing: relentless brain fog, a deep intangible aching inside, and an unshakable melancholy. But nothing seemed to fit.

She remembered when her great-aunt Julie was sick. How the medication she used to ease the pain would sometimes make her go all loopy and then when she was aware again, she didn't seem to recall any of her loopy antics. Her aunt would say it felt like her brain was always foggy and she couldn't quite grasp information the same. This memory was enough to inspire another question in the search engine.

What does being drugged feel like?

This time Google presented her with pages and pages of information that felt eerily similar to what she had been experiencing.

And digging deeper, her search brought her to online forums, where there were so many accounts that matched hers.

Strangers who had also gone to parties and had woken up with little to no memory of the night.

But she didn't recall taking anything at all.

These forums became Elizabeth's newest obsession. It was like reading these accounts were the only things that made her feel at ease in a world with so many unanswered questions.

It wasn't until days after the party, when she spoke to August again, that it became clear her searches hadn't been specific enough.

She had been given a detention for missing her homework due date and August was there supervising on junior prefect duty.

It was the first time they had been alone in weeks.

"Hey," she said to him. But he pretended not to hear it. Continued sorting through stacks of paper like she was invisible.

"It's very mature of you to pretend I don't exist," she said.

He scoffed. "Yeah, like you've been mature?" he said.

"What's that supposed to mean?" she replied, arms folded as she leaned back in her chair.

He looked at her finally and something about his expression was weird. He looked at her like she had something on her face that he was disgusted by.

"I mean that I'm sure sleeping with my best friend to get back at me is a very mature thing to do," he said.

Elizabeth shook her head at that. "I didn't sleep with Jude—" she started, but then paused as a random, fragmented memory filtered through.

Her in a dark room. Jude on top of her—

"It's also very mature to lie, I'm sure. I literally saw you guys."

She felt her heartbeat increase as more memories of the night replayed.

How cold she'd felt.

August's cruelty as he spat vile words at her.

"I hate you."

"Yeah, I thought so. You act like you're this holier-than-thou person, but really all you do is fuck people up. And when this all blows up in your face and everyone discovers the person you are, I'll be there watching you burn," he said with such a vicious cruelty she was certain that she had never known the guy she had loved for so long.

She felt sick.

She got up, ignoring August's calls for her to sit back down, and left the classroom without another word.

Panic overtook her as she stormed all the way to Franklin House, wanting to be alone. She could feel tears trickle down her face as she ran into the building and up the stairs. Soft cries escaped as she opened her room door and it slammed shut behind her.

Unfortunately for her, April was there and so was her boyfriend, Jude. They were both seated on April's bed watching a movie, attached at the hip as they had been throughout second year.

"Knock, much," April said.

Elizabeth locked eyes with Jude, who only smiled at her.

"S-sorry," she replied before grabbing her laptop and walking out of the dorm room quickly.

By the time she reached Baz's room, the walls of her chest hurt and her tears had dried on her face.

When Baz saw her, he knew immediately that something was up. And of course he did. He knew her better than most.

She went into his arms and he hugged her tight.

"What's wrong?" he asked her.

She couldn't bring herself to tell him. He was the only good thing in this whole cruel world. She didn't want to taint him like she had been.

"I got a bad grade on my bio test," she replied with a lie she knew he'd believe.

Given her scholarship, he knew how much she could lose if she slipped up.

He only hugged her tighter. "I'm sorry," he said.

She nodded. *Me too,* she thought.

They used to tell each other everything before she started dating August. She was sorry for breaking their one vow to each other.

She hoped if he found out someday, he'd forgive her for it before she could forgive herself.

"THAT'S A SERIOUS ACCUSATION, MISS Wang," Headmaster Webber told her after she had finished telling him everything.

"I'm aware," she said. "I wouldn't be making this accusation if I wasn't serious about it."

Webber folded his hands, placing his chin on them, giving her the impression that he was considering it.

She wasn't sure what there was to contemplate about the statement "I was raped," but apparently Headmaster Webber had to think it through before hearing her clearly. She had considered going to the matron first, but she figured Miss Blackburn would only go to Webber, so telling him straight up would cut corners and have him deal with Jude faster.

"You say that your memories of the night were not as clear as you would have hoped?"

She nodded. "Yes, I believe I was drugged."

"You believe you were or you were?" he replied.

"I was," she said.

He nodded. "Well, Miss Wang, I will certainly investigate all of this. I want you to know that I have taken your concerns to heart and while I have you here, I just want to remind you that if you did, indeed, attend a party of this nature, it could really put your scholarship at risk. I would hate to inform the school board about it. I know they won't like it."

"What?" she said, wondering if she heard him clearly. "Is that a threat?"

He shook his head, a grave expression on his face. "Not at all, Miss Wang. I just want you to know what was at stake here. I think you are brilliant and could really go far, so I want to make sure that you're thinking clearly about your future."

She thought thinking clearly about her future meant reporting boys like Jude, but apparently according to Headmaster Webber, it wasn't.

"I mean, of course the scholarship would be the least of your worries. As you may know, Mr. Ripley's mother, the countess, is a prominent member on the school's parent governing body, and I'm sure she would petition for your scholarship to be revoked and more. And I imagine, due to her influence, this would be effective," Webber finished.

Elizabeth couldn't believe this. "You're saying that I could be kicked out for coming forward about the truth?"

Webber winced at her use of "truth."

"I'm saying that as I haven't seen any evidence of the events that you've recounted, I suggest you focus on what I think could be very bright and promising futures instead of jeopardizing that for yourself and Mr. Ripley. I will talk to Mr. Ripley, ensure he knows not to be so silly again."

Elizabeth felt enraged and small and powerless all at once.

"If that's all, I wish you a wonderful rest of the week, Miss Wang. Miss Blackburn will escort you out."

Disbelief turned her blood cold as she left the office, her entire world completely off-kilter. As she passed the cold-natured matron on her way out, she swore she saw a mirror of disbelief on her face. But when she blinked, Miss Blackburn's expression returned to a cool, neutral state.

As Elizabeth drifted through the halls, like the dead thing she now was, it felt like everyone and everything had changed.

Life felt colored by a dull sepia filter, and nothing, after that point, felt real anymore.

THE ONLINE FORUM BECAME HER solace.

Reading about people like her, who had been through what she had been through, made her feel less alone in the world.

Like Webber instructed, she left it alone, tried to move on and focus on her so-called *bright future*.

As if it was easy to forget being violated.

To sleep soundly after that.

To focus in school.

To be okay.

She didn't mention it again to anyone, until she saw the post in one of the forums.

I wish Jude Ripley was dead.—PBJam08

It was buried so deeply within the thousands and thousands of posts she'd read in the weeks since the party. She almost couldn't believe it when she saw it.

Elizabeth usually used this site as a ghost, peering in on the lives of others without saying anything or commenting. Just using their experiences as a warm blanket to cover and validate her own.

But for the first time, she opened up the comment box and typed.

IT TOOK ELIZABETH LONGER THAN it should've to realize that Webber's advice wasn't advice at all. It was poison.

Doing something *did* matter—especially if Jude could hurt someone else the same way he hurt her. Even if the headmaster—the guy whose literal job was to protect all his students, not just a privileged few—told her otherwise.

So she did the opposite of what he'd suggested.

She looked into the Hawking parties. She figured her ex-boyfriend would be the best way into this secret world. August always kept the same password for everything. Phelps or 2004 or a combination of both. She logged into his message app on the computer and discovered the group chat of boys named the Fishermen where they'd send one another explicit things about the girls at their school. She began to decode their usernames but couldn't quite figure them all out. It was an obsession, but one she felt had more positives than negatives to it.

She decided she needed to move out of the room she shared with April, realizing she could no longer pretend and occupy the same space as Jude. She would miss April. Her icy demeanor would melt when they were alone, as if she was like a secret best friend.

But Elizabeth now knew that wasn't healthy. Another Owens who kept Elizabeth a secret.

And she was fed up being a secret.

April had walked in on Elizabeth packing her things, staring at her silently as Elizabeth packed.

"Is everything okay?" April asked.

Elizabeth wanted to laugh at that. What a question. She didn't turn to face April. She couldn't.

No, everything is not okay. Your boyfriend ruined my life, she wanted to say but instead settled on a straightforward "I'm moving out."

April crossed her arms. "Why?"

Elizabeth shrugged and continued to pack.

"Is it because of my brother? I told you he's a moron—"

"No, it's not August—well, it's not *just* him."

"What else is it, then? Stop being dramatic and look at me."

"Don't worry," Elizabeth said.

"Well, that's only going to make me worry more, isn't it? Can you just tell me what's wrong? So I don't think you've got cancer or something and are running away in the middle of the night to die. You're one of my closest friends, Liz. I care about you—"

"So much that no one even knows we're friends," Elizabeth muttered, turning to look at April now.

April seemed to flinch back when she saw her face. Like the answer was written across her skin in big red ugly ink.

Jude is a rapist.

"We can tell everyone if you want? You know I like making big announcements," April started, nudging her gently. "I never did before because I liked that we exist outside of everything in this shitty school, but I don't care about keeping this a secret. I just want to know what happened."

Elizabeth sighed, looking down at the floor and tucking a strand of hair behind her ear, her fingers shaky.

"You should break up with Jude," Elizabeth said.

This made April pause. "Why?"

"He's not a good person, that's all."

"What in the world do you mean by that, Elizabeth?" April asked.

Elizabeth wiped her face, her mind screaming the same three-word sentence over and over again.

He's a rapist. He's a rapist. He's a rapist.

"He—" she began. "We—uhm—" Why couldn't she say it? Why was this so hard?

April's face hardened. "Oh my god, August was telling the truth, wasn't he?"

"Wh-what . . ."

April looked angry, and Elizabeth could literally see the fire behind her eyes.

"He said you had hooked up with Jude . . . that he saw you guys . . . I told him to piss off, that you would never do that to me . . . but you did, didn't you?"

Elizabeth shook her head fast. "No—"

"So you didn't have sex with my boyfriend?"

Elizabeth went quiet and April nodded, with a smile. "You know, with friends like you, who needs enemies?"

Elizabeth's face felt warm and sticky from tears.

April moved toward the door and turned to look at her one last time.

"I want you and your shit gone before I get back," she said, before slamming the door hard in her face.

• • •

ELIZABETH WAS GRATEFUL WHEN SHE was granted the immediate transfer to Turing.

Instead of letting herself wallow from the fallout, she threw herself into research, staying in her room more than she ever had before. Avoiding the world and its judgments.

She wasn't always lonely—she had her new forum friend to talk to each night.

Their conversations started on the forum, before they moved to private messages and then to one video call, before her forum friend stopped appearing online. Elizabeth's messages were left unread.

She tried talking to other people on the forum, but it was never the same.

One user, DinosaurGuts222, told Elizabeth that she should seek professional help in response to her posting about being alone. DinosaurGuts222 even linked her to charities that helped young girls who had been through what she had.

But Elizabeth just wanted Jam to come back. She was the only one who really *got* it. Got how ugly Jude made you feel.

She didn't know PBJam08's real name, so she couldn't even try to find her anywhere else.

She thought she knew loneliness when April kicked her out. But now she was truly on her own, with no one she could speak to about the unrelenting hollowness inside.

7 WEEKS AGO

SECOND YEAR WENT BY IN a flash, and by the beginning of third, Elizabeth had so much information it surely had to be enough evidence for Webber to take it seriously. Or even enough to take past Webber and to the local authorities.

These boys were all rapists and abusers to some degree.

And it was time the world knew.

She was excited for this new year. She knew things were going to change; she could feel it in her bones.

She would be the biology club president; she'd finally expose the truth; and she'd finally be okay. On to that bright future she knew was waiting for her.

But what was that saying?

If you want to make God laugh, tell him your plans.

How true that was.

"SLUT," SOMEONE SAID UNDER THEIR breath as Elizabeth walked past.

She was on her way to the biology labs for the lunchtime bio club meeting, and at first she thought she heard them wrong, but when it was followed by snickers and staring, she turned to find two girls glaring at her.

"Can I help you?" she asked.

"Not sure you can. You must be so tired from helping yourself to my boyfriend," the girl said.

Elizabeth raised an eyebrow at that. She hadn't dated anyone since August and she had no interest in anyone either.

"You're thinking of the wrong person," Elizabeth simply said.

The girl looked like she wanted to punch Elizabeth in her face. "Oh, so this isn't you?" she asked, holding up her phone to Elizabeth.

On the phone was a photo she had sent August months ago, when they were still dating and he had asked her for something he could remember her by when she wasn't around.

Foolishly, she obliged.

And now that photo, alongside the last one that had gone around the school, had come to haunt her.

"Wh-where did you get that?" Elizabeth asked.

The girl scoffed at her. "Harry's phone, you know, my boyfriend who you're sleeping with?"

Elizabeth didn't even know a Harry. "I d-didn't—"

"Don't worry; you don't have to keep lying. I broke up with him, so now he's all yours! But remember, how you get them is how you lose them," the girl said, then turned around and walked away from Elizabeth, leaving her alone in the hallway.

In biology club, she was so distracted by her thoughts and the events that just transpired that she was too busy moping to notice the hamster fall out of the cage and splat on the floor.

"Fuck," she whispered.

THEODORE, THE VICE PRESIDENT OF biology club and her archnemesis, couldn't wait to have Elizabeth demoted, and between her no longer being president and the interaction with the girl from earlier, she had just about had it with the day.

When she got back to her room, she checked the forums as usual, hoping her friend had made a miraculous return, but her inbox was empty, again, so she refocused on something else.

Her Fishermen takedown.

E: Hey August, we need to talk.

Maybe it was a mistake her messaging him, but she felt like she had to. Before everything went down, she had to.

She knew how *Harry* got that picture.

She hadn't cracked all the names just yet in the Fishermen's chat, just enough to prove what was going on right under the school administrators' noses, but now she was going to.

6 WEEKS AGO

TODAY WAS THE DAY.

The day something about the Fishermen.

She had spent every moment of alone time working on cracking the code of the usernames. Sometimes she'd leave school, pull baggier clothes over her uniform as she scrolled through files at the cat café in town.

And then one night she finally reached the end.

She had a list of all their names. All fifty-four of them. Ranging from quiet boys in third year who posted the occasional misogynistic comment about some girl in his fourth-period history class that he'd like to have his way with, to the loud and proud Jude Ripley who did way worse.

They would all be taken down. They had to be. It was the only way she could cope with being here anymore.

As insurance, she began writing down the information she acquired with a UV pen, aka invisible ink. In case, for some reason, she failed, it would always be here, for someone to eventually see. She would have kept to her previous method of writing down everything on Post-it Notes but had been told she might be getting a roommate—seeing as she was the only third year in Turing without a roomie. And while the potential roommate had not yet shown up in the weeks since term started, she knew she would look unhinged if they had their first meeting and her room looked like a giant murder board.

Bzz.

Her phone buzzed loudly on her desk, nearly vibrating off it.

She picked it up, surprised to see it was a text . . . from August.

A: Hey, what do you want.

She had messaged him last week and hadn't gotten a response. Until now.

She paused to think before sending her reply.

E: I know about the fishermen and all the fucked-up shit you guys do, and so I'm letting you know now that when this all blows up in your face, I'll be there watching you burn.

She quoted his vicious words back to him. Then she blocked his number and pocketed her phone with a smile.

ELIZABETH WAS CALLED OUT OF class during third period by one of Miss Blackburn's messengers.

Apparently, Lady Death—the nickname ANA students had for her—requested her presence at the reception.

"Thanks for gracing us with your presence, at your own speed, Miss Wang," Miss Blackburn said when Elizabeth arrived—on time might she add.

But there was never any reason to argue back with her. You would certainly lose.

Elizabeth had no reaction at all, choosing the safe option.

"Your new roommate finally showed up. She's in there finishing her house test while I sort her admin and uniform out," Lady Death said.

Elizabeth's gaze moved to the door and then back to the matron's tired expression. "Why is she doing a house test if you've already sorted her into Turing . . . ?"

The matron narrowed her eyes a little at Elizabeth—as usual Lady Death never looked pleased when questioned. "Because, Miss Wang, I know you had some trouble with your past house, and so you out of anyone will know how important a welcoming environment is. She has not had an easy time before now . . . and without showing bias, I think the calmness of Turing might do her some good. I have also assigned you as house sister for her and you have been excused from your classes today to show her around and make her feel welcomed at ANA. Is that all clear?"

Elizabeth only had more questions, but instead of asking them and facing the matron's fiery wrath, she simply gave Miss Blackburn a thumbs-up, which she seemed displeased by, but honestly there probably wasn't a reaction she could have given that she wouldn't have been displeased by, so Elizabeth counted that as a win.

Miss Blackburn checked her watch and nodded to herself. "She should be done. I'll be right back."

As Miss Blackburn spoke to the girl on the other side of the door, Elizabeth stood and waited, letting her thoughts meander through her plans for the day.

After showing the new girl around, she would go to Webber after dinner with the evidence she had stored. She'd written everything down in Notepad with printouts so that nothing she did could be monitored by the school like her computer and phone were. Last time she had no evidence, but this time, it was more than just her word against Jude's. Even if Webber didn't listen, she had already scheduled an email to go out to all the contacts she could find, not only on the school board but the local police too.

Whatever happened today, the Fishermen would be done, once and for all.

The door opened and Miss Blackburn stepped out, followed closely behind by the person Elizabeth assumed would be her new roommate for the next two years.

"Sade, this is your house sister—and roommate—Elizabeth Wang. She will be showing you around and answering all your burning questions," Miss Blackburn said, but Elizabeth could barely focus on her words.

She was too busy staring at the familiar face of the girl in front her.

"Hi," the girl said.

Elizabeth was still frozen, wondering if she was somehow dreaming this.

How could it be that her forum friend, PBJam08, was here, right here in front of her?

"Hello?" Elizabeth finally said, realizing that if she had been quiet a moment longer it would have made things weird.

"See, you're already off to a great start," Miss Blackburn said, and then proceeded to tell the new girl—Sade—about meeting her after dinner or something.

It couldn't be her, Elizabeth decided. Because surely if it were her, she would say something too, but there wasn't an ounce of recognition in the girl's features.

This girl in front of her might have shared a similar face to her forum friend, but she clearly had no clue who Elizabeth was.

"All right then . . . quick tour?" she said, forcing herself to let it go. Shake off this uncomfortable déjà vu.

What was it that people always said? That each person had seven doppelgängers roaming about the earth?

It was possible that she had simply met Jam's.

PING!

Her phone went off for the first time during the tour of the school grounds.

Elizabeth had been showing Sade Turing when she received the message that would turn her whole world upside down.

Hello Elizabeth, this is the admissions office for Whitehall University. We received your message and endeavor to get back to you within two working days.

Message? What message? she thought. Whitehall was one of her top choices for university but she hadn't even begun the application process yet.

Her phone buzzed with another email, this time from an anonymous account.

Fuck with us and we fuck with your future

Attached to the text was a picture of her that August had taken, one she wasn't familiar with.

They wouldn't.

She felt the edges of her vision blur, but then she remembered she had company.

Elizabeth met Sade's concerned eyes and forced herself to smile. To carry on with the tour as though nothing was wrong.

When they got up to her room and she saw the dead rat, she didn't even flinch. She heard their message loud and clear.

If she said anything, they would hurt her.

And she had a feeling that the Fishermen could easily make good on that promise.

SHE RECEIVED MORE MESSAGES LIKE that throughout the day. Increasing in severity. The latest one shook her to her core.

It threatened her scholarship.

"Is everything okay?" Sade asked.

No. I'm not sure everything will ever be okay, Elizabeth wanted to reply. But instead she told Sade she had lab homework to collect and would see her later.

Elizabeth had hung out with PBJam08's look-alike for hours and decided that she liked her.

Maybe it was bias talking or the fact that she felt so sad and Sade had been so nice to her.

She hoped they could be good friends.

PING!

She was beginning to loathe the sound of her phone. Elizabeth hadn't left the greenhouse like she told Sade she would. She was too afraid to. Up here, no one could reach her—she had the key after all—and she would stay here forever if she could.

She had long ago unscheduled the emails to all the important people she'd planned on telling.

And she didn't bother going to see Webber. What was the point? When they could do so much harm to her?

Instead of reading the Fishermen's latest threat, she opened her phone and sent a message to a number she hadn't contacted in a very long time.

E: Hey, can we talk please

She was so sure she would be ghosted, but a long ten minutes later the phone buzzed in her hand with a response.

362

A: Okay.

Elizabeth felt herself exhale.

E: Usual place? 15 minutes

A: Okay.

A few minutes later, she found herself in the Franklin bunker.

She hadn't been here in almost a year—not since the fight with April.

It mostly looked the same, but it was clear that April still frequented the area. The décor had changed.

Elizabeth heard a thud as her former roommate climbed down the bunker's ladder into the dark open space.

"Hi," Elizabeth said.

April stared at her coldly. "You wanted to talk. I don't have long—Francis is waiting upstairs for me."

Elizabeth had heard that April had started dating Francis toward the end of second year. It was kind of a shock to her, seeing as Francis didn't seem to really be her type. She usually went for the uber-wealthy, preppy type, less so the rich-but-not-as-rich-as-her, unclean stoner type.

But to each their own, she figured. Perhaps it was his position as the headmaster's stepson that made him a suitable candidate for an Owens to date.

"I wanted to talk to you about Jude."

April rolled her eyes. "Not this again—"

"He raped me," Elizabeth said. The words slipping out with ease this time. Desperation made it easier to say.

April's face dropped. "What?"

"That's what August saw—and he, your brother, did nothing. He even sent Jude private pictures of me. I wanted to go to the school about it, but August and Jude threatened to hurt me if I did."

April didn't move at all. She just stared at Elizabeth silently, and it was then that Elizabeth noticed that something was different about April.

Something in her expression . . .

"Why did you contact me? What do you think I can do?" April replied coldly.

This wasn't the response she was hoping for.

"I . . . I don't know. I feel so lost and I don't know what to do anymore—I just, I need someone to help me."

Again, April said nothing. Just observed Elizabeth silently and then she looked away from her, moved back toward the ladder, and without another word left Elizabeth in the bunker all alone.

ELIZABETH KNEW IT WAS A bad idea. Anyone with a brain would know it was a bad idea.

But she was desperate.

After being left in the basement of Franklin by the girl she once thought was a friend, Elizabeth wandered around the edges of the campus, considering her options, and finally landing on the only one she hadn't attempted yet.

She pulled her phone out, her last resort.

E: Meet me in the usual place

She was going to speak to August face-to-face, in a place where he couldn't run or hide.

And for August, that place was the swimming pool.

IT TOOK A WHILE FOR her to get some nerve. She had gone back to the room to look over the walls on which she had written all her plans.

It was almost comical how confident she had been before.

She wiped her eyes and sniffed and then moved toward the window.

It was a well-known fact that the only way not to be caught going out just before curfew was to use the balcony. That way judgy Jessica couldn't catch you and reprimand you for being out so late.

Elizabeth slipped out quickly, trying to be as quiet as possible. It didn't occur to her until she was already on the ground that she'd left her room key behind. *Good job, Elizabeth*, she thought as she went on, walking through the school's blind spots to get to Newton Sports Center, where August spent so much of his time practicing.

Before she went inside, she scrolled to the Friendly Links app and sent Baz some sandwiches—their code for *something's wrong*—just in case things went left. If she got hurt, at least he would know where to find her.

She then swiped off the app and onto the recording app, hitting the red button for more assurance before placing her phone in her pocket.

Sometimes when she came to Newton, she'd find August in the main pool, already doing laps, obsessively almost.

Other times, most of the time, they'd hang out in the new pool area. It was under construction, which meant it was unlikely they'd be seen.

Meaning she could remain his secret.

However, when she arrived, he wasn't in the main pool or the new one either.

Could this day get any worse? Elizabeth thought as she stood, surrounded by scaffolding and machinery.

He hadn't shown.

Typical August. Disappointing and hurting her all at once.

She was about to leave when she heard footsteps.

And then, a voice. "Come here to start more trouble, Liz?" Jude Ripley's voice came out in the catty, controlled, and confident way it always did.

She turned to face him and was not surprised to see he had company.

Like some kind of twisted version of a guardian angel, Jude stood in front of August. Or more like Cerberus, Hades's demonic three-headed dog.

She felt her heart rattle.

Looking at Jude was painful, knowing what he did to her but having no memory of it. And even now he looked at her as though she were an object he'd like to once again consume.

She folded her arms over herself and stepped back. "I came to talk to August."

"About what?" Jude asked, stepping closer.

"Something personal," she replied.

Jude raised an eyebrow, looked her up and down. Before she could stop him, he reached into her pocket, pulled out her recording phone, threw it on the ground, and crushed it with the heel of his designer dress shoe.

Elizabeth's heart sped up as she watched it happen.

"That was a very, *very* amateur move. August doesn't want to speak to you; he told me about your little blackmailing scheme. And now I can see it for myself. It's endearing, a foolish endeavor, but still endearing."

This made her so angry, the way he spoke down to her, how nonchalant he was about everything.

"Why doesn't August speak for himself, then?" Elizabeth asked.

"I'm not—we're not the bad guys here, Liz, you are," August said, barely looking at her.

She peered around for any cameras. There had to be some in here. For a private school, ANA didn't have the best security, but this was a public place so it had to have cameras even if the pool was still being finished, right? She would be fine.

So she walked over to August without a second thought, going past Jude like he was invisible.

"Sharing those photos, watching me get assaulted that night, and doing nothing, that makes you the bad guy, August," Elizabeth said, her eyes glassy.

"Whoa, assault? Seriously, Liz? You're gonna pull that card," August said, looking shocked.

"It's not a card to pull. It's what happened," she replied.

He shook his head, clearly not wanting to believe a word she said.

"You know me, August. And I know you. You don't believe it. You know what your best friend is. He's a rapist—"

"Don't say that," August said, closing his eyes.

"You know you believe me, August. So please, help me," she said quietly, stepping closer.

She knew he was as guilty as every last boy in that group chat, not only because he sent the photos of her but also because he sat there and let so much happen to so many girls, including her.

Someone he once claimed to love.

If he did, if he does, he'd do something now.

She heard the sound of Jude's slow clapping, as though he was applauding some performance he'd just witnessed.

"Wow. It would be so easy to believe you if I didn't already know so many girls like you," Jude said. "This is the problem with you—all of you. You want to say it wasn't consensual when you face up to the consequences. You're the one who had been making advances on me for weeks, you're the one who wanted it. You don't see me complaining," Jude finished. There was a lilt to his tone that almost sounded like he found this all so humorous. He was even closer to her now. So close she could almost feel his breath.

This made her blood boil, and her vision red. She pushed him back and he stumbled slightly, slipping a little but still smiling. Like this was all a game to him.

"I hate you, and I hope you rot in a prison cell. I don't care about your threats or what you try to do to me. As long as you're behind bars, that will be the solace I need. Because you're a rapist, Jude. You're a rapist and a coward," she said, her voice as loud as the ache in her chest.

His face morphed. His eyes narrowed, and before she knew it, he was charging at her fast, grabbing her neck and pinning her to the tiled walls. Hard.

She thought she heard a crack.

"What did you say to me?" he spat, face red and hardened.

"Jude, stop—" August said weakly.

"You are *nothing*. Do you not get that? No one is coming to save you. Try to report those lies about me, and you *will* fail. You always fail," he said, his grip shaking as he squeezed the life out of her.

Suddenly, Jude let her go as August pulled him away and punched him squarely in the jaw.

Jude staggered back and held his face, staring at his friend with a look of shock and betrayal.

Elizabeth choked out a cough and wheezed hard, recovering.

Jude gathered himself, quickly strode toward August, and pushed him backward. "What the hell is wrong with you? I defended you against that slut," he said, pushing him again. "This is how you repay me?" Another push.

"I'll kill you," August yelled, attempting to swing at Jude again, but Jude was faster.

Elizabeth saw this as her opportunity to escape quickly, but as she darted past, Jude reached out to push August again, his hands finding Elizabeth instead.

She felt herself falling.

So far that she had to be falling into the gaping mouth of the empty, unfinished swimming pool. Her skull connected with the ground, and this time she knew the crack was real.

For a moment, everything went black.

In the distance, she could hear August ask, "What do we do? She's not moving."

"We have to leave her," she distantly heard Jude respond.

"Someone'll find her!" August replied.

"At least they won't find her alive," Jude said.

There was a pause. The sharp footsteps of Jude's shoes on the tiles, and then she heard a whirring sound. *Like a machine.*

"Why'd you turn the machine on? It's not going to work. They'll know you were in here—"

"Relax, Auggie. I'm not expecting the concrete to cover everything; it's just meant to show anyone who comes looking that *someone* was tampering with the machinery. Who's to say Elizabeth didn't sneak down here, fiddle with a few buttons, and *whoops* accidentally fall inside? She's not exactly reliable, is she?"

"But we can't just leave—"

"Let's go. It's too late for her," she heard Jude say as the machine whirred. She could hear the wet sound of something sloshing into the pool. Concrete.

She was going to be buried alive.

Elizabeth thought about what it would mean to suffocate to death. To lie here, no one knowing where she'd gone, possibly forever.

She tried to push herself up, wanting to fight, but with her throbbing head, it was too much.

She wasn't sure how long she had been lying there, but just as she was starting to accept her fate, she heard the sound of bickering hushed voices.

"What happened? Where is she?" a familiar voice sounded.

"Inside—she's inside the pool."

ELIZABETH BARELY REGISTERED WHAT HAPPENED next, her vision hazy from the fall. But here she was fully clothed in a warm shower, water falling onto her from above, drumming against her pounding head.

She was convinced she had died and this was some strange purgatory.

"What the hell is wrong with you, August?" the familiar voice said.

"I don't know," August replied, sounding tearful.

"I'll sort this out, like I always do."

"How?"

There was a sigh.

"I'll make some calls, arrange a car, and send her home. Keep her quiet and make sure this whole thing doesn't come out—"

Elizabeth slowly pushed herself out of the shower, disoriented as she crawled toward the slightly open bathroom door. Through the crack she could see that April and August weren't facing her. They were huddled in a corner.

She watched as April told August to get some sleep, then told him to leave through the back doors.

She watched as April sighed, looked up at the sky, wiped her face hard, and then walked toward the bathroom door. Elizabeth shrank back when the door opened wide.

April looked surprised to see Elizabeth on the ground out of the shower.

Elizabeth saw this as her chance to fight back. "I h-heard what you s-said t-to him," she said, her teeth chattering together. "You can't j-just sh-ship me off—"

"I wasn't planning to," April replied.

"I THOUGHT I WAS DEFINITELY done for." Elizabeth looked at Sade, her gaze unflinching. "I was waiting for the reaper to collect my soul, but she never came. I was somehow still alive. It seemed August felt guilty and told April and they rescued me, taking me to her dorm. April told August she was going to get rid of me, but seeing what had happened, it seemed she believed me after all. Believed all the things I'd said about her brother. She offered to get me real medical attention, but I was too scared to leave and risk them finding me. While I was in the bunker, Jude still thought I was dead and August still thought April had sorted things for him. I thought my head wound was healing; my concussion slowly cleared, and though I knew I probably needed stitches for the wound, my mum was a nurse and I remembered what she'd said about keeping wounds clean to avoid infection. But then it got worse and now I guess . . . here I am. Other than that, I had no plan really. But the guilt of letting Jude and the Fishermen get away with everything was heavier than the fear I had of being found. I just needed someone to see and expose everything. April wanted to help, but for her own reasons couldn't do it herself, and seeing as you were in my room with all the evidence, I figured that person could be you.

"I told her to get close to you in order to get your room key; I told her to break in and put the music box with all the notes I'd originally written somewhere you'd easily spot it. When that didn't seem to work, I had her get ahold of UV light bulbs so you were forced to see the writing on the wall. I had hoped you would've seen it all much sooner—"

"Why didn't April just tell me? Instead of planting things and waiting for me to do something."

"Would you have just gone along with it if a girl you didn't know told you things about a boy you didn't know?" Elizabeth asked.

Sade's eyes found the ground. Elizabeth didn't know the whole truth. That

Sade *did* know him. She knew exactly who Jude was and what he was capable of and if April had told her, she might've been able to find Elizabeth sooner.

But she didn't tell Elizabeth that. She couldn't.

Sade had so many questions she wanted to ask, and so she asked the loudest one. "Why me?"

"What do you mean?" she replied.

"Why didn't you ask April to plant them on Baz, or even send Baz a note? Why did you think a complete stranger would figure out what was going on?"

Elizabeth looked at her, like there was something she wasn't saying. Looked at Sade as if they knew each other.

"I just hoped you'd understand, and you did. Least I could do was tell the police the truth. I told them August must've killed Jude."

"And they believed you?" Sade asked. Elizabeth hadn't been there; why would they?

"Well, I told them what August and Jude had done to me. I told them about their fucked-up friendship and the way they'd always fight and how August would sometimes get so worked up with Jude that he'd threaten to kill him. I told them everything they needed to hear to doubt August's innocence."

Sade's eyebrows furrowed. "But you don't think August actually did it."

Elizabeth shook her head. "I assure you, he's far from innocent. Whatever happens to August now, he'll deserve it."

TUESDAY

BRIGHT FUTURES

THE SCHOOL BOARD HAD ALREADY reached a verdict on how to handle the Fishermen situation.

They agreed to put up posters about bullying around the school and had scheduled assemblies about the perils of drug abuse. Other than that, they would be taking no further action against any of the boys who had been singled out via the website.

Their answer was no answer. They didn't even mention the words *sexual assault* or *rape* once.

Which was, of course, unsurprising given that many of the boys had connections on the same school board that made this very "difficult" decision.

In their statement, they even said: "We can't just allow the promising futures of these boys to be wasted on baseless evidence and what seems to be a singular person pointing the finger."

Room 313 felt as cold and as haunting as it always did.

Though she knew Elizabeth was safe now, Sade felt the presence of Jamila watching her like she always did. Feeling her twin angry at her for not listening. For Sade not leaving the school when she asked her to. For digging into her past and going on this dangerous mission to ANA.

The boys had stopped updating the chat, likely aware that there was someone watching their moves now, given everything that was on the website. She highly doubted that this meant their shenanigans had stopped. They probably just migrated to some other, more secure host for their gentlemen's club.

Sade couldn't help but feel like she had failed everyone.

Yes, Jude was dead, but he'd been made a saint and victim by the police and the school. The other boys still roamed the halls, powerful as ever, while their victims were either dead, injured, or suffering in silence.

She couldn't get the contents of the group chat out of her head.

There were many pictures and they spanned years. It was hard to tell where it even began, and whom it began with, but this was not unique to the boys of ANA. This was everywhere.

In schools, where you were meant to be kept safe by teachers. Where sometimes even the teachers themselves were the danger.

Inside communities, where people abused the power they so easily wielded.

Inside homes, the world over.

Everywhere.

Boys with everything. The world had been and always would be theirs for the taking. Sade had learned to fear the men who had everything, because even the moon, the skies, and the earth could not sate them.

She found that she couldn't be alone with her thoughts for much longer and so she got up, pulled her boots and jacket on, and left the room and its ghosts behind.

"It's bollocks," Persephone said, her face screwing up.

Half an hour later, Sade was in the Seacole common room with Persephone and Baz, who to her surprise had immediately responded to her SOS text on their Brown Bitches group chat (Baz's idea), and were more than happy to keep her company and stop her from spiraling alone.

Basil was making tea and Persephone was holding Muffin in her arms. Upon first seeing the stolen rodent, she had frowned and asked Baz what the hell the thing was and why it was in his room, to which he'd responded:

"This is my guinea pig, Muffin," holding it up to her face so that she was at eye level with the small round animal.

"Basil, if you don't remove that guinea pig from my face, I swear I will kill you," Persephone had said. He promptly pulled Muffin away from her head.

But now, here in the common room, she had become well acquainted with the small pet.

"How the hell do cheap antibullying posters help the fact that so many students are being harmed right under the school administration's noses? We need to take this higher," Persephone continued.

Muffin let out a squeal and Persephone apologized to her. "Sorry, didn't mean to pull your fur. I'm just angry at the sexist knobheads sitting on the school board."

The student body had mostly been kept in the dark about Elizabeth. Everything was handled secretly. Sade wondered if the other teachers even knew or if that was something Webber was keeping concealed from them too. How would anything change if no one knew what had really happened?

"But what's higher than the school board?" Sade asked.

Persephone sighed, looking up at the ceiling for answers. "I'm not sure."

"Tea, anyone?" Baz asked, emerging through the doors of the adjoining kitchen moments later with a tray of tea and biscuits.

He had been doing much better since Elizabeth was found, though Sade suspected that Elizabeth hadn't told him all the things she had revealed to Sade.

"Why not," Persephone said in response to Baz, who happily poured her a cup of the steaming hot brown liquid.

Sade scrolled down their website on her phone, wondering how anyone could see all this and not want to do something.

If only Webber and the people on the board weren't as powerful as they let them be.

She remembered what Elizabeth had said about Webber, how it was her word against Jude's . . .

"What if it's our . . . or, well, the site's word against theirs . . . ," Sade said mostly to herself.

"What?" Persephone asked as she took a sip from her teacup.

Sade looked at her. "We were so focused on highlighting the alleged wrongs of the perpetrators. And we needed to, because we didn't talk to the victims; we didn't get their stories. But now it's time to change that. What's bigger than Webber and the school board? Us—we are."

Persephone and Basil shared the same perplexed expression.

She thought about that graffitied bathroom. The one with the carving that read: *Michael O'Connell is a rapist.*

"We need a new section of the website, one that lets people anonymously share their real stories about these boys."

"You think the school will care about that?" Baz asked. "Because they don't seem to care regardless of what evidence they're shown."

"I think we need to outnumber them. They will certainly care if this has the ability to affect their reputation. Imagine if a local newspaper saw that a school like ANA was ignoring the accounts of their students. Imagine if parents saw. We are more powerful than they want us to think. I say we use that."

IN THE MIDDLE OF THE night, she was woken up by an alert on her computer. She sat up, her heart thumping as she quickly pushed herself out of her bed and went over to her desk to open it.

At first, she expected another threatening anonymous email asking her to leave things alone.

But it was a different kind of anonymous message.

Not so Noble, I have a problem . . . , it began.

It was their first hit on the website's anonymous ask box she'd set up that afternoon when she was with Persephone and Baz.

Sade read, feeling a chill spread through her as she read the account.

Another alert popped up. Another student's account.

By the time the sun was rising, Sade was still awake under the covers. They already had fifteen hits, each story as harrowing as the last.

Sade couldn't tell if it was her anger at the situation, the time, or both, but she suddenly had an idea.

She tapped out of the website's dashboard and went to look for email addresses of the local newspapers. She then opened up her email and forwarded the website link to each one.

When she finally fell asleep, she dreamed about the whole school burning down, Sade holding the jug of gasoline, and Elizabeth the match.

WEDNESDAY

IT WAS DISTURBING HOW QUICKLY things moved on at the school.

There was no time to process any grief.

A student went missing, another student died, allegations of abuse . . . And yet nothing in the world could apparently stop the force of a pop quiz.

They were in English class, and Mr. Michaelides was out sick—he had been out all week—so the substitute had been giving them random bits of work to do.

Sade wished they were watching another movie like they had done the day before, so that she could sneak out her phone and check the hits on the site.

As of this morning they were now on thirty—some of which were oddly not from ANA students.

"I definitely failed," Sade said to Persephone when they were walking out of the class.

Persephone opened her locker to grab a book for her next class. "I'm sure you didn't."

Sade rolled her eyes. "You're literally the mark scheme. Everything you do is perfect."

Persephone turned back to her and gave a small smile. "Nice to hear you think I'm perfect."

Sade smiled back at her, ignoring the way her stomach somersaulted and her heart jolted in response.

The halls felt buzzier than usual. It was something she had taken notice of earlier in the day, but it only seemed to heighten as the pair approached the lunch hall.

"What's going on?" Sade asked, but Persephone only shrugged.

When they walked inside, her question was finally answered.

All the noise and the side-gazes were pointed toward one table near the back.

Where August Owens now sat, eating pasta in a casual manner.

As though he hadn't been arrested for murder on Monday.

August looked up, his eyes flickering over the crowd of onlookers, and then his gaze rested on Sade and she swore she saw him smile.

Checkmate, she imagined he'd say.

A chill ran through her.

"We don't have to stay here," Persephone said decisively.

Sade looked at the table where August usually sat with his sister and those she believed to be esteemed, but the table was empty.

Sade nodded, holding August's gaze. "Let's go."

They headed to the place where it always made sense to go: the library.

Persephone went to grab some vending-machine food while Sade sought out their usual space. Her mind was filled with so many questions about August's sudden return.

When she got to the table, she was surprised to see Baz there.

He looked nervous about something. She could tell from the way he was anxiously eating a whole row of biscuits.

"Baz?" she said.

He looked up at her, snapping out of his daze. "Oh, hi, I was hoping you'd come here at lunch. I've been texting you but I figured you'd have your phone off during classes. Is Persephone here?"

"Is everything okay?"

"They got Jude's killer," he said.

A confused mix of emotions swirled through her. Anxiety, relief, nothingness, overwhelm. Above all, the feeling of impending doom was the most prominent.

She could hear her heart beating in her ears. "Who? *How?* Is that why they released August?" It made no sense. He was still guilty for hurting Elizabeth.

Baz's eyebrows furrowed together. "They released August?"

"Yes, he's literally in the cafeteria as we speak, eating the lunch special," she said.

"I guess it could be their father. He knows people in high places and could probably easily bribe a judge since he is a retired one himself . . . probably got August off or something."

"Who did they get?" Sade interrupted, realizing that he still hadn't told her.

"April," he said. "She confessed."

I SLEEP, I DROWN & DISAPPEAR[8]

Dear Diary,

Am I too late?

_____

[8] An anagram

THURSDAY

THE QUEEN IS DEAD

APRIL WAS IN CUSTODY, AND it was the talk of the entire school.

The queen bee had fallen and, according to her confession, had not only killed Jude but was also the mastermind behind the website.

"Why is she lying?" Persephone asked, pacing the expanse of Sade's dorm room.

"Maybe she knows it was us who created the website and wanted to protect you. Her dad has influence over the law; maybe she knew she'd be okay?" Sade offered in response, but Persephone shook her head.

"There's more to it. I know her. There's something she isn't saying."

A knock sounded at the door and Sade went to open it but Persephone was faster. When the door opened, she looked perplexed.

"Who are you?" she asked.

"Uh . . . this is Sade's dorm, right? Baz told me to come and meet him here."

Persephone still looked at him suspiciously, but Sade immediately recognized the voice.

"Hi, Kwame, you can come in," she said.

Baz had meant to join them but it had been reported by an anonymous tip that he was harboring a stolen guinea pig in his room. He suspected it was his pleasant roommate, Spencer, who had finally turned him in.

"Where's Baz?" Kwame asked, taking out his laptop.

"Detention," Sade replied.

Kwame looked a bit concerned but not all that surprised. "I have the thing he said you wanted, the transcript. It came in this morning."

"Yes, thank you," Sade said, taking out her purse to pay him. "Did Baz already compensate you for your time?"

Kwame smiled and nodded. "Something like that."

"Okay, well, I actually have something else I need your services for . . . Can you get into student records?"

"Probably," Kwame said.

Sade nodded. "Can you find the record of these students, please?" she asked, writing down the names and sliding it over to Kwame.

TRANSCRIPT OF INTERVIEW
Uncensored

OFFICER: This interview is being recorded. I'm PC STEVENS and I'm based at Blackhurst Metropolitan Police. Please state your full name.
AO: Is it really necessary to record this?
OFFICER: Yes, for our records. You were forewarned that this would be recorded.
AO: Whatever, what was the question again?
OFFICER: Your full name.
AO: April Piper Owens.
OFFICER: Thank you, April. So, we talked briefly earlier and you told me that you were at that party, correct?
AO'S LAWYER: She was.
OFFICER: Sorry, could we hear the answers from April.
AO: Yes, I was.
OFFICER: And that the deceased, Jude Ripley, got you alone and tried to hurt you. Could you please, for the record, repeat your statement from earlier?
AO: My confession?
AO'S LAWYER: For the record, it's a statement, not a confession.
AO: I mean my statement.
OFFICER: Yes, that.
AO: Jude was high—like he usually was. He asked me to join him in his room to talk, because we used to date and I guess he wanted closure. I was wrong, he wanted to get back together. I told him I wasn't interested and he tried to harm me, so I defended myself and he stopped breathing.
OFFICER: How exactly did you defend yourself?
AO: He was trying to strangle me. I managed to fight back, then I got on top of him and held him down by his neck and then he stopped breathing.

OFFICER: Hmm . . . Well, you're right that his cause of death was asphyxiation, caused by strangulation, but your hands are much smaller than the hand marks on his body. Here's the picture of his neck and the indentation. The handprints here are thicker.

AO: I was wearing gloves.

OFFICER: To a party?

AO'S LAWYER: Sorry, how is this relevant?

OFFICER: It's just so we can paint a clear picture of the night.

AO: Yes, the gloves went with my outfit.

OFFICER: Okay, well. The gloves you submitted into evidence are still being examined. Would you be able to also submit the clothes you wore that night into evidence?

AO: I think my father sorted that out.

[Throat clearing]

OFFICER: I see . . . I must have missed that, then. Well, while we wait for that to process, please clarify something else too. You admitted earlier to creating that website that we're currently investigating? The one detailing the private lives of the boys at your school?

AO: I did. And I wouldn't call sexual assault their private lives.

OFFICER: That's all up for debate, isn't it? Well, just for the record again, we would like to know your reasons and justifications for creating such a website.

AO: I was bored.

OFFICER: Is that all?

AO: Yes.

OFFICER: Miss Owens, you do understand that these are serious offenses you're confessing to?

AO: Yes. I understand.

AO'S LAWYER: Again, this is a statement, not a confession. We also understand that this interview is just a formality kindly arranged by Mr. Owens and his colleague, who I believe to be your boss. She has complied, and answered all your questions, so it would be great if we could wrap this interview up, please.

OFFICER: I see. Well, thank you, April, for your time. As you are aware, I cannot keep you or your brother in custody. But we will be in contact with your father's lawyers.

AO: Sounds good to me.

SADE HAD GONE OVER APRIL'S interview transcript more than a dozen times.

Persephone was right. Something was *off* about it.

But Sade had always felt like something was *off* about April. A disconnect. This time, though, the off feeling came from her words and not her vibe.

It didn't feel like a confession to a heinous crime. There was no obvious guilt.

April was simply reciting what she seemed to know was factually true. She somehow knew that Jude had been strangled to death.

April *was* protecting someone.

But who?

Sade wasn't sure what to make of this situation or of April.

The website's alert sounded, and the notification bar popped up with the update that seventy-seven people had now sent in anonymous accounts. More and more of these kept appearing each day.

Sade found herself clicking off the police report Kwame had given her and back onto the clone phone data.

She clicked on the photos of April at one of the parties. It was the photo Sade had seen before that made her wonder about April's connection to all this. Sade hadn't stopped thinking about it. Especially now.

She pulled up the student records for Jude, Francis, and August that she'd asked Kwame to retrieve and looked between the photo and then the files.

As she stared at the photo, something about it gave her a weird feeling.

It was April's body language.

She zoomed in slowly.

If it wasn't for the fact that she had now seen what a dosage of Rohypnol does to a person, she might've never caught it.

April wasn't smiling along and laughing with the boys in the photo like Sade had originally thought. She was barely conscious.

April had been drugged too.

I SLEEP, I DROWN & DISAPPEAR

AN ANAGRAM:

A

P

O

R I

P

I

L W

S

P

I E

R

E

D

N E

S

A

D

APRIL PIPER OWENS IS DEAD.

46

FRIDAY

THE FRENCH EQUATION

APRIL WAS ESCORTED BACK TO campus by four black cars, giving her the appearance of some sort of charioteer for the four horsemen of the apocalypse.

She wore a long black trench coat over her uniform, boots, and sunglasses, creating an almost dramatic level of intrigue around her sudden return. And of course, the students of Alfred Nobel ate it up.

The same students who had relished in her supposed downfall were now cowering as they observed her casual return from the dead. People watched from classroom windows in reverence as their ruler returned.

April's arrival was like an omen. Sade could feel it sweeping through the buildings, turning the sky gray and dull as rain pelted down angrily on the gravel.

And April drew her umbrella and walked through the doors of the main building once again.

"That's enough nosing about, turn back to your textbooks, page thirteen." The sound of Mr. Lanister's voice rang through the psychology classroom.

She couldn't help but feel that something was coming, and she wasn't sure if that was good or bad.

SADE HESITATED BEFORE KNOCKING ON April's room door.

Instead of going to dinner, she had rushed right over to Franklin House, where she hoped April would be.

There was no sound, and Sade assumed that April was someplace else. Then she heard soft footsteps, followed by the rattling of the handle before the door yawned open and April appeared before her.

She was dressed in a silk robe and slippers and gave Sade a weary look as though she was one of the last people she wanted to see.

"Hi," Sade said. "Can we talk?"

April wordlessly gestured for Sade to step inside, and she did.

April's room looked very different from when she last saw it. It had a less gloomy appearance now, possibly because there wasn't a half-dying girl inside. She spotted a record player and a stack of vinyls with album covers she recognized from the posters on Elizabeth's side of the room, along with a giant jar of loose-leaf tea and an electric kettle on her desk. Glimpses of how April and Elizabeth might've been friends.

April stared at Sade expectantly as she sat on her bed, before going back to painting her toes a deep shade of red. "What did you want?"

Sade hesitated before speaking. "Did you know that statistically men choose more violent ways to kill?"

April raised an eyebrow at her. "No, I didn't know that."

"Well, they do. Women tend to use things like poisons. Men use stabbing, beating, or strangling someone to death—or other, more violent methods."

"Is there a point here?" April asked.

"I know that Francis killed Jude," Sade replied simply.

April paused, dipped the nail polish brush back in the pot, and began her second coat.

"Is that *all* you know?" she replied with a small smile, her voice dripping with sarcasm.

Sade ignored her tone and continued. "I know that Francis was kicked off the swim team last year because they found drugs in his locker. I know that the drugs weren't his; they were Jude's, and that Jude had a business going and Francis was a regular customer. I know that Jude and Francis fought a lot. My guess is that your boyfriend wasn't pleased with the amount of *product* he was given. And I know that on the night Jude died, they had a fight. Jude's cause of death was a mystery to me, but as you know because Francis told you, and also confirmed by the coroner, Jude died from asphyxiation. Your boyfriend, the addict, strangled him to death—"

"So what if he did? One less monster in the world," April replied suddenly, staring at Sade with that empty expression she always had.

A silence followed and Sade just stared at her.

What she'd always seen as a vacant iciness in April's gaze seemed to be something else entirely.

It was clear that April was somewhere else, replaced by a version of herself with steel armor and a sharp tongue.

"I also know what Jude did to you while you were dating, and I'm sorry."

There was an edging silence that followed as April reached out for her phone. "I don't know what you're talking about," she finally said, tapping away on her phone screen with one hand and gently waving the other over the polish on her toes to dry them. "You should probably go."

Sade had suspected that response would come soon.

She didn't push her on it. April clearly didn't want to talk about this. So she'd leave it alone. "I'm here anyway, if you ever want to tal—"

"You don't know half as much as you think you do," April said, looking up at Sade now, glassy-eyed. "You're always here, asking people too many questions, thinking you know everything. But you don't. You know nothing."

Sade wanted to laugh at the irony of it all. "April . . . I'm sorry, but *you're* the one who had been pushing me to ask all the questions. I wouldn't be here asking these questions if you hadn't made me seek answers out. I spoke to Elizabeth, and I know that you helped her. I know you approached me at lunch all those weeks ago to figure out how you could manipulate me into figuring out the Fishermen and helping you expose them because you couldn't do it yourself without arousing suspicion. Elizabeth even told me you watered her plants for her. You act so nonchalant, April, but I know you care," Sade said, instantly regretting how harsh her tone was.

April stared at her unblinking for a few moments, and then she finally wiped her face and smiled.

"Please leave my room now. We're done talking."

Sade didn't move at first, unsure whether to stay and apologize and offer help again or just go. In the end she chose the latter. Especially as April looked like she was ready to wring Sade's neck.

On the way out of April's dormitory, their conversation and everything it signified weighed on her. April was just as much a victim as Elizabeth and Jamila. Sade wanted to run back and do something, say something . . . But it was clear that she wasn't the person April needed right now.

She smelled him before she saw him.

The solid figure she bumped into as she rounded the corner leading to the staircase out of Franklin House. The familiar smoke mixed with Lynx body spray and, under that, a lingering smell of something sour.

She looked up and there he was.

Francis Webber.

Boyfriend of April. Stepson of the headmaster. And killer of monsters.

His pale eyes were bloodshot—and not in the usual way—his hair uncombed.

"Hi," he said.

Sade almost thought she had conjured him up in her head. But no, he was really here. Looking down at her, with this expression as though he was on the verge of throwing up.

"Hey," Sade replied, not quite sure what to make of Francis anymore.

Logically, she should've run in the opposite direction as soon as she saw him, seeing as he was a literal murderer. But for some reason, she stayed.

"I-is, uhm, i-is A-April okay?"

Francis had no idea that she knew his dirty little secret. He probably thought it was a thing just between the two of them. April takes the fall, her father's connections ensuring she would be okay. Sade wasn't sure what it was he was asking, then.

Her eyebrows furrowed. "What do you mean?"

His red-rimmed eyes were glassed over and unfocused. "I know you know," he said, placing a hand in his pocket and standing up straighter.

"Know what?" Sade asked, though her heart paused in her chest and she felt her head swimming.

"April told me; she messaged me. Said you knew . . . a-about Jude."

Sade didn't respond to that. She didn't know how.

Francis continued. "Listen, I won't blame you if you decide to turn me in. I wanted to turn myself in; the guilt was eating away at me, but April wouldn't let me. She said it would kill her. Which I don't get. I'm not sure why she likes me. I'm a good-for-nothing addict, and yet she does. She sees me and I see her. April means the world to me, so I let her go." His voice broke at the end of his confession and he repeated *I let her go* softly to himself. Then he roughly wiped his face, swearing under his breath. "I'm not going to stop you, but I ask that you think of April in your decision, whatever it may be."

Sade blinked at him, still unsure of what to say.

He had basically confessed to her. She should turn him in, right?

But who would that serve? Francis was an asshole, and yet he wasn't one of the Fishermen. She hadn't found any trace of him in the group chat, ever.

Apparently, he was simply a messed-up asshole who loved his girlfriend.

A very surprising revelation.

"I'm going to go," Sade said, and Francis's shoulders dropped and he nodded, as though accepting his fate now.

"Okay," Francis said, and then trudged up the rest of the stairs and began walking over toward the hallway where April's room was.

"Wait," Sade said, turning now and watching him slowly turn to face her too.

"Yeah?" Francis asked, and in the low lighting of the hall, he looked even worse than before.

"Why'd you do it?" she asked.

They both knew what she was asking.

Why did you kill him?

Francis was quiet for a moment, staring at her, clearly trying to figure out what to say and how to say it.

He cracked a broken, twisted sort of smile. "I'm a good-for-nothing addict, I told you," he said, then paused and added, "and I'd kill again for April Owens."

47

SATURDAY
FINAL GOODBYES

ELIZABETH WAS BACK FROM THE hospital.

Her return was not nearly as dramatic as April's had been.

She simply arrived and spent the day in Webber's office doing admin and avoiding the prying eyes of the ANA student body, most of which had heard about her strange return. Though it seemed the students hadn't yet pieced together how Elizabeth, Jude, and the website (which was still up and getting new messages every day) were all connected.

Sade saw her again on the roof of the science building before dinner. Baz had messaged her to join him and Elizabeth at the greenhouse for a super-secret showing of *Shrek the Third* on his laptop.

When she arrived on the roof, Elizabeth wasn't there yet but Baz was. "Help me set up. She'll be here in ten minutes; I told her I had to go and feed Muffin."

The stolen guinea pig had been returned to the science labs but had shown distress over being separated from Baz, so the school allowed him to keep the guinea pig in the same room as the Seacole mascot, Aristotle the Lizard, instead of his bedroom. He still had a month of detentions but it was better than *"losing Muffin to science,"* as he'd put it.

Sade helped him set up the surprise party he seemed to have planned for Elizabeth.

On the side of the greenhouse was a messily drawn banner that read: WELCOME BACK BETTY and on the ground were balloons with crooked smiles on them and little electronic candle lights Baz had found in town.

Elizabeth arrived on time. She walked through the doors of the greenhouse, looking both the same as she had on that first day weeks ago but also completely different. She was thinner and looked tired, but the masks Sade had seen on her face had mostly eroded away. Before them both stood the true Elizabeth Wang.

Elizabeth took in the somewhat distressing décor and proceeded to do something that surprised them both.

She cried.

And then she walked into Baz's arms and hugged him tight.

"I told you to never call me Betty again, Basil. It makes me sound like an old white lady," she said softly into Baz's shirt.

"My bad, won't do it again," Baz lied, squeezing her tighter as if he was scared that letting go would make her disappear again.

Despite everything that had transpired, Sade could never shake the feeling that she was always intruding on something between them.

"I'm glad you're back," Sade said to Elizabeth once she finally pulled away from Baz.

Elizabeth wiped her eyes with her sleeves and smiled at her. "I'm not staying. This is my last day at ANA," she said.

"What?" Baz said out loud, vocalizing Sade's thoughts.

"I wanted to tell you in person. I spoke with my mum, and we decided it was best I finish my studies at home and I can look after her and make sure she gets the help she needs. I was in Webber's office all day sorting out the details. He tried making me sign some nondisclosure agreement about not speaking out on any of this to the media—it was very weird. But anyway, in the words of Shakespeare, it's time to shuffle off this mortal coil or whatever Mr. Riley said that quote was. I think I'm done here at ANA."

Sade nodded, understanding why Elizabeth had to leave.

How could you stay in a place filled with so many bad memories, a place that had denied what happened to you and didn't protect you when you almost died.

Sometimes a fresh start was the only way forward.

"This shall be a goodbye party, then," Sade said.

Elizabeth nodded. "Or better yet, an au revoir party."

"Isn't that the same thing?" Baz asked.

"Au revoir means, *until I see you again*. It's less final," Elizabeth said.

Goodbyes were always so difficult for Sade because of their finality. Goodbyes were painful, and she hoped to not have to say goodbye to anyone else for a long while.

"I like that," Sade replied.

SADE WOKE UP FROM THE nightmare before it ended.

It always ended the same.

A shadowy figure would pull her out of the water and devour her whole, and then she became it.

"Are you okay?" a voice called out in the darkness.

Sade looked up, expecting the shadowy figure to emerge, having followed her from her dream like it sometimes did, but instead it was just Persephone. She seemed to almost glow in the dark.

"Yes, why?" Sade asked her.

Persephone sat at the edge of the bed. "You're crying," she said.

"I had a bad dream," Sade replied.

"Was it about your sister?"

Sade nodded. Her dreams were almost always about her sister.

Persephone moved closer to her, squeezing her hand.

"Why are you here?" Sade asked.

"You missed dinner, so I brought you a nutritional bar from the vending machines."

Sade raised an eyebrow. "How did you know I missed dinner?"

Persephone shrugged. "A guess."

Sade accepted the bar with a small smile.

There were a few moments of silence, then Persephone pressed her head to Sade's.

"Sade . . . ," she said in a gentle whisper, their faces so close.

"Hmm?" Sade replied.

"None of this is real."

"What?"

"Wake up."

She woke up on the floor of her room.

It had been years since her dreams had deviated from the one the day her sister died.

She looked around the room, expecting to see the shadow of Jamila, but there was nothing there.

Just a granola bar on her side table and a note.

Eat or you'll get an ulcer—P x

MONDAY
VIRAL

THE WEEK STARTED WITH ANOTHER assembly.

At this point it seemed that the student body was tired of hearing Webber's voice, and similarly, Headmaster Webber was tired of speaking to them.

"Good morning. I will try to keep this assembly as quick and to the point as possible. As you might have already heard, the website NotSoNoble.com has found its way to local and national news sites. A number of the articles published do not paint our school as we know it to be—a supportive, caring environment that listens to its students. Thankfully, due to our contacts, we have been able to get some of these articles removed."

Sade's heart stopped for a moment.

"We have also been made aware that a student, who we also assume is one of the creators of the website, was instrumental in contacting a number of these media outlets. This student will be immediately expelled from Alfred Nobel Academy."

The entire hall went silent, and Sade could feel her anxiety take over. Her legs moved restlessly, tapping the chair she was seated in, and her heart pounded so loud she was convinced everyone could hear it.

"That's all for today. You will all be dismissed shortly by Miss Blackburn. Sade Hussein, please stay behind," Headmaster Webber said, loud and clear, squinting at her in the crowd.

There was a low rumble of whispers as heads began to turn in her direction.

Persephone looked at her from across the hall where she was seated next to Juliette, April's usual seat vacant, and giving her a questioning anxious glance.

It felt as if there were thousands of spotlights shining on Sade.

As the hall cleared out row by row, she stayed put.

"Want me to wait for you?" Baz asked.

Sade shook her head. "It's okay. I'll be fine."

When the room was finally emptied, and only Headmaster Webber and Miss Blackburn remained, Sade got up and went to where they were waiting for her.

"Hello, Miss Hussein. I think you know already the nature of this conversation. I would like you to follow us into my office. We have much to discuss," Headmaster Webber said.

SADE SPENT THE ENTIRE DAY in Headmaster Webber's office.

By the end of it, it was already final period and a verdict had been made.

She had been officially expelled from Alfred Nobel Academy, after only two months.

It had to be some record.

She didn't contest it or defend herself. She merely stayed quiet during the whole exchange. And then, when it was over, she returned to her dorm room to start packing her things.

She had until Wednesday to arrange her removal from the school, as Headmaster Webber put it.

When she got out, she messaged Persephone and Baz the news, figuring it would be a lot easier than saying it in person. She'd be leaving for good.

Sade was tired of goodbyes, but it seemed they had yet to grow tired of her.

When she got inside her dorm, instead of moving to pack her things right away, she collapsed onto her bed, letting the quiet completely consume her.

Elizabeth was officially gone. Safe, but gone. And now Sade would be too.

No one but the ghosts on the walls of room 313 would exist here after this week.

A knock sounded at her door.

She found Persephone behind it.

She looked breathless and wet, as if she'd run all the way over.

"Hi," she said, bleary-eyed. Sade couldn't tell if Persephone was on the verge of tears or whether it was simply the rain.

"Hey," Sade replied.

"I got your message. Is it true?" she asked, and from the way her voice broke in half as well as the distant sound of raindrops tapping on her windowsill, it was clear her expression was caused by both.

Sade nodded. "I leave on Wednesday."

Persephone shook her head, digesting this new information. Sade had somewhat processed it. She wouldn't see her friends for a long time. And even then, they might forget she existed. The thought of Persephone forgetting her made her heart hurt.

Persephone stepped close to her and whispered the very question Sade had wanted to ask her for weeks. "Can I kiss you?"

Sade wanted to say *yes*, but it felt selfish to want good things for herself.

"I'm leaving. Won't that complicate things for you?" Sade asked quietly, as she felt herself involuntarily moving even closer to her.

Persephone brushed Sade's hair out of her face and shrugged. "Complicate them," she whispered.

So Sade pulled her in, closing the gap between them and pressing their lips together.

TUESDAY

BAZ CAME TO TURING DURING dinner the next day, naming the event the *Last Supper* since she would be leaving tomorrow.

He wore his green frog hat and a huge smile on his face when he saw her. She hugged him tight and then they went to eat today's special in the Turing dining hall. Pizza.

He insisted on showing her an array of Brazilian memes in order to cheer her up, professing that they were the best. Which Sade agreed they were.

As usual, Jessica was patrolling the hall and as usual upon seeing Baz she gave him a murderous glare.

"You need to go, Basil. This dining hall may only be used by Turing residents. I've told you this countless times before, but it is apparent that you love to make my life difficult," she said.

"And what a sad little life that is, Jane," he replied.

"My name is Jessica."

"This pizza is soggy," he said, ignoring her and turning to Sade, but then he proceeded to eat it anyway.

It was a weird thought to have, but she'd miss Jessica. There was something about the constant nature of her being there with her watchfulness that was comforting.

After dinner, they went to Seacole to hang out with Persephone, who said she'd meet them there.

They hadn't spoken much since the kiss yesterday, and Sade really wasn't sure what the future of their friendship looked like either, but she decided that would be for the future version of herself to worry about.

She would just attempt to enjoy the present.

The four of them (including Muffin) lay on the ground of the empty common room staring at the ceiling now.

It had been Baz's idea to recline. Apparently, it made all your thoughts rush into your brain and he reckoned that then they wouldn't forget to say the important things today.

"I read that sexist article," Persephone said suddenly.

"Which one," Sade said. So many had cropped up at this point.

As a result of the virality of the website, articles—both the good and the ugly—had emerged as a result.

One—*Let Sleeping Dogs Lie: Private School Boys and Their Sordid Hidden Affairs*—had sided with the victims, though everything was written in a way that made it seem like salacious gossip.

But an article written in response to it, calling out the website for its *harm* to the male population of the school, had also gone viral: *Where Sleeping Girls Lie: The Toxic Me Too Trend and Its Champions* by Jeremy Dierden. The article spoke about the apparent trend of girls and women with nothing more to offer than their beauty, seeking revenge on unsuspecting men and ruining the lives of these promising young boys. His post almost seemed like a parody, like he had read some manual on how to be the ultimate misogynist and regurgitated it.

"What a knob," Persephone announced, looking at her screen.

"Agreed," Baz said.

"Sadly, there will always be people like Jeremy Dierden. What matters is that there's a platform that the school has no control over where people can express things they couldn't before. While progress might not come right away, it's coming," Persephone mused.

Muffin squeaked in agreement.

"That's very optimistic for you, Persephone," Baz said.

"It's not optimism, it's just fact. I'm smart and so I know these things."

Baz nodded in agreement because Persephone was, indeed, smart. Possibly smarter than all of them combined.

"She has a point," Sade said.

"When I'm prime minister, I'm going to make sure that things finally change around here," Persephone said.

"You want to be prime minister?" Sade asked.

"Of course I do. What do you guys want to be when you're older?"

"I do not dream of labor," Baz said.

Persephone laughed. "What about you, Sade?"

Sade thought about it for a moment. She wasn't sure what she wanted to do with her life. For so long her life had been wading through endless waves of sadness and grief, and now it felt like she was on the shore, dry and safe.

"I think I just want to be happy," she said. "In a way, I guess I already am. Because I have you guys."

WEDNESDAY

A KNOCK SOUNDED AT SADE'S door on her last day at ANA.

She hoped it would be Persephone again, wanting to hang out or even kiss some more—she quite liked doing that.

But instead, it was Jessica with her usual displeased expression.

"Miss Blackburn wants to see you," she said.

"Why?" Sade asked, surprised that Lady Death wanted to be graced with her presence. She had assumed that Miss Blackburn would be celebrating and would never want to see her again.

"I don't know, but you should hurry; she doesn't seem like she's in a good mood."

Sade had already experienced Miss Blackburn's apparent good days; she did not want to see what she was like on a bad day, but it looked like she had no choice.

She quickly slipped into her shoes and rushed over to the reception area in the main building. Miss Blackburn was standing by the entrance when Sade arrived, waiting for her like on the first day.

"You're late, but I suppose I should get used to that now when it comes to you," Miss Blackburn said. "Anyway, follow me."

And Sade followed her into the reception office room.

Miss Blackburn closed the door behind her and told Sade to take a seat.

"I never agreed with Mr. Webber on the way he handled everything, I want you to know that. What you did was necessary and you don't deserve to be expelled for that— maybe your tardiness, but not that. Never that," she said, which again surprised Sade.

She had never in one million years thought that Miss Blackburn would be here telling her this, but she had learned that life was filled with surprises. She'd stopped trying to predict the curveballs it would throw at her.

Miss Blackburn didn't seem as though she was finished with her speech, so Sade said nothing.

"I have been contesting his role as headmaster for a while now. The board hasn't been happy with his performance for many months but has kept him around because of the sentimental value of having the role of headmaster be passed down to the founder's children and their children and so on. But it seems as of this morning they're ready to let him go. The summation of the many concerns we have had from parents and teachers alike over the safeguarding of the students at this school and based on some recent articles that have come to light . . ." Miss Blackburn paused, giving Sade what seemed to be an *approving* look. "It has been determined by the board that Mr. Webber is no longer a fit candidate for headmaster, so your expulsion has been paused and will be reviewed by them again. While I believe in the good that tradition can bring and I'm usually all for it, sometimes traditions should be disrupted. Your staying here will be determined by a trial of how your finals go, as well as teacher reports. You'll need three glowing recommendations, which two of your teachers have been willing to give. The third will come from me."

Sade couldn't believe what she was hearing; she almost couldn't speak.

She might get to stay.

But did she even *want* to remain at Alfred Nobel Academy anymore? After all, she had done what she set out to: get justice for Jamila—even if that came with more complications than wins. What else was there for her here?

But returning home felt like going back to a life where she was nothing more than her grief.

Despite the many bad things that had happened while at ANA, she was happier here than she'd ever been.

She thought about her friends, Persephone, Basil, and Elizabeth, and how in just a few short weeks she went from being lonely and filled with so much anger and guilt to having people she cared about and who cared about her too. Who didn't care that she was flawed and who made her feel like she deserved to exist in this world.

"Thank you, Miss Blackburn," Sade finally said, feeling somewhat choked up.

Then Miss Blackburn gave her what she thought might be a smile mixed with a grimace. "Don't disappoint me."

ONE YEAR (AND A BIT) LATER
EPILOGUE

IT WAS THE 14TH OF March, and the students of Alfred Nobel Academy were celebrating Pi Day as they did on this date each year. It was the second Pi Day Sade would be celebrating at ANA, though this Pi Day was a lot nicer than the last.

A lot had changed in sixteen months.

Headmaster Webber had been fired and replaced with Headmaster Laurens, who seemed to care for the well-being of the student body a little more than Webber had.

A number of cases had been brought against several members of the Fishermen, with a few leading to charges for possession and distribution of indecent pictures of minors, and immediate expulsion. Most charges were dropped, however; the systems meant to mete justice did anything but.

The remaining boys involved in the Fishermen had been put on academic probation and anyone found with explicit photos of another student would be immediately escorted out of the school.

The Fisherman were, in name, over. Though Sade had heard rumblings of another version of it where they'd meet in person in secret, which they called *the net*.

It was all a mixed bag of disappointment and triumph.

There was also a counselor now on campus, Miss Tate, who was hired so that students could have someone to talk to. There were one-on-one sessions held weekly as well as group sessions for those who had been victims. Sade knew about the latter because of Persephone, who had attended a few with April in the beginning.

Sade wished the counselor had been there when Elizabeth was around, then maybe she wouldn't have felt so alone. Jamila too. Maybe if Jamila could have spoken to someone, she would have known there were other options for her.

Sade had attended one of the solo counseling sessions herself after having a particularly bad anxiety day, running into April as she exited her own session. It was the first time April had looked at her since everything that had happened.

As usual, April's stare was blank, and Sade now knew why.

She offered a smile, but April flinched and moved quickly away from Sade.

She doubted that April would ever speak to her again, and Sade was okay with that. After all, April had counseling, Juliette, and Persephone, and Sade thought Persephone was the best person anyone could have in their corner.

It seemed April was doing better, and Sade was happy April had someone to talk to. Multiple someones.

April was still dating Francis, though Francis decided he couldn't cope with being at the school anymore and left to go to an all-boys private sixth form nearby.

August was, thankfully, no longer at the school either. Sade didn't know the details of it, but it seemed his parents decided it was best that he stayed at home and finished his studies from there. She wondered if April had anything to do with that too.

The charges against April for the murder of Jude had been settled quietly outside of court, which Sade suspected had something to do with a nice settlement paid to the Ripleys by the Owens. Sade hadn't reported the truth to the police about what really happened that night at Jude's party. After all, what was the truth? She wasn't sure she'd even heard the full story anyway, and she wasn't sure she ever would. In the end, she wasn't completely blameless either.

Sade knew that sometimes justice looked like this: It wasn't fair, and it wasn't just. But it was something. A start.

Thankfully, Sade had not been expelled from the school. With the space to focus, Sade had passed her finals and made the decision to continue on at the academy.

Now she was in her fourth year and was the vice captain of the girls' swim team, dating the head girl of ANA and president of the school's Shakespeare club, Persephone Stuart.

She still had awful dreams filled with shadowy figures that roamed the haunted halls of her mind. She suspected she'd always have these dreams. But at least they weren't as frequent.

For the most part, she was doing good.

But the thing about grief was that even one hundred good days were sometimes weighed down by an overwhelming guilt of forgetting. Sometimes she'd win a swim meet and for a moment forget why she was ever sad at all, and the guilt of not constantly being consumed by the weight of the loss she had experienced would be paralyzing. Other times, she'd feel the crushing weight of the past trying to drown her still.

Miss Tate would tell her in her sessions that she needed to let go of the idea that she was anybody's savior. In truth, her sister had been in a lot of pain and needed to speak to a professional. It wasn't Sade's fault. None of the deaths in her family were.

"Superheroes are a thing of fiction; you can't be one. You're human," Miss Tate had told her.

"You never know; I could get bitten by a radioactive spider or something," Sade had said in response.

"If that happens, I'll call you an ambulance," Miss Tate had replied.

Which was Miss Tate's way of letting Sade know she wasn't alone.

"Did you know that there are eight houses at ANA, because if you add up the numbers in the shortened version of pi, 3.14, they equal 8," Kwame said.

Kwame was a new addition to their circle. He and Baz were finally dating, after a while of what Baz told her was an arrangement of friends who kissed and watched Brazilian novelas together sometimes.

She'd told him that it sounded a lot like dating to her.

Today they were eating pies for lunch, as that was all that was on the menu in celebration of Pi Day. Sade had a veggie pie, Kwame a cottage pie, and Basil, blueberry—which she noticed Kwame steal bites from every now and then.

Most days the three of them would sit in the lunch hall together, and on occasion Persephone would join, but she mostly hung out with the rest of her unholy ones.

After lunch Sade made her way to the pool in Newton.

She no longer saw dead bodies floating alongside her. Nor did she panic when she went under.

But sometimes, she'd still feel the heaviness of her bones as she settled into the water. As though her memories and her trauma were carried inside her now, burrowing into her and sticking to the marrow.

The counselor had said that was what trauma could do. It got stuck and replayed memories on a loop sometimes in our minds and other times in our bodies. And it didn't mean Sade was broken or weak, it just meant that she carried an experience that shaped who she was now. She would learn how to live, in spite of it.

When she got into the pool, it welcomed her as usual, hugging her close and surrounding her.

She decided she wouldn't swim today, she would just lie back and drift until her mind was clear.

As her body glided across the water, she remembered the thing she told her sister that she sometimes told herself on the bad days:

Keep swimming. Or if that's too hard, at the very least, float.

THE END

ACKNOWLEDGMENTS

WHERE SLEEPING GIRLS LIE **IS** a story that simply would not exist without the guidance and support of so many people. I wrote this book over the course of three long, arduous years—most of which were in the height of a global pandemic when we were not only trapped inside and forced to face our own mortality for months on end but also when many of us experienced overwhelming and constant waves of grief. I lost several family members in the pandemic; it felt like every month we'd get a call that someone else had passed on, and I was convinced at points that we were all living in some twisted Groundhog Day where the end of the world kept arriving with no sign of stopping.

On the day I sold *Where Sleeping Girls Lie* (along with *Ace of Spades*) to my publisher in the United States, I'd heard that my great-aunt Ariat had passed away. I couldn't really celebrate the publishing news when something so earth-shattering had happened—and would continue to happen all throughout the pandemic. I was also still in university, somehow working on my undergraduate thesis and final essays while launching *Ace of Spades*. I think all of this, combined with the fact that sophomore novels are notoriously difficult, meant that when it came to working on *Where Sleeping Girls Lie*, I was so burnt out from the real world I couldn't even fathom trying to create a fictional one. And yet, in the words of Kamala Harris, "We did it, Joe!" The *we* in question being the amazing people I'm about to talk about below.

First and foremost, I would like to thank my brilliant editors Foyinsi Adegbonmire, Becky Walker, and Rebecca Hill, as well as my UK and US publishers (Usborne and Macmillan) for being so patient with me and this book. Thank you to Foyinsi, Becky, and Rebecca for not giving up on me and constantly being so willing to jump on a late post-work call to try to help me fix the chaos that was drafting and editing this monster of a book (145,000 words of monster, I must add). I honestly think editors are wizards, with Foyinsi, Becky, and Rebecca being the queens of wizardry, of course, and this book would not exist if it wasn't for their craft.

As always, thank you to my agents Molly Ker Hawn and Zoë Plant for reading the hundreds of early draft ideas for what would become *Where Sleeping Girls Lie*. (When I say hundreds, it's not that much of an exaggeration.) Thank you for always being in my corner and thank you for being wizards too and sharing your wizard wisdom with me.

Thank you to Jean Feiwel and Liz Szabla for their continued support of my stories and career. Thank you to Dawn Ryan, Trisha Previte, Elizabeth H. Clark, Allene Cassagnol, Melissa Zar, Naheid Shahsamand, Katie Quinn, and Morgan Kane, who, without their wizardry, this book would also cease to exist. Thank you to the uber-talented Aykut Aydogdu for illustrating one of the most beautiful covers I have ever seen. I have been such a huge fan of his work for years and I am so chuffed to be able to have his work as the cover for this book.

Now on to my wonderful friends:

Thank you to the brilliant Louangie for all your undying support. Sometimes the impostor that lives in the deepest, darkest corners of my mind wants to come out, and Louangie tells that impostor to politely F off.

Thank you, Terry, for believing in my work more than I do and reading early pages I sent over and telling me to keep going. Thank you to Adiba for being the best friend and writing partner anyone could ask for. Thank you for all the late-night calls and letting me rant to you for hours on end about fictional issues. Thank you for reading the terrible first draft of this monstrous book and threatening to slap some sense into me when I tried to give up. Honestly, if I went on about all the things Adiba does, I fear it would be longer than this book itself.

Thank you to the wonderful people who helped with sensitivity issues in the story: The Survivors Trust, Basil Wright, Jim Anotsu, and Write Up.

Thank you to Pippin (@hitchikerhobbit) and Hanna (@hannakimwrites) for lending your expertise on guinea pigs as I wrote the ever-important character, Muffin.

Thank you to my mum for being my biggest supporter.

And lastly, but not least(ly), thank you to my kettle, Steve. Still going strong and always reliable for a nice cuppa at the end of a deadline.